Praise for Reavis Z. Wortham

Hard Country

"A stunning success! *Hard Country* checks all the boxes: a nonstop thriller plot, characters that are so real we're sure we've crossed paths in real life, and a breathtaking portrait—both searing and sympathetic—of a small town, from an author whose compelling voice and keenly observant eye transport us there. Wortham is known for his protagonists, and Tucker Snow is one of his all-time best: sharp, uncompromising, wry, thoroughly human, and the one thing we don't see enough of nowadays: a dyed-in-the-wool hero. I was going to set aside a weekend to read the book. My problem? What to do with the rest of Saturday afternoon and Sunday—yes, *Hard Country* is the definition of a one-sitting read. Bravo!"

—Jeffery Deaver, *New York Times* bestselling author of *The Bone Collector* and *Hunting Time*

"*Hard Country* crackles with authenticity as Tucker Snow shows us what it takes to be a lawman, and a good man, in a sprawling state like Texas. I'll read anything Reavis Z. Wortham writes!"

—Marc Cameron, *New York Times* bestselling author

"An action fan's dream. Nonstop excitement. Wonderful characters. A terrific locale. And a startling bulletin about how your car is watching you."

—

"*Hard Country* is easy to love, a beautifully crafted and fully realized thriller of rare depth and pathos. The debut entry in Reavis Wortham's new series is structured along classic lines reminiscent of the best from Ace Atkins, Don Winslow, and even James Lee Burke. This is thriller writing of the highest order that grabs hold from the very first line and doesn't let go until the last. As timely as it is terrific!"

—Jon Land, *USA Today* bestselling author of the Caitlin Strong series

The Texas Job

The Ninth Texas Red River Mystery

"Reviewers taking on a Wortham novel will make heavy use of cowboy-movie images. The unkillable Ranger goes from hero to superhero, 'a man made of hard bone and corded wire.' None of this will put off Wortham's admirers, who can't get enough of 'the sweet natural cologne of leather.'"

—*Booklist*

"Readers who've already seen Tom grown old in earlier installments of Wortham's Texas Red River series will be rubbing their hands in eager anticipation of what happens next. A...powerful tale of a solitary hero confronting a web of conspirators against hopeless odds."

—*Kirkus Reviews*

"Set in 1931, this well-crafted crime novel features Texas Ranger Tom Bell, a supporting character in *The Right Side of*

Wrong. Authentic settings and richly drawn characters complement Wortham's striking depiction of the Texas oil boom and the unavoidable corruption, greed, and anarchy that accompany it. Hopefully, Bell will be back in a sequel."

—*Publishers Weekly*

Laying Bones
The Eighth Texas Red River Mystery

"Wortham adroitly balances richly nuanced human drama with two-fisted action, and displays a knack for the striking phrase ("R.B. was the best drunk driver in the county, and I don't believe he run off in here on his own"). This entry is sure to win the author new fans."

—*Publishers Weekly*

Gold Dust
The Seventh Red River Mystery

"Center Springs must deal with everything from cattle rustlers to a biological agent that the CIA said was safe but were wrong, and a real fight between the government and those who actually know what the term 'gunslinger' means. Murder is everywhere and readers will never forget this Poisoned Gift once they see it in action. Wortham has created yet another Red River Mystery that hits home in a big way, making it all the more terrifying."

—*Suspense Magazine*

"Richly enjoyable...reads like a stranger-than-strange collaboration between Lee Child, handling the assault on the CIA with baleful directness, and Steven F. Havill, genially reporting on the regulars back home."

—*Kirkus Reviews*

"It's a pleasure to watch [Constable Ned Parker and Texas Ranger Tom Bell] deal with orneriness as well as just plain evil. Readers nostalgic for this period will find plenty to like."

—*Publishers Weekly*

"Reading the seventh Red River Mystery is like coming home after a vacation: we're reuniting with old friends and returning to a comfortable place. Wortham's writing style is easygoing, relying on natural-sounding dialogue and vivid descriptions to give us the feeling that this story could well have taken place. Another fine entry in a mystery series that deserves more attention."

—*Booklist*

Unraveled

The Sixth Red River Mystery

"The more I read of Reavis Wortham's books, the more impressed I am by his abilities as a writer... His understanding of family feuds, how they start and how they hang on long past their expiration date, is vital to the story line. Wortham's skill as a plotter is demonstrated as well. He's very good at what he does, and his books are well worth reading."

—*Reviewing the Evidence*

"This superbly drawn sixth entry in the series features captivating characters and an authentic Texas twang."

—*Library Journal*

"Not only does Wortham write exceptionally well, but he somehow manages to infuse *Unraveled* with a Southern Gothic feel what would make even William Faulkner proud... A hidden gem of a book that reads like Craig Johnson's Longmire mysteries on steroids."

—*Providence Journal*

Dark Places
The Fifth Red River Mystery

"Readers will cheer for and ache with the good folks, and secondary characters hold their own... The novel's short chapters fit both the fast pace and the deftly spare actions and details... The rhythm of Wortham's writing, transporting us back in time, soon takes hold and is well worth the reader's efforts."

—*Historical Novel Society*

Vengeance Is Mine
The Fourth Red River Mystery

"Wortham is a masterful and entertaining storyteller. Set in East Texas in 1967, *Vengeance Is Mine* is equal parts Joe R. Lansdale and Harper Lee, with a touch of Elmore Leonard."

—*Ellery Queen's Mystery Magazine*

★ "Very entertaining… Those who have read the author's earlier books, including *The Right Side of Wrong* (2013), will be familiar with Center Springs and its rather unusual denizens, but knowledge of those earlier volumes is not required. This is a fully self-contained story, and it's a real corker."

—*Booklist,* Starred Review

The Right Side of Wrong
The Third Red River Mystery

"A sleeper that deserves wider attention."

—*New York Times*

"Wortham's third entry in his addictive Texas procedural set in the 1960s is a deceptively meandering tale of family and country life bookended by a dramatic opening and conclusion. C. J. Box fans would like this title."

—*Library Journal,* Starred Review

Burrows
The Second Red River Mystery

★ "Wortham's outstanding sequel to *The Rock Hole* (2011)… combines the gonzo sensibility of Joe R. Lansdale and the elegiac mood of *To Kill a Mockingbird* to strike just the right balance between childhood innocence and adult horror."

—*Publishers Weekly,* Starred Review

"The cinematic characters have substance and a pulse. They walk off the page and talk Texas."

—*Dallas Morning News*

The Rock Hole

The First Red River Mystery

"One of the 12 best novels of 2011. An accomplished first novel about life and murder in a small Texas town... Wortham tells a story of grace under pressure, of what happens when a deranged and vicious predator decides that they're his promised prey...a fast and furious climax, written to the hilt, harrowing in its unpredictability. Not just scary but funny too, as Wortham nails time and place in a sure-handed, captivating way. There's a lot of good stuff in this unpretentious gem. Don't miss it."

—*Kirkus Reviews*

"Throughout, scenes of hunting, farming, and family life sizzle with detail and immediacy. The dialogue is spicy with country humor and color, and Wortham knows how to keep his story moving. *The Rock Hole* is an unnerving but fascinating read."

—*Historical Novel Review*

Also by Reavis Z. Wortham

The Texas Red River Mysteries

The Rock Hole

Burrows

The Right Side of Wrong

Vengeance Is Mine

Dark Places

Unraveled

Gold Dust

Laying Bones

The Texas Job

The Sonny Hawke Mysteries

Hawke's Prey

Hawke's War

Hawke's Target

Hawke's Fury

HARD COUNTRY

HARD COUNTRY

A THRILLER

REAVIS Z. WORTHAM

Published by Poisoned Pen Press, an imprint of Sourcebooks
P.O. Box 4410, Naperville, Illinois 60567-4410
(630) 961-3900
sourcebooks.com

Library of Congress Cataloging-in-Publication Data

Names: Wortham, Reavis Z., author.
Title: Hard country : a thriller / Reavis Z. Wortham.
Description: Naperville, Illinois : Poisoned Pen Press, 2023.
Identifiers: LCCN 2022061927 (print) | LCCN 2022061928
(ebook) | (trade paperback) | (epub)
Subjects: LCGFT: Thrillers (Fiction) | Novels.
Classification: LCC PS3623.O777 H37 2023 (print) | LCC PS3623.O777
(ebook) | DDC 813/.6--dc23/eng/20230109
LC record available at https://lccn.loc.gov/2022061927
LC ebook record available at https://lccn.loc.gov/2022061928

Printed and bound in Canada.
MBP 10 9 8 7 6 5 4 3 2 1

DEDICATION

This one is for two brothers who spent a career in Texas law enforcement: Sergeant Rick Easterwood, Special Ranger, Texas Department of Public Safety (DPS), Criminal Law Enforcement (Ret), and his younger brother, Assistant Commander Dan Easterwood, DPS Narcotics Service (Ret).

Though this is entirely a work of fiction, it was their unique working situation as undercover narcotics officers under special dispensation from then–Texas governor Mark White, and the stories they told me long after they retired, that gave me the idea for the two characters in this book.

These two exceptional men are legends in Texas criminal law enforcement, and it is an honor to call them friends.

"It was a good career."

—RICK EASTERWOOD

"As the younger brother, I think you should dedicate a page about how much better looking and smarter Harley is than his older brother."

—DAN EASTERWOOD

"Society questions the police and their methods, and the police say, 'Do you want the criminals off the street, or what?'"

—KURT RUSSELL

TSCRA strongly supports and defends a free enterprise system, protecting private property rights, and protecting and enhancing our natural resources.

—TEXAS SOUTHWESTERN CATTLE RAISERS ASSOCIATION

Chapter One

A trio of angry voices washed over the gravel county road in front of our restored Victorian perched on a low Northeast Texas hill. They carried onto our wraparound porch as if piped in on the cool easterly breeze.

"You don't tell me what to do! Either of you!"

I couldn't see the individuals a couple of hundred yards from where I sat in the swing, but the man's furious tone rang with menace.

It was early fall, and the countryside was a riot of autumn color around our new sixteen-hundred-acre ranch. It was a lot of land, more than I ever thought I'd own, but my late wife, Sara Beth, had a million-dollar life insurance policy she'd bought on herself without telling me. I guess that's how she splurged, playing the odds and providing for me and the girls.

Who would have thought that someone in such a potentially dangerous line of work in law enforcement like me would still be standing, when my wife and baby daughter died in a car wreck caused by someone's stupid addiction to meth?

An ancient, sun-seasoned barn made of notched logs rested

on another slight oak-covered hill across the county road on a separate piece of our property. Wood ducks passed over the house on their way to a heavily timbered pool just out of sight past the barn, and birds called from every tree.

The Realtor told me the original house ten miles from the town of Ganther Bluff partially burned a couple of years earlier, and the owners moved away once the new place was finished. My sixteen-year-old daughter Chloe and I toured the property in late summer when the trees were thick with foliage. It was exactly what we were looking for, and I thought the house was isolated when we signed the papers on the place.

I couldn't have been more wrong.

A woman's voice thick with anger and decades of cigarette damage fired back. "You don't think worth a *dayum*!"

Family arguments weren't anything new to me after a career that first began as a trooper for the Texas Department of Public Safety, but I didn't expect to hear them so close out there in the country. I wondered at the weird confluence of wind and weather conditions that brought me the family dispute.

His response was immediate. "You have *two* jobs, to keep the house clean and cook. You don't do either one! Get off your ass and do something besides moon over that old boyfriend of yours! He's not here, but I *am*!"

"That's not what we're *talking* about." Her voice cracked when she emphasized the word. "You keep coming back around to that and I'm tired of..."

The fierce teenage female voice that cut her off rang sharp and shrill. "You two shut up! Shut *up*! I hate you both!"

I was already beginning to feel the same way, and I didn't even know who they were.

I'm not sure why I bought so much land after my wife and

youngest daughter were killed by an addict high on a new kind of meth called gravel. Looking back, I think it was because the ranch house seemed to fill the bill for me and Chloe at that moment in time.

The ranch was a cattle operation before I signed the contract, but I had no intention of raising beef. By the time we moved in that autumn, not one cow grazed in the creek-bottom pastures where coyotes yelped and wild hogs rooted at night.

From the high front porch, there wasn't another real stick-and-nail house in sight, though across the road at a forty-five-degree angle from where I stood was the ratty house trailer where the noise originated. I thought of the place as despair on wheels.

Maybe that's what sparked the disagreement, hopelessness.

The rusting wreck had been there so long the tires were gone and the single-wide structure sagging in the middle was on cock-eyed cinder block supports. Other blocks under rotting railroad ties held up the stripped carcass of a cannibalized pickup.

It was surrounded by trees in their bright foliage, and tangles of blackberry vines, making it impossible to see from ground level unless you stopped at just the right spot by their gate. I didn't have to drive down the road to do that. The view we had from the second floor was like peeking into a junkyard. After idly glancing out the window on the day we moved in and seeing stacks of trash, metal, and defunct household appliances, I tried not to look their direction again.

The invisible woman's voice broke with emotion. "I'm going to town!"

"No you're not! I need the truck in a little bit and don't intend to wait around for you to go stringing off to Brenda's house and come back stoned to the gills."

It was Friday morning, and all I wanted to do was sit outside to drink coffee while Chloe slept late. Someone once told me that it takes two years to start getting over the loss of a loved one, and I couldn't imagine eighteen more months of such intense pain.

For weeks I'd felt embarrassed by my own inability to control my thoughts and feelings. There were days when I wanted nothing more than to rest and stare into the distance, reflecting on our loss with the knowledge that I'd never hold Sara Beth or our baby daughter again.

I wandered through life in a trance and did my best not to let Chloe see it. She'd been close to her mother and little Peyton and had a harder time in her own way. Teenagers are strange beings anyway, and her overwhelming grief and emotions swept back and forth like the tide.

Wilted from grief, I took an extended leave of absence from my job as a special agent for the Texas & Southwestern Cattle Raisers Association, the oldest livestock alliance in Texas, and we moved. We're also known as Special Rangers, stock agents, and brand inspectors, depending on who you're talking to. I'd worked my way up from the highway patrol to undercover narcotics for the DPS, and finally to the position I'd always dreamed of.

Instead of the peace I needed that morning, the voices cut the still air with the harsh rasp of a blue jay, coming through loud and clear on the light breeze.

"Get back in the house!" The man must have turned away, because a sentence or two was swallowed by a shift in the early morning breeze. "...customer coming...call that ex of yours and have him come get y'all then!"

They may have both been rolling around on the ground after that, because all I heard were occasional well-defined cusswords.

A door slammed, and I figured the teenage girl decided not to referee the fight.

Disappointed at the realization they were so close, I took my coffee around to the back porch overlooking the wide pasture and a line of trees reflected in the two-acre stock pond several hundred yards away. No one was arguing there, so I settled into a rocker as a skein of Canada geese cupped their wings and landed on the still surface of the water.

I took a sip of coffee made in the new pot and watched the geese paddle to the bank and start grazing up the slope like cattle. Movement caught my eye as a line of wild hogs emerged from the distant trees and hurried across the pasture.

A Remington 7mm mag rifle stood in the corner behind my bedroom door, and I thought I'd drift down there about dark and pop a couple of them. Chloe was familiar with firearms and a pretty good shot. Maybe she'd be interested in learning how to hunt. It'd be a good skill to have.

There's over three million wild pigs in Texas, and the damage they do to land and crops is staggering. Shooting one or two wouldn't put a dent in the population, but at least it was something to do, because I never was one of those guys to sit in front of a TV and watch the alarmist news.

The crunch of a vehicle on the county road out front brought me back into the present. From where I sat around back, I couldn't see Rock Hill Road, but they were going way too fast. Pebbles popped and rattled against the undercarriage as it passed the house and decelerated at a slight rise over a concrete culvert bridge. It slowed again seconds later, telling me it was pulling through the battling neighbors' wire gate to follow the weaving two-track dirt lane to the crumbling, rusting trailer.

There was no other turnout until a mile farther on, where

the road intersected with still *another* gravel county road and the home of Bud Grubbs and his wife, Clara. I'd seen Bud pass in his little Toyota pickup that morning, and he was never in a hurry, always driving with the window down and his elbow hanging out in the breeze.

We waved each time, because that's the way neighbors act. They'd stopped by the first week I was there to say howdy and welcome me in, offering to help if I needed anything. After that, I saw him up at the little country store at a highway intersection about ten miles away, where we picked up a few staples such as milk, bread, and eggs, along with a smattering of local gossip.

The geese heard the car pass, too, and stopped grazing and turned their heads to watch for danger. When the sound stopped, they went back to pecking at the ground and I took another sip of cooling coffee.

My relaxed mood vanished minutes later at the crack of a gunshot coming from the direction of the trailer. Out in the country, gunfire's as common as mosquitoes, and most folks pay it little mind because people often shot at pigs, varmints, or were sighting in a rifle.

One shot, or maybe two, was normal. But it was the *cadence* of the gunfire that caught my attention. The distinctive sounds told me there were likely two different firearms involved.

The flat report of a single round, a pause, and then two shots in quick succession weren't target practice. Several more shots on top of each other were followed by one last round.

There was a gunfight in progress.

Chapter Two

Wearing my faded T-shirt that read, "When a Man Tires of Discussing Politics and Women, He Can Always Hunt Ducks," Chloe came through the back door, dark hair tousled from sleep and looking annoyed as only a teenager can. Though it was Friday morning, she was home, the happy recipient of the school's four-day week due to changing educational practices.

"What was all that shooting?" She checked my hands and glanced around to see if I had a gun laying on the arm of a lounge chair or a rifle leaning against a post, likely to use it as evidence to chastise me for waking her up.

"It wasn't me." I pushed past her into the house to where I kept my service weapon on top of a barrister bookcase near the front door. "It came from that trailer over across the road. You stay here, and I'll be back in a minute."

She followed me, padding on bare feet. "Why're you going?"

"Somebody may be in trouble."

"You're off on leave."

"Not in situations like this. I'm not working right now, but I'm still commissioned." I threaded the holster onto my belt and covered the Colt with a black T-shirt under an unbuttoned denim shirt. Tucking my badge into the shirt pocket, I headed out the door. "Call 911 if you hear any more shooting."

"Do we have 911 up here?"

"Good question. Dial it anyway."

A new white Dodge replaced my government issue truck, and it was parked near the house. In seconds I pulled through the open side of our eight-foot pipe gate and steered right. The window on my side was down, and damp fall air blew into the cab.

Before I reached the culvert bridge over Long Creek, a covey of bobwhite quail erupted from the grass. Any other time I would have stopped to watch the little six-ounce birds set their wings and scatter in the pasture, because since the early 1990s they'd become almost extinct in our part of the world. There was no time to watch the birds, though.

I was over the bridge and halfway to the neighbors' gate when a faded orange RAV4 fishtailed on the loose rocks as the driver shot through the gate and hammered the accelerator. I let off the gas, fully expecting the back end of the little SUV to whip around and slap the front end of the truck, but the long-haired man behind the wheel regained control and passed, throwing up a spray of rocks and fine dust.

He passed so quickly I was unable to absorb any more details before the rooster tail of dust obscured his license tag. The only thing I got was the make and model of the vehicle.

Watching through the side and rearview mirrors to make sure he didn't turn into my driveway, I slowed and kept an eye on the receding cloud before swinging onto the neighbors' drive.

A hand-painted sign nailed to a hackberry tree beside the bob-wire fence read, BACKHOE SERVICES. Going a little faster than I should, I followed the two-lane track through the trees and came out into what amounted to a clearing, where an angry man and woman argued nose to nose not far from the trailer. They were both dressed in the uniform of that part of the state, faded jeans and camouflage hunting shirts.

It was hard to determine their ages because he'd spent much of his hardscrabble life in the sun, leaving him with a weathered look. She, on the other hand, had the emaciated look of a chronic meth head. I'd seen it a thousand times, and my younger brother, Harley, would always shake his head in wonder, more than once voicing the opinion that it'd be easier on everyone if they simply put a gun to their heads and got it over with before they destroyed everyone around them.

Two years behind me, Harley and I worked for DPS narcotics as an undercover team before I joined the TSCRA and he retired after being seriously injured on the job. We cut a swath through Texas drug dealers for years, working together under special dispensation from the governor, who barely raised an eyebrow at two brothers who reveled in the danger and adrenaline of putting criminals in jail.

We especially hated meth users and dealers.

Methamphetamine eventually wreaks havoc on addicts, etching their faces with ravine-deep wrinkles, loosening and rotting teeth, or creating yawning, oozing sores on their bodies. Every time we arrested the cooks or users back in those days, Harley and I often wondered how anyone voluntarily breathes in enough toxic smoke in one puff to give the EPA a rigor.

It's made from the corrosive cleaning materials you can find under the average homeowner's kitchen sink, including in some cases lye, battery acid, and acetone.

They give it cool street names like crystal, ice, LA glass, and now this newest drug whipped up in hell that took my wife and daughter, gravel. They sell it to weak-minded people with addictive tendencies who slowly kill themselves with it by smoking, swallowing, snorting, or injecting that garbage.

Appearing to chastise the couple, a teenage girl a year or two younger than Chloe stood spraddle-legged beside them in a white blouse and shorts, waving her smooth arms and stomping a bare foot to emphasize her point. The sun was behind them and in my eyes, but it did nothing to make the scene pleasant other than to halo the girl's tangled blond hair.

When the man saw my truck, he turned his back and handed something to the teenager. She hesitated for only a moment and he pointed at the trailer. She whirled and flew up the steps as smooth as a deer running through the woods.

My law enforcement training kicked in, and I wondered what those two were hiding. Had it been a real emergency, the older woman I assumed was his wife or girlfriend would have already headed my direction, looking for help. Instead, she remained where she was with her own bare feet rooted to the sandy ground.

Leaving the engine running, I shifted into park and opened the door. Keeping it between me and the couple, I put one foot on the running board and spoke through the open window. "Hey, folks. I'm Tucker Snow. I just moved into the house across the road there and heard some shooting that didn't sound like target practice." I glanced around as if looking for a shooting station. "You guys all right?"

They took longer than normal to absorb my comment and question. The woman started to answer around the half-smoked cigarette dangling from her lips, but the guy interrupted. "We're fine."

She shot him a look and waited, as if undecided about what to do.

I'd seen that kind of behavior in the past, while questioning people about a variety of transgressions. Women often deferred to the male standing nearby, letting him speak for the both of them. I found through the years that men who leaned toward spousal abuse wouldn't let their partners talk. Likely ingrained through violence, even if I specifically directed questions toward the woman, it was second nature for them to look to their husbands to answer.

The way she waited for him to speak irritated the hell out of me, but I wasn't there in an official capacity, and because of that, hadn't yet identified myself as a law enforcement officer, so I let it go. "Well, the shots sounded different to me, so I wanted to make sure you didn't have any trouble."

The guy with greasy hair cocked his head like a dog examining a strange new critter. He spat to the side and I tried not to think about the thick green glob that looked as if might have a spine. "What're you? The law?" His words were flat, accusatory.

"Depends on who you talk to."

"We were just shooting at a skunk that's been hanging around."

"Like I said, it sounded like two different guns from over there."

They exchanged a look, and the woman flicked the still-lit cigarette at his foot before she spun on her heel and headed for the trailer, weaving past a defunct washing machine. She climbed the wooden steps, and the door slammed behind her. I gave the rest of the yard a quick glance to make sure no one was hiding behind the junk or the two rusting vehicles up on blocks.

I'd always wondered how people could let their home places turn into junkyards. My dad grew up in a dirt-floor shack in the river bottoms with his brothers and sisters. He said they were dirt poor, but that was no reason not to be proud of what little they had. He always shook his head in disgust or wonderment when we passed houses squatting amid yards full of cast-off garbage, cars, and appliances.

The man stepped closer, likely for intimidation, and for the first time I got a good look at the guy of average height. He'd lost his razor a week earlier, and his comb before that, probably about three months after his barber died.

It wasn't the unwashed hair or beard that made me wary, though. Or the thin arms that weren't much more than corded rope and wire. It was his eyes, glassy and hot, the eyes of an angry dog that wanted nothing more than to bite the first appendage it could clamp onto.

They read drugs and danger.

His hand rose and seemingly flicked of its own accord. "I said we're fine. We don't much like city people getting into our business here in the country."

"I saw a car flash by." I kept my voice even, so he wouldn't think I was nervous. Humans are like animals, and sensing weakness either through fear or nervousness, they use it in whatever way works best for them. "It looked like he was in a hurry."

He stuck both hands into the front pockets of his faded jeans that hung off skinny hips so low that I was afraid they'd slide down and I'd see his willy. He could have benefited from a belt. "Just a misunderstanding. It was my cousin. He owes me money, and he's got a temper. Blew up when I asked him to pay it back and started waving a gun around after he was here for a few minutes."

"He shoot at y'all?"

"Naw. 'Bout that time a damned skunk came out from under the trailer, and he busted one at it."

"You too?"

"What? No, like I said, I tried to kill a skunk and missed. Them other shots was him's all." He was scrambling, trying to remember what he said only moments before.

"The cadence was like a shoot-out."

"Cadence?"

"The pattern of shots."

"Echoes. He can't hit shit with a pistol, and that made him mad when he missed." The guy paused, and I could see he was working out a story as he talked. "Tried to shoot something bigger and it was that washer sittin' over there. Missed it too. He was already aggravated when he got here, and when he missed it, I laughed at him and that made him madder, so he shot a couple more times."

"He shouldn't be shooting that way. My house is over there. One of those rounds could have hit my daughter, or me."

"Well, I said he shot at the washing machine, but it was really the ground. I don't know why I said that, 'cept you looked like the law coming up on me and all, and it made me nervous."

"I was. Special agent for the Cattleman's Association. Took a leave of absence." The blinds behind one window twitched, telling me someone was watching through the dirty, cloudy glass near the front. "Well, sorry we had to meet like this. I should have come by and said howdy when we moved in, but the truth is, I wasn't sure if anyone lived here."

"What're you saying?"

"I can't see your house very well from mine." I gave him a smile to settle the guy down. It must have worked, because he visibly relaxed and didn't seem as inclined to attack. "Lots of cedars between you and me."

"We do." He toed the ground with an untied sneaker. "Live

here, I mean. Got me a little backhoe business, and I take odd jobs ever now and then when we need a little more cash. Thanks for coming by."

I'd seen that before, too, when a liar is trying to cover a bad story and offers way too much information. "You bet."

As I settled under the steering wheel and backed around to leave, he remained where he was, standing in the open as if to block me from charging the house. Motion at a window at the rear of the trailer caught my attention. The blond teenager's face appeared for a second before I finished my turn.

The last thing I saw before the trees closed in behind me was the guy who still hadn't introduced himself by name, standing right where he was, watching.

Chapter Three

As soon as Snow turned around and left, Jess Atchley's common-law wife, Priscilla, came out on the rickety wooden porch deck and called across the yard. "What'd he want?"

He hated those kinds of questions, preferring instead to wait until he was inside to tell her in his own good time. Annoyed that she was shouting demands at him, Atchley balled his fist and kept his back to her, refusing to answer the woman who only brushed her hair about once a week, and that was when she went to town. He couldn't take it right now, to turn and see her in that oversize camo shirt and worn-out jeans that made her look more like the white trash she was.

Hell, he was white trash, too, but at least he didn't think he looked so much the part. Tense as a wound-up mainspring from the shooting, he listened to Snow's truck pull onto the county road.

"Did you hear me? What'd he want?" The shrill voice became sharper and snappish as she waited for the answer that wouldn't come. "All right then, but I'll tell you something. Don't you ever put me or my daughter on the spot like you just did. If he'd seen that pistol, he could call the laws and Jimma'd be the one who goes to jail for shooting at somebody's car."

He drew a long, deep breath to calm down.

Twitching and moving from the constant stream of meth in her body, she wouldn't quit. "I'd turn you over in a minute, you know. You're the one with the gunfire residues on your hands. I watch enough cop shows to know that, and they could get me for conspiracy to hide the facts, but I'd tell everything I knew to stay out of jail!"

Atchley considered his answer. He could explain that they would both be going to the pen if the DEA or the DPS showed up. They had enough meth stockpiled in the house to get both of them convicted of trafficking, so the self-educated bitch who spent most of her time watching reality television could yammer on all she wanted, and it wouldn't make any difference.

Dammit! A typical tweaker, she talked all of the time in an endless flow of the same local gossip over and over, or continually rattled on about people he didn't know or care about. Instead of being drawn into still another argument, he consciously tuned her out to think back about what Snow said and how he looked.

Who did that guy think he was, driving up like he owned the place to start asking questions? Atchley smelled po-po from the moment he got out, and then the dude actually told him he was cattle police. That's the laws for you, sniffing around where they weren't wanted, butting into people's business and stopping him from selling what people wanted. Who said the government could decide a substance was illegal just because they wanted to?

It was his job, and he intended to continue the family tradition of selling to those who needed something a little different.

Back in his granddaddy's day, the old man was a bootlegger and provided whiskey to anyone who had a few coins in their pocket. Why not? The drugstore shelves back then were full of products marketed to relieve pain, treat chronic illnesses, or help children feel better. The main ingredient was alcohol, but other patent medicines back then contained cocaine, heroin, or opium. So what was the damned difference?

Doctors routinely prescribed billions of pills with OxyContin at the top of the list. So why not something that worked quickly and was a helluva lot cheaper in the long run and you didn't have to pay no expensive doctor to get what you needed?

"Are you listening to me, Jess?"

He turned and studied her stringy dishwater-blond hair for a moment. "Shut up." There was no power, no venom in his response, but she apparently heard something she didn't like. She deflated and went inside without another word.

Why couldn't a person buy what they wanted? They lived in a free country, and if somebody wanted to smoke meth to deal with life's problems, it was their business and nobody else's. Hell, if it made you feel better so you could put up with another day of life, then suck it in. He provided a service, like prostitutes. Prostitution was illegal, just because a bunch of Bible-thumpers didn't want consenting adults to do what they wanted behind closed doors.

Damned laws. Had to wear a seat belt. Had to have a license just to drive. Had to pay taxes on land they owned. Had to pay taxes on what people made on their daily jobs. Had to pay taxes on most of what they bought at Walmart.

Atchley brought himself back to the moment and stalked toward the trailer. Stomping up the steps, he paused on the warped porch. From his elevated position, roughly three feet off the ground, he could see the upper half of the old Berry house, where Snow said he just moved to.

Only half of what Atchley told Snow was the truth. It wasn't a relative who showed up making trouble. It was that Lawrence idiot who didn't have enough money for two hits of crystal and tried to negotiate a deal, trading some damned hot rims for enough crank to get him through the week.

Everybody knew he didn't trade. His was a cash business, and he told him so. Dealing in stolen goods was a quick trip back to the pen, and he wanted none of it. Told the kid, but the dumbass started waving a gun around and fired off a round over the house to make a point. It didn't work, because Atchley wasn't afraid of shit, and he snapped, snatching a Glock from under his shirt and putting two past the dumbass's ear to show him who was running things.

He'd kill the son of a bitch the next time he showed up too. You don't piss off a country boy who knows how to shoot and owns a backhoe.

Taking a deep breath because he still didn't want to fight with Priscilla at that moment, Atchley reached for the doorknob at the same time a security bar fell into place. The familiar thump made him madder'n hell.

The anger building behind his eyes exploded as he twisted the knob and threw his shoulder against the cheap hollow core door. "Open up, dammit!" He backed up and gave the weathered plywood a kick.

Priscilla shouted from the inside. "Not till you stay out there and cool off for a few minutes. I knew you were working up to a mad!"

Atchley threw his weight against the door again, pissed that the steel bar he'd installed on the inside held as solid as a boulder. It was supposed to keep narcs and robbers out, at least until they could grab a pistol or dump their stock, but not *him*! "Open the damned door!"

Her voice came through, soft and scared. "No, Jess. Give us a couple of minutes alone in here, will you?"

"Priscilla, if you don't open this goddamn door, I'm gonna kick it off the hinges before I beat the ears off your damned head. Now, let me in!"

"Please don't be mad at me."

"I'm not mad, just pissed that you won't unbar the damned door."

"All right, but just take a deep breath before you come in." A couple of seconds later he heard the bar slide free and thump onto the floor. The dead bolt snicked back, and she opened up, moving back a step.

Atchley gave her a smile. "There, see? It's all good." He stepped inside, immediately enveloped by a stew of cigarette smoke, soured food, unwashed dishes, and garbage that should have been taken out a week earlier. He closed the door behind him. Jimma peeked around the corner, eyes wide and scared. "Hey, I'm not mad at y'all, Jim-Jim." It was his nickname for Jimma, his stepdaughter by common-law cohabitation. "I know I'm hard to live with, and I'm sorry I yelled at you both, but that Lawrence kid got me all stirred up. Just don't ever lock me out again."

Priscilla relaxed and built a tentative grin that disappeared when his fist snapped her head back. She hit the floor like a felled timber, and he kicked her out of the way. Jimma disappeared into her back room, slamming the door.

Atchley leaned over and pointed his finger at the stunned woman lying on the floor. "This is my goddamned house, and *nobody* locks me out." He chuckled. "You better be glad I'm *not* mad."

Priscilla rolled onto her side, curled up in anticipation of even more violence. Instead, he ignored her, took two steps into the kitchen, and plucked a Busch Light off the fridge's top shelf. Stepping over her prone form, he ignored her familiar sobs and dropped into his recliner. Tugging the phone from his back pocket, he punched up a name and waited for the call to go through.

"Lloyd, I have a job for you tonight." He and his second cousin had worked together for years, even before Lloyd got out of the army, and the things he learned there served them well in their growing business. Atchley outlined the night's activities and hung up, knowing Lloyd would do what was needed.

Satisfied, Atchley walked outside and punched up another number as he climbed into the cab and started his truck.

The blunt, rough voice on the other end was abrupt. "What?"

"This is Jess." Atchley climbed into his truck and turned around.

"Yeah, I know that. Your name just came up on the phone."

"Oh, yeah." Atchley hated it when he said or did something stupid around Butch, who'd been to college and was one of the most successful and important members of the family. "Listen, some guy moved into the Berry place across the road and heard something a little while ago that made him suspicious. He drove over here to the house and we talked, but I think he's some kind of law. Said he's a special agent."

"What kind?"

"Works for the Southwestern Cattle Association."

"He's a brand inspector."

"Okay, so what?" Atchley turned right and drove slowly toward the Berry place.

"Those guys are part of the DPS, and they're even known as Special Rangers. Hell, maybe more. They have the authority to investigate and make arrests up in *Oklahoma* if they want to."

"Oh, shit." Atchley felt himself deflate. He watched the big house pass on his left. "That's bad, huh?"

"Probably. He do much sniffing around?"

"Nope. Just said his name was Tucker Snow and he wanted to know if everything was all right, I just don't trust him is all."

"You didn't say anything stupid, did you?"

"I know better than that." No one was outside the Berry place. His green Expedition and white Dodge truck were parked out front. He wondered how many people were inside.

"Umm hum. Anything going on there to make him wonder?"

"Not that I know of."

"Bullshit. I hear it in your voice."

Did the man on the other end somehow know Atchley was scouting the house in the bright daylight? "Well, me and Priscilla were arguing in the yard and he was eavesdropping, and then I cranked off a couple of shots from my Glock when that dumbass Lawrence kid came by, 'cause he made me mad and I wanted to scare him. Bastard wanted to trade some hot rims for a couple of rocks, then he pulled a damned peashooter and...and we weren't really shooting at each other...but that's all. Anyway, I called Lloyd and he's gonna check around over there at that guy's house tonight. Just wanted you to know...and ever'thing..." Atchley sometimes drifted off and ended with awkward ways to fill in the gap when he was talking to people who intimidated him, and there were a handful of people like that for sure, especially Butch.

"I wish you hadn't done that."

Atchley reached the corner where the Rock Hill intersected

Blue Creek Road. Using one hand to turn the wheel since the other held the phone to his ear, he pushed the accelerator and the little truck sped down the road in a cloud of dust. "How come?"

"You're liable to screw this all up."

"Lloyd's good. All he's gonna do is look around."

"We don't need him messin' around over there. Just leave it alone."

"You know Lloyd. He's like that blue genie. Once I let him out, I can't get him back in the bottle."

"Well, don't do anything that'll cause me any grief. I don't want to have to come out there."

Atchley felt a chill go down his back. Even though Butch was another second cousin, the man was still someone you didn't want to tangle with. "You won't. Bye bye."

He hung up, silently cursing himself for sounding like a little kid on the phone. He'd worked long and hard to build his reputation as a solid man, and that kind of slipup didn't help at all.

Bye bye.

Shit!

Chapter Four

In jeans and an oversized orange sweatshirt, Chloe waited at the door with her phone in hand when I pulled around to park the truck on the circle drive out front. Though she'd changed out of the T-shirt she'd slept in, I noticed she stood barefoot on our hardwood floor, and it seemed as if she did something every day that reminded me of her mother. Sara Beth hated to wear shoes at home, so unless we were going somewhere, she'd pad around in bare feet with her red toenails showing.

Chloe was speaking before I killed the engine. "What happened?"

"Nothing." I got out and gave her a little hug. The way her hair fell around her face was a mirror image of Sara Beth, and my stomach ached with misery. She patted my back and we stood on the porch in order to maintain enough elevation to see what little of the nearby trailer was visible.

She waited while I studied the trees. "I'm not sure I believe that. One time, Mom explained the way you're looking right now, and she said it's your thinking face. You know, you're not as good at hiding what's on your mind these days."

"Um, humm." I couldn't see as much of the trailer as I wanted. "Let's go upstairs."

She followed as I went inside and up to the second floor, but she peeled off into her room. I went into the southeast bedroom overlooking the front lawn and Rock Hill Road. What I thought of as the guest room was an exact flip from my master suite that overlooked the pasture behind. The higher sight line gave me a good look at most of the upper half of the trailer and a good part of the yard full of junk.

I plucked the phone from the back pocket of my jeans and took a photo of the area, then increased the magnification and shot another. With it in my hand, I thought about calling Ganther Bluff's emergency number, but then what would I tell them?

That I heard gunshots in the country?

That I talked to the landowners and they denied anything other than shooting at a skunk and a clothes washer?

Sighing, I tucked it away, and half a second later it rang. I checked the screen to see that it was Harley. "What's up, little brother?"

Harley's the exact opposite of my own personality. He was always the one who laughed at the devil when his train went by, while I was the most cautious. We were an unusual pair, twenty years earlier, country boys who wound up in big-city law enforcement as undercover narcotics officers for the DPS. Arrests, fights, gunfights, car chases, and living two distinct lives apart from our families finally caught up with us, and we figured we'd used up most of our luck on the day he was shot.

The kid he never grew out of was still in him, and it showed through in almost every way with wisecracks and eternal optimism. His eyes always smiled even when someone irritated him, and his whole demeanor was always lighter than mine.

However, once he got a mad on, you better hunt a hole. He's the kind of person who'll shoot a bad guy, piss on him, and go have breakfast without another thought.

"Nothing much. Checking on you after Chloe called and said there was a lot of shooting around your place."

In the back of my mind, I kinda expected him to call, even though I hadn't reached out. We thought alike, reacted alike, and operated so well together we each knew what the other was doing or planning to do. Whenever we had to include other officers in our operations, we were as on edge as a cat in a room full of rocking chairs.

All those years, we were seldom injured, and even then it was in bruises, cracked ribs, or scratches and sprains, though we exchanged gunfire more times than we wanted. Then one hot, humid Dallas night, some punk put two rounds in him when a buy went bad.

They planted the shooter the next day, and the department offered Harley a desk job, but Harley couldn't sit behind one of the things if you nailed him to a chair. Through bureaucratic red tape, they finally pushed him into retirement. One weekend he agreed to train a mixed group of male and female citizen students to survive what he called "urban chaos." It quickly became a must-take course for hundreds of people in North Texas, and he soon launched Lone Star Tactical, a one-man company training police, SWAT officers, and military contractors.

I grinned at the humor in his voice. "Folks across the way there were shooting, all right. I thought it sounded like a gunfight, but when I went over, they denied it was anything."

"Only you would buy a house next to a gun range."

"It's not a range, but I think the guy was lying to me. It's something else."

"What?"

"I have an idea, but I'll let you tell *me* when you come over."

"You in trouble?"

"Naw." I watched the still-unnamed man come outside and cross the cluttered yard to a beat-up old blue Ford Ranger pickup. He climbed inside, turned around, and pulled out onto the road that passed our house. "I was just being neighborly."

"Some people might call that being nosy."

"Some might."

The faded pickup rolled slowly past the house, so close I could see enough dents to make me think it'd been through a demolition derby. The hood and top of the cab were as dimpled as a golf ball from one helluva hailstorm.

He passed slowly while talking on the phone and giving the house a good once-over. I was glad we weren't still on the porch. With one hand on top of the steering wheel, he tilted his head up, and it felt like he was looking straight at me through the closed window, though I'd backed up a couple of steps, confident the reflections off the glass prevented him from seeing inside.

Harley's voice rose when he repeated a question I'd missed.

Coming back to the conversation, I had to concentrate on what he was saying. "What was that?"

"I said, we have some steaks in the freezer. How about if we come over tomorrow night and throw you a housewarming party?"

I glanced over at Chloe leaning against the doorframe, intent on the phone in her hand. "Sure. It'll do both of us some good to see y'all."

"Great. We'll be over around five or so."

"I'll have the charcoal ready."

"Just have the beer cold."

"I have to supply the beer at my own housewarming?"

"It's your job to take care of your little brother."

"The *little* brother who's so much bigger than me he can pick up a refrigerator by himself."

"Right. That one."

"See you later." I hung up and watched the truck continue toward the T intersection at the far end of my property line where the two county roads come together, realizing I still didn't know the greasy-haired guy's name. "Hey, kiddo, you up for a trip to town tomorrow?"

Chloe heard me and came out of her room, only looking up from her own phone when she walked into the spare bedroom. "Sure. Where we going?"

"The grocery store, a stop at wherever you want, and a quick run into the county tax office."

She frowned. "I knew there'd be a catch."

"Well, I just want to find out who lives over there." I pointed over my shoulder at the trailer.

She rolled her eyes and tapped on her phone's screen. "You old people just kill me."

"Why's that?"

"You don't have to go to the tax office for that information. It's all on the internet." Her voice trailed off for a second and I watched my little girl who stood on the cusp of becoming a woman. A sharp jolt punched me in the gut when I realized I'd have to deal with all of those hormones and questions by myself, instead of relying on Sara Beth's expertise as a woman and mother. I was about to put Harley's wife, Tammy, on speed dial.

Chloe was sharper than I gave her credit for. She held the phone out so I could see the screen. "Here you go. The guy who lives over there is Jess Atchley."

Chapter Five

Phone signals in the country are sometimes spotty at best. Chloe was still poking at hers when I checked my screen and saw that I had full bars. Without thinking any further, I punched the number for the sheriff's office. I'd already keyed it into my contacts list from sheer force of habit.

The female voice that answered was pure country. "Sheriff's office."

"This is Agent Tucker Snow, stock inspector. I recently moved into the old Berry house out here on Rock Hill Road."

"I heard that place sold. How can I help you?"

"I wanted to report suspicious gunfire not far from the house."

"Suspicious how? You're out in the country, you know."

I swallowed a sharp answer, knowing dispatch gets a lot of calls from city people moving from the suburbs. Those calls are a fun topic of conversation when country LEOs, law enforcement officers, get together. People have been known to report coyote and bobcat sightings, "abandoned" fawns, or injured rabbits and squirrels that in their opinion, needed transportation to a veterinarian.

"Who am I speaking to?"

"This is Mary Lynn Davis."

"Mary Lynn, I've been in law enforcement for twenty years and was raised in the country, so I know the difference between target practice or hunting."

Chloe's eyebrow rose at my tone, and she gave me a half grin as she listened.

The woman's condescending attitude immediately evaporated at my slightly sharper, but still polite tone. "I understand. Hold just one minute."

I glanced out the window again at the neighbor's yard. The young girl appeared and stepped down the warped deck and walked out into the yard. She backed up to the abandoned washing machine and hopped on top. I wondered what she was doing until I realized she came out for a smoke. I found my brow furrowing at the thought of a girl two or three years younger than Chloe sucking a trash fire into her lungs.

The room was getting stuffy, so I opened the windows while I waited. A cool cross breeze filled the room. A mockingbird perched on the limb of a hackberry tree about thirty feet from the house went through her repertoire of songs. I was just about to hang up and call back again when a husky, phlegmy male voice brought me back into the room full of stacked furniture and unopened boxes packed with clothes and household items.

"Chief Deputy Lomax. How can I help you, Mr. Snow?"

"Special Agent Snow. Texas and Southwestern Cattle." I went through the same recitation of what I'd seen and heard while he listened without interruption. "The family is named Atchley. I talked with Jess and told him who I was." There was no need to discuss the man's attitude at that particular moment.

"I know the family. Has there been any further disturbance?"

"Not since about thirty minutes ago."

"Do you feel as if you're in any danger?"

"No. Like I said, based on my experience, it sounded like a conflict, but he explained that it was a disagreement with a cousin."

Lomax chuckled and I got the sense that he was a smoker. "We get a lot of that out here. If I had a nickel every time we got called on family disagreements I could retire in a couple of years. Every time we show up, they're all lovey-dovey, and all we get is deflection."

"I know the drill." I'd already given up. We were in the commiseration stage of the discussion. "I just wanted to let you know what happened, that and the fact that there's a lot of traffic on the road that runs past my house day and night. Mostly at night. It sure seems like there's more cars coming and going out here than you'd expect in our area."

Lomax took several beats to answer. He finally drew a deep breath. "I'm not sure what you're saying."

"Just making an observation that might tie into what I just told you."

"Mr. Snow, are you calling me as part of an investigation? You planning on taking official action on this information?"

There was that "Mister Snow" thing again. I had the feeling he was dismissing both me *and* the badge, putting me on notice. Had I not been on leave, that was exactly what I'd be doing. TSCRA Special Rangers assist in recovering stolen livestock and equipment, and arresting the thieves. We also investigate the thefts of cattle, horse, saddles, trailers and equipment. Essentially, anything having to do with the farm and ranch business.

Chloe's eyebrows rose, and I once again realized that young peoples' hearing is astronomically better than what us older folks have, or people who've shot a lot of guns. Nearly a year earlier, she'd downloaded the mosquito ringtone that adults can't hear. As soon as Sara Beth heard about it, she demanded that Chloe delete it while she watched.

"Not at all. I'm not working right now and this is nothing to take action on."

"Come again?"

"Took a leave of absence." He didn't need any more info.

"So, you're not working."

I bit off a sharp reply. The guy was making me clarify my statement for some reason. "No."

"Oh, okay." Did I sense relief in his voice? "Well, enjoy your time off and call if I can do anything else for you."

You haven't done anything yet, I thought, but again pounded down the response. "You bet."

My daughter and I remained where we were in what amounted to a temporary storeroom, listening to the mockingbird sing through the open window's screen. The sound of a vehicle on gravel came to us and we turned toward that same window to watch Jess Atchley pass again on his way back home from nowhere.

We were quite a ways out in the country. There was no way he could have gone anywhere in that short amount of time.

We were under surveillance.

Chapter Six

The air cooled quickly after the sun sank below the trees on the far side of what I came to think of as the lake out back of the house. After a supper of Hamburger Helper, Chloe and I sat in lawn chairs and watched the high air currents sweep yellow and orange fire across the sky with long brushstrokes, changing it to red, and finally blending into grades of blazing pink until the light faded.

A low-flying skein of honking Canada geese circled the pool before cupping their wings to settle into the middle, where they were safe from predators. When they landed on the surface, it sounded like someone throwing buckets of water across the still surface.

"I think I'm going to build a real firepit right there."

Chloe lowered her phone and looked where I was pointing. "Why?"

"Summer's gone, and I'd like to sit out here beside a fire. It's cooling off pretty fast, and I'd rather stay out here with you a little longer."

Her eyes flicked from me to the patch of grass. "I'd like that."

"We can build it together."

"Is it hard?"

"Nope. While we're in town tomorrow, we'll pick up some of those curved landscape bricks. That's all we need. By the time Harley'n them get here tomorrow afternoon, we can have a firepit. The boys can roast marshmallows."

"Good, I've been missing Aunt Tammy and the boys." Always rough as cobs, Harley's six- and seven-year-olds, Danny and Matt, were always into something. "Uncle Harley always makes me feel better when he's around."

An owl hooted down in the creek bottoms, a deep, soothing sound. There was still enough glow on the horizon to reflect on the water, silhouetting the geese. She watched them for a few moments. "Let's go to the grocery store too. I have an idea for some recipes."

I looked at her in surprise. "You're going to take over kitchen duties?"

"You shouldn't have to cook all the time." She gave me a grin. "And I'd like a little more variety than what we had tonight."

"That was my famous Hamburger Helper. I spiced it up with those green peppers."

"Dad's famous dishes." She smiled. "Everything you cooked had that name. Dad's famous stew. Dad's famous spaghetti. You had Peyton believing that you were a great cook, and it was all out of a box."

I didn't react to Peyton's name. It was the first time Chloe had spoken her name aloud since the accident. Maybe the loss of her mother and little sister was fading, at least a little, instead of always being a painful jolt. "She liked my famous scrambled eggs."

"Well, she was four." Chloe's eyes sparkled in the dim light. "I'll take care of the cooking duties if you'll handle the dishes."

"You mean you don't want to load and unload the dishwasher."

"Right. And I'd like something fresh, with fewer calories and more nutrition."

I studied my daughter, still frightened by the prospect of her next few hormonal years. "It's a deal."

"Dad, I'm sorry I've been so hard to live with since Mom..."

The crunch of gravel under an approaching vehicle broke the peaceful evening. I stood and walked to the end of the house to see who was coming by. Two quick honks came from a pickup. Though they couldn't see us on the opposite side of the house, it was Bud and Clara Grubbs's country way to say howdy without stopping on their way home. Though they probably weren't looking toward where I was standing beside a tall pecan tree, I waved anyway and the pickup passed, leaving a small cloud of dust in its wake.

"What were you saying, babe?"

She reached out and took my hand. "Nothing, just I love you."

"Well, I love you too."

We passed the time in comfortable silence. For once, she put down her phone and allowed her eyes to adjust to the darkness. I'd been watching the sky, and she tilted her head to study the stars. That far out in the country, the clear sky was filled with billions of bright lights and the cloudy sweep of the Milky Way.

After almost an hour, Chloe spoke. "It's beautiful, Dad, but how can we have smog way out here?"

"It isn't smog, baby. It's the Milky Way. This is what it's supposed to look like at night. People have watched the stars for thousands, if not millions of years. It looked like this a couple of hundred years ago, only I bet it was even brighter then, when there was nothing at all in the air except for smoke on occasion."

"I wish they were here to see this."

My eyes burned, and I blinked away tears, knowing who she was talking about. "They're looking at it right now. My grandmother, your Mama Esther, would say they're right here with us."

Her phone buzzed with an incoming message, but since it was lying facedown on the arm of her chair, the light didn't interrupt the night. Out of character, she didn't check to see who was texting, and we shared even more of the evening until the air cooled.

Chloe shivered and stood up. "I'm getting chilly, and I haven't finished my homework." We had enrolled her in school on Monday a week earlier, and she was already out for fall break, but she was always one of those kids who wanted to get her lessons out of the way as soon as she could, instead of waiting until the last minute.

She gave me a hug and crossed the yard. "Night, Daddy. I love you."

Fighting the ache in my chest, I hugged her back. "Love you too, babe."

She went inside, and I watched the stars for a little longer before going in and locking the back door. We had one of those K-cup instant coffee machines in the kitchen, so I turned it on and waited for the water to heat. When the blue button blinked ready, I dropped in a cup of Angelino's brand coffee and waited a few seconds for my mug to fill with the Hawaiian blend. When it was ready, I walked through the living room and out onto the front porch and settled into one of the rockers.

Taking a sip of the hot liquid, I relaxed in the shadows, propped my feet on the rail, and watched more stars pop out. Barely moving the swing and enjoying the coffee, I caught a glimpse off to my left of oncoming headlights flickering through the trees on Blue Creek Road. They turned down Rock Hill and passed with a rattle of rocks against the undercarriage.

The dark Toyota sedan didn't slow until its headlights lit up a reflector on the Atchleys' gatepost. Brake lights flashed, and it turned into the drive. Taking another swallow of the cooling coffee, I checked my watch.

It was a quick turnaround and lights flashed again, coming back down the drive. Like anyone else in the country and at that time of night, it didn't stop, but rolled out onto the road and accelerated past the house.

I looked at my watch again. Ten minutes.

Just enough time to pick up a date? Naw, the girl was too young, I hoped.

Based on my experience, it was just enough time to make a quick drug buy, that is, if the sellers knew the buyers. Had it been strangers, or a big buy, the exchange might have taken longer.

Harley and I had been on both ends of those kinds of deals when he and I were working undercover. They were our bread and butter, but no matter how many arrests we made, more of the same kind of people kept coming back over and over again.

The coffee was cold. I pitched the dregs over the rail and stood. Despite the reasons Chloe and I were there, it was a good place to live, and I was glad to get her out into the country where it was safe...for the most part.

At least two more cars passed by the time I locked all the doors and turned out the downstairs lamp. As I climbed the stairs, the slim glow beneath Chloe's door went off.

She'd helped me hang simple curtains over the windows in our rooms the second day after we moved in. It was stuffy in mine, so I pulled them back and opened two windows for a little cross breeze. Coyotes yipped in the distance, chasing their supper through the woods. I slipped under the covers and lay there, listening to the chase that faded in the Long Creek bottoms below the house, which wasn't much more than a glorified wash.

Some of the men up at the store brought me up to speed on the area the first time I went to pick up a loaf of bread and they realized I'd bought the ranch. Long Creek seldom held water, not like Catfish Bayou only a couple of miles south. Most of the time, the creek contained only muddy pockets that dried up in the summer.

Our ranch was created by the previous owner who bought up several small farms over the years, taking down some of the fences to provide access to pastures that were once cotton and cornfields. Looking at our place on the map, it was mostly a two-mile square, except for the hundred acres across the road.

Nights in the country are never truly quiet. In addition to the coyotes, owls, and geese, the air was filled with the sounds of crickets and tree frogs. A whippoorwill called, adding to the orchestra and reminding me of nights at my grandparents' house not far from Crockett, in Deep East Texas.

A dog barked in the far distance, barely heard through the wire screens. Hands behind my head, I stared at the ceiling, wishing for what would never be again, and uncertain about my future, and Chloe's.

Chapter Seven

Dressed in dark clothes that clung to his wide shoulders and slim waist, Lloyd Belcher stood in the damp early morning darkness beside the five-strand bob-wire fence separating the old Berry house from the south pasture. He waited, listening for a dog to bark from inside the house.

Reaching for the ever-present pack of cigarettes in his shirt pocket, he paused. Lighting one right then was impossible. Choking down his obsession, he returned them to his pocket and took out a blister pack of nicotine gum. Punching four of the squares free, he popped them in his mouth and chewed fast as a chipmunk to release the drug.

Night creatures filled the still air with their songs as the nicotine flooded his bloodstream. An owl hooted from the creek bottom at the same time a pack of coyotes chased supper in those same lowlands. Listening to the pursuit, he took a deep breath as the jolt hit him.

Now he could get busy. He started to duck between the wires and paused at the sight of headlights flicking through the trees. Cursing, he dropped flat onto the ground, confident the dark clothes would blend with the shadows as the vehicle passed. He almost chuckled when the truck turned into the Atchley drive.

Another customer.

As long as he was lying in the shadows, Belcher unsheathed a knife and rapped it twice against the steel fence post. The sound rang clear, and he waited several more minutes for a dog to come around the house to investigate the noise.

After ten minutes he relaxed when nothing happened, except for the vehicle that pulled back on to the road and disappeared with the flicker of taillights.

Still chewing with almost frantic speed, he remained on his belly and crawled under the bob-wire fence like an alligator. Liking the way it felt, he covered several more feet that same way before rising and moving across the grass light as smoke. Belcher made a full circle around the dark house, searching for an unlocked window or door. Finally, back at the edge of the porch, he glanced upward.

Hoping the owner was careless like most people who lived in two-story houses, his next attempt would be through the second floor. Stepping onto the porch rail, he pulled himself onto the roof that ended under windows along the front.

The first window Belcher saw was open, and he removed the screen with slow, deliberate motions. It rose with barely a sound. Less than a minute later he was standing in a room full of furniture and boxes.

It was time to go to work.

Chapter Eight

I'm not a deep sleeper, never have been, and it was harder and harder to get more than three or four hours a night. That's why I heard Sara Beth's voice in the darkness, soft in my ear.

Tuck, wake up.

I awoke from a light doze, chilled by the current of autumn air flowing through the screen like a river.

You need to check on Chloe.

Turning my head to look at her, I snapped completely awake. The pillow beside me was fluffed and smooth, the blanket lying flat on the mattress. Sara Beth would never sleep next to me again. That familiar ache of loss swept through my body, and I pulled the covers higher. Sleep was out of the question, and a few minutes later I needed to visit the bathroom.

Sighing, I swung both feet out of bed and paused at the sound of a creak.

Sitting there in the darkness, I wondered if it was the house settling as the night cooled, or if Chloe was up. I checked the clock on the nightstand. It read 3:13. I stayed where I was and listened.

When the sound didn't repeat itself. I reached for my jeans and pulled them on. Barefoot and shirtless, I crossed the room and opened the door. There were no lights coming from under her door, but the spare room full of boxes and furniture was half open. I tried to recall if I'd closed it earlier that day. A jolt hit my stomach when I remembered the window was still up after we finished watching the road and the Atchley's house.

I went to close it and found that the screen was off.

I stopped, senses jangling. My Colt was still on the nightstand beside the bed, farther away than I preferred. Remaining where I was, I scanned the room, squinting into shadows. The moon was bright, providing enough illumination to see into the corners. When I was sure no one was hiding there with a machete or a chainsaw, I crossed to the window and peered outside.

The screen lay on the porch roof. It could have fallen after we left. It could have happened naturally, pushed loose by a breeze, or the expansion or contraction of the window. But the more suspicious part of my mind told me it would be easy for an athletic intruder to climb onto the porch rail, pull himself up onto the roof, and then through the window.

I willed my heart to quit beating so hard. Glad to be barefoot, I hurried down the hall on the balls of my feet and ducked back into my bedroom to get my pistol. Turning the knob as carefully as possible, I opened Chloe's door and peeked inside. She lay on her back, mouth slightly open and breathing softly. The blinds were down and the curtains were drawn. There are a lot of places to hide in a dark room, and I wasn't about to leave until I was sure she was alone.

A seashell night-light from a weekend in Galveston two years earlier provided enough glow to see. After checking behind the door, the obvious place for bad guys to hide in the movies, I slipped around the end of her bed. No one was crouching on the other side. I knelt and did a quick push up to peer underneath.

Her dark closet was partially open with no boogeyman in evidence. Pushing the adjoining bathroom door open until it touched the wall, I scanned the interior with the aid of another night-light on the counter. The shower curtain was pulled back, the tub empty.

Clearing a house was one of my least favorite things to do, especially with my daughter there. Gently closing the door behind me, I held the pistol at high ready, the natural and familiar way I'd learned to carry it in such circumstances.

It took another five minutes to check the rest of the second floor, and I felt better to know she and I were alone up there. Maybe there was no one at all and I'd worked myself up for no reason, but experience weighed heavy on my mind. I'd seen too many instances of B&Es going bad, resulting in injury or death. Night weighs heavy on people, and oftentimes we experience more dread and danger in the darkness, than the day. We've all been awakened in the night by some sound, and more than once laid in bed, imaginations running wild.

It could have been my subconscious, but Sara Beth's voice told me it was real. *Check on Chloe.* Something was threatening her, and I wasn't going to allow anything to happen to either of us.

I paused at the head of the stairs. For a moment I swore a shadow passed at the bottom from left to right on the first floor, but it could have been my imagination. I had to make the rounds down there too.

Descending stairs is a little safer than going the other way. They're shooting galleries for anyone waiting at the top, but going down, the higher position gave me a clear view of the dim hall and doorways below. Halfway down, I paused. Instead of peering directly into the darker shadows where someone might hide, I looked slightly off to the side.

Used to the darkness, and because I hadn't turned on any lights, my night vision was intact. It was wise to move slowly, listening every two or three steps. I wanted to think someone was there, but there was no concrete evidence one way or the other, yet.

Straight ahead was the front door. Still locked.

Turning back to the interior, I had a living area on the right and the formal dining room-turned-office on the left. I chose to clear the living room first, and it was empty. When I was crossing back to the office, the hair on the back of my neck prickled, that sixth sense of unseen danger that came from our ancestors who fearfully squatted in caves and the darkness.

Something wasn't right.

It was then I caught the strong odor of cigarette smoke, like the scent that emanates from the bodies and clothing of heavy smokers. My senses heightened, and that warning jangling in the back of my mind went into overdrive. I worked through the office and into the kitchen. Still no one, but the lingering smell wasn't my imagination. Someone toxic in more ways than one had been in the house.

The back door was unlocked, and I knew I'd turned the dead bolt when I came in for the night. Twisted tight as a clock spring, I made a second round on the ground floor, double-checking that the windows were locked and making sure no one was in the closets or even under the cabinets.

The cigarette odor was strongest in the kitchen, and I figured that's where the intruder spent most of his time for whatever reason. I wondered why, with the whole house open to investigate. What was the guy after?

Finally, sure the intruder was gone, I stepped out onto the back porch. The boards were smooth and chilly under my bare feet. Still cautious, I waited with my back to the outside wall. The silver moonlight was bright and clear, with sharp, defined shadows under the surrounding trees. I watched for several minutes, hoping to catch movement from the corners of my eyes, but there was nothing.

A pair of my old sneakers sat on the floor beside the door, and I slipped them on without tying the laces. Feeling a little better that I wasn't barefoot, I went inside and flicked on the kitchen and back porch lights. The windows were bare, with nothing more than vinyl pull-down shades to block the view from outside. I went around the ground floor, closing them all.

Relaxed now that no one could look inside, I turned on the rest of the lights on that floor and made another round. When I was finished, I went upstairs and eased Chloe's door open once again to be sure she was still asleep, then lit up the second floor also and made the rounds one last time.

Her door opened by the time I finished and her sleepy head poked out. "Dad, are you all right? What's with all the lights?"

"I heard something and wanted to look around."

"With every light in the house on?"

"I didn't turn on the closet lights."

"Funny. You woke me up."

"Sorry, kiddo. You know how my paranoia is."

Bathroom.

It was Sara Beth's voice again in my head, and I suddenly had a sickening thought. I pulled her bare arm rougher than I intended and pushed past her. "Stay right here for a minute."

The locks on her windows were engaged, and I flicked on the lights. Her closet door was still open, but the light revealed nothing but hanging clothes and a mound of laundry on the floor. Still unconvinced, I went back to the bathroom and flicked the switch.

It was there I found a damp chunk of mud in the clean white tub. My stomach flipped as I picked it up. I've tracked enough mud into the house to recognize it as a piece that came from that space between the heel and instep.

My stomach flipped again when I realized the intruder had already been in my daughter's room before I came in the first time. Choking down a wave of nausea and dread, I palmed the chunk of mud so she wouldn't realize the intruder had been in her room and came back out.

Chloe leaned against the wall, one foot against the inside of her opposite knee like a stork. She was back in my faded old T-shirt, and it swallowed her. "Are you finished?"

I finally relaxed. "For the time being."

"I'm going to the bathroom then. Have you made sure there aren't any boogers in there? Don't want anything coming up through the toilet to bite my butt while I'm sitting there."

I swallowed. The boogeyman had been in there. "It's fine, and don't be a smart-ass."

She threw me a sleepy grin and disappeared inside.

I went downstairs and back into the kitchen to start over. Someone had been in my house, and I was determined to check every square inch. That's where I saw a sprinkle of what looked like powdered sugar on the baseboard under the light switch by the back door. The powder also dusted a tiny section of the floor. Moving closer, I followed the trail up to the light switch. Slight scuff marks on the screws holding the faceplate drew my attention.

Touching one of them with a fingertip, I felt a tiny burr and slight warmth. Someone had removed the plate and at the same time had dislodged dust, paint, and plaster powder.

Wall switches shouldn't be warm. I flicked it off, cutting the light in there by half. Using a screwdriver from our junk drawer, I took the screws out and removed the faceplate. Instead of the pair of black-and-white wires I expected, the switch box was filled with a snarl of unfamiliar electrical spaghetti. Heat radiated from the inside, and I worked through what I was looking at.

The warmth, strange wires, an unidentifiable tiny glass tube, and an intruder equaled something I couldn't have imagined before that moment. Someone broke in and booby-trapped the light switch to burn the place down.

Experience with basic house wiring came to my aid. I flipped the breaker in the pantry and removed the little device and rewired the switch to the way it was. That done, I went to the bathroom to relieve the pressure on my bladder, then sat up the rest of the night with the lights out and my pistol in hand, watching out the window after thanking Sara Beth for waking me up.

Chapter Nine

Daylight filtered through the Atchley trailer's filthy windows and around stained paper blinds that were always closed. A baggie of cocaine sat in a glass ashtray on a cluttered table alongside half a dozen tiny baggies of meth measured out for sale.

Lloyd Belcher and Jess Atchley sat at the table in the trailer's tiny dining room, which was separated from the kitchen by a low pony wall. The counter was full of condiments, empty beer bottles, dirty pots and pans, and an assortment of cheap knickknacks. Smoke hung low from the ceiling as Belcher made up for the cigarettes he couldn't smoke while he was in Snow's house.

Beside them, small twists of tissue paper held about a quarter gram of gravel that sold for two hundred dollars, twice the price of crystal meth. Each hit was enough to ramp up a user for about twelve hours, giving them enough superhuman chemical energy to make them feel capable of doing anything they could think of.

Two semi-automatic pistols rested near each man's hand. A pump shotgun and an AR-15 leaned against the wall beside the front door.

The dismal kitchen beside them needed to be burned out and rebuilt. Food-encrusted dishes filled the equally dirty sink. Trash overflowed from the trash can onto the floor like lava from a volcano.

"That was one of the easiest jobs you've ever called me on." Belcher lit another toonie from the stub between his lips and stubbed out the butt. "If you want to get a little deeper into this with them, I bet I can get the Farm Boys to pay me for that little gal in there. She's a cutie, and they'll turn her out pretty quick down on the border."

Atchley didn't much like dealing with that crazy bunch of neo-Nazis belonging to the Aryan Brotherhood. He worked with them from time to time, but those rattlesnakes were unpredictable and dangerous.

His eyes flicked to the dark hallway where Priscilla and Jimma slept in two separate rooms. "Keep your voice down."

"Fine then." Belcher drew another lungful of smoke and chased it with two large swallows of bourbon, finishing his breakfast. "How'd this guy piss you off so bad in the first place?"

"Got in our business."

"So did that farmer who lived there before."

"It was fine after they rebuilt the house. He learned his lesson for sure."

Belcher chuckled. "It took him longer than it should have to straighten up. I don't have to have a house burn down around my ears to figure out who to leave alone."

"Yep, it worked the first time for sure, but I figured we'd be hearing sirens by now on this one."

"It might take a while for him to hit the switch. It's the one beside the back door, so he might not turn it on until night. He sure pissed you off, didn't he?"

"He did." Atchley drained his beer and slid the can across the table to join half a dozen other empties. "Butch says he's for sure the law, and I don't want him around any longer than it takes for him to drive off. Having a lawman across the road's too damn close for comfort."

"Cop? Thought you said he was some kind of cowboy lawman."

"He is, and we can't take the risk. He's too close, and I bet the son of a bitch spends half of his time watching cars come down the road." Atchley raised an eyebrow. "Anyway, it worked before."

"Maybe you should've let Butch handle things. All it takes is a little money in a man's pocket to help him see things our way."

"That works some of the time, but this guy's a stock inspector, and he don't work for Butch. They have so much power they can cross into Oklahoma and investigate anything they want. If he somehow traces everything back up to McCurtain or Pusmahata County, we'll be blowed up." Atchley fired up a joint and held the smoke for several seconds before letting it out. He opened another rodeo-cool beer from the half-empty twelve-pack carton on the table. "Can't risk it."

Belcher chuckled. "Hell, those guys just deal with cows. He ain't no threat to you."

"He came over here asking questions. I don't like nobody with a badge."

"Well, come tomorrow, he won't be worrying about *you*." Belcher poured another shot of whiskey for brunch and threw it back like John Wayne, his hero. "They'll be looking for another place to live."

"That's what I want." Atchley glanced up at the black cat-shaped clock on the kitchen wall. Its tail twitched in time with its white eyes, and Atchley hated it. He kept intending to throw it out, but it was something Jimma was fond of, and for once, he felt a little sentimental about what she wanted. There wasn't any need to stir her up.

It had been a couple of hours since their last customer, and users didn't usually come by in the early morning hours. It was time to turn in after a long night. "You going home?"

"Naw." Belcher flicked a finger toward the living room. "Figured I'd sleep on the couch tonight."

"Fine then." Atchley put the roach out in a full ashtray and stood. "See you when I get up." He flicked off the kitchen light and padded down the hall, passing the room where he and Priscilla slept, and turned the knob on Jimma's door.

Chapter Ten

It was nearly noon when I pulled up in front of the sheriff's office. Someone in the 1970s decided to bulldoze the old office building and construct a "modern" monstrosity so out of place with the surrounding old-school architecture that it was jarring to look at.

The chill of autumn was in the air, and I looked forward to the first blue norther of the season when winter arrived to blow out the last remnants of summer.

The small-town square was busy under a bright, blue sky. The stores were doing a bustling business, and it reminded me of the old days our parents talked about when everyone came to town on Saturday. Most towns dried up after bypass loops came into being, taking the vast majority of businesses to the outer edges, but Ganther Bluff didn't yet have one of those choking beltways, and so that old-fashioned way of living was still in place.

Being new to town, I didn't know anyone, but more than a few folks threw up their hands in a friendly wave that I always returned.

Chloe looked up from her phone when I shifted the Expedition into park under an elm tree shading the sidewalk. She drew a long breath. "What're we doing *here*?"

I ignored that long-suffering sigh teenagers have perfected over eons. "I need to visit with the sheriff for a minute."

"You said we were going to the store so I can get something to cook."

"We will, but I need to tell him about what happened yesterday."

"The shots or the boogeyman you heard last night? That why you called that lady this morning to come and give us an estimate on window treatments?"

"Yep. Folks ought not be to able to see in at night, and you're right, I'm concerned about the people who live across the road."

She rolled her eyes. "Come on. They were just arguing. I doubt there's a family of pervs living over there."

I considered telling her about the chunk of mud in her tub but decided she didn't need to know. I couldn't stand the thought of the horror that would cross her face when she knew a stranger had been in her room while she slept.

To make sure it never happened again, I also called a home security company while she was in the shower and scheduled a time for them to come out and put up cameras. I didn't bother to bring that up right then either.

"People come and go there at all hours of the night. Something's up. I need to talk to the sheriff for a few minutes."

Dealing with teenagers was something I did better with Sara Beth's help. She was the one who understood teen angst and emotions. I simply wasn't geared toward those types of issues or young hormonal girls. Most of my adult time was spent dealing with vermin, not youngsters with bright futures.

Call me when your stock trailer was stolen, or someone loaded up your cattle from a remote pasture, and I was your guy. Someone buys a show steer online and finds out it didn't belong to the seller who didn't know they were being used in the scam, I'm on it. But dealing with those female-related issues was beyond my experience.

She crossed her arms in that time-honored tradition of disagreement between fathers and daughters. "Do you know how many times I've had to sit in the truck, or in an office, or a cafe to wait while you talk to ranchers or farmers or the highway patrol?"

Chloe went everywhere with me when she was a young tomboy. Some ranchers knew her well enough to nickname her Sidekick, a nod to Guy Clark's song, "Desperados Waiting for a Train." But through the years, she gravitated toward her mom, who filled in those areas where I was ham-handed and unfamiliar with how young women think.

"I know, but it won't take but a minute."

"We're not going to look like friendly neighbors if you're already ratting them out for something you suspect."

I sighed. I hadn't told her about what I'd found in the switchbox either. Making a B&E report that would carry consequences, or alleging attempted arson, was out the window because I'd removed the device. I should have left it there and made the calls, but after being so jacked up in the night, I screwed everything up.

Everyone makes mistakes, even experienced law enforcement officers. Special Rangers are supposed to be the best of the best. That's why we're hired, for our experience as lawmen in other agencies before joining the unit, and that makes us an elite force. Since Sara Beth's death, my mind struggled through a continuous fog, and the little device in a zippered plastic bag was a physical example of not thinking clearly.

Chloe sighed and pushed the button to lower her window and punched up one of her Sirius radio channels, interrupting a Mark Chesnutt song. "Please don't take too long."

"I won't."

The reception area was just as ugly as the exterior, so ultra-modern it looked like an IKEA showroom. The young deputy manning the front counter looked up. He quickly absorbed my starched jeans, light-blue shirt with the badge above the pocket, the silverbelly hat, and the Colt in the leather holster on my hip.

The name on the tag above his badge said R. Schneider. "How can I help?"

"Is the sheriff in today?"

"He's not, sorry."

"That's fine. I'm here to see Deputy Lomax anyway. Name's Tucker Snow."

His eyes flicked back to the round badge on my shirt with its distinct longhorn in the middle of a five point star. "You a new agent here?"

"Nope. Moved outside of town a few days ago."

"You know Robby Taylor? This is his district now."

"Sure do, but this is something else." The truth was, as a member of the TSCR, I could have reported the break-in to Taylor, but I wanted to keep this issue off his plate for the time being.

"Deputy Lomax know you're coming?"

"I doubt it."

"Hang on a minute."

He picked up the desk phone and punched a button. "There's a stock inspector here to see you. Name's Tucker Snow."

He listened, nodded, and hung up. Pointing with a forefinger, he gave me the go-ahead. "Right through there."

"Much obliged."

Deputy Lomax put down his pen when I rapped on his door and walked in. "Hello, Agent Snow. You caught me just in time. I was about to go out for a smoke."

He didn't have to tell me he was a smoker, because I could smell it on his clothes and caught a whiff of the mouth spray he used to cover it up. I had the uncomfortable image of him in my house, sneaking around in the dark, but shook it off. Though he reeked of cigarettes, whoever had been in my house was the kind who *sweated* nicotine.

One of those guys who saves smiles for special occasions, Lomax flicked a finger toward two uncomfortable-looking wooden chairs across the desk from where he sat. "Have a seat." His hat lay crown-down between us. He leaned forward and slid it to the other side. "Has Robby been promoted?"

Guys like us usually find the job as Special Rangers to be exactly the right position for our expertise and that exact time in our lives. Positions seldom come open unless someone retires due to age or gets promoted. "Naw, I took some time off from my old district. Robby's on the job here."

He eyed the badge and my clothes. "I'd think you wouldn't dress the part if you weren't working."

"This is how I dress. A lady once told me she liked my outfit, and I had to explain to her she was in the country, and I didn't wear costumes. But I thought the badge might be appropriate in this situation."

"You following up on that call you made yesterday?" He

sighed and glanced toward his hat. I did the same and saw a pack of Winstons in the crown. He needed a smoke, and I intended to finish our conversation. I almost grinned.

"I am. Figured I needed to talk to you in person."

Sometimes people who are addicted to a substance will hurry a conversation and get to a point to get rid of someone like me. I figured this was the case. I once grilled a guy for four hours and he wouldn't budge, but then his stomach growled, and I knew I had him. He confessed to stealing the trailer I was looking for about sixty minutes later, and I figured it was because he was hungry. Since Lomax already needed a cigarette, I hoped to get some kind of quick promise to look into my concern.

"Like I told you, I doubt it was much more than someone having target practice."

"No. I came to report a break-in."

His eyebrow went up. "Really?" He leaned back and smoothed his thin starter mustache, one that most men grow when they're younger than he and trying to get the look that older men have long forgotten. He picked his pen back up. "What happened?"

I told him in as much detail as possible. When I was finished, he frowned down at the pad in front of him. "Broken locks? Glass?"

"No." I didn't like what I was about to admit. "I'd left an upstairs window open. I figure that's how he got in."

"I'd think you'd know better."

"I do."

"Nothing was taken?"

"Nope. Found some fresh mud in my daughter's bathtub." I reached into the pocket of the barn jacket I'd laid over the other chair and placed the plastic baggie on his desk. "Whoever it was, he wired this to the light switch in my kitchen."

He slid the bag close with a fingertip. "What is it?"

"Not sure, but it looks like something designed to start a fire."

"How do you know that's what it's supposed to do?"

"I don't. Just a suspicion is all because the switch was getting pretty hot when I found it."

He looked up, raising one eyebrow. "How'd you come to find it?"

"He didn't have time to clean up his mess, probably because I heard something and went downstairs to investigate."

"You searched the house on your own? You should have called 911."

"Could have, but I didn't feel like hiding in my bedroom or staying upstairs until someone showed up twenty or thirty minutes later."

A filter behind his eyes slammed closed. "That's a little harsh."

"We live in the country." I shrugged. "You know the facts. Responders coming to a house so far from town won't be there as fast as you want. Besides, like you, I'm not the run-of-the-mill citizen."

"We? Your wife?"

"Widowed. My daughter lives with me."

He grunted and turned the bag to examine the contents. "Have you shown it to the fire marshal?"

"No. We have a volunteer department out our way, and those boys aren't experts in cause or sophisticated ignition devices, as far as I know. Figured I'd show it to the chief here in town."

Lomax laid the pen down and laced his fingers. He appeared to find some interest in the wall to his left, but addressed me anyway. "Agent Snow, you haven't been in that house for long, have you?"

"No."

I never did like a man who side-eyed me.

"So that means you likely haven't taken a look under all the faceplates in your house. I don't mean to be rude, but this thing could have been there before you bought the place. You know, building codes don't extend all the way out to where you live, so for all I know, it could be something new that's supposed to save electricity."

"You're right about me not looking under all the plates, but this thing is new, and the switch was already getting hot a few minutes after I turned it on."

"I lived in an old house when I was a kid. Sometimes the electrical outlets got warm when we had too many things plugged in. Again, with all due respect, there's not much I can do right now but take this report." He laid his pen down, and I figured it was to make a point. "You didn't see an intruder. You aren't missing anything. There's no damage from someone entering through a door or window." He spread his hands and put his palms on the desk surface, as if ready to stand and end the meeting. "You know better. You should have left this thing where it was so someone with experience could get a look at it. Now it's just an unknown…device?"

Dammit. He was right, and it infuriated me. "I agree. Leaving it there would have been best, but at the same time, it was hot like I said, and I couldn't afford to let it detonate, or spark, or whatever it's designed to do."

"You're an officer of the law, Agent Snow, you understand my hands are tied."

Sara Beth spoke to me again and I heard her clear as a bell inside my head. *"Chill, pill. You remember how to play poker. Stay cool like old school."*

She had little ways of using music and old timey sayings to make me laugh or feel good. When she did, the tip of her tongue always touched her upper teeth and those gorgeous eyes crinkled with fun.

Clamping my teeth to keep from saying something I'd regret, I took a folded sheet of paper from the inside pocket of the coat and dropped it on the desk beside his pad. He tilted his head like a dog looking at a new pan, then met my gaze. "What's this?"

"A report I wrote this morning." I'd written hundreds of those and wanted to get it all down on paper while it was still fresh in my mind.

Irritation flickered across his face. "You could have given this to me when you came in, then I wouldn't have needed to take all these notes." The pad in front of him contained only a few sentences, mere highlights of what I'd told him.

"This gives you two copies, mine and yours. I have another dated and notarized, just in case we need it."

He laced his fingers again and studied the unopened report. "Well, thanks for coming in."

"You know, I'm gonna run those Atchley folks. I suspect they've had trouble with the law in the past." I still had access to the state's database and could run names and license tags.

"Why? Legally, you can't do that if you're not on the job, and you don't have any solid evidence on that family."

"My old granddaddy said knowledge is power."

"I'd advise you not to go over there and start anything. That family has been around a long time, and there's a lot of 'em. They have plenty of friends around here too."

I like to say the back of my brain tickles every now and then with something I can't identify. That happened right then, but like a recollection on the edge of your mind, one you know is there but can't recall.

A rap on the door was followed by a soft voice. "Butch?" It was Deputy R. Schneider from the front desk.

Lomax's eyes flicked over my shoulder. "What?"

"Sorry to interrupt. There's been a bad wreck out on North County. Sounds like they're gonna need a supervisor."

"Fine. Thanks."

Our conversation was done. I tapped the report and stood. "I look forward to meeting Sheriff Jackson. Would you ask him to give me a call after he looks this over?"

Lomax nodded. "I'll be glad to. Right now he's down sick for the next week, at least. Give us a holler if you need anything else."

"You bet."

The chief deputy reached for the device but I picked it up instead. He met my eyes, frowning. I tucked it back into my jacket. "Since there's no investigation, it's mine. Right?"

He drew a long breath, reminding me of Chloe's sigh. "It's not mine."

"Thanks."

Chapter Eleven

Frustrated by the all-too-familiar wait at the curb, Chloe dropped her phone onto the Expedition's console and plucked a thick book from the floorboard. She read the title, and was flipping through to the dedication. She always liked to see who was important to the author.

It was the latest Stephen King novel from her dad's collection of first editions. He collected two things before her mother's death: King's complete printed works (he still needed *Carrie,* but the pride of that list was the limited edition of *The Dark Tower*), and firearms because he was a hunter and loved to shoot at the range.

The hardbacks were still packed away in moving boxes stacked against the spare bedroom wall. He'd lost interest in reading after the funeral. The guns were in the safe, where he put them the day they moved in. He kept four out, a short-barrel Remington 870 shotgun and an M4 rifle he carried in his truck at work, a 7mm Mag rifle for hunting, and his ever-present side-arm, the Colt 1911.

A flicker of movement in the corner of her eye caused her to look up. A skinny girl slightly younger than Chloe stood rooted to the sidewalk, watching her through the windshield. The youngster in cutoff jeans and an armless blue buttoned shirt looked immensely sad, as though a heavy weight lay across her shoulders.

It was the intensity of her stare and a head full of blond hair that needed attention that made Chloe hang her elbow out the window. "Hi. Are you all right?"

There was silence between them for several seconds before the girl nodded. She licked thin dry lips and absently smoothed a thick eyebrow. "I'm fine. You're the girl who moved in across the road from us."

Chloe's breath caught. After her dad's interaction the day before, she wondered if she should admit who she was. The slender, forlorn girl with hair that desperately needed combing waited for an answer, as if her whole world hinged on what she would say next.

Closing her book, Chloe checked the glass entrance to see if her dad was coming out. "On Rock Hill Road?"

"Yeah. The old Berry place. Y'all just moved in."

"That's us. I'm Chloe."

Anchored in place, the girl pulled a strand of hair behind one ear. "My name's Jimma. We're neighbors then. I've never had a neighbor so close by who's my age."

Chloe grinned. There was something about Jimma that reminded her of a kicked puppy that needed someone to pet it. "Y'all live in that trailer...mobile home, then."

"Yeah. It's the nicest place we've ever lived. Y'all live in a mansion, though. I tried to get Dad...Jess to buy that place, or at least the house, but he said he'd have to be rich to just afford the downstairs."

Swallowing a hitch in her chest, Chloe took a moment to get

a grip on the raw emotions that lay just below the surface where they'd been since her mom's death. "It isn't a mansion. It's just a house."

Jimma stepped closer. "I watched y'all move in."

"I don't remember seeing anyone on the road." Chloe noted she was barefoot with tiny flecks of red paint on her toenails.

"Well, we can see your house from that little rise behind the trailer. I sat there and watched you through Jess's rifle scope."

The hair rose on the back of Chloe's neck at the thought of a rifle pointed in her direction. She was experienced in firearms, because her dad made sure she knew how to use every weapon in the house. She liked to shoot with a little Remington .243 he bought her when she turned ten. It was the perfect size for her.

"That's a dangerous thing to do."

"To watch people?"

"No, to point rifles at them."

Jimma giggled. "Oh. Don't worry. I didn't have my finger on the trigger, and the safety was on too."

Chloe's stomach tightened at the thought of a loaded rifle pointed in her direction. Most rifles could easily shoot far enough between the two houses to cause considerable damage when the bullet struck. "Jimma, were there bullets in it?"

"Sure. Atchley says a rifle ain't no good if it ain't loaded."

She shuddered, and her granddaddy's grin flashed through her memory. *Possum run over your grave?* Chloe swallowed. "You really shouldn't have pointed it at me. Does he know you touch it?"

The girl laughed. "Shit, no. He'd take a belt to me if he knew I messed with his guns, but I do it all the time, and I always put it right back where I got it. He never knows. He has three ARs in the house and a bunch of other pistols. He wouldn't notice if I switched them around just to aggravate him."

Chloe licked her lips. Her skin crawled, and a strange tickle began in the middle of her forehead at the thought of an AR's crosshairs lined up on her head. She shuddered again, as if chilled. "Will you do me a favor?"

"Sure. What?"

"Promise me you won't ever point your dad's rifle at our house again, or anybody else. I have some binoculars you can borrow if you want to see something far away. Okay?"

The girl shrugged. "Sure."

"And another thing, it's not really nice to spy on people. If I let you borrow those glasses, you promise not to look at things you're not supposed to with 'em?"

Jimma's pleasant expression evaporated. "I just wanted to know what you looked like."

"You don't have any friends close?" A wash of sadness was almost too much for Chloe to take.

The girl's face closed. "No. There's one or two girls who live a couple of miles away, but they're older and never wanted to hang around with me. I have a couple of friends at school, but since we live so far from town, it's just me and Mom most of the time."

"Kinda lonesome out there, huh?"

Jimma stepped off the sidewalk and stopped beside the Expedition's door. Her hesitant approach was exactly like that of a wary doe living a lifetime on the edge of flight. "We get plenty of company, but most don't stay long, and I don't like any of 'em anyhow."

"I meant kids our age."

"Oh, yeah. I get lonesome for people. I like to talk, but Jess don't want me talking to anyone anyway. Says I might say something that'll get us in troub..." She paused, eyes darting from side to see.

Chloe saw Jimma'd almost spilled something she shouldn't and got her out of an embarrassing moment. "You can come by sometime, if you want."

"I can?" Jimma's eyes widened in surprise. "I'd love that. I'll text you later. You busy this afternoon? What's your number?"

Immediately regretting the invitation, Chloe saw she was committed and gave her the number. "Don't call after nine at night. Dad really doesn't want me talking late on school nights either. But you can text whenever you want to, just don't expect me to answer right away."

"I won't. I know how rules are."

"No, it isn't like that. Dad's pretty laid back when it comes to phones and stuff. How about you come over when we get a little more settled?"

Jimma's face closed even tighter. "I can't give my phone number to anyone. Jess says we need our privacy."

"But if you call me, I'll see your number."

"It's a cheap flip phone. Jess calls it a burner, and the number won't come up. He blocked it in some way."

Glad her dad wasn't like that, Chloe nodded. "Okay, but give us a few days, and you can come over. How about that?"

"I'd love that!" Jimma's pleasant expression returned, and Chloe thought she was experienced in emotional flip-flopping. "Can we have a sleepover?"

"We'll see." It frustrated her that she'd used an adult's lame response to get someone close to her age to stop asking for something.

"Oh." Jimma looked down for a moment.

To Chloe, it seemed that the girl's emotions rode on a roller coaster.

Jimma brightened just as quickly as her spirits fell. "What does your dad do?"

"He's a stock inspector."

"A cowboy? The last guy who owned the Berry place ran stockers."

Chloe spent so much time with her dad when she was younger that she recognized the cattleman's term for weaned calves purchased at the lowest price possible, then grazed for several months to add weight before selling them for slaughter.

"No, he's a lawman. He goes to sale barns and checks brands, investigates farm and ranch thefts, things like that."

"Oh." That concerned face returned.

"What about your dad, Jess? What does he do?"

"He's not my real dad. He moved in a few years ago, and I kinda grew up with him around. He hires out to do farm work, cutting hay in the summer, working odd jobs when we need money, mostly. He has a backhoe."

"I see he has a lot of friends. Lots of cars in and out at your place."

"Uh, yeah." Jimma quickly ended the conversation over that observation. "Well, I gotta go. He'll probably be out in a minute or two."

"Jess's in the courthouse?"

"Yeah, visiting a cousin." A startled look crossed Jimma's face again, and Chloe saw she'd spoken out of turn. "Uh, he's in jail…his cousin."

"My dad's inside too. He'll be out in a minute."

Jimma ended the conversation when she turned and walked back to the shade of an elm tree at the same time Chloe's dad pushed through the doors, setting his hat against the bright sun. He was behind the wheel in a second, and as they backed out,

Chloe saw her new friend with her back against the tree trunk, watching them drive away.

She looked so sad that Chloe had to again fight that hitch in her chest that threatened to make itself known, but she wouldn't have that. She had to stay strong for her dad in all ways.

Chapter Twelve

Chloe had a look on her face when I came out that made me wonder if she'd gotten mad about something while I was inside. I slipped behind the wheel and raised an eyebrow. "You all right?"

One corner of her mouth turned up and that told me everything was good. "Yeah, I just met a girl, and she's a pitiful little thing."

"How so?"

"I think she has a sad homelife. We just talked for a couple of minutes and she made me think she'd get in the car and go with us."

"You're like your mama. Always wanting to adopt strays."

"I don't think she's really a stray, she's just lonesome."

"Well, I 'magine you'd make a fine friend for her, if it works out."

"Maybe." There was something else she started to say, but closed up for some reason. I knew better than to ask. If I did, she'd clam up tight. She started to glance down at her phone, but stopped. I'd been talking to her about being in the moment, and not letting that device in her hand distract her from in-person conversations. "We going to the store now?"

The lilt in her voice told me I'd disappoint her for a few more minutes. "I'm finished in there, but I need to ask a couple of people some questions."

"You're not working again, are you?"

"Not per se, but I need a little more info about our neighbors the Atchleys."

She started to make a comment, but then stopped. There it was again. She had something to tell me, but was weighing it in her mind. Chloe's theory of life had always been to be quiet if she didn't want to engage. Her silence spoke volumes, but I knew better than to press her on it.

She cleared her throat, as if choking back a sigh. "Where are we going?"

"Don't know yet. Where do you think's the best place is to get information in a small town?"

"Online?"

"Well, that's what y'all might do, but I need something a little more personal."

"Mama would have said the beauty parlor, then, but I doubt you're going in there."

"You're right about that, but the barbershop's a good place to start. After that, I think we need to stop by the Beef House to eat lunch."

That was the name of the café in the sale barn. Since it was a Saturday, there'd be plenty of farmers and ranchers I could visit with.

"So I can eat alone and you can talk to some old farmers about cows."

"And one or two young ones, if they'll talk." I raised an

eyebrow, hoping she'd realize I was talking about *young* cowboys her age. "Let's stop by the barbershop first."

I didn't need a haircut because I keep it pretty short. Most guys who wear hats get what my dad used to call a Men's Regular. Your hair don't look quite as bad if you take your hat off after wearing it all day, though my cowlick in the front tends to stand up because of that.

A sharp pain was like a punch in the gut when that thought came into my head. From the time we first met, Sara Beth'd see that stick-up and laugh and wet her palm with her tongue and try to smooth it down. Now she was gone, and I'd never have that pleasure again. I shook off the rising sadness and drove to Main Street.

Of course there was more than one barbershop in town, and Lord knows how many hairdressers and spas, but I wasn't going in one of *those* looking for information. That'd be like going into one of the two or three dozen nail salons I suspected were in town.

I'd seen a barber pole on the square and figured that's where I'd start first. The town was so old hitching rings were still cemented into the sidewalk that was almost knee-high from the street. I parked nose-in, and Chloe opened her door, surprising me. "Where you going?"

"There are a few boutiques and some girly shops here. I'll look around while you're inside."

"How'll I know where you are?"

She rolled her eyes and waved her phone. "Dad, just text me."

"Fine then."

She went one way, and I went inside the barbershop bracketed by a donut shop and an H&R Block. A bell tinkled overhead and the familiar smell of old-school barbershops enveloped me like an almost forgotten blanket from the past. I knew I'd found what I was looking for. Breathing deep of witch hazel, Barbicide, and aftershave, I raised a hand in greeting to everyone there. Three men older than myself were sitting in a line of chairs backed against the wall, talking and laughing. To a man, they all raised a hand in greeting.

"Gentlemen." I took an empty chair nearest the door.

The lone barber, as bald as a cue ball, was working on a customer in one of the two old-fashioned chairs in the shop. When I didn't take my hat off and hang it on the wall with a couple of others, he raised an eyebrow. "I'll be with you, but it'll be a while."

"I don't need a haircut right now, I just wanted to come in and say howdy. Just moved out of town into the old Berry place. Name's Tucker Snow."

He nodded and went back to snipping at the thin head of hair occupying very little space over a skinny man's head. "I heard it sold. What brings you to Ganther Bluff?"

"Life changes." I thought about how much to tell him, but if I didn't give them any details, I figured they'd clam up. "Wife passed away. It's just me and my daughter."

A silver-haired man with the grayest eyes I've ever seen reached out to pat my leg. "I'm sorry to hear that. Bless your heart." He stuck out a hand. "Trevor Crawley, Pastor of First Baptist."

We shook, and the two on the other side leaned over to shake. Pastor Crawley took it upon himself to introduce the rest. "That's Ramsey Dolittle in the chair, and the barber trying not to cut his ear off's Pete Alessi. You can see his head's smooth as a newborn, so be careful what you say around him; my daddy always said to never trust a bald barber."

Everyone laughed at that old joke. Pete waved the scissors

and went back to his work. "What's your line of work, Mr. Snow?"

"Tuck will do. I was a stock inspector, but I've taken time off work."

"Sometimes a man needs to step back and heal." Pastor Crawley's voice went soft.

"I believe you're right." The concern in his face was genuine, and I had to look away. "I think we're gonna like this town."

"It's a good place to live." The pastor nodded in the general direction of the street. "I hope to see you in church soon."

"Just might. It'll give me the opportunity to meet some more folks. I met one of my neighbors today. Jess Atchley."

The silence that filled the barbershop was thick and uncomfortable.

Alessi chewed at something between his front teeth for a moment. "I know him. Don't come in for a haircut very often."

"Yeah, it's a little long." I waited for someone to make another comment, but everyone found something else to interest them. "Met his wife too. I think his daughter's close to my Chloe's age."

Dolittle wiped some hair off his eyebrow and slipped his hand back under the dark cape covered with clippings. "I've heard that little gal's about half wild. My son told me once that she cuts more classes than she goes to."

Alessi turned, filled his palm with hot lather, and applied it to Dolittle's cheeks and the back of his neck. "That's what's wrong with kids today. They cut school and don't listen to their parents and spend all their time with their noses stuck in their phones." He picked up an old-fashioned straight razor and went to work on a sideburn.

I knew the conversation about Atchley was over. The tension lifted and the barber and customers alike outlined and solved the world's problems in the next ten minutes. I rose when Alessi whipped the cape off to the side, and Dolittle stepped out of the chair.

It was the perfect time to leave.

Chapter Thirteen

Tucker Snow was barely out of Lomax's door when Jess Atchley came in through a side entrance from an adjoining office. His face red with anger, Deputy Lomax glanced at the door to make sure it was closed and jabbed a forefinger at his cousin who slouched like a cur dog. "Can't you do anything right these days?"

Atchley froze in place, stunned at the fury in the man's coarse voice. "It ain't my fault, Butch."

"Are you on that damn stuff you're selling?"

"Some, but I can control it."

"You know better'n that."

"I *can*." Atchley's voice shifted to a whine.

"Then what's going on? You've screwed up from the time Snow woke up yesterday. Shootin' at people in broad daylight. Coming up with some lame lie a ten-year-old wouldn't believe."

"I thought Lloyd took care of things last night. The damn house should have burned down already. I was just as surprised as you to see it still standing when I got up."

"When you got up." Lomax leaned back and rubbed his forehead. "You figured you'd *sleep* through a house fire?"

Atchley pondered his feet. He couldn't tell Lomax the truth, that he was using pretty bad and had been up for the past two days. It was the worst thing he could do, and he knew it, because that's how you got caught. Selling was one thing, but using the product you were selling was nothing short of idiotic.

"I don't know what to say."

Lomax opened a desk drawer and produced a burner phone. He punched in a number and walked to the window. Snow came into view on the street below at the same time a voice answered. "What?"

"I got a job for you."

"Where?"

"Wherever you want to do it. Guy by the name of Tucker Snow. He moved in just outside of town." Lomax read off the rural address from his pocket-size notebook. "He has a daughter, so don't do it here. Pick him up when he leaves and follow him somewhere."

"The usual fee?"

That meant that Lomax was expected to look the other way when a load came through town. "Sure. What is it this time?"

"We have a delivery coming through tomorrow." The man gave Lomax the description and license tag of a car. "This one's packed solid for a drop in Dallas. We don't need anybody stopping him."

Lomax wrote the info on the palm of his hand with a pen. It was safer than writing it on paper. No one would ever see that hand, and once he had the details hidden in the pages of an old law book in the case across the office, he'd wash up, and it would be gone. "Deal."

The phone clicked off, and Lomax turned back toward Atchley. "All right. I got this handled." He paused at the sight of his cousin's pale, fear-stricken face. "What?"

"Belcher was going over there while I was here. Said he was going to get even with Snow for not cooperating."

"Good God. Call that idiot and stop him."

"He was going in the minute Snow left the house."

"What'd he plan to do?"

"Who knows?" Atchley shrugged. "I'm not his boss, Butch."

"Son of a bitch! I oughta shoot both of you."

Chapter Fourteen

Trucks and cattle trailers filled the dirt parking lot in front of the Bethany Auction Company. More trucks turned in and parked their empty trailers to form a ragged line in front of the sale barn, planning to have them filled with stock by the time they left.

The crisp fall air was thick with blowing dust, bellering cattle, and the smell of cow shit. I took a deep breath, comfortable with everything around me. I never minded the smell of fresh manure because it's nothing but grass and water, but those with finer sensibilities don't get it.

Chloe faked a gag as she got out and walked with me to the entrance. Inside the 67,000-foot barn was a busy lobby full of cattlemen going back and forth between the offices, the sale arena, and the café. It took a while for us to cross to the Beef House because I knew so many of the ranchers, farmers, and stockmen through my job as a special ranger.

More than one shook my hand and visited for a while, noting the lack of my .45 and gold badge. Most knew what happened, and I could read sympathy in their eyes. Chloe endured the small talk, comments about how she'd grown, and business conversations.

The smell of manure, dust, and cattle disappeared in a delicious wave of frying onions and fresh coffee as we stepped through the glass door separating the reception area and the café. Just as I'd hoped, Agent Robby Taylor was sitting at a booth, talking with a grizzled old cowboy who looked as if he'd herded cattle on the Chisholm Trail. He cut a bite of steak and looked up from under the brim of his hat. "Good Lord, a cattle cop."

There are places in Texas where a man's required to take off his hat when eating: in public restaurants, in a friend or neighbor's house, and for sure in his mama's house, but it wasn't in the Beef House. To a man, everyone eating in there still wore their hats.

The grizzled old cowboy wasn't eating, just visiting. He slipped out. "I need to go. Y'all go ahead and sit down."

I shook his hand, though neither of us had introduced ourselves. "Don't mean to run you off."

"You ain't. I need to get back to work before they fire me."

He flashed a bright smile at Chloe, which she returned, and left. Robby waved his fork toward the empty bench seat. "Y'all sit down and eat. Hey, gal."

"Hi." Chloe slid in first, and I took the end.

Robby chewed and swallowed. "That was old Clint McCoy. He knows more about cattle than most of those rich stockmen sitting in the arena."

"I know him. Y'all looked intense there for a minute."

"Yeah, he caught some stolen cattle here last week and called me."

"How many head?"

"Fifty."

"Damn. That's more'n most of these people run." The average size of a Texas herd is only thirty-seven to forty head.

"Yeah, they were from three different ranches. I poked around after he told me and checked the sale logs. Didn't take much sleuthing to find out where they were stole. What're you doing here? I figured you'd keep some distance between you and all this for a while."

"Doing okay covering for me." We'd worked adjacent regions for years and knew most of the farmers and ranchers who flowed through the sale barns.

He chuckled. "I'm just filling in 'til you're ready to come back."

"I don't know if that'll ever happen. I dropped in for a little information from some of these boys, but you might be able to help."

The slender waitress with helmet hair came by with her pad. She matched the men around us in jeans and a Cinch shirt. We stopped talking for a moment and ordered. A chicken-fried steak for me, and a chicken salad for Chloe.

The name on her shirt read Mavis, and I'd known her for a year without any personal knowledge. Her eyes twinkled as she wrote Chloe's order. "That's the first chicken ordered in here this month, and it takes a sharp gal to do it."

She left, and Robby took a swallow of sweet iced tea. "What kind of information?"

"I met my neighbor yesterday and something seemed a little greasy about him. Came to town to talk to the sheriff, and decided to ask around about him."

"What's his name?"

Mavis arrived with our drinks that had already been poured and sat with a dozen others on the counter. It was an old-school way to stay ahead of the rapidly evolving crowd.

"Jess Atchley."

Robby hadn't heard of him and shook his head no.

Mavis's look was pure disgust as she caught the man's name.

She set the red plastic cups down and acted as if she wanted to say something, but pursed her lips instead.

I had to know why she looked like she'd just kissed a pig. "Mavis."

She looked down at me. "You need something else?"

"Yeah, an answer to the way you set your jaw when I said that name."

She looked around to see if anyone was listening. It didn't make any difference, because the place was busy, and men were packed close and loud enough we couldn't hear other conversations even if we concentrated. "That's 'cause he's useless as tits on a boar hog."

Chloe grinned, but I wasn't surprised. Waitresses who worked with mostly men day in and day out were usually rough as cobs. "You wanna tell me why?"

Concern crossed her face. "You're not kin to him, are you?"

"Not hardly."

"If he's been within reach, you better check your back pocket to see if your billfold's still there. That man'll steal anything that's not nailed down."

Robby put down his fork. "I haven't run into him."

"That's 'cause he hasn't stole from the right people lately." She dropped her voice. "I hear he's also selling drugs."

Now she had our attention. Robby was suddenly on point. "In here?"

"Naw. He's dumb, but he ain't that stupid. It's just hearsay, and I probably shouldn't have said that at all, 'cause I don't know for sure. I just despise the man."

"That's pretty strong." I could almost feel the venom coming off the woman who'd been cheerful and sweet only a minute earlier.

"I know it, and I oughta be ashamed of myself, but his wife, Priscilla, worked here for a while, and ever now and then she'd come in with bruises on her arms and a couple of times on her face. She always said she bumped into something and it was nothing, but my first husband did the same to me, and I knew what I was looking at."

Robby raised an eyebrow. "Bet he didn't do that to you for very long."

"Nope. Put him in a shallow grave."

She said it so matter-of-factly that I wasn't sure if she was kidding or not. I decided not to pursue it any further.

Mavis kept on as if she hadn't surprised us. "Priscilla quit after a while, and I think it was because he made her..."

She wanted to tell us more, and I gave her a nudge. "What else?"

"She got into drugs."

A thick voice called from the kitchen. "Mavis, order up!"

"I gotta get that. Hang on a minute." She spun on her heel and left.

Chloe couldn't hold it in any longer. "Oh, my."

I grinned at my daughter channeling Sara Beth, who always used that same expression when she wanted to be funny and quaint.

Robby nodded and went back to his steak. "You said it, kiddo."

Conversation between us drifted for a while from one subject to another, none giving me much more information than I had when I came in, and that made sense. Robby was only filling in for a while and hadn't run into much more than he'd already told me.

Before long, Mavis was back with our plates. She slid them

in front of us and leaned down so others couldn't hear. Her top three buttons weren't fastened and being eye level, I had to make sure where I was looking.

She was so close, I could smell her perfume. "Little story about that guy."

Chloe adjusted her plate, positioning it in some mysterious teenage alignment only she understood. "You're talking about Atchley?"

"You bet. It'll give you a little background on that son of a b...son of a gun. Ten years or so ago, him and his ex-father-in-law got their hands on an old-fashioned printing press. I don't know how they did it, but they got some old-timer who knew how those presses worked, and he... I don't know what you call it...etched some twenty-dollar plates. I hear they printed up a couple million in counterfeit twenties.

"Anyway, it was Atchley's job to get rid of the press while his daddy-in-law went to clean the money. Might have gone to Vegas, I don't know for sure. Anyway, instead of dumping the plates into a river or ditch somewhere, he decided to sell the thing and make a little cash. Well sir, that dumbass forgot to take the plates off the press when a buyer picked it up, and he wound up doing time for counterfeiting. But the best part is that he rolled over on daddy-in-law for a lighter sentence, and both of them wound up in a federal prison." She chuckled. "Wouldn't have mattered anyway. They say they used regular paper that woulda got 'em caught anyways."

Chloe's eyes were wide. "What'd his wife do?"

"Why, she left him, honey, moved in with another feller and filed for divorce while Atchley was in the pen. She disappeared about a month after his time was up, and no one's seen her since." She leaned even closer, and I *really* had to look her in the eye. "I think he used that backhoe of his and put her in the ground somewhere."

I didn't mention that she'd confessed to the same thing earlier, and it made me think she'd been kidding. I hoped so.

Robby kept eating, as if he'd heard that story before. "But that part's all supposition."

"It is, but my suppositions are usually right." She straightened, much to my relief. "So there you go. You didn't ask me, but I figured you needed to know anyway, since y'all live so close to him."

I tilted my head. "I didn't say we were neighbors."

"You didn't have to. This is a small town, hon. You can't blow your nose without everybody knowing whether it was in a handkerchief or a Kleenex. Now, if you want to hear about how that preacher at that independent church and his secretary was caught at his house in his boxers and her in a towel," she leaned down again, "said they'd been making chili dogs and got it all over themselves and their clothes were in the washer, I can give you all the gory details." She slapped my shoulder. "Ain't that a hoot? Look, it sure is good to see you back in here, Tuck, but y'all be careful around that guy."

Chapter Fifteen

Two hours after we left the Beef House, the SUV's rear cargo space was filled with bulging paper grocery bags. Chloe was happy with a Yeti cooler full of fish, chicken, and beef, along with unidentifiable vegetables with strange names. Well, one was familiar, but I had no intention of eating kelp, or anything else I hadn't grown up with.

There were four different county roads off the main highway winding and merging like an org chart drawn by a kindergartner. I typically used Blue Creek because I liked the country we drove through. The landowners had their pastures and woods looking like showplaces.

We came to the T intersection a quarter mile from our house, but instead of turning onto Rock Hill, I braked and studied our fence line half a mile further on.

Chloe looked up from the phone. "What are you doing?"

"Something's up with the fence down there."

She shifted forward in the seat. "Like what?"

"Like somebody's cut the wire." I accelerated, and the damage became clear as we rolled closer. The gap in the bob-wire fence spoke volumes. Two metal posts were bent flat on the ground, and broken wire stretched and curled in long tangles.

"Dad! Somebody drove through the fence, from the *inside*."

I stopped in the middle of the road to work things out. It wasn't the first time I'd seen something like that in my business. Most of the time it's someone driving *into* a pasture, either by accident or design.

Deep tracks in the soft ground led from where a truck came out, across the bar ditch, and east, in the direction we came from. We'd have met them had we been earlier. I backtracked the ruts in the pasture's coastal Bermuda grass leading at an angle through a low draw, then up a slight hill toward the house.

"What were they doing in the pasture in the first place?"

"Stealing my truck." Shoving the SUV's transmission into reverse, I punched the accelerator and looked through the rear glass, shooting through my own dust to the T intersection. Whipping around, I floorboarded it down the road and slid to a stop at our turnout.

"Dad! Our gate!"

The twin eight-foot pipe gates were now nothing more than twisted and bent pipes. The padlocked chain securing them together and the welded hinges held what looked like more than one impact from the inside. To our left, seventy-five yards of securely rooted heavy pipe posts and cable fencing kept them from driving through the yard.

Hand over her mouth, Chloe took in the damage. "What kind of shape is the truck in after all this?"

"Probably came close to totaling it."

"Who would do something like that?"

"Meth heads, most likely." I shifted into park and handed her my phone after punching in a number. Opening the door,

I hit the button to lock the doors. "Stay here. When Dispatch answers, ask for Deputy Lomax and tell him I'm checking the house. Then call Robby Taylor and tell him what happened. The number's on that notepad in the glove box."

The Expedition wasn't nearly as outfitted for work as the truck, but I kept a few things in there like notepads with phone numbers, emergency equipment, and a weapon. I stepped out with my pistol in hand. "Slip over here behind the wheel. If anything happens, get out of here and drive to the sheriff's office. There's a Colt in the console. That's a last resort."

My raised eyebrow anchored the point so that she knew to leave it alone until absolutely necessary. To her credit, my daughter didn't look panicked, or even scared. Her eyes were wide, though, and I knew she was twisted up tight.

Chloe knew how to shoot. She was coming into her own person, and wasn't the child she'd been in my mind on the day Sara Beth and Peyton were killed. She'd been around my work all her life, and more than once I had to take her with me if an urgent request came through.

In front of our damaged gate, she had the phone to her ear when I dug the keys from my pocket and unlocked the padlock holding the mangled gates together. One side didn't move, but the other gaped open wide enough for me to slip through.

Although I was confident the bad guys were gone, I walked up the drive with the Colt in my hand. To the right was the empty bunkhouse, barn, and cattle pens. All the gates were closed, and the front door leading into the bunkhouse/storeroom was still padlocked.

Circling the house, I saw that everything was still secured. Whoever had paid us a visit wasn't interested in breaking and entering, not right then at least. They wanted the truck.

I made a complete loop, coming around into the front yard to find two vehicles bracketing the drive and blocking the Expedition. My stomach clenched, and it was all I could do not to charge across the lawn to Chloe.

One of the vehicles was Jess Atchley's little blue Ford Ranger pickup. He was standing on the off side with the truck between us, leaning over the hood and staring at the house. A frail girl I took to be his daughter sat slumped in the passenger seat, intent on something in her hand and ignoring everything else around her.

A sign on the small SUV came into view as I got closer. THE SEEING EYE. It was the security company I'd called. A hair too late.

Atchley feigned concern. He scratched a four-day beard. "Something happen here?"

The guy's demeanor was completely plastic, and it immediately pissed me off. I wanted to cut loose on the man, but Sara Beth always said to keep your friends close, and your enemies closer. I took her advice, slipped the .45 under the belt in the small of my back. "Looks like the sun was too hot and the gates warped."

"You don't need to be a smart-ass about it. I was just concerned. Your daughter all right in there? She looks scared to death."

"She's fine. Probably doesn't like to be hemmed in."

Exaggerating his actions, he leaned back to see the other vehicle, then turned his attention back to me. "You need help?"

"No. We're fine. Thanks for stopping by."

He slapped the hood to end our discussion. "Well then, suit yourself." He opened his door and spoke over the cab. "Putting in a security system?"

"Just getting an estimate. Wouldn't want the place to catch fire and burn down if I'm not here. These new systems call the police and fire department at the same time and notifies me that something's wrong."

"Um humm. Oh, hey, I hear you were in town asking about me today."

A cold fist wrapped around my chest. I'd forgotten how fast the local grapevine worked, and never once imagined that the few people I talked to would get word back to him. Was that what happened here? Instant retribution? It wasn't that I was afraid of him; I just didn't like surprises.

"I like to know my neighbors."

"You could ask me anything you want. I'll tell you. You didn't have to go stringing off spreading my name around."

"It wasn't like that. I visited with some folks in the barbershop." I decided to throw him a curve. "And while I was at the sale barn, I talked to the stock agent. Thought you might buy and sell goats, since you have a couple, and your name came up."

"Them stupid goats are hers." He nodded in the girl's direction and the same time something flickered behind his eyes. "Well, I guess that's all right. Catch ya' on the flip-flop." He cranked the Ranger and drove away.

The security technician walked around the back of his SUV, hands in his pants pockets and a bag full of tools over his shoulder. "Looks like I was almost in time."

I winked at Chloe to let her know everything was all right. She lowered the lid on the console, hiding the revolver inside. "I believe I might need the deluxe package."

A car coming down the road with the lights flashing caught my attention. It was a sheriff's car with Chief Deputy Lomax driving.

Chapter Sixteen

Harley cracked a Bud Lite out back of my house, staring over the five-strand bob-wire fence toward the lake reflecting the gold and pink clouds lit by the setting sun. The evening was pleasant, cooled by a slight north breeze that pushed the humidity back down to the coast where it belonged.

Harley's boys, Danny and Matt, were fishing for crappie when their Labrador, Kevin, loped over a nearby rise and launched himself into the murky water. With that, the fishing was over. The boys shouted at the big lug to get out of the water. They knew he'd be muddy, and their job was to wash him off before they left for home.

"Come on in, boys!" Harley waved. They pretended not to hear him and chased the dog across the pasture, only to tangle with the Lab that cut in front of them. They landed belly-first in the grass with whoops of joy. Excited, the dog made a full circle and knocked Danny down again as soon as he regained his feet. Unflustered as Matt lay laughing on the ground, Danny stood again only to get sideswiped again by the ecstatic dog, who circled back around.

"Kevin!" Harley hollered. "Get away from those kids, you dumbass!"

I watched them grab at the dog in fun. "Only *you* would name a dog Kevin."

"Hey, it fits him. He *looks* like a Kevin."

"He's gonna kill the kids before we get to eat."

"Naw, he'll just toughen 'em up."

Always the class clown when we were growing up, Harley spent an inordinate amount of our public school years either sitting in the hall outside of his classroom, or waiting in the principal's office. He and Principal Patterson got to know each other well enough in high school that on occasion Harley simply walked into his office and leaned over for the obligatory three licks, and *then* handed him the discipline slip.

He never told Patterson, but Harley always said it was the principal who both liked and disciplined us that kept him from getting into even more trouble.

Steaks sizzled on the Weber grill, and the campfire we built nearby burned the grass away where I wanted to build the firepit that day. The shaped concrete blocks intended to contain the flames were still stacked in the back of the Expedition, forgotten for the moment.

Tammy and Chloe were inside, away from all the male chaos, and I figured they were deep into conversations I had no business hearing. Glad my daughter had her aunt to confide in, I hoped she'd open up and unload anything she wouldn't, or couldn't, tell me. Tammy was good with kids, and having only boys, she always enjoyed talking to my teenager. Now with Sara Beth gone, she was a godsend.

Harley turned from the boys to check out the new security cameras. The technician located them high, under the eaves. "Well, you have the system in, so it looks like we're going to work."

I took a sip of my Coors and toed a stick of firewood close to the middle of the flames. "I've already started, like you saw."

The security technician was finishing up when they all arrived at the ranch and the boys boiled out of their truck with fishing rods in hand. They charged across the pasture while Harley walked around the house, studying the cameras positioned to cover every inch of the immediate property, and most of the surrounding area. He'd spent half an hour quizzing the installer on the service and response time in the event of an emergency.

I watched him corner that guy and had to shake my head. Harley could talk to people for hours, asking questions and digesting their information as if it made a difference in his life goals. People opened up to him, too, because he was such a good listener, and they usually felt he had a genuine concern for them. He did, but not in the way they'd expect. He processed all that information and at some later time it usually helped in our work.

Standing there in jeans, Cinch shirt, and hat, he looked like a rancher, but we'd never raised a single head. With our jobs, running stock would be difficult at best, due to the hours we worked and the little time we had off. We both owned land when we worked, though, and leased it out for grazing or hay. That's why I didn't want either responsibility going on here at the new place. I wanted things to be different.

He pointed at the boys who were once again trying to fish. "Matt's gonna fall in before we eat. You can bet on it." He positioned himself between the fire and the lake, watching and warming himself at the same time. "Good thing he learned to swim. Well, I have a couple more ideas you didn't think of."

"Such as what?"

He studied the kids for a moment. "Those numbnuts are gonna hook that dog if they're not careful."

As if Kevin heard him, the dog swam a great circle around the boys and emerged on the muddy bank, shaking water that showered both kids. They squealed and laughed.

He was in another world at the moment, so I asked him again. "What were your ideas, little brother?"

"Well, we need to do more than fort-up. Playing defense is one thing, but now it's time to go on the offense at the same time." He pointed with a finger holding the beer can toward the unseen trailer.

"We can't go charging off over there."

"Not what I had in mind." He took another swallow. "Your bill from the security company's gonna be a little higher than you expected."

I sighed. It was classic Harley. "What'd you do?"

He jerked a thumb back toward his truck and watched a car pass on the road. It disappeared behind the house, and he turned to see it emerge on the other side. The pickup passed Atchley's drive and continued south. It was one of our neighbors I still hadn't met who lived some distance away, down on a bayou that flowed into the Red River. "I got two more wireless cameras and a repeater."

"What for?"

"After it gets dark, we're gonna creepy-crawl across your pasture down to the bridge and install one to record the road not far from his house."

"You could have done that out front here."

"Nope. You see anywhere we could mount a camera that couldn't be seen?"

I thought about it. "Well, we could have put it in a birdhouse."

"Right, and we could put up a sign that says, 'Look into this hole,' or how about. 'Smile, you're on *Candid Camera*.'"

"Fine then. You think there's a better place?"

"Sure, farther down on your property where all those vines have grown up on the fence. We can hide it there."

"And the other?"

"That'll be a little more dicey. I think we need to put it right across from Atchley's drive. They'll link with the repeater, and you can check them with your phone, just like the others around the house."

I considered his idea. "Surveillance on private citizens is a no no. I believe we need a court order for that. We still live in the United States, little brother." Good Lord, sometimes he frustrated me to no end. Those were the kinds of ideas that kept us in trouble back in school, and nearly got us shot a time or two when we worked undercover.

On the way home from town, I'd called my supervisor, Jimmy Meeks and talked with him about the house and Atchley. Because I didn't have any concrete evidence, or to say it in a better way, no real crime had been committed. All Jimmy could do was recommend that I "hide and watch," in his words. He also reminded me that I needed to bring Robby Taylor up to speed.

He rocked back and forth from one foot to the other, an old habit that arose when he was thinking. It helped back in our undercover days when sellers assumed he was an addict, bleeding off nervous energy or jonesing for a hit.

"They've been in your house. As far as I'm concerned, all bets are off. This isn't official. It's personal."

"You're getting pretty deep here awful fast. That's also what Jimmy Meeks told me, that I was too close to it already and it *had* become personal. He suggested that I work with the sheriff's department and when I told him what Lomax said, he just sighed."

"Well, that don't make no difference. I'm damn mad now."

"They didn't do anything to *you*, you know."

"Yeah, they did." His usually pleasant eyes went narrow and cold. "They messed with my brother." Harley's seriousness passed as quickly as it came when he laughed loud and long. He pointed toward the pasture. "I told Tammy one of those numbnuts would fall in."

He whistled, loud and shrill. Instead of Matt, it was Danny who slipped and fell in the stock pond. He rose in the knee-deep water, and Matt turned toward the house. Harley waved. "Y'all come in and clean up! Supper's ready." He chuckled and drained the beer. "Boys stink anyway, and they're both gonna smell worse with that mud all over 'em. Tammy'll have a conniption fit when they get here."

He thought for a second, studying his sons with that look only a dad has for the kids he loves. "You know, I'll just hose 'em off out here. It'll be colder'n a well-digger's ass, but maybe it'll make an impression on those two peckerheads."

"I suppose she brought some more clothes for them."

"Of course she did. Whadda ya think, we're new?"

By ten o'clock the boys were dry and asleep on a pallet on the floor. Kevin curled up beside them and was snoring. Tammy was in my room, which I'd given up for the night, reading and talking with Chloe, and waiting for Harley to come to bed. I planned to sleep on the couch, but much later.

Harley stood up from the kitchen table where we'd been talking quietly. "Where'd you put your tactical gear?"

"Spare bedroom beside Chloe's."

"Still got some stuff that'll fit me?"

"I do."

"Good. Won't need it, though. I brought my own. Just made sure you still have your gear."

I raised an eyebrow in question.

He didn't clarify. "Time to get busy."

Dressed in all black gear thirty minutes later, we moved slow and quiet along the inside edge of my fence, taking care to stay in the shadows and looking for just the right place to install the first small solar-operated night-vision camera. It was new technology I'd never heard of, and I was looking forward to seeing what the images looked like when we downloaded the video.

The darkness was filled with the familiar night sounds that identifies the damp country of northeast Texas. A whippoorwill called, and in the distance, soft grunts told me wild hogs were rooting up the low-lying pasture. A cow lowed and coyotes again chased their supper through the creek bottoms.

We wore our usual sidearms, plus several backup weapons. Between us, we carried ten firearms, reminding me of the days when we went creepy-crawling around meth houses.

Harley knelt beside a hackberry and spoke in a whisper. "This one'll catch 'em coming and going, giving us license plates and hopefully a good look at those inside."

The cameras were camouflaged, perfect for what we had in mind. I was familiar with bulky game cameras, but these sleek, decidedly smaller devices were a cut above. Lucky for us, the trees and brush still had their leaves and that helped hide the little box.

Neither of us used flashlights, but the dim glow from the face of the cell phone cupped in my hand was enough for Harley to attach the camera to a tree with a zip tie. The crunch of car tires gave us enough warning to push back and lower ourselves into a low depression on our side of the fence. I buried my face in my arms until the vehicle turned into Atchley's drive to make sure my white face didn't glow.

Harley chuckled. "Smile, peckerhead, you're on *Candid Camera*." He watched the car disappear into the cedars screening the house. "So this goes on all the time?"

"Every day and night. It slacks off in the early morning hours."

"Only *you* would get a place right next to a buy house."

"We don't know that for sure."

My little brother grunted. "Right." He rose and led the way through the shadows along the edge of the pasture and we followed the fence to the dry slough directly across from Atchley's drive. This time the fencerow was overgrown, something I planned to clean up later in the year when the weather cooled.

Fencerows and the ditches alongside country roads reflected the owners' pride in their land. The Atchleys let their ditches grow up to catch trash and litter. They were those kind of people who didn't clean the weeds and scrub brush from the fences and allowed it to eventually become overgrown.

When we reached the section of fence directly across from his drive, Harley started under the lower wire and I grabbed his ankle. "What are you doing?"

"It's so thick over there, I'm putting the phantom sneak down the edge of their drive and using this other camera to keep an eye on the house."

"Nope. That's trespassing, and we're not doing that right now."

"Dammit." That soft chuckle came again. "Right now. You realized you qualified it when you said *right now*."

"I sure did. Put the camera here on my property where it aims down his drive. That's not illegal."

"But you won't see much more than what we'll already have with the other one."

"It'll be enough. We'll have straight shots of them coming and going. That'll double our chances of getting good images. Might even get some faces through the windshields."

He paused, thinking. That could either be good or bad with Harley. He finally sighed and was rising up to position the camera when the glow of headlights on the returning vehicle flashed through the cedars lining Atchley's drive.

We again dropped into the long grass and scrub brush, hiding our faces as the oncoming sedan pulled through the gate and turned back toward town. I raised up to watch it drive away and saw the brake lights flicker over the little culvert bridge.

My blood chilled when the brake lights again flickered as they slowed in front of my drive. Tensed to jump up and run, I thought the strange car would turn in, but it accelerated with the roar of a big engine and was gone.

Harley's voice came low and tense. "Wonder what that was all about?"

"It's about how lucky they were they didn't stop."

He was silent for several moments. "That'll do it. Let's get back where we can check these cameras. They started this dance. Now let's get to finishing it."

Chapter Seventeen

Cool air flowed through the open windows of Atchley's trailer, where he and his second cousin Lloyd Belcher again sat at a table full of empty beer cans, dirty plates, and assorted liquor bottles. It was the first clean air to wash through the house in months, but did little to overcome the stench of cigarette butts and kitchen garbage.

Priscilla and Jimma were in their rooms where they belonged when Atchley had company. He figured he'd roust Priscilla out of bed a little later to fix him and Belcher something to eat. At least she knew how to cook, even though she couldn't clean or sweep for shit. As far as Jimma was concerned, he didn't care what she did as long as she didn't aggravate him.

Beside the dealers on the cluttered table were a dozen tiny test tubes not much longer than the end of the first joint on a man's little finger. They contained pink crystals similar to rock salt, or maybe contaminated rock candy.

Atchley poked a forefinger at one of the fragile plastic tubes capped with a red plug. "Have you tried this stuff?"

"Damn sure have." Belcher's eyes glistened, cold and glassy.

The ever-present cigarette hung from his lips. "Gravel. Man, this stuff's a magic carpet ride. People love it, and so do I. These are for you to try out. Get it to some of your customers, and they'll never go back to crystal again."

"I've heard about it. They say it makes you crazy."

"I've heard a couple of stories, but those dumbasses probably OD'd, or I figure they were already high on something else and it didn't mix well."

Atchley considered the tiny tubes, thinking that maybe he'd let Priscilla use one of them first. A kind of scientific test. If it hit like Lloyd said, she might be easier to live with. If it went bad, well, no great loss.

"I don't want to kill my customers. That's bad for business. I'd like to keep them coming back, dumbass. That's how you make money."

The insult flew over Belcher's head. "It only has that reaction with a *few* people. Man, this stuff is sweet. I had a hit just before I came over here, and I feel like I can move the *world*! It greases the tubes all the way down into my *soul*."

"Uh, huh. I can tell. This shit opens doors to worlds we don't need to see into."

"Just have your customers give it a try. I guarantee it'll sell better than anything you've ever moved, and for a helluva lot more money too. Man, it'll sell for ten times more than it costs to make." He drew on the cigarette and let the smoke out through his nose in two long streams.

"What's in it?"

"Hell-if-I-know. Someone said it has something Grandpa distills from wasp spray, but I don't know if that's the truth. Probably not." He barked a laugh, "If it is, though, it'll be better than having to show your ID to get some cold medicine."

He laughed, louder. "Can you imagine showing ID to buy bug spray!" He grew thoughtful. "Like I said, Grandpa up in Oklahoma cooks this shit, but you can bet your ass I won't be around those silos."

He giggled like a schoolgirl.

"If that tin can goes up, it'll be in orbit for a *month*. That's why I don't make it, I just sell the stuff." Belcher's eyes seemed to move in different directions of their own accord. He brought them back to focus on Atchley. "You know who's making it, don't you?"

"I heard it was coming out of Lamar County, so I guess I was wrong."

"You are. Guess who's cooking it."

"Said I don't know."

"Give up?"

Frustrated, Atchley threw up both hands. "Sure. I give up."

"It's your man, Lee Quattlebaum."

"No shit? They call him Grandpa?"

"I shit you not. He's tricked out that lab up there in the Choctaw Nation up in Oklahoma, not far out of Cloudy. Man, it's a slick operation like I've never seen. Big fifty-five-gallon stainless-steel drums with heating mantles. They turned all that into giant cooking vessels and fitted the drums with custom-made stainless-steel cooling condensers that stand eight feet tall. Man, it's something to see."

Atchley ran fingers through the stiff, dirty hair that stood up all over his head. "Look, I need you to listen to me."

"I'm listening." Belcher's eyes were locked on the tube style television on a table in the corner. The sound was down, but the snowy picture had his attention.

"No. Lloyd! Listen to me."

Belcher's eyes drifted back to Atchley's face. "Listening."

"All right. You've screwed up twice across the road. First thing was that the house is still standing."

"It's not my fault he found the igniter."

"Didn't say you had any fault, but you're right." Atchley flicked a finger. "He found it and now the son of a bitch knows we're onto him. I can feel him looking this way every time I think of it."

"You seen him watching us?"

"No. That's not what I said. I can *feel* him, if that makes any sense, but you really screwed the pooch when you stole his truck. What'd you do that for?"

"He made me mad, going to Butch with this, so I figured I'd make him bleed a little."

"By stealing his truck."

Belcher lit another cigarette from the butt and crushed it out in an ashtray. "Hey, I didn't steal it, Curtis did. I wanted to do more. I intended to get inside and take all his guns. I bet a guy like him has a ton of guns I could turn over, and maybe some cash. He has to be loaded, but when you told me Butch called and said the guy... What's his name?"

"Snow."

"Yeah, Snow was on his way back, I didn't have time, so I took his truck."

"Did you have to try and drive it through the gate?"

"It was locked. He hit the damn thing three times, but it held. Pipe gates are tough."

"So you *and* him plowed across the pasture and went through his fence."

"Seemed like the thing to do at the time."

Atchley studied his cousin for a moment, wondering how he

could be related to someone so dumb. "Why'd you come over here right after? You know Jimma saw you drive up in it. She's not dumb. She knows where that truck came from, and there's always a chance she'll let it slip to somebody."

"Who the hell cares?" Belcher's head lowered, the way a drunk reacts to too much whiskey. He watched Atchley from under his thick eyebrows. "*Let* it slip. Curtis was driving, like I said."

"I care, and you were in there with him when he stole the damn thing, so whatever slips is gonna get on you too!"

"Well, me'n Curtis needed to see you for a minute."

"You just wanted to show me what y'all did." Curtis was a con who'd already been to Huntsville twice. His sheet was several pages long, reaching back to when he was a kid, stealing bicycles in town. "You were both high, and I need you straight. You can't do your job like that."

"It don't matter none. Curtis has the truck, and it's gone. Nothing to worry about. I just wanted to twist that guy's tail a little bit."

"Well, I'm afraid you twisted a panther's tail, because Lomax said..."

Atchley's cell phone blared to life with a Florida Georgia Line song. Seeing who was calling, he punched it alive and put it on speaker. "Hey, Butch."

"You at home?"

"Yep. Sitting here with Lloyd. What's up?"

The tinny voice coming through the speaker was sharp and angry. "You two dickheads are in trouble."

Atchley went cold. "What happened?"

"The highway patrol pulled Curtis over down on 75, just north of Dallas."

"So?"

"So, he was driving a stolen truck registered under the name of Tucker Snow. Does that ring a bell?"

Atchley thought fast. He had to sound innocent. "The guy across the road."

"Don't try to act like you don't know who I'm talking about. You remember I said those guys are a branch of the DPS, don't you?"

Atchley met Belcher's eyes that were wide in surprise. "Uh, no. Why'n hell would I know something like that? I've only seen those guys up at the sale barn, but I've never talked to one. All they do is look at brands on cows. What does any of this have to do with me anyway?"

"You might get your chance to talk with this one again soon." Butch's voice was sharp. Accusatory. "He'll be at the impound lot pretty quick to get what's left of his truck. He's a lawman, and when he finds out Curtis's last name, I'd expect he'll do a little digging. You're on his radar, and if he connects him to you, or Lloyd, then all hell's gonna break loose, and I doubt I can do much more than save my own ass when that happens."

Belcher licked his lips and leaned forward to get closer to the phone. "Uh, this is Lloyd. Does Jackson know anything about all this?"

"I know who's talking, you dumb shit. Not yet. But Sheriff Jackson will when the report comes across his desk, because I won't be able to intercept it. This one goes straight to him, and I'll have to do some fast talking to cover up the fact that I haven't let him know what's going on out there."

"But you're the chief deputy. Why can't you handle the whole thing by yourself?"

"Because, dumbass, the report'll bypass me and go straight

to his desk, sick or not. Grand theft reports go out to *everyone.* It's on the computer, and all we have to do is log in to the website and read it."

They all knew Sheriff Waylon Jackson was blissfully unaware of how Lomax manipulated the system by intercepting many of the reports on their relatives by either trashing them or burying them under drifts of paperwork. Jackson was relatively new to the job, having been elected only a year earlier. An old-school lawman who'd been sheriff in two other Texas counties before he moved to Ganther Bluff, he trusted his deputies, and most of them were old hands at playing the system.

"Curtis'll say he borrowed it. I know him. They can't connect it to us."

The phone was silent for a minute. "Which one of y'all drove the truck?"

Belcher laced his fingers and leaned forward, hovering over the phone. His head swayed slowly back and forth like a wounded bull. "Curtis did, why?"

"Were you with him?"

Belcher frowned. "Yeah."

"So I imagine your fingerprints are all over it."

"Nope. Wore rubber gloves. Any prints belong to that dumbass Curtis."

"Good to know. At least I won't be defending kinfolk."

Atchley had a thought. "Hey, if anyone tries to get warrants with our names on it, you'll let us know, right? Since they'll go through Grayson, he'll tell you, right?" His third cousin was Judge Jimmy Lee Grayson who believed in family and did all he could to keep them safe.

"Family can only do so much, but yeah, I'll let you know if any of it gets on us."

"Good. Thanks for calling. We're gone." He punched the phone off at the same time headlights flashed through the windows. Atchley rose. "Customers."

When he returned, Belcher was gone out the back door.

Chapter Eighteen

Autumn mornings in Crystal Springs were historically quiet, especially in Lucy and George Lavaca's small post–World War II neighborhood. They'd lived in their little frame house for over forty years and knew almost every neighbor on both sides of their street.

The home on one side was always quiet. Ruth Hall was a widow and seldom came outside. Jay and May Roberts on the other side were ten years older than Lucy and George and like them, their kids were grown and gone.

The Rush family lived directly across, and they always reminded Lucy of the Cleavers on the old TV series *Leave It to Beaver*. Their girls were also grown and married. Though some of the other families on the two sides of the block had children, it was too early for them to be up.

Lucy filled a cup from their old-fashioned percolator and breathed in the aroma of freshly ground coffee. For once George wasn't up before dawn, so she had the perfect morning to sit out front and watch the world wake up. Still in her housecoat, she unlocked the door and stepped outside.

The pier-and-beam foundation provided enough elevation to see most of the street in both directions. George's old Monte Carlo was parked out front. She intended to give him another nudge after dinner to clean out the garage so there was room for the sedan. She hated to look out and see cars parked at the curb.

They had an old metal swing rocker beside the door that George sanded down and refinished and painted turquoise. Though it was a little chilly, she sat on her usual side to enjoy the silence before starting breakfast. She didn't mind cooking, loved it actually, and preferred to eat at home rather than be like so many folks these days and go out. Wasting money on food she could make herself was foolish, in her opinion.

Lucy longed for the days when paperboys passed on their bikes, flinging the morning edition up on the steps with accuracy. She recalled when the milkman pulled up in front with a smile and a wire metal carrier full of bottled milk. Folks waved back then when they walked or drove past, and the Saturday morning sound of lawn mowers filled the air along with the pleasant odor of freshly cut grass. These days it was mostly delivery trucks bringing packages.

Movement caught her eye, and she paused with the cup halfway to her lips. Steam rose and she tilted her head so it wouldn't fog her glasses. There was someone crouched on the far side of George's car, and they were up to no good.

She stood to get a better angle and saw a man's head bent to his work. "Hey! You! What do you think you're doing to my husband's car?"

Her voice activated something in the man who stood straight up with a screwdriver in his hand. For the first time in her life, Lucy understood what people meant when they referred to a feral look in someone, or some*thing*'s eyes. The would-be thief wearing only a pair of faded jeans was a man all right, but even from a distance his eyes were wild and dangerous.

"Huh!?" His guttural voice came from some dark hell she'd never dreamed of.

He edged to the front fender and stopped. There it was again, that animal look. His lips rose in a lion's snarl at the same time his chin lowered. She'd seen that before in dogs before they attacked.

She backed up a step, and then sidled toward the door, unsure of what was about to happen or what to do. She'd interrupted a break-in, and now there was no reason for him to stay. Maybe he'd made his point and would go away.

He should run away.

But he didn't. Instead, a savage growl rose in his chest and the raging man charged.

But people don't go crazy and attack women for no reason... do they? Barefoot, he was halfway across the lawn and up the walk before she realized this was real. His teeth were bared like those of a werewolf, and if she had to describe what she saw, it was fangs in a human mouth. She yelped and dropped the delicate china cup she'd used for years, spinning fast enough to twist out of her house shoes as it shattered on the concrete.

"George!" Her terrified scream came from deep inside her, like the shriek of a wounded rabbit. She hadn't closed the door on the way out, and that gave her just enough edge to put precious distance between herself and the insane man whose growl rose in intensity.

Lucy shot through the door in a flash. Instinct encoded into her DNA after a million years of evolution told her there wasn't enough time to shut and bolt the door. She had to flee, and to her cave she went.

"Help!" She planted her left foot into the carpet like a fullback and lurched to the right, down the short hall to their bedroom. The growling man had reached the front door, and it slammed back with a flat pop when he shoved through hard enough for the handle to bury itself in the Sheetrock.

"George!" Her shrill intensified, and tomorrow her chest and throat would be sore from the effort, but she had no control over what was happening to her. Now words failed, and her mounting terror devolved any form of communication into a pitiful howl of despair.

She flashed past the open bathroom door, knowing there was no time to hide in that pink retreat full of soft towels and lotions. No time to lock herself in there. She wailed and rushed into the bedroom, not sure if she should run to George, or make the hard right into their closet.

Her eyes took in the room, their king-size bed directly ahead, bracketed by matching nightstands and lamps. On her side was a clock, her Bible, and a glass of water. His also had a clock, the remote control for the television mounted on the wall, and his Bible. But there had also been one more item that rested within reach for their entire married life.

Thin gray hair tousled from sleep, George sat up with a Smith & Wesson semi-automatic pistol in his grip. The muzzle rose as she entered the room and looked down that black hole. Knowing her husband, she flung herself forward at the same time a flat report drowned out her screams.

The pistol roared again and again with three quick pulls of the trigger, and the man chasing her dropped to the ground. Frantic to get away, Lucy crawled on her hands and knees and shrieked again when the insane monster grabbed her ankle.

Pulling himself to his knees, the man launched himself

toward her again at the same time three more loud bangs filled the room. The man collapsed on her legs, but continued to pull at her gown.

She sensed George standing beside them in his pajama bottoms.

The next gunshot was much softer, as if muffled, and she looked back over her shoulder to see her attacker lying still on the carpet with blood and gun smoke pouring from his temple.

Blood-splattered, George leaned forward and shoved the muzzle against the man's head a second time, but there was no need to fire the gun again. He knelt, shoved the corpse off her legs and pulled Lucy close. "What the hell just happened?"

Sobbing, Lucy curled up like a baby in a crib. "I don't know."

Chief Deputy Fred Bronson, two deputies, and a pair of paramedics gathered in the Lavacas' living room, looking down the hall and into their bloody bedroom. The body lay as it fell, and the room strobed with lightning again and again as a photographer documented the scene.

Bronson leaned against the doorframe, his back to the shocked husband and wife sitting on the couch in their small living room. A paramedic knelt beside them, talking softly as she took their blood pressure as a precaution.

"What was his name?"

"Pate. Duane Pate." His deputy read from the iPad in his hands. "Twenty-two. Several arrests for possession and use of methamphetamine out of Dallas, and three DUIs in Sulphur Springs. No assaults, though, and nothing even remotely violent."

"This is the same thing we had back in June, when that stock inspector Tucker Snow was here."

"That was before I got here, but I heard a little about it." The deputy closed the iPad's cover. "What do you mean?"

Bronson tilted his hat back and sighed. "I'll bet my job it's that damned gravel again. I need to call that stock agent, Tucker Snow. He'll want to know this stuff is everywhere now."

"He the one who lost his wife to that car accident here-while-back, the one driven by some guy on this crap?"

"It is."

"Why does he need to know?"

"Because the two of us ran into something like this a few months back, and I think he should know about it."

Chapter Nineteen

Stomach twisted in knots, I looked at Chief Deputy Fred Bronson's name on my phone. He'd hung up only a minute earlier after calling with the news about another incident involving gravel. Once again I was on the front porch, leaning back in a chair and couldn't get my mind off an incident that happened only two days before I lost Sara Beth and Peyton.

It was the last time I'd acted in my official capacity as a stock agent in the little town of Crystal Springs. A deputy manning the front desk ushered me into the sheriff's office where Venetian blinds opened onto a cracked asphalt parking lot. Yellow light from old-school globe lamps did little to add to the daylight coming in through the window to illuminate a scarred wooden desk, two wooden chairs, and a couple of file cabinets.

In an 8 by 10 color photo on his desk, the partially nude body of a young man lay sprawled on the sidewalk in front of a small frame house that needed painting fifteen years ago.

He saw my interest. "Recent murder. That there's the killer. You don't want to see the other guy. Since it happened in town, I doubt that's why you're here, Agent Snow."

I'd expected to speak with Sheriff Hal Newsome, but the well-respected sheriff of Hopkins County was temporarily relieved of his duties for a few days while the Texas Rangers completed a routine investigation into the officer-involved shooting. That's why Chief Deputy Bronson was behind the desk.

"You're right." I picked it up and studied the painfully white figure in a pair of dingy jockey shorts. "So all he was wearing was his drawers?"

Bronson's bicep stretched the material of his green and brown uniform shirt as he ran fingers through his short hair. I bet he spent a lot of time lifting iron, but then again, he could have been born with it like the old television star who played Cheyenne in the 1950s, Clint Walker.

He grinned from under a thick mustache. "I haven't heard that term in a while." His graying hair was so short it barely creased from the straw hat laying crown-down on his desk.

My own hat rested upside down on his inbox. I couldn't figure out why the guy didn't have a rack in his office to hang 'em on. "I was raised by a tough old man who should have lived in the late eighteen-hundreds. Name's not Michael Joseph Lyon, is it?"

"Nope, but they look a lot alike, 'cept I 'magine Lyon's still sucking air."

"It was Sheriff Newsome who that killed this guy?"

"Yep. Feller killed his daddy and then attacked the sheriff who let the air out of him. All because of a new kind of meth called gravel. What do you need Lyon for?"

"I have an arrest warrant for him."

The chief deputy raised an eyebrow. "He's crazy as a Bessie bug."

"That's what I've heard. Thought you might have a little more background for me before I pick him up."

"Take a posse with you. He'll shoot the minute he sees a badge. What're you gonna pick him up for? He stealing cattle now?"

"Saddles. Burglary and stolen property."

His cell phone rang and he plucked it off the desk "Bronson." He listened for a moment and pointed at the photo so I'd know what he was talking about. "Yep. Sheriff Newsome was coming back from lunch at home when he got the call. It came through as a family disturbance and when he rolled up, the suspect was on the front porch, peeling his clothes off, or what was left of them."

He held up a finger as a polite "excuse me" and returned to the call. "The suspect is Carroll Hill, a meth head, and became a murderer." He frowned. "According to Sheriff Hal Newsome's statement, he arrived at the scene only moments after Carroll Hill finished chewing off the fingers on his daddy's right hand. When he saw the sheriff, Hill ripped off what was left of his T-shirt, leaving nothing but a pair of underwear.

"Following protocol, the sheriff stepped out of his county-issued SUV and circled around to the sidewalk, ordering the suspect to drop the weapon and get on the ground. Hill shrieked like a panther, then screamed that no one was ever going to lay a hand on him again. All right, shrieking like a panther wasn't in the report, Carl."

He mouthed "local reporter" at me and continued his conversation. "But that's how Hal told me it sounded. Sheriff Newsome ordered him down again and called for backup. The deceased charged the lawman with an Old Hickory butcher knife raised in what we all call the 'ice pick' position.

"The next two seconds were corroborated by a witness watching from next door who stated that Sheriff Newsome shouted "no" over and over again as the enraged man sprinted off the porch. The witness stated that Hill crossed that distance in two to three seconds and the sheriff retreated until he was against his vehicle. In my opinion, the sheriff waited until almost too late, because his attacker was only five to eight feet away when he discharged a Glock 40 until Hill fell when one of the slugs severed his spine. He was at that time only two feet from the sheriff, and despite his wounds, he continued to move his arms and mumble for more than a minute before he bled out."

Bronson nodded as if the person on the phone could see him. "That's all I can tell you, Carl." He slipped a forefinger through the thick handle of a coffee-stained mug and took a sip. "It was a righteous shooting, sir. Obviously self-defense. Fine. I'll let you know if I hear anything else."

He thumbed the phone off. "Sorry about that, Special Agent..."

"Tucker Snow. Call me Tuck. How's Hal doing, by the way?"

"He's fine. I don't think the shooting bothered him a bit because he's fishing today."

I knew better than that. There might not be any psychological damage on the surface, but deep down below, I figured he was dealing with it as best he could. A sheriff usually won't show emotion over something like that, but I can bet you a dollar to a donut hole that he was working it out with that fishing rod in his hand. Sometimes fishing isn't about catching anything.

I'd done the same thing in the past because I've been involved in more than my share of trouble; it was a familiar way of working out problems that couldn't be solved by sitting in front of a television.

"I'll go out with you to pick up Lyon, and we can stop by and talk with a witness for a minute." Bronson flicked a finger toward the old-school half panel and glass door. "I need to hear one part of his story again about the sheriff's shooting, just to clarify a point."

I was in no hurry. "Sure."

"Mr. Ben'll enjoy visiting with us." He took a sip of what looked to me like cold coffee. "He's outlived almost everyone he's known, and the old feller doesn't have much family. He spends most of his days on his front porch, watching the neighborhood." He sipped again from the stained cup and grimaced. "I wish we had more of those folks out there keeping an eye out for us."

"You're right. I had a college professor way-back-when who said our society began to deteriorate when air-conditioning became common and architects quit putting front porches on houses. In his opinion, he said crime increased after that because folks stayed inside and didn't come out to keep an eye on their neighborhood, or their neighbors."

"That's for sure. People don't hardly know one another anymore in their neighborhoods." Bronson seemed determined to finish that coffee for some reason, or maybe he was trying to learn how to like cold coffee. I never could understand how anyone paid good money for something I pour out. "I have a few folks here in town who keep the phone hot, but most of the time it's their imagination. It works, though. We haven't had much crime here other than the usual small stuff, at least until meth started showing up here while back."

"Cooking or using?"

"One leads to the other. We busted a meth lab here-while-back set up in a trailer out in the country about five miles from here. You'd think they'd get farther away to cook that crap."

"Someone turned them in?"

"Sure enough. Guy feeding his cows smelled something coming from across his fence. He knew the trailer was there, and didn't much like the people living in it. Called 'em river rats, and said they were the trashiest people he'd ever seen. We got a warrant and popped 'em. I've never seen anything like the inside of that place, but as soon as we shut 'em down, somebody else started up a lab somewhere else and that crap just kept rolling out."

Some cookers were the descendants of backwoods bootleggers and moonshiners who learned to make whiskey from *their* grandparents, sort of a family tradition. It was like most families. Some were good at marketing, so they took up that aspect of the business. Others were lazy and wanted to sell that crap instead of working. Then there were those good with their hands, and they modified what the old folks did generations ago, and produced product. People using their strengths.

I picked up my hat, getting ready to go, when his cell phone rang again.

"Hang on a minute and I'll walk out with you." He answered. "Bronson."

I watched his chiseled face harden as he listened to the caller on the other end. He clicked the end of a pen. "What's that address?" He scratched it down on a pad and I tilted my head to read his surprisingly neat handwriting.

"Fine. Stay inside. I'm on the way." He hung up and grabbed his hat. "You're here at the right time. I might need your help since it's just me in town right now. This sounds like a repeat of the Hill incident. Guy named Mickey Fuller's a meth head, out on the east side of town. We've picked him up a dozen times. His mama called to say he's on the way to kill his wife, who's shacked up with another dope head on College Street. Fuller's acting nuts, complaining that he's burning up inside and red mad."

I set my hat and we pushed into the sheriff's small reception area. Though TSCRA special rangers are officially part of the Texas Department of Public Safety or the Oklahoma State Bureau of Investigation that has no jurisdiction in regards to civil matters, we *are* certified peace officers charged with maintaining a safe town for good people to live in.

"Annie!" Bronson's bark was soft, but authoritative. A curly-haired woman behind a desk outside his door looked up. "Get me some help out to the east side of town, South Fall Street." He gave her an address. "Man with a gun."

All business, the one-person dispatch nodded and turned to make the radio call.

"That's not what you wrote down." I followed him outside and we high-stepped it across the parking lot. "You wrote someplace else."

"We're gonna cut him off before he gets there."

"How do you know where he's going?"

"I know this town, and the people in it."

"I'll follow you."

I was barely in my pickup when Chief Deputy Bronson squalled out onto the street, lights flashing on his agency-issued truck. I slipped on a pair of Oakleys to block the early summer sun and pulled in behind his Ford. We darted around slow-moving traffic, zigzagging through the small-town square and out on the other side. Two minutes later he slid to a stop in the middle of a cracked asphalt street, and I pulled up behind him and stepped out.

To our right, a line of tired-looking frame houses in need of a wet paintbrush squatted on large overgrown lots. Cars parked haphazardly in the scraggly yards were the order of the day, along with sagging chain-link fences, rusting cars, rotting sheds, and tire swings hanging from huge shade trees.

To the left, a mixed windbreak of hackberry, cottonwoods,

and cedar elm trees separated us from a two-lane highway running parallel about forty yards away. I heard a heavy truck growl past. It flickered through the trees and was replaced by a white car passing in the opposite direction.

There was no one on the street, and I wondered what Bronson had in mind. "One of these his house?"

"No, but about a hundred yards on the other side of those trees is where his wife is laid up with that dope head." He pointed the opposite direction. "Fuller lives two streets over that way with his mama."

Bronson saw the puzzled look on my face.

"Fuller can't drive. His brain is so fried that he has trouble with depth perception. He walks everywhere he goes, and the best route's between those houses and across this lot." He pointed. "There he is."

It was a brilliant piece of police work, the kind that comes with knowing your town and those in it, but neither of us were prepared for the frantic, barefoot young man in faded jeans and a shredded T-shirt hanging off one shoulder. He reminded me of the dead man I'd read about in the sheriff's report.

Fuller stumbled from between two houses, arguing with himself just below the decibel level of an AC/DC concert. "I told you she was no good! You did not! Yes I did! She's a tramp, and I'm going to kill that bitch! I'll kill her first and cut her head off, but I'm so goddamned hot!"

I'd heard of split personalities before, but had never seen a man actually argue with himself. The guy's hair looked like it was combed with a garden rake, and his sunken face had that ravaged look that came from inhaling vaporized chemicals whipped up from cleaning products people store under a kitchen sink. His eyes burned with the glassy look of meth addicts.

It was the big revolver in his hand that had my attention the most. It looked like an old-school Colt Python, and the hammer was back.

He saw us and stopped. "I said get *away* from me!"

I waited, hand on the butt of my still-holstered Colt 1911.

"Mickey Fuller." Bronson slowly raised his left hand. "Easy, Mickey, you know who I am, don't you?"

The tweaker's voice cracked and rose on every third or fourth word. It reminded me of Bobcat Goldthwait doing one of his comedy routines. "I know you. Leave me alone, Bronson. I ain't done nothin' to you."

"That's right, but you look a little upset. Come over here and let's talk about it."

"No!" Fuller ran fingers through his greasy hair. "All you want to do is put me in handcuffs again, and I can't take a jail cell right now. It's too damned *hot*! I ain't going back to prison, neither. Who is that with you? You brought a *cowboy*?"

Bronson tilted his hat back like Will Rogers. I've done the same thing while talking to agitated individuals. It makes you look more relaxed and friendlier. "I didn't say a word about going to jail. I just want to find out why you're upset."

"What makes you think I'm up*set*?" Eyes flashing like lightning, he sidled toward the line of trees. "Leave me *alone*!"

From behind the Oakleys, my own eyes were on that big gun hanging in his hand. I stayed quiet and let Bronson handle it.

"Your mama called and told me you're a little put out." Bronson's voice was low enough to put a baby to sleep. "Set that ol' gun down, and let's talk."

Fuller seemed surprised to find the Colt in his hand. "No!" His face grew beet red and looked as if was going to explode. His expression changed, as if he remembered why he had it in the first place. "I'm gonna *kill* that bitch with it!" He wiped at his sweating forehead.

It was hot all right in the June sun. Cicadas sang in the trees, and the guy's skin under his ripped shirt looked like a boiled lobster, as if he'd been sleeping nude in the full sun.

Keeping his voice calm and under control, Bronson advanced a couple of steps. I was impressed with his demeanor. "Look, calm down a little, Mickey. We're just visitin'. I want to hear what you have to say."

Using the man's first name to increase a sense of familiarity, the chief deputy was doing his best to defuse the situation, and it would have worked most any other time, but the twitchy guy was stuffed to the gills on something pulsing through his body like hot acid. I've seen addicts before, but this was a tweaker times one thousand.

"No!" His high, strained voice cracked again. "I'm not going to jail before I kill her!"

"No one said anything about jail."

"Why is he here? Who is that guy?"

Bronson patted the air in a calming manner. "He's a livestock inspector. Don't worry about him."

"I don't *like* it!"

The tweaker's pistol rose, and we drew our weapons. The checkered grips on my .45 felt cool in my palm, and one part of my mind wondered how that could happen on such a hot day.

A blue jay flashed behind Mickey Fuller and across the street. Somewhere a dog barked, and a wooden screen door slammed. The world was normal beyond our narrow, focused view.

"Mickey. Put that gun on the ground right now. Tell me what you're on. Is it meth? We can get you some help." Chief Deputy Bronson had his weapon at low ready, pointed toward

Fuller's feet so he could keep an eye on the man's weapon. If he was aiming at his chest, Bronson's own weapon might have obscured Fuller's hands. We all watch hands and eyes.

My weapon was aimed slightly higher, at Fuller's midsection. *Aim for center mass.*

From a screened window on the house only fifty yards away, the opening rifts of the Rolling Stones' "Gimme Shelter" floated across the still yard. I'd heard the same song just before a shoot-out erupted on an East Texas highway only a few months earlier, and I wondered if some higher force had decided the song was now my curse to bear every time things went south.

Chief Deputy Bronson spoke loud enough to be heard over the music. "Son, tell me what you're on so we can get you some help."

"Gravel!"

The guy's face grew even redder, a frightening, unnatural plum color. Sometimes people's faces looked like that when they die and aren't found for several hours.

I expected his head to explode at any second.

The next thing we knew, he put the muzzle to his temple and the situation became surreal. "I'll kill myself! I'll do it before I go to jail!" Keeping his bloodshot eyes on us, he crossed the crumbling street, moving sideways like a crab in slow motion, and stepped into the uncut grass. "Leave me *alone*! It makes me crazy!"

"You said gravel? Is that what you're using?" Chief Deputy Bronson swiveled in place to keep his weapon trained on Mickey Fuller. Heart pounding, I shifted to my right past the lawman to maintain a clear sight line. "Put the gun down, buddy, and let's talk in the shade."

Fuller continued his strange crab-walk toward the trees. "Don't make me shoot my hostage! I'll do it! I'll kill him! I surely will!"

It was a bizarre comedy routine come to life.

A car door slammed on the other side of the thin strip of woods. I hoped whoever was getting in or out of the vehicle over there was moving fast enough to get clear of the situation that was fast spinning out of control.

Fuller stepped into the trees with the gun still at his own temple and we followed into the understory full of sticks and fallen limbs. I didn't like the idea of him using those big trunks as cover. My voice was soft. "Bronson, you have a clear eye on him?"

"Yeah, he's on a footpath through there."

Guns ready, we followed.

Fuller stepped behind a tree. "Get away from me!"

"We can't do that, Mickey." Bronson's voice remained sweet as sugar. I was glad I didn't have the lead on that one because I was sure my own voice would crack from the tension. "Drop your weapon and come out to us with your hands up where we can see 'em, buddy."

I angled to get a better sight line, twigs crackling underfoot. By that time Bronson and I were fifteen yards apart, and I stepped into the woods. Finally, the meth head's side was to me as he leaned against a tree. I could see most of his right shoulder. He still had the gun against his head. Lining the sights up, I took several deep breaths to slow my heart.

His attention on the chief deputy, Fuller pulled at the remains of his shirt, tearing it the rest of the way off. "Hot!"

But it wasn't, especially in the shade. A dove flapped hard in the tree limbs overhead and peeped away through the treetops. Gnats danced in front of my face as the music from the house behind us rose in volume. Someone was enjoying the music that I didn't need right then.

To my right, the trees abruptly ended at an open grassy area bordering the two-lane highway. A pickup passed, catching my attention, and I realized I could ease into the open and have the angle on Fuller if he started shooting.

Before I could move, a highway patrol cruiser pulled up on the shoulder. A trooper stepped out and rounded his front bumper, walking toward the trees as casually as if he were strolling in a park.

He couldn't see much past the understory brush growing at the edge of the timber. I waved an arm to get his attention, but he was concentrating on the sound of Fuller's voice. Unaware of our situation, he was gonna walk right into Fuller.

Without any provocation, the meth head cut loose with a shriek that sounded like someone was ripping off a body part. "No!" He spun and took off through the trees and into the open.

The startled trooper saw an armed man burst through the trees. He drew his weapon. "Freeze!"

Seeing the officer, Fuller raised his weapon toward the trooper.

"No!" The officer fired three times, and Fuller stumbled.

"Special agent! Drop your weapon!" I pushed through the brush, hoping the rattled officer would recognize me as law enforcement and not shoot at *me*.

Incredibly, Fuller regained his footing and despite three center mass shots, the tweaker planted his feet and charged the officer, firing as he ran. The big cannon in his hand jumping with every shot. The trooper fired again and again. Most of the rounds struck Fuller in the torso.

My .45 thundered twice, both shots taking Fuller in the right side of the chest as he ran, but he slammed into the trooper like a fullback, knocking the man backward. His engine room completely destroyed, Fuller was already dead, but he still didn't know it.

Screaming himself, the officer grabbed Fuller's gun arm and stuck the muzzle of his service weapon under the enraged man's chin, and pulled the trigger.

In a vapor of gore, Fuller went limp, and dropped on top of the shaken lawman.

I rushed forward and flipped Fuller's body off the trooper, who scrambled to his feet, shocked at the sight of the addict's shattered corpse. White as a blood-spattered sheet, he staggered back against his vehicle.

Holstering my weapon, I wiped at my face, suddenly exhausted. That was my first exposure to a new, incredibly dangerous drug with the street name gravel that indirectly killed Sara Beth and Peyton only days later. And now, it seemed, it was just down the road from the new life I was trying to build.

Chapter Twenty

Harley and I were in the Expedition, headed to the Collin County impound lot. A call came in at nine the night before from a highway patrol officer named Charley Rhodes, who told us they'd recovered my truck near Dallas. He said I could come to McKinney to pick it up, and Harley went with me.

Chloe was with Tammy, who'd agreed to pick her up after school. I wasn't going to send her away for an extended length of time, it would be too much for a kid suffering through so many changes, but I needed to be gone all day and didn't want her there alone when she came home. It was hard on Tammy to drive so far, and harder on the boys who had to ride along without much to do, but we all knew it was the right thing.

Impound lots are interesting places at any time of the day. I've been to more than one at night, when folks are in line to pick up their towed vehicles after the clubs close. It's quiet, organized and strained chaos where owners show up so drunk or high there's no way the officer in charge could release their property to them, or dozens of angry owners insisting their rights were violated and the fines should be dismissed. I once watched a woman in a tutu dance around like Glinda the Good Witch as no one paid any attention to her antics.

I expected something similar on that bright day, but we were the only two in the building at that hour. I showed the officer behind the window my badge and ID, along with the police report. He stamped the paperwork and slid the receipt through the slot. "Sorry about your truck, sir. It took a beating." He gave a smile. "It's in row eighteen."

"Much obliged."

Leaving the Expedition parked and locked in front of the building, Harley and I walked onto a field filled with rows of vehicles ranging from simply impounded to wrecked. It reminded me of rusting metallic crops. We soon found what was left of my pickup. Harley gave a low whistle. The once-white Dodge looked like it'd been through the wringer. The black brush guard was dented and pushed back into the grille in two places. One fender crumpled almost against the tire, and long scratches down both sides were evidence of encounters with the gate and bob-wire fence. The interior wasn't much better.

The lab boys did us a favor and expedited their investigation after they picked it up. Fingerprint dust was everywhere, and you could see where they lifted a couple of prints. Oftentimes they don't even do that with returned vehicles, but when the investigative officers found out who it belonged to, they did it more for a favor than anything else.

We climbed into the cab. Harley shifted his weight in the passenger seat and looked around. "Bet that crack wasn't in your windshield day before yesterday."

His sarcasm made me grin, despite what we'd found. I looked down at what I took to be seed holes in the upholstery. A cigarette burn in the material beside my leg added character.

"It wasn't, but I'm kinda glad the seats are still in here. I had a friend lose his truck like this once, and he got it back from down in Brownsville. They took it across into Matamoros, where they used it as a taxi for a while before somebody stripped the seats out to pack more people in. Probably taking 'em up to the border."

"How do you know it was a taxi?"

"Because someone painted the word TAXI on the side with a brush."

"Now that's just funny." He laughed and trash crackled underfoot. "But I wonder how anybody can be such a pig and do all this in only one day?"

"It doesn't belong to them, so they don't care." I pointed at the dash. "Don't touch that. It looks like blood. Someone may have been shooting up in here."

He shifted his boots on the floorboard. Empty fast-food wrappers, cups, cans, beer bottles, and crumpled articles of clothing also made me wonder how many people had been through the truck from the time it was stolen until the officer pulled it over.

"Where we taking it to?"

"West of Fort Worth to a friend of mine."

"How long do you think it'll take to download all the info?"

"About three minutes, probably."

New vehicles these days have several features most folks aren't aware of. In addition to the black box that records information in the event of a crash, another program loaded into the onboard computer records where the car or truck has been by identifying GPS and cell towers.

I'd called my supervisor again and told Jimmy that I planned to investigate the theft as a stock agent, or if he gave me static about it since I was on a self-imposed leave, I'd look into it as a private citizen. Either way worked for me, because I didn't care.

He asked if Harley was helping, and when I told him yeah, he sighed into the phone and said all right, but to keep him updated.

The side of the steering column was in shambles. Harley leaned over and twisted a couple of wires. "Stick the key in and give it a turn."

Not believing it would work, I turned the key, and the engine growled to life. Something sounding like plastic rattled under the hood, but the engine ran better than I expected. "We'll leave the Expedition here and pick it up on the way back. No reason to take two vehicles to Fort Worth."

"What if the truck don't make it?"

"Uber can get us back here."

"Whatever you say." He leaned back, crossed his arms, and appeared to doze for the next thirty minutes.

We pulled up to a light in a busy intersection in far north Dallas that bright afternoon when the sky was so blue it didn't look real. A cool wind brushed the air clean and washed some of the stink out of the cab, telling us summer was over and winter was on the way, or at least what we call winter in Texas.

I'd been away from the city long enough to forget how congested it was. Instead of a small town, where people weren't in a hurry and trees lined the streets, we were in a world of concrete, box businesses, and traffic stacked up bumper to bumper.

Sitting at the light, Harley suffered awed looks from other drivers who likely wondered what we'd been up to in the battered truck. He sat over there, nodding and smiling like he was enjoying the attention of everyone who gaped at us through windows we couldn't roll back up.

Careful, Tuck.

We were a couple of miles from DFW airport on Highway 121 when Sara Beth's voice again came to me as real as if she were in the truck. I shot a look at Harley who was still dozing. The voice was in my head, not in the cab.

A chill ran down my spine and I glanced into the rearview mirror. A blue Chrysler with dark-tinted windows slipped in behind us. I'd noticed him pacing the truck from the adjacent lane for several miles, neither moving ahead nor falling back. That explained the voice inside my head. It was my subconscious jolting me into paying attention to what was going on around us.

"Uh-oh."

Harley side-eyed me. "What's up?"

"Car behind us looks suspicious."

"How?"

"Been following since we got into the city limits, but now he's right on our bumper."

"May be completely innocent." He flicked a finger in the direction of the airport. "Probably in a hurry to catch a plane."

"Could be, but my Spidey senses are tingling." I didn't want to tell him that just maybe Sara Beth was talking to me. "I think I've seen that car go by the house."

"Badges." Harley dug his retirement shield out of a pocket, and I pinned mine just over my shirt pocket.

Still facing forward, his eyes flicked to the side mirror. "Four-door. I think there are two in the front, but maybe more in the back."

I took the next exit and merged onto the service road. A traffic signal up ahead turned red.

Dammit.

I slowed. "When we get to the light, I'm gonna make a right and then whip into that convenience store."

"Need to pee?"

"Very funny."

I shifted into the turn lane and braked. No one was coming, so I turned right on red, then steered into the convenience store's parking lot. The dark car also made the turn, but continued on past and pulled into a coffee shop's lot.

"Maybe you were wrong." Harley kept his eyes on the retreating sedan.

"Could be." I looped around the gas pumps and back onto the two-lane. The dark car was nowhere to be seen. I relaxed and we drove on.

A minute later it was back behind us. We were still on the service road, and I was done with their little game. "I'm pulling into this K-Roger's lot. You ready?"

"Drive slow." He punched his cell phone alive and hit the speaker icon.

"911. What's the nature of your emergency?"

"This is special agent Tucker Snow, TSCRA."

I cut my eyes at him using my name, then realized the call would carry more weight from me than from a retired officer. He gave the operator my badge number and our location. "Send a couple of cars to the Kroger parking lot. There's going to be some trouble."

I heard Dispatch ask what kind of trouble.

"Probably a lot of shooting. You might want to hurry." He punched off and drew the Beretta M-9 from beneath his untucked shirt. "This is why I like riding with you. I never know what's going to happen next. Damn! I'm glad to be back in the middle of things!"

Chapter Twenty-One

"Jimma, come here."

Atchley's gruff voice penetrated the thin walls of the trailer house and half a minute later, the youngster stepped out of her room, hesitant as a doe. She half-tilted her head to look down the dim hallway, a habit she'd gotten used to over the last couple of years. She hated to be called out by him because there was always a demand for something.

Sometimes he was hungry or thirsty and was too lazy to get up and fix something, and every now and then it was the thing she hated the most, but that only happened when her mother wasn't there or was passed out.

He and Lloyd were sitting at the table full of dirty dishes, beer cans, and full ashtrays. This time instead of drugs and piles of cash filling the remaining spaces, there was a small piece of electronic equipment lying beside Lloyd's hand.

Atchley nudged it with a finger. "I have something for you to do."

Relieved it wasn't the Thing She Hated the Most, Jimma shifted her slight weight from one foot to the other. "What is it?"

"Not much. Lloyd and I just want you to go over to that girl's over there and knock on the door."

"For what?"

"To see if they're home. That's all."

Suspicious, she glanced at Belcher, who wouldn't make eye contact. He tilted a beer can and drained the contents. Every time he asked her to do something for him, there was a fish-hook, and because of that, she was overly cautious.

"What if they are?"

Atchley showed his yellow teeth in a grin. "Why then, you just hang around with that little gal for a while and talk about whatever it is you girls talk about. You know, boys and clothes and school."

Suspicious, she frowned. "I didn't think you wanted me to have anything to do with her."

"I don't, much. Just stay there for a little while and then come home, but don't you tell her nothin' about what goes on over here. It's nobody's business but your old daddy's."

Jimma couldn't help herself. "You're not my daddy." When she heard the words spoken aloud, she wanted to cover her mouth so nothing else damaging would come out.

Atchley's eyes went diamond hard. "Do you know who your real daddy is, smart-ass?"

She swallowed. There was no answer, because her mother didn't know either.

"That's what I thought. You're in my house, so I'm your old man, and you're my daughter. You ever hear of common-law marriage?"

In the back of her mind, their conversation was as mindless as two five-year-olds playing house. She didn't like where they were going. Nothing would come of it, no matter how much they argued, and in the end, one night her mom would be gone again for a few hours and Lloyd too, and Atchley would come into her room and make sure she knew who was boss.

She shivered. If he did that, she somehow knew he'd make her call him Daddy at some point and she'd scream. "Okay. Whatever you say."

Something was wrong, but she knew better than to ask too many questions. The idea of getting out of the trailer was appealing, though. Jimma thought of the single-wide as an aluminum dungeon, and getting away from the foul-smelling trailer for a while would be like a cool shower on a hot day.

Going to Chloe's, Jimma could see how clean people lived, and that was almost as exciting as the thought of turning sixteen and making a run for it. She always thought of others as "clean people," while her life was nothing but dim, dusty, and full of fear.

"Good. Then go ahead on."

"Okay."

She turned to go back down the hall and Atchley's voice stopped her cold. "Where you going now?"

She glanced down at the dirty white T-shirt she'd selected that morning from the pile of clothes on the floor by her bed. That and her ragged cutoffs weren't what she wanted to wear over to Chloe's. She didn't want to talk about clothes with that man, though. "I need to get my flip-flops."

"You run around here half naked and barefoot all the time. I've seen you go out and piddle around the yard without your shoes a thousand times."

Embarrassed about the "half naked" comment, her eyes flicked to Lloyd to find him staring at her bare legs. His tongue peeked out and then disappeared. For anyone else, it might have been someone simply wetting their lips. From him, it was obscene.

"Fine." She spun and reached for the door handle, but froze when he spoke again.

"Wait a minute. I'm not through with you."

Taking a deep breath, but not letting him see it because he hated when she sighed, Jimma turned and looked at him with the one eye that wasn't covered by hair hanging over her face. "What did I do?"

"Nothing, yet." He picked up a small clear disk the size of her thumbnail. It looked like one of those tiny suction cups people used to hold items on tiles, or a mirror, except where the hook should have been was a tiny black disk. "Put this in your pocket. If there's somebody home, leave it where it is. If there ain't, I want you to put it in the corner of one of the windowpanes in the front. Don't make a big deal out of it, and don't look around like you're doing anything wrong. Stick it there and just come home."

She couldn't help herself. She was a teenager and full of questions. "What is it?"

"None of your business. Just stick it on and leave."

She studied the little disk between his fingers. "Stick it on the glass."

"Yep. And come straight back."

"Is this something illegal?"

Lloyd giggled, a high, maniacal sound that shouldn't come from a grown man. "Sure 'nuff, but not something that'll get you put in jail. Hell, if you get caught you wouldn't even get a ticket or nothin'. If somebody does see you, just tell 'em you found it somewheres and thought it'd be a good idea to stick it there. You're a teenage girl. Nobody understands how y'all think."

Atchley extended his hand, and Jimma took the device from his fingers as gentle as a baby's breath. It was so light she could barely feel it. Knowing she couldn't refuse, she tucked it into the front pocket of her jean shorts and again turned toward the door.

Lloyd's voice stopped her. "Hey."

Keeping her face blank, she looked over her shoulder to see him leaning forward on his elbows with a gleam in his smoke-filled eye. "It might get pocket lint on it in there, so when you take it out, give that suction cup a little lick before you stick it on the window."

He demonstrated with that foul tongue of his again, then laughed and dissolved into a coughing fit.

Fighting a shudder, she opened the door as gently as possible to show them she was unaffected and stepped out into the daytime glare.

The walk down the sandy drive was comfortable, despite her bare feet. There weren't any sandburs in that area, not even a goat head sticker, and those hurt like the devil when you stepped on them. Jimma figured it was because of her two Tennessee fainting goats, Skye and Rocky, that acted like living lawn mowers, eating everything within reach. Their names came from *PAW Patrol,* her favorite cartoon when she was younger.

Skye trotted over to see if Jimma had anything tasty to eat. Pulling a strand of hair behind her ear, Jimma paused to rub the little goat's black-and-white forehead and between her ears for a moment. She sighed. Most kids her age had cats, dogs, and maybe parakeets for pets, and here she was with these two sawed-off little fainters.

Atchley delighted in coming outside and making sudden loud noises that triggered a preservation instinct in the goats, causing them to fall over in what appeared to be a dead faint that lasted twenty to thirty seconds. They were still conscious as they lay still, but Jimma couldn't bring herself to torture the little animals. Though they suffered no harmful effects from the genetic condition, it infuriated her that he would do that.

Skye closed her eyes in ecstasy, but Rocky stayed where he was in the shade of a hackberry tree. Jimma gave the little doe one last pat and ducked between two strands of the bob-wire fence separating their property from the county easement.

Hissing at the sharp rocks, she tiptoed across the road and sighed when her feet found soft crabgrass on the other side. The folks who owned the ranch before Chloe and her dad bought the place were good about mowing the sides of the road, preventing weeds and johnsongrass from getting a foothold. Jimma almost shivered in relief.

From there it was a quick walk down to Chloe's crushed granite drive, easier on bare feet, but so expensive she'd never seen anyone who had enough money to use the material that packed smooth and hard. It was still rough, though, so she stayed on the grass on both sides of the damaged gate, and that exposed her to only a couple of feet of compressed rock. She slipped through the cable fence and danced across the lawn and up to the front steps, hoping someone would see her and come outside.

The house was silent as she bounced up the stairs. It was nice and cool in the shade of the porch. She turned back, thinking how it would be to live in such a wonderful house with a wide lawn in front and a beautiful view out back over the little lake that was usually full of geese in the wintertime and fish in the summer. Jimma really wanted to sit in one of the rockers and enjoy the view, but that would have to wait until late some night when she could sneak over and pretend she lived there.

Still no one came outside, and she knew they'd installed security cameras, so Chloe or her dad should have been watching, maybe with soft alarms going off inside to tell the homeowners that someone was at their front porch.

A new doorbell had a built-in camera. Pushing the button would activate it, and whoever had the app on their phone could answer. Instead, she rapped on the door with her knuckles.

It was silent inside the house. Disappointed her new friend wasn't home, Jimma almost turned to leave before she remembered the device in her pocket. Understanding dawned on her. That's why they'd sent her over to the house. No one would think twice about a teenage girl coming to visit a friend. Even if the cameras around the house were activated by motion, all anyone would see was a visitor.

Jimma plucked the little round device from her pocket and studied it for a moment, not understanding what it could be. It wouldn't be much of a crime to simply stick it on the front window and leave. What could it hurt?

But she was there because Atchley wanted it done, and in that case, it was illegal at the worst, or wrong at best. A tickle in the back of her mind told Jimma that Atchley would know if she didn't put it on the window, and she'd pay the price when she got back. It'd be easier just to do it and go home.

She started to touch the tip of her tongue to the concave side of the rubber disk when an image of Lloyd's tongue made her stop. What if he'd already licked the piece of soft rubber? Stifling a shudder, she wet her index finger and ran it around the disk before thumbing it into the lower left-hand corner of the front windowpane.

Wanting to get gone, she whirled, jumped halfway down the front steps, and sprang out onto the lawn. Seconds later, she took the shortest distance back to the trailer, trotting at an angle across the lush green grass to a distant corner fencepost and ducked between the two lowest of five cables strung tightly between white steel posts.

A car was coming down the intersecting road with a crunch of gravel when she hopped across the shallow ditch. A plume of dust rose behind the vehicle and she figured it was someone coming to their house to make a buy. Hissing at the pain in her bare feet, she danced across the gravel, slipped between the sagging bob-wire strands separating Atchley's land from the county easement, and waited behind a thick cedar until the car passed.

It wasn't a customer after all. It was that Evans woman, who lived in the house at the end of the road. She worked as a teller at the bank and had two boys who were grown and married.

Skye and Rocky trotted up to see if she had picked up anything to eat while she was gone. She paused again to rub their heads for a moment before making her slow way back to the false safety of her room.

Chapter Twenty-Two

The far end of the grocery store lot was mostly empty, though dozens of vehicles were parked near the entrance. I pulled across several lanes as far away as possible, hoping the police would arrive before anything happened.

The dark-blue Taurus came up behind us and stopped about fifteen feet back. We sat there as if we had all the time in the world to talk. Seeing them drive in behind us, Harley rested his elbow outside the window, his Beretta hanging limp in his hand. Relaxed and unsuspecting.

I waited for what I expected might happen.

All four of the sedan's doors opened as if choreographed. Heavily tattooed men with shaved heads and automatic rifles were halfway out when I slammed the transmission in reverse and floored it.

I heard Sara Beth's ghostly gasp of breath in my ear. Her warning gave me a half-second head start. "Brace yourself!"

"Shit!" Realizing what I was about to do, Harley slid low in his seat to take advantage of the headrest that usually only knocked his hat off.

I did the same and tried to push the foot-feed through the floor.

Bad guys count on their victims to freeze or ask what's going on in confusion. Most never expect anyone in the herd to bring the fight to them, but that's just what we did, because our motto has always been, "Attack, attack, attack."

The Dodge's mistreated engine roared, and we shot backward with a squeal of big tires. The two-inch ball on my trailer hitch plowed through the Taurus's plastic grille with a bang and into the radiator, releasing a thick cloud of white steam and the distinctive odor of hot radiator fluid.

The tremendous impact crumpled the hood, knocking the lighter vehicle backward. Two men in the back seat were almost out, and the others had one foot on the ground when we hit 'em at thirty miles an hour. Like giant fly swatters, the open doors slapped all four of them at the exact same time with the force of a charging locomotive.

An AK-47 rifle went flying across the parking lot at the impact, and a semi-automatic handgun squirted out from under the driver's door and slid in my direction. Shouts of surprise punctuated by a high shriek of pain cut through the air.

I jammed the transmission into park, and Harley and I were out and advancing on the damaged car in an instant, pistols at high ready. The driver was sprawled half under his door when I lined him up, down the sights of my 1911. "Special agents! Stay down! Hands! Hands! Show me your hands!"

Similar orders came from Harley. "Po-lice! We're the po-lice! Hands in the air!" Shouting that we were special agents might not register with someone who's on the razor-thin edge of a fight, so he was doing his best to keep us out of a shooting war.

It didn't matter what we said; the commands were cut off

by the staccato pops of another automatic rifle from behind the sedan. I was shocked that the guy from the passenger seat could even gather himself enough to fire. He was much of a man for sure, but Harley's weapon responded with a long string of gunshots at the same time the dumbass driver lying on the ground raised a pistol in *my* direction.

Our little piece of the world filled with gunfire as my sights lined up on center mass and I fired again and again. The heavy rounds impacted the skinhead's torso, fluttering the cloth of his shirt. He sunfished and twisted in pain before he stilled. Next target.

The back-seat passenger on my side with a shiny shaved head regained his feet and took a knee behind the open door, intending to use it as a shield. Those guys were tough, if nothing else, but getting bitch-slapped by a car door affects your ability to focus. He was too slow in shouldering his rifle.

I'd already anticipated such a move, and the Colt bucked in my hand, walking holes up the door and into what I could see of him. Some of the first rounds punched through the sheet metal and glass, striking the man and causing him to rise up in shock, giving me a clear target.

I ran the pistol dry and thumb-dropped the magazine that rattled on the concrete at my feet. Slapping a full mag into the butt from one of two holders on the left side of my belt, I thumbed the slide release to chamber a fresh round and checked to make sure Harley was all right.

He'd cleared his field of fire and stood there absently rubbing his chin as if bemused by the whole situation.

Sirens wailed in the distance, and I watched cars flee the parking lot. We kicked our assailants' weapons out of reach, as if they could actually start breathing again.

"I don't think they were Boy Scout sponsors with these prison Nazi tats." Harley tilted his hat back. "Aryan Brotherhood. You *know* any of these guys?"

I shook my head. The guy at my feet had a hole in his cheek, but it didn't change his appearance that much. Only a couple of feet away, the driver was lying on his stomach, but the half of his face I could see didn't look familiar at all. His eye was already drying out, and I wondered who, or what, he'd seen in a misspent lifetime that led to that moment. "Not a one. But they were irritated at us for some reason."

"Should have controlled their anger."

What I imagine the first responding officers saw when they power-slid into the parking lot were two armed cowboys standing beside a battered pickup with four sprawled bodies not far away.

Harley holstered his weapon and covered it with his shirttail. He raised his hands and held his badge so it was visible. "Looks like we've been busted, partner."

I slid mine back into the holster, and we waited for the two officers who stepped from the vehicle and took cover behind their partially open doors. The patrol car's speakers came to life as the driver followed protocol. "You two beside the truck! Hands on your heads! Turn around and back toward my vehicle!"

"We're special agents!" Harley put his hands on top of his hat and did as he was told. His little white lie was designed to get those guys to stand down.

I did the same, turning my head toward the officers to repeat his statement. "Special agents! We're on the job!"

They didn't budge. "Down on your knees, facing away, and then on your stomach! Do it now!" I followed the officer's shouted orders.

"He said we're cops, guys!" Harley's head swiveled toward me and I saw something in his eyes I didn't like. That flash of anger reminded me of when we were kids and the powder keg that was my little brother was about to explode.

I tried to cool him down. "Easy, hoss. We'd do the same thing if we were in their shoes."

"Nope. They see our badges. These assholes are overreacting."

"Don't make any difference." I did as we were told, and after a couple of heartbeats, Harley sighed and followed suit.

The uniformed officers moved up behind us. One of them seemed more twisted up than the other. "Don't move! Hands out to your sides!"

I had to get them to understand who we were before one of them did something dangerous and pissed Harley off. Like me, he was buzzed on adrenaline, but he handles it differently than I do. He's always been like those guys who're allergic to alcohol. A couple of drinks and they're looped.

He maintained, but everything about my little brother was amped up, hot and electric. If he'd gone the wrong way when we were kids, he'd have been that bad guy everyone feared. If you see an electrical outlet with two bare wires sticking out, don't touch it. I was afraid the two police officers were going to touch his wires that sizzled with electricity. "Guys! Hands are already out."

We were relieved of our firearms anyway, and the next thing I knew, they had us cuffed. I thanked their lucky stars they didn't drop a knee onto Harley's back or neck. The youngest DPD office held up Harley's Beretta like a trophy. "Gun, partner!"

Harley snorted. "Of course I have a gun. That's what I just used to shoot those two."

The officer finished patting him down and jerked him to his

feet, and Harley grunted when he drove a fist into his kidney. "Shut up until I ask you to talk."

Electricity crackled in Harley's eyes, and I took the chance. "Don't, little brother."

The officer opened the back door to his unit and pushed Harley into the seat. "You have anything else to say, tough guy?"

"Yeah, you hit like a girl, and I still have two more guns on me back here."

I couldn't help but laugh. The older officer took our badges, told his partner to stand down, and helped me to my feet. While he called it in, I leaned against my truck.

The door to the cruiser was still open, and Harley twisted toward me. "Maybe *I* should have been first to tell them who we were. Let me do that next time."

A trickle of blood leaking from one of the bodies made its way toward us across the concrete. "I hope there's not ever going to be a next time."

Chapter Twenty-Three

"Didja get it done?"

Atchley and Lloyd were still at the table when Jimma returned, but they'd cleared the table and the only thing on the sticky, crumb-covered surface was a laptop computer. Stickers covered the backside of the screen, covering up the brand's logo—"Be Rad" on a smiley face, fingers in a "hang tight" gesture from the Ron Jon Surf Shop, REI, NASA, Papa Murphy's Pizza, Murge Records, a colorful dragonfly, Positive Vibes, and a shocking green pickle with the words "I'm Pickle Rick"—told her the device was almost certainly stolen, traded for drugs.

Jimma saw their idea of cleaning off the table consisted of pitching everything on the floor, chairs, or the lumpy, stained couch sitting only three feet away. George Strait music came from an old, cracked radio on a shelf behind them. "You told me to, didn't you?"

"Don't get smart with me." Atchley scooted closer to the table. "Fire it up."

Lloyd squinted at the screen and spoke through smoke rising from a cigarette between his lips. "Working on it."

"You said you knew how to do this."

"I'm-a doin' it, ain't I?"

"I'm not sure what you're doing right now."

Alien-sounding noises from the laptop's speakers sounded almost like the tone from an old dial-up internet connection that resolved into a squeal, and then nothing.

"Dammit, Lloyd, it doesn't work."

"Wrong."

"I don't hear nothing."

"That's because there's nobody home right now." He used two hands to manipulate the finger pad. "Listen."

Despite herself, Jimma moved closer to see what they were doing. Neither man noticed when she drifted around into the kitchen where she could see over the thin dividing pony wall holding empty beer cans.

Instead of images she expected, the screen was divided in two. One side was a list of commands, and the other was filled with an oscilloscope. She remembered the name from an experiment her science teacher demonstrated about sound waves. Her family thought she was dumb as a box of rocks, but she ranked near the top of her class, despite cutting classes on those days she couldn't bear to go.

Lloyd plucked the cigarette from his lips with two fingers and pointed. "See that tik popping up and down?"

"That little hill?"

"If that's what you want to call it. Each time it pops up, it shows me a sound."

"But I can't hear anything."

"That's because it's the bass beat from a radio that's turned way down. That little split-tail must've left it on, probably thinking it would make a big bad burglar think there was somebody home."

Atchley and Belcher laughed and high-fived like a couple of teenagers.

It's a listening device, Jimma thought. *I bugged their house.*

Chapter Twenty-Four

It took a while before the PD confirmed who we were, but the arresting officers finally realized the bad guys were all lying really, really still in the parking lot and removed our cuffs. Harley and I sat on the dented tailgate of my truck, and I was glad we had our hats back on. Even though the weather was relatively cool, the sun hammered us, and the thin spot on top of my head would have blistered faster than a redheaded baby's butt.

There was lots of activity going on as a small army of first responders worked the shooting scene with practiced, methodical precision. Yellow crime tape fenced us in with our vehicles. Four bodies lay under bloodstained white sheets, and two uniformed officers snapped photos of the shooting scene.

Like flies drawn to a fresh cow patty, a news team showed up and the reporter almost jumped from the van in excitement. He waved an arm toward the covered bodies and a squatty guy in a T-shirt and cargo shorts fired up his camera while the talking head made sure his hair looked good. A police officer charged with maintaining the area drifted over to push them back a ways.

The Texas Rangers arrived, standing apart from everyone

and talking with the first officers in the field. They're always on the scene of any officer-involved shooting, and that included us. Both were easily recognizable to most Texans in their light-colored shirts, khakis, distinctive hand-tooled gun belts holding .45s, and of course, Cattlemen or Rancher-style straw hats.

One of them was familiar, because TSCRA agents have a strong working relationship with those guys, and in fact, we're related deeply enough that our badges are very similar. Our turn to talk with them was coming next, but the team of Rangers was getting statements from the local authorities first.

It was a good thing, too, because Harley was still worked up over being treated as a criminal. "My damn badge was in plain view." He tapped the bulge in his pocket for emphasis. "These guys need to be more observant. Hell, if we'd rolled up on something like this when we were highway patrol, you can bet we'd see the badges and treat a brother *right*."

"Are you gonna be mad all day?"

"Probably. I don't like to have guns throwed on me, especially in the hands of..." he raised his voice so the Dallas officers standing beside their car could hear, "...the *po*lice who're on our *side*!"

"Chill out. It's all right." I raised a hand in a wave. One of the older, more experienced officers gave me a grin, and I saw he probably thought like us, that the younger guys should have taken in what was happening just a little faster.

It was as if his grin turned off Harley's anger. That's how he'd always been. Fighting mad one minute and laughing the next. On the other hand, I built up with a long sizzle and held grudges forever.

I shifted on the tailgate to keep an eye on the Rangers and on Harley too. Finished with their interviews, the Rangers joined us at my truck. They could have been typecast directly out of a

Hollywood movie—the older, more experienced officer, and a young man who looked as if he might be thirty, but not a day older.

The guy with short gray hair at his temples closed a notepad and slipped it into his back pocket. "Howdy, Tuck."

"Earl." I jerked a thumb toward Harley. "My baby brother, Harley."

"I've heard of you." Earl and Harley shook. "You did undercover work with Tuck back in the day."

"I did."

"Good work. Name's Earl Gray, and I don't want to hear any comments about tea." He grinned to let Harley know he was half kidding. "This here's Ranger Lucas Martinez."

We shook hands all around and everything settled into normalcy. Earl nodded with his hat at the bodies the paramedics were loading onto stretchers. "Aryan Brotherhood. What'd they swell up at y'all about?"

"Not sure, but I suspect it's because we're poking around a little business they're running across the road from my house." I explained where I lived, what I suspected was going on at the buy house, the break-in, and what happened with my pickup.

Face impassive, Earl nodded. "Looks like you brushed up against a yellow jacket nest."

"I wish it was as simple as that. I think this is just the tip of the iceberg. Harley and I were headed over to a friend who used to work at a Dodge dealership. He has the tools and a computer to download what's on the truck's black box. I'm hoping there's something I can use to find out who stole it. Then I'm gonna start pulling on the string until I find the end of it."

"Have you called your supervisor on this?"

We were suddenly in dicey territory. "I took a leave of absence after my wife and daughter were killed."

His eyes filled with sorrow. Brothers and sisters in arms always felt for each other and our families. "I'm sorry to hear that. So, you're not acting in an official capacity."

"Right, but that don't mean I'm sitting on my hands."

"I wouldn't either."

Harley shifted his weight to speak. "We should have called the agent in charge of our region, but we know what we're doing, and I figured we'd leave Special Agent Taylor out of it to go on and help other folks while we investigate." He was trying to deflect some of the blame.

Young Ranger Martinez spoke up for the first time. "You should have called the sheriff's department at least, then."

Now there's one thing you don't do in our profession, is offer "should haves" to experienced agents or officers. Putting it to us in the form of a question would have taken the accusation and sting out of the comment. Instead, it thickened the air, sharp and bitter.

I felt Harley tense, and to stop him from saying anything I might regret later, I half-slid off the tailgate until one boot rested on the ground. That move put me a little more between him and the younger Ranger.

Ignoring the ill-advised statement, I directed my comments to Ranger Gray. "I contacted the sheriff's office right off, more than once. There's a lot more going on than I'm going to talk about right now, but thanks for the advice, Lucas." The younger Ranger's eyes slid off, and he studied the notepad in his hand. He got the point, so I addressed the senior Ranger. "You need us for anything else, Earl?"

"Naw. We have everything for now. I'll give you a call if there's anything else."

"Good." Harley slid off the tailgate and slammed it shut a little harder than necessary, a harsh period to end our conversation.

I shook Earl's hand. "We're out of here, then." Slapping Harley on the shoulder to break his gaze off the younger Ranger, I gave a half nod to Martinez as a goodbye. "Let's get gone."

Chapter Twenty-Five

Don Wells was in his shop about a hundred yards behind his ranch-style house surrounded by pasture and mesquite trees out west of Weatherford. A hundred years earlier, everything west of Fort Worth was prairie as far as a person could see, but time and civilization pushed ranchers and cattlemen farther away.

Don's house was in the country for the time being, where cities and suburbs end and the real Texas begins. In twenty years, if Metroplex growth continued at the rate it was going, folks around him wouldn't be raising cattle any longer, because the land only a few miles away was sprouting rows and rows of houses that buried the land and all the history of that region.

The garage beyond the one-story red brick house had everything an automotive mechanic wanted or needed. Two lifts, a paint booth, a storage area, and a full bathroom filled the main floor. The second floor contained a bedroom, living area with a huge flat-screen TV, and another full bath. It was his home away from home.

Don operated the shop like a small business that wasn't. Cars were his passion, and when he retired from the dealership, he couldn't just quit. Don loved to work on cars, and there was always a list of people who wanted him to make repairs as simple as changing a headlight to a complete engine overhaul.

One bay door was open when we passed the house and followed a wide concrete drive down to the shop. Standing beside a tool bench stretching the length of the back wall, he directed me over the lift with minimal hand movements, holding a palm flat to stop us in just the right place.

It didn't look like any mechanic's garage I'd ever seen. Everything was clean and appeared to be freshly painted. The floors gleamed brighter than most restaurant floors.

He hit a button on the wall, and the overhead door closed with very little noise. Hands in the pockets of his overalls, Don walked around to my window. "Leave it running. From the looks of it, the damn thing might not start again today, and I got too much to do than to get it going again."

He'd been blunt, almost gruff, from the time I first met him, but I quickly saw through it. That was back when he worked for a dealership that didn't know what they had. He asked for a raise one day, though he didn't need it because family money made him and his wife filthy rich, but the shop manager turned him down, saying he could hire two young guys for the same salary.

Don closed his tool chest that day ten years earlier and rolled it toward the door, telling them to go ahead on and that hell would be refrigerated if he ever worked for anyone again. Doing one better, he never set foot in another dealership after that and spent most of his time collecting neon signs and rebuilding cars for folks he liked.

I introduced Harley, who turned to look at the metal car signs and lights covering the walls, advertising everything from oil to tires to product brands. Vintage neon beer signs scattered through all the memorabilia gave the place a museum feel. "Glad to meet you. I'm the good-looking brother."

Ignoring him, because I imagine everyone who ever entered the shop for the first time did the same thing, Don used both hands to tighten his gray ponytail and walked around what was left of the truck, studying all the fresh scratches and dents.

He whistled low and slow. "Did somebody take a sledgehammer to this son of a bitch?" I'd told him what happened and what to expect when I called, but seeing the truck was a shock. "Front end's out of line. The frame's bent too. Y'all looked like a crab coming down the drive. What they did to this fine truck's a shame."

He stopped at the rear and studied the twisted tailgate and trailer hitch that was still damp and oily from radiator fluid that had leaked out of the Taurus we'd left dead in the Kroger parking lot. "This didn't happen when the truck was stolen, did it?"

"Nope. On the way over here. We had a little...incident back in Dallas." I told him what happened and his eyes widened.

"You boys live a whole different lifestyle, don't you?"

Instead of answering, Harley pointed toward a wooden door with the stick figure of a man peeing on a Biden/Harris bumper sticker. "Gonna use your bathroom."

"Go ahead." Don waved a hand and picked up a blue plastic device about the size of a cell phone from his workbench. "Well, they screwed up a perfectly good truck."

"That's why I'm here. I want to see what you can tell me about the person who stole it."

"You're not wanting to know just that, are you?"

"Nope. I think he was part of something bigger. He's working for a bunch of meth heads who live across the road from me."

"A man who treats a truck like this oughta be horsewhipped."

Don leaned under the steering wheel and plugged the device into a portal.

"How long will it take?"

"About finished. Hold your horses."

The bathroom door opened to emit the sound of the commode flushing in the background. Harley came out, and Don raised up to peer across the cab and through Harley's open window. "You wash your hands?"

Taken aback, Harley paused. "Uh, no, but I only handled my own."

Don chuckled and jerked a thumb in my direction. "You're just like he said."

He unplugged the device from under the dash, killed the engine, and walked over to a brand-new desktop computer on the built-in bench. He perched a pair of readers on his nose and inserted a pigtail line from the computer into a port and we watched the wide screen come alive. The Dodge icon popped up at the top first, then was followed by so much info I couldn't keep up.

"This box used to be called a crash data recording device. Some now call it an event data recorder, but that's not all it does."

I wondered about the glasses perched on his nose because he looked over the top.

His fingers danced over a keyboard, and I noticed there wasn't a spot of grease under any nail. "When they first came out, black boxes were set to only record about fifteen variables like vehicle speed, throttle position, steering angles, whether brakes were applied in a crash, airbag deployment times... things like that."

Whistling through his teeth along with "Sweet Home

Alabama" playing through the speakers mounted on all four corners in the shop, Don frowned and tapped some more. "Then they added about fifteen more points to study, but after that, things went dark."

Harley and I watched over his shoulder as he scanned through lines of data.

"That's not nice." He was talking to himself, and neither Harley or I answered. He abruptly flipped the ponytail out of his collar and tapped several more keys and watched the screen change. "You're not giving me what I want. Why don't you behave yourself and cough it up?"

Harley turned his head to me and mouthed. "He's talking to a computer."

I shrugged, and Don tapped some more and the screen went blank before it lit back up. This time there was no Dodge logo on top. The screen flickered and divided into two, then four segments.

"There you go, little buddy. *That's* what I wanted." He typed faster than anyone I'd ever seen, then did some more magic. "Now we're cooking with gas."

I recognized an icon that looked like it could be a search engine, and he clicked a few more times before slapping the Enter button with a forefinger. "There." Data downloaded from his blue device and even more cryptic info popped up.

Without taking his eyes from the screen, he pointed at a symbol I didn't recognize, followed by pages of flickering data. "This is stuff manufacturers don't want you to know they have."

"It's moving too fast for me to make anything out." Harley leaned forward. "Like what?"

"Everything about Tuck that he didn't know was downloaded on the truck's computer. Look here." He turned to a second, larger monitor and used the mouse to point. "There are two levels to what I'm looking for. These are places you've been. The GPS keeps track of everywhere you drove."

I didn't like that one bit. "You're kidding."

"Nope. The black box in there's been tracking you since the day you drove off the lot. Here are the speeds you ran from Point A to Point B. They say it only records and holds the info for a short while, but it's a lie."

Harley chewed his bottom lip. "How long has this been going on?"

"Since 1994. It started out innocent enough, like everything else the government does, but then they started adding stuff on. The data was used to track how cars performed in crashes, but then they went off the rails with it. They'll tell you it doesn't track where you're going, or record audio and video, but they're lying through their teeth.

"See here? It even tells when you're wearing your seat belt or not." He tsked-tsked through teeth like a parent admonishing a toddler. "You spend a lot of time without your seat belt, my friend."

"I spend a lot of time driving through ranches and on dirt roads."

"You disabled the warning bell, huh?"

"You showed me how once, remember?"

He grunted. "It couldn't have been me. I'd never do something like that."

He scrolled through more lines of information and kept talking like a surgeon teaching a class full of first-year interns. "Now they're into data mining. Right now there are over seventy-eight million cars on the road with these recording devices. I 'magine ninety-eight percent of the cars sold will be tracking their owners within the next ten years, and probably doing more than that.

"That's where the technology gets out of hand. More recent vehicles record your habits, where you go, and when. Here's one I don't like." He paused the scrolling screen and pointed with the cursor. "Cameras in cars now track your eyes when you're driving to see whether you're watching the road, and not your phone or any other distractions. They do it in the name of safety, but I don't believe that for one minute.

"What I'm looking for is even deeper, and more disturbing. They're downloading your taste in music and your voice commands. They search your history, looking at apps such as Waze, Apple CarPlay, Pandora, or Music Box…which is where I am now. You like big band music, huh?"

I felt the hair on the back of my neck prickle. I *do* like big band music and only listen to it when I'm in the truck by myself, but the idea of the car recording my listening habits was uncomfortable, to say the least.

"Folks are driving giant smartphones these days. The minute you pair your cell phone with the truck, either by Bluetooth or through a USB port, they tap into everything with personal data, anticipate your needs, and even log into apps that have credit card information and who has access to all that info that shouldn't be out there."

He poised and glanced over his shoulder at me. "I can find your credit card numbers if you want, 'cause I bet you've ordered stuff through your phone."

"That comes through the truck too?" Both eyebrows bumped the brim on my hat.

"Boys, you're watched twenty-four seven. Big Brother is here, and people feed him info every day without a shrug or a raised eyebrow. Give me an old '56 Dodge truck anytime."

"All that from your vehicle?"

"Some. But like I said, the rest comes from that phone in your pocket."

"How?"

"Weren't you paying attention? Bluetooth. When your phone links up with the vehicle, or a laptop you have that's on in a briefcase, all that data is downloaded. Hardly anyone reads all those pages of legal gobbledygook on apps or when they download something. We wouldn't understand it if we did, so nearly everyone scrolls to the bottom and hits 'I agree.' So that's what I'm doing, looking for your bad guy's data cause it's in here too, and he never knew what he was doing." More clicks. "And here it is, starting two days ago."

He pointed with his finger. "Feller by the name of Curtis Bailey stole your truck and needed some getaway tunes, probably because he watched *Baby Driver* a hundred times while he was laid up between jobs or meth hits, so he used Bluetooth to play HotBox." He clicked a couple more times. "He must have taken the time to pair up with the truck so he could listen to Monkey Snatch, the Oozes, and Dirty Nil for about fifteen minutes before he parked the truck at..."

He clicked the keyboard. A satellite map popped up. "Here. Looks like a trailer house on Rock Hill Road."

I swallowed. "That's across from where I live. You mean he stole the truck, drove through a fence, and only went a few hundred yards before stopping?"

Don nodded without taking his eyes from the screen. "Why would he do that?"

Harley spoke up. "To make a buy. Probably traded something from the truck for meth."

I tried to read the lines on the screen, but Don's fingers were too fast. "Where'd he go from the buy house?"

Don tapped on the keyboard again. "To here." Another window opened on the screen and he typed in the address. A satellite picture appeared, with a blue dot that blinked over one particular house. "I'd bet the guy lives here, or he went and laid up with some gal, because the truck stayed in one place for about eight hours before it left again."

"Hold on and let me write that down."

"No need." Don hit the Print button and page after page rolled out of a laser printer. We had Curtis Bailey's entire history in the palm of my hand.

Harley lived for those moments "Let's go get him." His eyes gleamed.

I thought for a minute. "You think we're gonna violate Curtis Bailey's right to privacy when we pick him up from all this?"

"Yep." Harley nodded. "And that's only the *first* thing I'm gonna violate on this guy."

Don swung around on his chair. "You want the rest of it?"

Harley frowned. "What do you mean?"

"I have his credit card info, taxes, passwords, and banking info."

I shook my head. "No."

"Yes." Harley held out his hand. "Phone records. Print all that. This guy's ass is *mine*."

Don Wells tapped a key, and his printer hummed to life. "Right here."

Chapter Twenty-Six

Chloe's phone vibrated and she glanced at the screen. She was sitting at the granite-topped island in Aunt Tammy and Uncle Harley's kitchen in the nearby town of Bonham. The boys were playing basketball in the backyard, giving Chloe and Tammy the opportunity to talk about school and the move to the new house while it was quiet.

It was a text from Jimma.

Went by 2day but your gone. U gonna b home soon?

Glad that the younger girl hadn't called, Chloe texted back, her thumbs moving quick and sure. Jimma was kind of pushy, and Chloe wasn't sure she wanted to get too close to anyone right then, especially with someone who had parents like hers.

Not sure. With my aunt. C u later.

There. That should be a kind enough dismissal.

Used to phones and kids texting, Tammy barely looked up

from cutting up a chicken to fry for their supper. Chloe loved to hang out with her aunt who was raised in the country and always said she was old school and preferred to cook the way she'd learned from her grandmother.

Chloe put the phone down to watch Tammy on the other side of the island. It reminded her of those happier days when she came home from school to their old house and did her homework and talked with her mom while she fixed supper. Sara Beth grew up the same way as Aunt Tammy, and also enjoyed cooking from scratch.

The teenager's eyes burned at the thought of what was lost to their family. She swallowed a lump thinking about what was lost to what was *left* of their family. Some of the best moments in her life were spent with Mom in their own spacious kitchen, learning to cook, but those days were gone, snatched away in a heartbeat.

Her mind went back to the new house that loomed dark, large, and ominous, a strange, possibly dangerous structure far away from where she grew up. It was just four walls holding up a roof, and nothing more. Houses needed people in them to live, and the shell that now held their belongings was cold and sterile, even worse, since there were no children to run and shout and play.

She missed little Peyton most. The rambunctious four-year-old bundle of energy was bright, funny, and full of life. Chloe loved her so much she sometimes ached when she watched her little sister play house, and every time Chloe came in from school, Peyton ran into her arms, shrieking with excitement that her big sister was home and they could do hair, or nails, or simply snuggle up on the couch to watch *Bubble Guppies*.

Tammy saw Chloe watching and had registered the phone's vibration. "Everything all right?"

"Sure." She blinked away a tear. "It was a text from Jimma, who lives across the road."

"Already made a friend, huh?"

"Kinda. She's younger than I am, but I think she needs a friend more than I do."

Tammy frowned and cut the pulley-bone from one chicken's breast. "No one her age close by?"

"No, and she lives in that house with those meth heads Dad doesn't like."

Tammy severed a thigh from the carcass. "Sounds bad."

"It is. I feel sorry for anyone who has to live like that."

"I know, but you be careful getting close to her. Kids like that are pitiful, and we need to help them as much as we can, but they can drag you into their world without you or them knowing they're doing it."

Chloe nodded. "Have you heard from Dad or Uncle Harley?"

"Not yet. But you know how those two are. They get busy and forget to call. I bet they got wrapped up in picking up Tuck's truck and lost track of time."

"They'll find out who took it."

"They sure will, but I swear, I don't understand people who steal like that."

"It's nothing new for Dad, though. That's what he does… did, all day long. A year ago, we were driving through Chisum, Texas, when a call came on the radio saying a shooter took himself hostage in a grocery store parking lot right next to the high school.

"Dad had to go, so we hurried on over there and pulled into the far end of a parking lot that was full of emergency response vehicles. I stayed in the truck while he talked to a SWAT guy and a deputy for a minute. They weren't too concerned, because the bad guy was sitting on a white car with the barrel of a revolver stuck under his chin. There was an officer talking to one onlooker after another, and I wondered what he was doing.

"Dad talked with the guys for a little while longer and came back to the truck. When I asked him what was going on with the uniform talking to all the civilians, Dad said he was looking for the owner of the white sedan. His plan was to hit the panic button on their key fob, so it would startle the nutcase to pull the trigger, then they could all go home."

Tammy cut her eyes across the seat. "Cold-blooded."

"Yep, but funny in a way. I asked Dad if he'd ever done anything like that, and he said no, but Uncle Harley would do it in a heartbeat."

Knowing her husband, Tammy barked a laugh as she glanced out the sliding doors to check on the boys. "I'm glad you're here. It's good to have a girl in the house. Ya smell better too."

Chloe laughed, temporarily forgetting her earlier sadness. "I like it here with you. Talking to Dad is all right, but I miss Mom."

"I know you do." Tammy didn't offer lame platitudes that had little meaning. "You want to help me cut this chicken?"

"You'll have to show me how."

"It's a lost art, but it's something you can do."

The sliding door just off the kitchen opened with a bang, and the boys ran inside, full of energy. The yellow Lab, Kevin, loped in behind them, tongue lolling. Sweaty and dirty, Danny jumped on a metal bar-height stool and leaned on the island. "Mom!"

"Just leave the door open, boys."

Danny missed her sarcasm. "We already did."

Tammy stopped splitting one of the chicken breasts and gave an exaggerated sigh that made the kids grin. "What?"

"We just saw the biggest lizard *ever*!" Danny extended his arms as wide as possible, much like a fisherman exaggerating the day's catch.

Matt joined his brother holding his hands a little closer to each other. "It was big as a dinosaur."

"A small dinosaur." Danny clarified. "Like a velociraptor."

"Yeah, but one of the *bigger* velociraptors in the whole world."

Tammy chuckled. "Where was it?"

"In the garden," they said in unison.

Matt turned to Chloe. "You want to see it?"

Putting off her cooking lesson, she stood and stuck the phone in the back pocket of her shorts. "Sure."

"I'll show you!" Danny spun his stool.

Everything was a competition between the boys. "No, I will!"

They dropped off the stools with twin thumps and rushed toward the door. Danny tripped over Kevin, and the dog who'd been laying in front of the door leaped to his feet. Danny grabbed Matt to steady himself. Laughing, Danny wrapped his arms around his brother, and they wrestled each other to the tile floor while the dog danced around, barking.

Smiling, Tammy called them down. "Boys! Knock it off. Somebody's gonna get hurt."

Chloe laughed and kicked the sole of Matt's sneaker. She grabbed Kevin's collar and pulled him back. "Hey, you guys. I've never seen a real live dinosaur. Let's get out there before it gets away."

Springing to their feet, they boiled out into the backyard without closing the door. Chloe paused when Jimma's text popped into her mind. The girl who was a couple of years younger than herself came by their house because she was probably lonely, being an only child and essentially friendless. Jimma was looking for company, and here Chloe was, in her aunt's house and enjoying the chaos around her.

She plucked the phone from her pocket and thumbed a quick text to Jimma.

You good?

The reply came instantly.

Sure. Just wanted to talk.

Be home later.

Snap me if you get the chance.

K. Then u can come over

Bet.

Kids never ended a text with a goodbye or see you later. They simply quit typing.

Feeling better and pushing away the concerns about the break-in at her house, Chloe followed the boys across the yard.

Chapter Twenty-Seven

The warm day evaporated as I returned to the ranch and pulled up to my damaged gate. The wind that had been out of the south laid for about half an hour before turning from the north, bringing a freshness that only came in the fall. Shifting into park and hoping the transmission would hold and not let the pickup roll back into Harley and the Expedition, I unlocked the twisted and bent pipe gate and wrestled the two sides back far enough for the truck to get through.

We parked on the circular drive looping past the front porch, and by the time we stepped out of the vehicles, Special Agent Robby Taylor had turned in the gate and parked behind us. I'd called him as we drove from Weatherford to McKinney to pick up the Expedition.

He was close, on his way back from the sale barn in Overbrook, Oklahoma, where he was looking for a trailer-load of stolen calves. Adjusting his hat, he stepped out and we shook hands. "Looks like you need a new gate...and a new truck."

"The results of our visitor." I thought about kicking the tire to put a period on my comment, but decided not to, just in case it might fall off. We leaned over the bed of my truck, Harley on one side, and Robby hooked an arm over the tailgate.

A sedan rolled past, throwing up gravel and dust. "There you go, Robby. Just what we're talking about."

We watched the car slow and turn in Atchley's drive. Robby plucked a small notebook from his back pocket and made a note. Harley's eyes flicked to me, and I gave an almost imperceptible shake of my head. Robby was jotting down a description of the car and the time, but I was afraid Harley would tell him about the cameras we'd installed. I wanted to keep that invasion of privacy between us.

"Was that anyone you might suspect?"

I watched the dust settle. "I suspect everyone over there right now."

"Did they take any stock? Tractors? Equipment?" That was *just* the TSCRA's business.

I knew what he was asking. If any of those items were taken, he could delve even deeper into the investigation. "Nope. The owner sold everything off before we signed the papers on this place. I'm not in the mood to run cattle for a while, neither."

He gave me a solemn nod and pulled a round can of Skoal from the back pocket of his jeans, tapping it hard against the palm of his hand to pack the contents. "At least you'd have sense enough to brand your own stock. I swear, these lazy son of a guns won't take the time to mark their cattle, but then call me when they're gone..." Robby drifted off, realizing he was preaching to the choir. He twisted the silver lid off and pinched out a dip. Tucking it into his bottom lip, he made the can disappear once again. "I got a call says you two were in a gunfight. Over this?"

Harley nodded. "We figure, but neither of us knows why. Look, I know this is your region right now and you'll look into it, but neither of us can just sit back and do nothing. We think the break-in and theft of the truck has something to do with that house over there, but there's more to it."

"Aryan Brotherhood," I added.

"That means drugs." Robby tightened his lip to pack the Skoal. Some men are always fooling with it, spitting on the ground, out truck windows, or in empty plastic soda bottles. He was more discreet.

Harley nodded. "It do."

In the time-honored tradition of farmers and ranchers studying on a problem, Robby leaned on the tailgate and appeared to be studying the toe of his boot. I knew different. He was selecting his words with care.

"Guys, this is a strange situation. Any other time, it'd be me telling y'all I'd do what I could to find the people who busted up your fence and gate, and took the truck, but you have it back, and I figure you two know who you're looking for by now. I can't tell you *what* to do, but be careful a-doin' it, and keep me updated. Oh, I suppose you made a report to Sheriff Jackson."

I didn't want to lie, but he didn't need to know everything. "I did, but he's been away from the office. I told Deputy Lomax."

Robby's eyes changed. "You boys're from the country. You know everybody's usually kin to everybody else."

He was telling us something without saying it. "Meaning?"

"Just what I said." His cell phone vibrated. He plucked it from the back pocket of his jeans and glanced at the screen. Uninterested, he tucked it away. "Y'all holler if you need me, and I'll stay out of your way. Oh, by the way, Jimmy Meeks told me last night that Region Seven's coming open. Hector Jiminez is stepping down. They want me to fill in until they pick someone to take his place. I guess that means they're hoping you come back soon."

Uh-uh.

There was a little voice in my head again, the one that sounded like Sara Beth. Instead of arguing with Robby, I chose my words with care. "Thanks. I'll keep that in mind."

"A lot of folks miss you. They're always asking about you."

"You know, my big brother here didn't seem to mention meth too much, before he…stepped down." Harley wasn't finished. "You running into very much of that crap, other'n this around here?"

Robby's first response was a grunt. "Shoot. It's everywhere. I took a kid in a couple of days ago. A family called me and said that he passes their gate every day at about eighty miles an hour. Ran over their dog, and that's what made 'em call me. I drove out there and waited in their drive. Sure enough, here he come, right on time, and he was a-flyin'.

"I followed him to work, and when he got out, had a little talk with him. He was high as a kite, you know, twitchy and all, and kept opening his mouth wide like he was trying to crack his jaws. That's one I'd never seen before, so I patted him down. Didn't have anything in his clothes, but I asked if I could look through his truck. There was two rocks on the floorboard, and I dug around a little after that, because if you find meth dropped and forgot, you're onto something.

"Before long, I saw the trim on the dash light above his windshield was loose. Pulled on it, and about two ounces of crank was packed tight up in there. Got him for dealing, and he'd just turned twenty-one and worked for a road crew, so yeah, it's everywhere."

"He was on his own stuff?" Harley's question pricked my interest. Most dealers had enough sense to stay away from their own product.

"That's what he said. Had to feed his own habit, so he turned to dealing, but said he'd never felt any crystal like this new crap of his. You know, watching him reminded me of how a yellow jacket looks after you hit it with wasp spray. The longer we talked, the more animated he was until the guy was twitching like a zombie. It wouldn't have surprised me if his head hadn't come so far back it would have touched his spine. Never seen anything like it, and hell, all I ever wanted was to work ranch crimes. Well, the city's in the country now."

"He give you the name of a supplier?"

"Nope, but it was likely somebody new. I'd never seen crank that color. It was a distinctive pink hue. Turned it in to Chief Deputy Lomax since Jackson's still out, and they're gonna test it all and said they'd get back to me."

He could have called it crystal, ice, chalk, wash, dunk, or no doze, all regional street names for crank, and we would have known what he was talking about. Robby watched us from under the brim of his hat and I saw it again, a look the same as if he were examining me from the corners of his eyes. It was the same way our old granddaddy would look at us when he was pulling our leg about something, or judging our reaction to a story.

"I bet there's a new formula somewhere." Harley worked through it aloud, the same as when we were kids. "When me and Tuck were working undercover, he found out everyone has their favorite recipe for making meth, like a chocolate cake recipe. No matter what ingredients they use, though, will get pretty much the same results. When the results come back from the lab, I'd say he has a higher pH level than what we're used to seeing."

"How do you know that?"

"Saw something similar once. The kid have a name for it?"

"Yeah, called it gravel."

Chapter Twenty-Eight

It was dusk when Tammy drove Chloe to pick up a few things at her house, leaving the boys to go with friends to a local game center. Though the sun was down, the sky was still on fire, red and orange mixed and sweeping to the horizon. A cold front settled in, not a true blue norther, but substantial just the same.

Most of the trip in the Suburban was on pavement until the two-lane forked. A hard left led to the next rural community ten miles away, while the right fork turned to gravel and ran arrow-straight between alternating fields and tree-lined pastures.

Tammy raised her foot off the accelerator and slowed at the Y, when the smooth hardtop shifted abruptly into a washboard lane in desperate need of grading. A plume of dust rose behind the SUV, and she slowed even more to lessen the rattle.

Darkness was approaching fast when they passed a pickup parked in a gate turnout. Two young men sliding long guns into canvas cases paused to wave from the tailgate of their truck.

Familiar with hunting seasons, Tammy lifted a finger from the steering wheel as they passed. "Squirrel season is open.

Guys hunted in the mornings when I was a kid, but I bet those two came out here as soon as they left school."

Chloe watched them recede in the right-hand mirror. "I wish Dad would get this idea out of his head so we can move back to civilization."

"He's doing what he thinks is right for the two of you."

"I didn't ask to move out here."

"I know you didn't, but you need to remember he's hurting too. Moving out to the country is what you both needed right now."

"He talks about being in the country all the time. That's what he does, but we always lived in town or the city when I was little. I don't know these people." She pointed a forefinger back. "Boys who get out of school and go hunting. Why aren't they playing football, or something else?"

"They're closer to their roots here. It's easier to get outdoors when you live out like this, and maybe they like hunting more than organized sports. It's a different way of life in the country, but one that's more like it was when your daddy and Uncle Harley grew up. That's why they left the city, and I would guess it's the reason he came out here. He needed space and a slower way of life."

"Well..." Chloe thumbed her phone awake, checked for messages that weren't there, and flicked it off. "Nothing's been right since Mama and Peyton died and we moved out here."

"And it will never be the same. What'll feel right will come later."

Her aunt's calm demeanor took the spark out of Chloe's irritation. She checked her phone again, a habit that repeated itself without conscious thought. It wasn't all about her, and more than once during the last few months she tried to understand how her dad felt. It was hard, though, because he seldom showed any outward emotion.

The drive through the October evening would have been relaxing at any other time, but to Chloe, the whole area felt unfamiliar and sinister, and she wanted nothing more than to leave and spend more time with her aunt.

The wave of sadness and guilt that gripped her stomach was almost physical. Her dad was all Chloe had left, and it was selfish to think that way. He needed her, probably as much as she needed him, but she was torn. Her chest hitched, and she turned her face toward the window so Aunt Tammy couldn't see the tears that burned like cayenne pepper.

Wide fields and pastures gave way to thick trees growing along both sides of a shallow runoff creek. After the drive through fairly open country, hardwoods crowded in and threatened to whip the SUV's sides. The leafy tunnel blocked the remaining glow from the sky and narrowed even more at a concrete weight-restricted bridge without rails. The SUV's automatic headlights came on.

Already familiar with the area, Tammy slowed to cross the bridge and looked through the gathering gloom for the intersecting dirt road that would take them to the ranch. As she turned right, the lights swept across an overgrown fence and illuminated a black Toyota sedan running without lights in their direction. Traveling way too fast on the narrow country lane, the other driver jerked the wheel to avoid the much larger vehicle, but the conditions worked against him.

Tammy gasped and instinctively took to the ditch on their right in order to avoid the oncoming car. Chloe saw a dark streak as the sedan passed, then the flash of taillights when it slewed left as the driver overreacted and fought to maintain control.

"Oh, my God!" Tammy slammed the brakes. Her car skidded

on the loose gravel and came to a parallel stop only inches from a bob-wire fence.

The sedan's back end broke, its right-side tires skidding into the ditch. It flipped in a crunch of metal, rolled once, and came to a rest when the roof slammed into a sycamore tree. At the impact, an avalanche of dust fell from the leaves, filling the air with a thick cloud that covered the wrecked vehicle.

Tammy jammed the transmission into park and shouldered the door open. "Call 911!"

Chloe was already punching buttons by the time Tammy was out of the SUV. Her aunt left the door open and ran down the road toward the cloud of dust that partially obscured the car. With the phone to her ear, Chloe twisted to look through the back glass.

"911. What is your emergency?"

"This is Chloe Snow. We're on Blue Creek Road, close to Rock Hill, and we almost hit a car that just flipped over."

"Are you hurt?"

"No, but there's probably somebody that is. I see a guy crawling out of the windshield and somebody else is coming out too. It's so dark over there I can't see anything else."

"Hang on, Chloe."

She heard the dispatch operator talking on the radio.

"Chloe. Is there anyone in your car that's hurt?"

"No, ma'am. They missed us and rolled the car."

"Us. How many people are in the vehicle with you?"

"Just my aunt. She was driving."

"What's her name?"

Chloe told her.

"Do you know if anyone in the other vehicle is injured?"

"No. It's so dark now I can't see anything."

"We have an ambulance and an officer on the way. Are you in a safe location?"

Chloe barked a laugh. "Not really. We're halfway in a ditch, and there's meth dealers and dope heads driving up and down this road all day and night. There'll probably be another coming around before long."

The operator perked up on that one. "What makes you say that?"

"My dad's the brand inspector who called in about it a couple of days ago." Her teenage attitude rose dark and ugly. "We're the ones who were broke into out here, and they stole his truck. That ring a bell?"

"Stay on the line with me until help gets there."

—

The car came to rest on its side, and the odor of gasoline filled the still air. Tammy rushed through the dusk, hoping the vehicle wouldn't explode from spilled gas. They always did in the movies, and if there was still anyone in the car, she wasn't sure she could pull them out.

Two loud bangs reached her ears as someone kicked out the shattered windshield. She saw a flash of reflected light on what little of the glass was visible. She'd unconsciously turned on her hazard lights when they went into the ditch and the red flashes gave the scene a surreal feel as a young man crawled out on all fours.

"Son of a bitch!" He stood, holding one hand against his bloody forehead. "Brock! Are you all right?"

A voice cut sharp and clear. "Hell, no." A second man of similar age appeared beside the first. He rose and held himself steady with one hand against the wreck. Blood soaked the leg of his jeans and ran down onto his shoe. "What'n hell happened, Dylan?"

The driver leaned against the car and pointed at Tammy who'd stopped several yards away. "She almost hit us."

Her face flushed hot with anger as she registered the young men somewhere in their early twenties. "It was *you* who almost hit *us*, and y'all better get away from that car before it catches fire. How bad are you hurt?"

Her cautionary words sparked the men to push away from the wreck and in her direction. Brock held on to Dylan's shoulder, limping. "We need a doctor. You know the way to the hospital?"

Tammy paused and glanced back toward her car. "Yeah, but we've called 911. Somebody should be on the way."

"Shit! No! We don't need the laws. Just take us to the doctor."

She held her ground as they stopped a few feet away. "Nope. I can let the tailgate down on the Suburban, and y'all can sit there until we get some help."

The men exchanged glances, then moved as one toward her. Dylan jabbed a finger at Tammy. "Nope. You're driving us out of here."

Fear shot through Tammy when she realized there was more going on with the two strangers than she knew. She thought back to her revolver in the Suburban. An experienced wife of a law officer, she never went anywhere without a weapon. The little Smith & Wesson .38 Special Airweight was within Chloe's reach, but she probably didn't know it was in the center console.

She whirled and ran back to the open door. The guys in the road were both injured and woozy from the rollover. It would be easy to beat them to the vehicle and drive to safety.

Startled, they stopped when Tammy jumped behind the

wheel. The door slammed as dirt and gravel flew from under the spinning back tires digging into the soft sand. She kept the pedal on the floorboard and buried the heavy Suburban nearly to the hubs. She flipped open the console and grabbed the little revolver.

Brock and Dylan were almost to the door when headlights appeared. She glanced into the side mirror to see the men stop in the middle of the road. Shifting her attention to the oncoming vehicle, lights across the top of the cab told her it was a dually pickup. Running lights on the big truck illuminated a trailer loaded with round hay bales. She almost collapsed in relief at the appearance of a local rancher.

The big truck slowed even more as it approached the accident. The diesel engine rattled as the driver eased forward, lighting the scene with the high beams until the cattleguard on the front bumper was mere feet from the Suburban. The driver let the engine idle. In Tammy's mind, he was studying the bloodied men in the road, the SUV, and likely, her and Chloe.

The door opened and the dome light came on to reveal an older rancher in a broken-down straw hat. Another man was with him. The rancher climbed down and paused in both sets of headlights. "Anyone hurt bad?"

Tammy almost wept. It was all she could do not to throw open the door and rush toward him. She rolled down the window. "Thank God you're here. Both of these guys were in that car. They're hurt and bleeding. They want me to take them to the hospital, but they don't want us to call for help."

Still letting Brock lean on him, Dylan jabbed a finger in their direction. "They ran us off the road. Dylan's hurt pretty bad."

"I'll call for an ambulance."

Chloe opened her door and stepped out of the car, keeping it between her and the accident victims. "I already have."

With the rancher there, and the other man in the big truck, Tammy felt safer. Pistol in hand, she slid out of the seat. "These two are trouble."

Still trying to make sense of what was in front of him, the rancher ignored the pistol, if he saw it at all, and spoke to Chloe. "I know you. You're Tucker Snow's daughter."

"That's right."

A powerfully built young man in an equally battered hat climbed out of the truck and into the lights. In jeans and a dirty white T-shirt, he stepped forward and pointed at the revolver. "You think you need that, ma'am?"

"I did. The way they were acting."

"We're not acting no way!" Brock's voice rose. "They came barrelin' 'round the corner, and we had to dodge 'em. They almost killed us."

"I'm Dan Birdsall." The older man's voice snapped like a whip. He pointed to the ground. "I know this girl, and I don't have any idea who you two are, and I doubt you're from around here, the way you're acting. Y'all need to sit right there where y'are until help comes. This here's my boy Taylor. Son, they come another step closer and you put 'em on the ground."

Brock held his head and moaned. "Oh, God! I'm burning up."

"What's wrong?" Dan Birdsall's voice was still sharp, authoritative.

Dylan dropped to all fours, head hanging low. Panting as if he'd run a marathon, his entire body quivered.

"You heard him, boys." Taylor Birdsall tensed and stepped closer to the two young men, putting his bulk between them, the girls, and his daddy. "Do what he said. I don't want to have to hurt one of y'all."

When Brock looked up at the two men, his face was white

and feral. Eyes wide, his head shook violently. Saliva ran from the corners of his mouth. A strange, keening moan came from his open mouth.

He rose into a tackle position and the high moan changed to a guttural growl. "I'll kill you!" Eyes wide and glassy, he charged Taylor.

Big as a refrigerator, Taylor Birdsall sprang forward and swung a ham-sized fist at the other man's jaw. It rocked Brock back, but the young man bared his teeth, dug his feet in, and charged again.

Taylor swung an uppercut that caught Brock under the chin with the crack of bone and teeth. Brock seized up. Stiff as a mannequin, he collapsed. Green puke poured from his mouth onto the gravel, and he slipped into unconsciousness.

The distant wail of a siren filled the air. Seconds later, a sheriff's car crossed the concrete bridge and stopped.

Chapter Twenty-Nine

I plucked a beer from my fridge and handed one to Harley. The house was dark when we got home, and I was concerned. Tammy was supposed to bring Chloe and be there when we got back. "They oughta be here by now. I tried to call Chloe, but it went straight to voicemail. That's kids for you; they don't want to talk to anyone."

"They'd rather text."

"I did, but she hasn't answered yet."

"I tried Tammy." He twisted the cap off. "She didn't answer when I called, so I left her a message. Hope it went through. I didn't have a good signal. You should've had 'em put in a stronger repeater while they were installing your security system."

"All this is draining my bank account pretty fast. I'll have one put in later."

"It'd make it easier to check those cameras we installed too. It takes way too long to download the images."

"You getting much off them?"

Harley loved his gadgets and couldn't wait to see what the cameras captured during the day. "Sure 'nough." He punched at the screen for a minute, then turned the phone so I could see. There must have been twenty images of cars going into and coming out of Atchley's drive. There were twice as many other photos of pickups going down the road. Some pulling cattle trailers, others of trailer loads of hay. In one, a tractor passed. In another, two kids in a four-wheeler.

"Action's picking up this evening." Harley used two fingers to expand the image on his screen. "Here's one shot just before dark. Look here at this. Two guys in a black Toyota sedan. They weren't there five minutes."

"Long enough to make a buy. Look here at this camera." Located near our gate, it covered the drive and the road. "They pulled in and look what they did." He was right. The sedan nosed in to our gate and a few seconds later, the interior flashed as someone struck a lighter. "They made a buy, then pulled in here so one of them could fire up a pipe and take a hit. Then they hit the road and fogged it. Look at all the dust and gravel he threw up."

I tilted the bottle and swallowed. "I can't believe they pulled into my gate to do dope."

Harley stuck the phone in his pocket. "This beer's good, but I need some water." He put down the bottle and found a glass in the cabinet. He pushed it against the ice dispenser set in the refrigerator door, and the mechanism rumbled without producing one single cube. "You know, I'm thinking you need a dog here." He pushed the lever harder, as if more pressure would help. "What's up with this thing?"

"There's something wrong with it. Must have made it mad when we moved everything. Just open the door and get your ice from the bin."

Ice rattled again as he dug a handful from the freezer.

"Anyway, I think Chloe should stay with us." He turned to the sink. "And Kevin can stay here with you."

"I was thinking the same thing. You think he'll be all right away from y'all?"

"I don't know why not. All he ever does is eat and sleep."

My phone buzzed with an incoming call, and I answered.

Chapter Thirty

Atchley looked up from the laptop on the kitchen table. "This thing don't work like it's supposed to."

"It's picking up a lot." Lloyd Belcher leaned a little closer to the screen, putting his head close to Atchley. "She said she put it on the living room window."

"I can hear some things, but there's too much noise in the way and the damned heater or something kicked on once." Atchley turned his head to escape the acrid smell of his friend's breath. The only reason he could sit so close to the toxic man was because Atchley and Priscilla smoked too, dulling their olfactory senses as well as their taste buds. Even then, Belcher reeked from the nicotine and smoke in his clothes, hair, and pores.

He almost laughed. Belcher kept two or three containers of breath spray in his pocket and was constantly pumping blasts of the minty fluid into his mouth without result. It only made his breath smell like minty smoke and the alcohol content dried his mouth, adding still another layer of odor to his exhalations.

Atchley studied the screen as if he could make sense of the sound graphs, frequency displays, and digital meters. "Is it still on?"

"No, it went off about the time they started talking, but they got away from the mike. Every now and then a few words come through. They're drinking beer, I know that, but I think they're in the kitchen. I figured they'd come back in the living room, but it looks like they're gonna stay where they are."

"*We're* in the kitchen. I think most folks like to sit around a table and talk. We should have told Jimma to put it on a different window."

Atchley looked around the dismal trailer. Yep, they were in the kitchen, and at the same time, the dining room and the living room. He snorted. Priscilla watched that damned HGTV all day and everybody was tearing down walls so they could have an open-concept house, or building what they called tiny houses, and here he was, almost sitting in three rooms at the same time.

"We didn't tell her which one to stick it on. She just decided herself. We're lucky she didn't put it on some bedroom window."

The rattle of ice ended when the speaker turned. The sound came through crystal clear. "...and Kevin can stay here with you."

Belcher shook his head at the comment and lit another coffin nail.

"Dammit!" Atchley stood and went to the wheezing refrigerator. He plucked a barely cooled beer from the nearly empty shelves and cracked the tab. "That's a third guy to deal with."

"What do you want to do?" Belcher pitched the lighter onto the cluttered table and sat back in his chair.

"Kill 'em all, but when I'm good and ready." A customer pulled up out front. Atchley picked up a pistol and stuck it into the small of his back. "Hear that?"

Belcher turned his head like a dog, listening. "Just the car."

"Naw, you're missing it."

"Missing what?"

"The sound of money. That's money out in the yard, because this new crystal's selling like there's no tomorrow. *Ka-ching!*"

Chapter Thirty-One

I was fit to be tied when the sheriff's department called to tell me Tammy and Chloe were in custody. My heart dropped when the deputy identified himself and said they'd been in an accident but weren't hurt. Years of training kicked in, and I went from shocked to a dispassionate emergency manager. It took a few questions to collect all the details, but I soon had the picture.

I'm glad the deputy called me instead of Harley. I absorbed the information and told the voice on the phone Harley was with me and he didn't need to make another call. Getting my jacket, I explained the situation in as few words as possible. I knew how he reacted to stress.

Tense as an overwound clock, my little brother rode quiet on the way to town, and that's a bad sign. Imagine a pressure cooker without a vent in the top. That was Harley, and I tried to think of some way to bleed off a little steam before we got there.

"They're all right. That's what matters the most. We'll figure the rest of it out once we get there."

"All right. My wife and your daughter are in jail, and that's all *right*?"

"They're safe, is what I meant. We know they're safe…"

My comment went without response. I was glad I was carrying a pistol. I figured I might have to shoot Harley in the leg at some point to slow him down if he decided to go in hot.

It was after midnight. Leaves blew across the deserted street under the harsh streetlights. The chill settled in deeper. True autumn had arrived with the first norther of the season. I rolled the windows down, hoping the breeze might blow some of the heat out of that tensed-up body beside me.

I steered into an angled space in front of the sheriff's office. Harley was out before I shifted into park, slamming the door and heading inside like a heat-seeking missile. I knew the detonation would come soon after he blew through the door.

"Harley!"

"What?" He spun as if I'd stung him with a hotshot. The one-word question was a slap, sharp, like a man running a dog out of his yard. If he was snapping at me, Lord help those inside.

I climbed out from behind the wheel. "We need to handle this together, and you have to be cool." Like him, my first inclination was to go in like a bear, but we had to play this as calm as possible.

"The girls are under *arrest*."

"That's what the officer told me, but let's stay cool and see what's up before we start knocking heads."

Jaw set and eyes like crackling electricity, he nodded and waited for me to lead the way. I still hadn't taken my badge off and was glad. A little extra oomph would help in the coming minutes.

As if he were waiting for us, Chief Deputy Lomax stood in the tiled foyer, talking with a highway patrol officer and some slimy-looking guy who made me think of a used-car salesman. I figured him for a lawyer.

Harley's bootheels echoed off the hard tile surface of the building constructed back in the 1950s, evidence that he was heading toward Lomax like a rodeo bull after a throwed rider. Lomax squared his shoulders when he saw us. His eyes flicked from me, to my badge, to Harley and the pistol on his hip. "Gentlemen."

I spoke before Harley could get started. "Where's my daughter and his wife?"

Focusing his attention on the two of us, Lomax didn't see the skanky lawyer disappear through a door behind them as if a vacuum sucked him out of the lobby. "They were involved in an automobile accident. Chloe's in my office." He spoke to me instead of Harley. "She's fine. I'm afraid Tammy's situation is a little more serious."

His eyes flicked to the holstered pistol on Harley's hip, then to me. "You need to keep your hands clear of that weapon."

Harley planted his feet and flipped out his retirement badge. "How's Tammy's situation more serious? Was she injured? Is she in the hospital? Tuck said she was in custody."

Lomax finally turned his full attention on Harley. "And you are?"

"Harley Snow. Tammy's husband. I'm retired, but I work for law enforcement on contract now."

Lomax wanted to press further, but it wasn't the time, and he chose wisely. "How about we go into the sheriff's office and talk?"

I looked around. We were the only people there at that time of night. I had no intention of giving Lomax the chance to put a desk between us, creating the illusion that he was in control. I wanted to keep him as off balance as possible. "We're fine right here."

Lomax shrugged. "Well, guys, Tammy tried to flee the scene of the accident this evening."

Harley's expression went flat. "Keep talking." My little brother's jaw was set.

"This is Deputy Baker." Lomax pointed with his hat at the uniformed officer beside him who looked as if he'd bitten into a green persimmon. His little pinched mouth wasn't much more than a slit. He also had eyes and features that reminded me of the banjo-playing boy in *Deliverance*.

"Deputy Baker was the first to respond to the scene after your daughter dialed the emergency number, Mr. Snow. When he arrived, he identified two male individuals as the occupants of the other car, which was overturned. They were injured, and your wife, Mr. Snow, was holding them at gunpoint in the middle of the road. I arrived on the scene a few minutes later and observed the SUV she was driving buried up to its hubs in a ditch. From the fresh dirt thrown up behind the vehicle, it was obvious she'd tried to drive away after the accident. As you know, leaving the scene is a serious offense."

A twitch at the corner of his mouth was the only reaction he got from Harley. I wasn't sure if he was fighting a grin or was about to launch himself at Lomax. He drew a breath to speak, but I interrupted him.

"Go on."

Deputy Baker took a deep breath. It might have been nerves, or just to spout out the rest of the report, but I detected a slight shudder. "There were two men on the ground and they looked to be in bad shape. One had been assaulted by an individual named Taylor Birdsall and was unconscious. The other victim injured in the accident told me what happened, and I took immediate and appropriate action at that point."

I'd heard that kind of memorized rote before. "Victim?"

"They were the ones making the report."

Lomax nodded in an effort to put a period on the end of Baker's assertion. "That's it then, Snow."

"Deputy Lomax, let's start here. I'm *Agent* Snow. Harley was *Lieutenant* Snow when he retired from the DPS, so let's use those titles."

His eyes turned to flint. "Fine."

Score one for us. I didn't like Lomax one little bit, and the whole dick-knocking scene was tiresome, but it had to be done. We weren't about to back down, and we had to set some ground rules right at the beginning.

"What makes you think she was trying to flee the scene?" Harley's voice was soft. A bad sign. When he lowers the volume, you can bet something's about to happen. "Spinning tires might say she was trying to simply pull out of the ditch and back on the road. Or maybe she'd tried to get away from some danger. If she was holding two men at gunpoint, she obviously wasn't trying to run."

Lomax shuffled his feet. "Uh, according to witnesses..."

"What witnesses?" It was my turn. We were alternating, keeping Lomax off balance by playing back and forth. It'd worked with us for years, and we fell into it naturally.

"The local rancher. Dan Birdsall and his son, Taylor, who like I said, assaulted one of the victims. They came upon the scene to witness the weapon in Mrs. Snow's hand."

"I've met them. So you're not referring to witnesses outside the scope of the event."

"Well, there were just the five of them, two victims, the Birdsalls, and Tammy." Lomax swung his attention back to Harley and frowned, likely wondering just how much Harley knew about the area.

"My daughter was there."

"She's a minor, so I didn't count her."

"We can count her." I watched Baker fidget. "The Birdsalls have a good reputation, I hear. I've talked to them before. They seem solid enough. Those kind of people mind their own business and don't go around beating up on folks."

Dan Birdsall and Taylor'd stopped by the house on the first day we were moving in and welcomed us to the area. Taylor pitched in and helped carry in some of the heavier items like the washing machine and dryer.

Weathered to dry leather by the sun, Dan was a perfect representation of the ranchers and farmers I'd worked with through the years. Taylor was a seventeen-year-old hoss already big enough to take the refrigerator from the back of a truck all by himself. He still wasn't through growing, and you could bet it took a lot of groceries to keep that big machine in motion.

I wasn't going to turn loose. "You're saying my *sister*-in-law actually threatened the *victims* with a weapon after, as you say, Taylor Birdsall *assaulted* the *victims*?"

The deputies exchanged glances at my question and the way I hammered those words. I read volumes into the looks.

Lomax switched back to me. "Well, no. The two accident victims said they were threatened by her after they exited their wrecked vehicle. When Birdsall and his son arrived, the weapon was unholstered and in her hand, though, then they were beaten by Taylor when he and Mr. Birdsall arrived." That last part flowed as if rehearsed.

Time to switch it up on them a little. "Is Taylor or Mr. Birdsall in custody? If they are, I'd like to post bail for them."

"Um, well, no." Deputy Baker looked to be wound tight as a watch spring. I kept waiting for Harley to break from his stance and shout boo, just to see the skinny little guy jump like Barney Fife. "Since the boy's a minor, we released him to his dad."

"Released him." Harley hadn't moved, though, but I'll be damned if he didn't look like he was a step closer to the deputies. "So the young man who laid hands on these…victims was released while my wife was arrested."

"She threatened them with a deadly weapon."

It was my turn again. "Did the ranchers say she'd pointed her weapon *at* them?"

The story was unraveling, and an increasingly nervous Deputy Baker cleared his throat. "We really shouldn't be discussing this right here."

"Did the ranchers say she'd *pointed* it at the victims?" We were in dangerous territory here, asking all those questions without any legal representation present, but we had Baker off balance, and I wanted to press it as hard as I could while we had the chance.

Baker shook his head. "No."

"Would you like to tell me why my wife said she needed a weapon, Deputy Baker?" I still can't figure out how Harley looked as if he were advancing on those two without moving a muscle.

"She said they threatened her, but Birdsall advised that he saw nothing that would indicate that she was in any danger."

"What were Birdsall's exact words?"

"Well, I didn't write them down."

"I would have." Harley crossed his arms. "You know I'm gonna call him tomorrow and ask for what he said. You want to think about that for a second."

Baker licked his lips. "Well, maybe he didn't actually say those words…"

"Two grown men against one little gal who ain't no bigger'n a minute." My volley. "Then why did young Taylor hit…which one?"

"Brock. Brock Horner."

"Okay. Why did he strike Horner in the first place?"

"That's part of an ongoing investigation we can't divulge at this time." Lomax squared his shoulders.

"Fine then." I flicked a hand as if waving off a fly. "That's off the table. What happened to cause the wreck anyway?"

"Mrs. Snow took a corner too fast, and the other vehicle had to swerve." Deputy Baker took a small notepad from his shirt pocket but didn't open it. I wondered if anything was really written down at all. "It rolled and injured the two passengers who exited the car and asked for her to render aid. That's when she tried to flee the scene."

"Who's the other one?"

Lomax's attention flicked back to Harley, as if watching a tennis match. "Dylan Kehoe."

I circled back, which is what we always did in questioning someone, hoping their story would change even a little bit, showing a chink in their story. "Your only witnesses to this accident itself are only two men who were *involved* in the accident?"

I swear Harley looked bigger. He was fast swelling up like a mad coon.

"Mr. Snow, we've already been over that ground and it's late..."

"Deputy Baker." Harley was tired of Lomax already. "You're talking to fellow officers. Cut the shit." His eyes narrowed. "What time did this accident occur?"

"Right at dark."

That's when Harley and I were already back home waiting for the girls.

"What kind of car was involved?"

"Toyota. Black sedan."

Harley tilted his head back, barely opening his mouth. I could tell he understood then.

"Were they intoxicated or chemically impaired?"

I saw Lomax reel as he looked for the words. His eyes flicked up and to the right, where liars are said to look. "They didn't show any signs of being drunk or high."

"No alcohol or drugs in the car."

"No."

Harley turned to me. "You remember what we saw while we were in the kitchen tonight."

He was talking about the surveillance photos. I nodded.

"What was that?" Lomax looked back and forth between us, waiting for an answer.

"Family joke." I was tired of Lomax too. "I don't suppose Sheriff Jackson's here at this time of the night."

"No. He's still not completely up to snuff."

"Just what is wrong with him?"

"Cancer. The radiation treatment seems to be worse than the disease."

"I thought you said he had some kind of bug earlier." Harley's eyebrow nearly reached his hat.

"Well, I didn't aim to tell his business."

Right at that moment wasn't the time to get into another man's illness, so I changed the subject. "Have you called him about this?"

"I don't call him every time we make an arrest, or when there's an accident. He'll get a full report."

Harley leaned in. "You have my wife in custody for fleeing the scene."

"For *attempted* fleeing."

"Then you can release her right now."

"I can't do that. We've already started the paperwork."

"Have you booked her in? Photo. Fingerprints?"

"Not yet."

I heard something in Lomax's voice that told me we had him. "Then she's being detained. I guess that's why we didn't get a call from Tammy or Chloe."

He had to think about that one for a moment. "We held her for questioning."

"Was my wife questioned?"

"No."

"Did she ask for a lawyer?" Harley knew what Tammy would do.

"Yes."

"It wasn't that chicken-necked geek who squeezed out of here a minute ago, was it?"

"He's an attorney."

"Not ours. Now, you go bring my…"

"Deputy Lomax…" I had to keep Harley off him. "We're all brothers here. How about a little professional courtesy? We all know what likely happened tonight. Deputy Baker, I'd bet my ranch that those two individuals in the other car were questioned and released, right?"

He swallowed, and those narrow eyes of his became slits that flicked from me, to Lomax, and back to Harley, who he probably expected would come unglued at any moment. "Well, I talked to them while we waited for an ambulance, and then… You're right, they were treated and released."

"Um hum. And how are they kin to you and Lomax?"

His mouth opened and closed like a fish. I'd had enough. "That's what I figured. Deputy Lomax, I'm coming back here tomorrow, and I expect to talk with the sheriff."

"We don't just let civilians tell us what to do, and like I said, he probably won't be back tomorrow."

"Oh, he will. We're all going to talk in the morning, peace officers to peace officers."

He snorted. "You're on leave, remember?"

"Not anymore." Even though it was the middle of the night, I punched a number on my phone and put it on speaker. My supervisor's voice came through after the third ring was sharp, strong, and concerned. "Tucker? You all right?"

"Fine, Jimmy. You're on speaker with Harley and two deputies who need to hear this. Gentleman, this is my supervisor at the TSCRA, Jimmy Meeks, on the other end of the line. I just wanted you to know I'm ready to come back to the job."

"You sure? I thought you needed time?"

"I had enough. Now I'm on a case, and I'd like you to phone Sheriff Jackson here in Red River County and tell him Harley and I need to come in and talk with him in the morning."

There was a long pause on the other end and I waited as he figured things out. Jimmy Meeks was one of the sharpest men I'd ever known, and he had the fastest mind I'd ever encountered.

"Harley's working on this one with you?"

"He is."

"I am." Harley leaned in to the phone without taking his eyes off Lomax. "Sorry to wake you up, Jimmy."

A chuckle came through the phone's tiny speaker. "No problem, boys. This involve the break-in at your house, Tuck, and your stolen truck?"

"Maybe. Not sure yet, though. Right up my alley, ain't it, rural crime?"

"Well, you're in luck. Hector Jiminez sent me his retirement papers two days ago. I've been meaning to call you, so this works out just right. Region Twelve is yours again as of right now and I'll transfer Robby out there to cover for Jiminez until I find a replacement."

"Thanks so much. Now, about calling the sheriff..."

"I'll call him first thing. Welcome back."

"You bet." I hung up and met Lomax's gaze. "That gives you about eight hours to nut up and make your own call."

He spoke to Baker without taking his eyes off me. "Go get Mrs. Snow and Chloe."

The deputy turned and I stopped him with a question. "Deputy Baker. You any kin to the Atchley family or Curtis Bailey?"

He paused and threw the answer I'd been expecting over his shoulder. "Curtis is kin on my mama's side. The Atchley folks on Daddy's side."

"That means you boys are kinfolk too, then. Let me guess, y'all don't look enough alike to be first cousins, and I doubt second, so I'd figure you for third."

Lomax's faced hardened, and I knew I had 'em by the short hairs.

Chapter Thirty-Two

It was dark when Frank Cornelison, better known as Spyder to his gangster friends, tilted a can of Natty Light and drained the contents. He lobbed it in the general direction of a trash can at the end of a gas pump bay. It bounced off the rim and rattled on the cement. Leaving it there, he pulled the hoodie up over his head to break the chilly wind.

The fuel island's harsh blue lights reflected off the shiny paint job of a white Prius, washing the area in an artificial shadowless glow. An elderly man filling up the hybrid frowned at the tattooed convict. His mouth opened, and when Spyder glared at him, the man shut off the pump and hung up the nozzle. Seconds later he pulled out of the OklaTex bay and vanished into the darkness behind an incoming eighteen-wheeler that plowed a hole in the North Texas darkness.

Spyder positioned himself against the side of a jacked-up Dodge pickup so he could keep an eye on the busy station. He'd parked the truck at the edge of the lot, nose to nose with a Ford pickup belonging to another gangster named Flea.

The descriptive nickname was dead-on, because Flea was

barely five foot tall. However, it was five full feet of sheer meanness. His diminutive size belied the violence wrapped in such a small package, and more than one opponent in a Huntsville prison learned the hard way.

A line of tattooed teardrops falling from his left eye and down that cheek was a record of corpses left behind, starting with his first kill at fourteen years old. Flea slipped both hands into the kangaroo pocket on the front of his hoodie. "What do you want me to do about it?"

They'd been discussing the failed hit in the Dallas parking lot. Spyder was almost out of control, thinking his men had been set up by Atchley and Belcher. He couldn't imagine they'd accidentally tied into two lawmen, who had eliminated half his men with as much ease as kids playing cops and robbers.

Spyder crossed his arms and leaned against the Dodge, feeling a 9mm semi-automatic heavy against his stomach. "I'm not sure what to do, but we're gonna do *something* and to several people."

"The whole thing was Atchley's fault. He didn't tell us those guys were pros."

"I doubt that dumbass knew it himself." Unable to get a handle on what happened in the Kroger parking lot, Spyder swung back and forth on what to do. There were too many unknowns with their target who'd laid waste to his best men. "We can't let them go, not after killing four of our guys. That makes us look weak, and I can't have that."

"You want me to take 'em out?"

"Them lawmen?"

"Yeah."

"I do, and then kill Atchley."

Flea nodded and scanned the fuel center. "He has Belcher around all the time. He's a tough son of a bitch."

Spyder studied the smaller man. "So are you. Cap his ass too."

Flea shrugged. "How and when?"

"Tomorrow. You can do it, or contract it out, for all I care. I just want those two hillbillies dead."

"Just them?"

Spyder studied on the questions. "Yeah. This ain't no family deal."

"Make it look like an accident?"

"Make it look any way you want."

They paused as a highway patrol car appeared, cruising slowly through the buzz of cars and eighteen wheelers rumbling in and out of the lot. It headed into a parking space near the front door. The state trooper stepped out, glanced around, and went inside.

Spyder reached into his truck bed and opened an RTIC cooler. Withdrawing a dripping can of beer, he closed the lid and pulled the tab. He took a long sip, keeping his eyes on the glass doors. Inside, the trooper filled a cup with coffee and joined the line of customers waiting to pay.

"When we get finished with this, let's head up to the farm and spend some time. Our boys need to practice their shooting and technique a little more. Those four we lost showed me we're not as ready as I'd like to think. And Grandpa has a shipment ready to go. Big one. I'm gonna call in the Czechs on this one. They have the contacts to move something this big."

Flea turned one side to the gas station. It would make them look like a couple of guys just waiting for someone to come back out. "I'll get two or three of the boys to go with me."

"They all you'll need?"

"I don't need them. I can do it myself, but I figure it won't hurt to give them some experience."

The state trooper came out and returned to his cruiser. He backed out, and seconds later left the lot with his light flashing. Spyder made a gun with a forefinger and thumb and shot at the car as it pulled onto the highway.

"I hate cops."

Chapter Thirty-Three

Chloe had been up for barely an hour and was still curled up on her bed when her phone vibrated with a text from Jimma. She hadn't been able to sleep all night, still amped up from almost going to jail. She was awake when her dad left not long after daylight, and kept rolling the events over in her mind from the day before.

Hoping the text was from Aunt Tammy or a friend from her former school, she punched the screen awake.

Want to hang out today?

Emotionally drained from months of chaos, Chloe initially wanted to ignore the message, but her text was pitiful. Another came in almost immediately.

Need 2 c u

With a sigh, Chloe decided she should spend time with the other girl who looked so lonely she could fade away. But not in the house today. Having Jimma there right then would require more energy and attention than she was willing to give.

They needed to meet somewhere else, somewhere...neutral.

The text came in while Chloe stared out the window at the old wooden barn across the road. Shaded by old, wide red oaks that hadn't yet lost their leaves, it was somewhere she hadn't yet explored.

To tell the truth, she hadn't seen much of the property other than what they passed driving between wire fences, and what was visible from the porches. The old barn looked like it might be interesting to explore, and her dad said the western section of the ranch was thick woods full of deer and squirrels.

Back when they lived in town, she used to take long walks whenever she needed to get away from people and think. Maybe there were paths through the woods. Dad said the place was once a working cattle ranch, and she'd been around cows long enough to know they made trails through pastures and timber and stuck with them. If the paths were old enough, it should be easy to walk without fighting too much brush.

She'd like to take a walk, and she and Jimma could do some exploring, and maybe fish a little. Chloe loved to catch crappie, back before all their troubles. Surprising Dad with enough fish for supper would be fun.

Jimma sent another text.

Free all day. Cant be here.

A blue jay flew past the barn and disappeared into the trees that lined one bank of a wooded pool. It was the first time she'd thought of the little impoundment since her dad took her on a tour of the ranch. She was having to get used to calling it a pool.

Tank came to her lips first because that's what some people called water meant for livestock. She'd been out west with her dad and on family vacations enough to know they called them tanks out there.

A tall dam separated the larger pool from one-half its size, and beyond that was another line of trees and then the Atchley trailer. Chloe decided she wanted to keep the trails through the woods to herself, and the pool close to Jimma's trailer was the perfect place for them to meet. A place to sit and talk without being in the house. She sure had no intention of stepping foot in the Atchley trailer.

She tapped the keys with both thumbs.

K. Like to fish?

The answer was immediate.

Hate it.

More than a little frustrated, Chloe stared at the screen. All right, fine.

Here, then.

now ?

Hour. were going for a walk

Need to run form this place something weird is going on. My goats are blue

?

and stpdad you cant beleve what he did

K

help

Chapter Thirty-Four

"Does Sheriff Jackson know we're coming out to his house?" Harley was barely in the seat before he reached out to adjust the vent on his side of my rattling truck, once again reinforcing the fact that he couldn't sit still for more'n a minute before fiddling with something.

I rested a hand across the steering wheel. The gauges on my instrument panel said it was ten thirty in the morning and the temperature was fifty-two degrees. It had been falling all morning behind the cold front.

It was fifty-six at daylight, so the average drop was about a degree an hour, not unheard of in our part of the state. We've seen it plummet in Texas from a high of sixty down to sixteen degrees in a little over twelve hours. I hoped we weren't going to see that kind of extreme weather in the next few days, though. It was likely too early in the year for that.

"Nope. Didn't want to bother him too early since he's sick. I figure Jackson'll already know we're coming if Lomax called like I told him to, but I doubt it. No matter what, we'll drop by and say howdy." I turned right out of my drive.

Harley pointed in the opposite direction. "Town's that way."

"I wanted to drive past Atchley's house so he can see the truck."

"Kinda poking the bear, ain't you?"

"Just making our presence known." A flash of color between the cedars in Atchley's pasture caught my eye. I slowed, though we weren't going more than fifteen miles an hour, and braked. The two normally white Tennessee fainting goats I was used to seeing were a bright blue. "Would you look at that?"

Harley scanned the road ahead. "What?"

"Here." I pointed out my window "Those goats are *blue*."

He leaned forward to see around me. "Well, I'll be damned. They *are* blue."

"Wonder why someone would dye them. And what'n hell would you use to do that?"

He laughed. "Probably hair dye. I wouldn't use paint if it was me doing it, 'cause that'd be bad for their coats, but dye now, that'd be easy and it eventually washes out. They look like Easter eggs out there, don't they?"

I know my brother, and his pleased tone spoke volumes. "When did you do that?"

He frowned as I accelerated. "What makes you think *I'd* do it? Those aren't my goats."

"All of a sudden you know a helluva lot about hair dye, and I don't think Tammy colors hers, and if I recall, you dyed Billy Thompson's Catahoula dog one time when we were kids because he wouldn't pay you for that bicycle he bought off you."

Harley grunted and leaned back, appearing to be disgusted, but it was all an act. "Just one little time, and now you think every animal in Texas that's changed color was done by me. And in my defense, he owed me fifteen dollars, and I don't think a purple dog looked that bad in the first place."

I started to accelerate, and he reached out a hand. "Hang on a second."

"Why?"

He leaned on the truck's horn loud and long. Both blue goats stiffened and fell over sideways at the sudden blast of noise. I hit the gas and got us out of there while Harley laughed like a loon. "They really *do* faint."

"You're just mean, and they don't faint like people do. Their muscles stiffen up and they fall over when they hear sudden noises."

"You seem to know a lot about fainting goats yourself. Maybe you changed their hair color."

"Not hardly. Chloe saw them over here the other day and asked if she can have a pair."

"You gonna get her some?"

"Nope. I don't think a five-strand wire fence'll hold those little guys in, and I don't intend to spend a lot of money on cattle panels."

"You can string an electric fence."

"I'd think you'd want to stay away from those after what happened when we were kids." I felt a chuckle rise, and it was the first in a long time, but then again, that's what guys think's funny. One of us gets hit in the nuts, and everybody laughs. Catch a shin on a trailer hitch, and we all howl, because it's happened to every one of us and we all know there's always a hitch sticking out the back of a pickup.

Harley frowned at the memory. "Hey, you pee on a live wire once in your life, you'll be careful with fences until the day you die."

Had there been anyone in the back seat, they would have wondered if we'd lost our minds. Here we were yapping away like a couple of kids, while dealing with the aftermath of the night before, and heading over to a see a sheriff fighting cancer to tell him I suspected his deputy, and maybe others, were walking on the wrong side of the law. It was a device we'd developed years earlier, a way to bleed off anxiety and fear by talking about everything but the task at hand.

It started when we were working undercover. We played our silly Abbott and Costello routine for each other, riding to a buy, to a meet, on stakeout, or to serve a warrant. A few guys we'd worked with in the past thought we were nuts, but Harley and I would rather bat each other around than sit in morose silence, thinking about the worst that could happen.

Only a couple of those brother officers chose to work with us with any regularity, and that was fine for us. Our ease and absolute trust with each other tended to put up an invisible fence between ourselves and others that they simply couldn't get through.

We drove on past Howard Petain's ranch. Howard was using the tailgate of his truck as a workbench and waved as we went by. We waved back, and I had an idea. "That time you colored Billy's dog blue, that stuff got under your fingernails and you had a devil of a time trying to get it washed off before someone noticed."

I watched from the corner of my eye as his left hand curled into a loose fist. The fingers of his right curled as well and I laughed out loud. "It *was* you that dyed those goats to mess with Atchley, wasn't it?"

"I ain't saying I did, or I didn't, and I really like the color blue, by the way, but it looks to me like somebody got his goat for sure."

"And you accused *me* of poking the bear."

—

Sheriff Jackson lived off Oak Street in a well-maintained neighborhood that reminded me of Mayberry on the old *Andy Griffith Show*. I used the map on my phone to find it and we pulled to the curb. A well-used ten-year-old Ford pickup was parked in the drive.

Gray clouds scudded across the sky as Harley set his hat and opened the door. "How do we do this?"

"I'm not sure. The guy's been sick, so I don't want to hit him hard with a bunch of accusations. I think we just visit for a while and go from there."

"That means you don't have any idea how to approach this."

"Pretty much, but let me lead." At least Harley was over his mad from the night before, but sometimes he's lacking in subtlety.

I scanned the Craftsman house that looked as comfortable as an old shoe. Two rockers on the left of the front door and a porch swing on the right told me Jackson and his wife enjoyed spending time outside, likely watching neighbors and the world go by. It was a little piece of lost history that many of us would like to see again.

I rapped on the mahogany door under three little staggered windows that descended left to right at eye level. Sheer curtains on the other side kept me from looking in. The sound of a vacuum cleaner told me somebody was home.

After a few moments, a soft female voice came through the door. "Who is it?"

"Stock Agent Tucker Snow, ma'am. My brother's with me. We'd like to speak with Sheriff Jackson on business, if we could."

I imagined her on the other side, thinking. The sheer curtain on the lowest pane disappeared as she peeked through to verify my claim. It fell back into place once she was satisfied. After a couple of moments, the lock clicked and the door swung open to reveal a woman stout enough to whip both me and Harley without breaking a sweat.

She noticed my badge and raised an eyebrow. "Can I help you?"

"Mrs. Jackson?"

Her wide face beamed in a grin. "Naw. I'd've already been a widow a second time if I was married to that ornery old coot. I'm his next-door neighbor, Loretta Gaines. Waylon's not here. He and Estelle went to Dallas for a doctor's appointment. He'll be back, directly, though."

"I heard he was sick."

"More'n sick, but he's tough."

"If he went to Dallas, it'll be late when he gets back." Some of the wind went out of my sails at the news. It was over two and a half hours one way, and that could increase depending on the route they took.

"You never know." She wiped her hands on a damp dishrag hanging over her shoulder, and then rubbed the side of her face with one palm. I noticed she had dimples on her knuckles. "Sometimes they eat dinner before they come home if he's feeling up to snuff. If he ain't, they make a beeline back here so he can go to bed."

I heard Harley step onto the porch. "He's in pretty bad shape, then, huh?"

Her brown eyes flicked past me, and her forehead wrinkled in what I took to be concern. "He is, but he don't want nobody to know it. You a lawman too?"

"No, ma'am, not anymore. Retired, but I train officers now."

He didn't usually volunteer so much, and it spoke volumes about how he felt about the lady.

"Ma'am, do you know if Deputy Lomax called him this morning before they left?"

Her mouth pinched like a church lady at the chief deputy's name. "I wouldn't know about earlier, they were leaving when I came in the back door, but he hasn't called while I've been here."

"We can come back tomorrow." I made to turn, but she stopped me. "Mr. Snow, tomorrow won't be good, neither. That's when his home health care folks come by. By the time they leave, he's usually plumb wore out."

"Cancer?" Harley was always one to cut to the chase.

"Yessir, I guess he wouldn't mind me saying it. Everybody on the street knows, though I doubt many folks are talking about it in public. There's not a day goes by I don't open this door and find a covered dish, or a pie, or a cake that somebody's left." She flicked a finger past us both. "This yard gets mowed every week, but not by the same person. There's always somebody who comes by to do a little something for Waylon, or Estelle."

"And you're over here a lot, I bet."

The dimples in her cheeks deepened in a smile. "I am. Me'n Estelle's been friends since we were kids. They bought this house when Ed was alive, he was my husband. There's a path between this back door'n mine, and we keep it hot, me more these days since she has to stay here with Waylon so much. When they're gone, I come over and pick up a little, you know to help her."

Harley was at my shoulder. "Picking up a little includes vacuuming and doing more than that, I expect." I wondered if he intended to go inside and start sweeping. He'd sure taken a liking to that lady we'd only known for a couple of minutes.

"Times are hard for those two, and I had to live the same life when my Ed got sick and passed. I know how it is, and any little bit around the house helps."

"Well, we won't bother you anymore." I took a manila envelope from inside my jacket and held it out. "Would you please give Sheriff Jackson this envelope?"

She took the thick packet and turned it over to see his name written on the front. "Do I tell him what it is?"

"You can. It's a report I think he should read." I took a step back. "We'll talk to him later. My phone number's in there. I 'magine he'll want to call me when he's finished."

"If it's important, you know you can call that *deputy* of his, if you need something."

The way she said "deputy" spoke volumes. It was as if she was talking about a water moccasin, and I guess that's how I thought of Lomax too. "You don't seem to think much of him."

"I despise the man." Her face hardened, but in a soft, interesting way that I couldn't explain. It was as if a two-year-old was unhappy. "He's always wanted Waylon's job, but he'll never be half the man, or sheriff, as Waylon."

"You know him very well?" There was vintage Harley, pushing in a subtle way.

"Well enough to know Lomax is the kind of man to leave his tools out in the weather. He's only been over here once, and that was the other day to get Waylon to look at some papers. Oh, he calls all the time, but he won't be bothered with visiting."

Harley stepped in a little more than I would have liked. "You know what kind of papers?"

Loretta shook her head. "Just legal papers is all. Folded up. Waylon wasn't feeling good, and he didn't even look at 'em. Signed every one and handed them back without knowing what they were. He ought to know better'n that."

"All right." I stepped back even farther, hoping Harley would take the hint. "We'll leave you to your cleaning. I'll call later and make sure he's home and can take visitors."

"You do that, but don't wait too long, if this is important. I'm afraid he's on the downhill slide and won't see Halloween, let alone Thanksgiving. Lordy, this house'll be dark and dreary come Christmas, and it's always been so full of life. Good to meet y'all."

She was already closing the door as we headed down the stairs. Harley stopped at the truck with his hand on the fender. "Well, this was a water-haul."

"In some ways."

"How's that?"

"I feel better now about Jackson. This whole town thinks a lot of him, so I don't believe he's mixed up in anything. Our problem's with Lomax."

"That's for sure."

Chapter Thirty-Five

Gray clouds hung low when Chief Deputy Lomax slowed his cruiser and steered around the traffic jam that stalled all four lanes of the east/west highway. He flicked on his light bar and pulled onto the shoulder behind a highway patrol vehicle, two ambulances, and an equal number of fire engines also flashing their emergency lights.

Already knowing what he would find after speaking with Deputy Baker by cell phone, he nodded hello to a couple of firemen standing between two emergency vehicles and went on past to another knot of men surrounding a barely recognizable Chevrolet pickup and a completely destroyed Dodge Charger. The roar of machinery filled the air as a team of firefighters used a hydraulic cutter called the "jaws of life" to reach two bloody corpses pinned in the mangled Chevrolet.

He paused to look left along an asphalt county road that bisected the highway lined by hardwoods beginning to change color. On the other side was an elevated railroad crossing that paralleled the four-lane. Following an imaginary line, he visualized the speeding Charger hitting what he considered a ramp where the county road's incline led over the tracks.

In his mind a speeding car launched itself at the apex of the elevated crossing, sailing over the two lanes on that side. As gravity overcame velocity, the flying car speared the silver Chevy truck with the force of a swinging wrecking ball. The impact was so violent it launched both the Charger's driver and his passenger through the sedan's windshield and through a five-strand bob-wire fence with horrifying results.

"Dayum!"

One of the paramedics watching the firemen cut away sheet metal in the pasture caught Lomax's eye as it swept back over the wreck. He exaggerated a glance toward the bodies of a man and woman still belted into the Chevy's bloody seats and the Charger's rear end that had fallen back to rest on top of the couple. He shook his head.

Mentally counting his steps, Lomax walked through the overgrazed grass, past the tangled mess and broken glass, and through the fence someone had cut in order to provide easy access to the two bodies ejected into the pasture. He joined Deputy Baker beside the Charger's still forms and whistled. "This is nearly a hundred feet."

"For *that* part." Baker was writing in his ever-present notepad. He nodded his head to point with the brim of his hat at a small piece of blanket covering a body part. "I'll need a tape to be sure, but I make that arm to be about a hundred and nineteen feet from what's left of their windshield. Those boys were flying low when they hit that railroad track."

Lomax stiffened when he registered a number of smaller pieces of material covering an assortment of lumps. Someone had cut up an old blanket and used the pieces to keep prying eyes away from the results of the horrifying accident strewn across the pasture.

The clouds fractured for a second, admitting a shaft of light that brushed across the accident scene before closing up again. He knelt to lift one edge of a bloodstained sheet covering the nearest body and hesitated when Baker warned him. "Butch! You might not want to look at that one. You know him, or what's left after he went through the fence."

"Who is it?"

"Brock."

"Brock Horner?"

"Yessir." Baker pointed with his pad. "The other one's his buddy Dylan. We should have put 'em in jail last night instead of lettin' 'em go."

"You know we couldn't do that."

"So we turned 'em loose and they made another buy."

"How do you know that?"

Baker cut his eyes back toward the activity around the mangled cars. He reached into his shirt pocket and pulled out a tiny plastic baggie. "This."

"Where'd you get it?"

"From Brock's shirt pocket."

"Anyone see you do it?"

"They saw me looking at him, but I slipped it out without being seen." Baker handed it to Lomax, who examined the crystals inside the bag.

"Pink."

"Yep. I 'spect it's gravel. Color's the same as what we've been finding. Look down by my foot."

Lomax did, and saw a used syringe. "They shot up."

"Yep. Looks to me like they graduated from smoking it to this. Faster high."

The chief deputy stepped on the syringe and ground it into

the grass. "We don't know if they just made a buy, or've had it for a while."

"The Charger belongs to Jack Cruise, or did before they stole it sometime this morning around three. You ever hear of Cruise?"

"Nope."

"Owns a cow-calf operation up near the river. Said he woke up this morning and found it gone, it and a couple of saddles from the barn where he kept the car."

"That means he called a stock agent."

"He did. Robby Taylor sent word he's on the way," he cleared his throat, "even though Snow's back to work. Looks like two agents might be working on this one together."

"Dammit!"

Baker flipped the little pad closed. "Brock and Dylan likely went straight to Atchley's after we turned 'em loose. They were probably hurtin', I bet they spent the next two or three hours smoking that shit until they were so amped up they thought they were invincible. Then they stole a car and went joyriding at daylight, just in time to kill a man and woman driving to work. Damn, those folks didn't deserve this.

"You're gonna have to talk to Jess." Baker lowered his voice, despite the rattle of the rescue equipment. "You and I both know he's the only one selling this formula. This stuff's nasty. One witness said Brock never touched the brake. Said it looked like he was trying to *hit* that car."

"How could anyone know something like that?"

"They had the windows down and the witness said he heard 'em screaming and laughing like a couple of lunatics."

"I'd have been screaming too if I'd been in that car."

"Me too, but the witness says one of them said '*woo hoo!*'" Baker's voice rose in what sounded like excitement on the last two words. "Don't sound like they were scared to me. Butch, I know Jess is kinfolk, but we may need to hammer 'em, and before Sheriff Jackson gets back in the office."

"They're not *making* the stuff." For some reason Lomax felt he had to defend his cousin, even if they weren't close and never had been. "They're just selling a product people want."

Family was family, and Lomax's mama expected him to take care of all their relations, and his position as a law officer dictated this requirement. His granddaddy made whiskey for years before he got too old. There was good money in it, just like there was good money in selling drugs, if you were positioned right.

It was always about money. *Everything* was about money.

Lomax's mama had never lived in anything other than small frame houses only seconds away from falling down. The furnishings were always hand-me-down or items picked up from the curb. When Lomax started bringing home good money from his salary, and even more in cash, their way of life improved exponentially.

Lomax had more money to spend, and he bought his mama a brick house, something she'd always wanted. She didn't ask any questions about how he could afford two homes on a civil employee's salary, but the house and new furniture seemed like gifts from the citizens of their county.

Lomax watched the firefighters work. "We have to be careful. We lean on Jess too hard, he might roll over on us, or that ignern't Belcher'll decide to do something stupid. We can't have that."

"Belcher scares me."

"He should. He's a demon." Lomax watched the paramedics pull one of the bodies from the truck. "He's the only man in this *world* that scares me. Some people make me nervous as a preacher in a whorehouse, but at least I can handle whatever they throw at me."

"Does that mean Tucker Snow too?"

"I can deal with him, but then again that brother of his is a loose cannon. There's something about that guy that tells me we need to worry about him more than Tucker."

"What are we gonna do, then, about all this?"

Deputy Lomax studied the ground at his feet. "I have an idea."

Chapter Thirty-Six

My phone buzzed as Harley and I drove back to the house under cloudy skies. It was Don Wells, the mechanic out of Fort Worth. "Don, what's up?"

"Hey, man, I just wanted to call and give you a little more information I dug up from those files I downloaded from your truck."

"I thought you told us everything." I punched the phone so Harley could hear. "What'd you find?"

"More than I expected. It was kinda fun, digging around to find out about Curtis Bailey. I ran some stuff through a couple of sites I pay for and found out that guy's been in the pen half a dozen times."

I wondered where he was going with that. We had what we needed on the guy who'd stolen my truck, and I wasn't sure any of his amateur sleuthing would get us anywhere. "Guys like that usually are."

"Well, I imagine he met somebody else there in Huntsville that you might be interested in."

"How so?"

"Curtis wasn't the only one to connect up to the truck's entertainment system. Do you know anyone named Frank Cornelison? Is he a friend of yours that might have been in your pickup at any time?"

"Nope. Don't know anyone by that name. It was probably another meth head with him."

"Well, Curtis only popped up because he was the first one to log in, but somewhere along the line Frank Cornelison might have gotten tired of hearing that rock crap Curtis was playing and he punched up some relaxing metal music. Or maybe his phone was dying and plugged into the truck's system to charge it up, but no matter what or how, he was in there."

Now he had my interest. "I bet you dug around a little on Frank Cornelison, huh?"

"Yep. He apparently deals in cash. There weren't any credit card accounts linked to that name, and for the life of me I can't figure out how he pays for that phone and the music he downloads, but he doesn't buy anything through it."

"Probably has an alias account to pay for things like that."

"Could be. I don't know a lot about that kind of stuff, but he was definitely in your truck, so if you get a warrant for Curtis, you can add Frank to it."

"Good to know. Harley and I are going to town right now to a judge's house. We'll get that one drawn up too."

Back in our undercover days, we had a couple of judges who worked on the right side of the law. We could call them at work or at home at any time of day. Judge Elliott Hiragana was our main guy, and we drove to his house more than once when we had enough evidence or probable cause to wake him up and get a warrant for some bad guy we intended to take down.

I felt we had enough on Curtis to meet Judge Hiragana at

his office and get both a search and arrest warrant. If what Don was telling me about Frank Cornelison proved to be right, we'd gather him up too.

Harley leaned in. "Don, this is Harley. Can you send that info to me in an email? For Bailey and Cornelison both? We're gonna need it to show the judge."

"What's your email address?"

Harley told him, and his phone beeped a couple of seconds later to let him know the email was through. "I got it. Thank you, sir." He sat back to read what Don sent, essentially checking out of the conversation.

"You bet. Tuck, you let me know if you need anything else."

"I will. Maybe you better keep digging around for a little while longer. We might have more info on other guys too."

"I think it's just the two, but one thing I found out, Cornelison is connected to a neo-Nazi group called the Farm Boys."

Harley and I exchanged glances.

"He has several aliases that I found when I dug around in some arrest records. They've called him Michael Day, Daniel Day, I guess he thinks he might be an actor sometimes, Charles Savins, Bill Carleton, but my personal favorite is his nickname, Spyder." He spelled it. "I kinda like that one myself."

We pulled into town. "Thanks, my friend."

"You bet."

He hung up and Harley turned his phone so I could see the screen, and a mugshot of Spyder. It was part of a wanted poster spread, and two of the six people in the photo were familiar.

"We shot those guys."

"Yep. Too bad Spyder wasn't with them."

Chapter Thirty-Seven

A cold breeze blew over the broad Red River fifteen feet below where Deputy Butch Lomax and Jess Atchley met under gray skies hanging low over the steep southern bank on the Texas side. Nothing but a wide sandy beach lined by thick hardwoods defined the Oklahoma side of the wide oxbow.

Up and down the river, sweeps of sugar-sand bars framed the muddy water, making the landscape a living, yet abstract painting. A raft of mallards followed the waterway, only feet above the surface. Their wings sounded like tiny jet planes.

Their trucks were parked nose to nose on the two-track pasture road paralleling the muddy river. The twin tracks drifted eastward away from the river through drifts of sand, disappearing into thick timber.

Judge Lee Dawson often let his colleagues and law enforcement officers hunt or fish the five-thousand-acre ranch whenever they wanted. Completely off the grid and so far away from microwave towers that cell phones couldn't acquire a signal, the sprawling ranch was also used for a variety of clandestine meetings or the occasional tryst.

Huddled deep in their heavy coats, the cousins squared off beside their trucks, positioning themselves to see behind the other so both ends of the two-track were covered. Lomax looked over Atchley's shoulder at the upward slope leading to the hidden highway half a mile away and pointed a finger at Jess Atchley's chest.

"Call off your dog, now."

Atchley turned to see what he was looking at, and the only thing he found were buzzards hanging low under the clouds. The drug dealer leaned against the fender of his pickup and lit a cigarette with enough nonchalance to fire up the chief deputy's anger. "You know I can't do that. Once he gets on the trail, that man's a bulldog. I can tell him to stop, but I can guarantee he'll keep on until that stupid stock inspector's cold."

"This ain't how it's supposed to happen. The whole thing's spinning out of control, and we're about to get our asses handed to us."

"What makes you think that?"

"Snow and his brother came in last night to collect those two women. Snow says he intends to tell the sheriff everything he knows today, and that'll tear our playhouse down. He called his supervisor at the cattle association and told him he was coming off leave. He's the official cattle agent for this region now, and that puts him right up our asses."

Atchley took a deep drag on the cigarette and watched one of the buzzards bleeding off altitude, likely to investigate something in the tall grass. Blowing smoke through both nostrils, he nodded as if committing those words to memory. "I have an idea."

"I don't need any more of your bright ideas. That's what got us into this in the first place. You were supposed to sell that shit and keep your head down until after Sheriff Jackson's looking at the inside of his casket, and that won't be long, neither, because if the cancer don't kill him, the chemo will."

"But not fast enough. You said Snow's going to see him today?"

"That's what he said, and I believe him. The only thing on our side right now is that Jackson has doctor appointments in Dallas, and he's not gonna be home until this afternoon. That still don't give us much time, though."

"Then it gives us time to plow Snow under."

"I don't need to kill a stock inspector right now with all this attention on him and us. That's why I'm a-tellin' you to call off your *dog*."

"It ain't that stock inspector I'm thinking about. Let's send that dog somewhere else."

"Like where?"

"To help Sheriff Jackson along." Atchley liked being one step ahead of his cousin for once. "Belcher can push him on over to the other side, and then you can have the killer dead to rights."

"I don't get it." Lomax frowned, unsure where Atchley was going. "What do you have in mind?"

"Here's my idea. How about I get a little of that gravel in Belcher to fire him up? I'll get him high and drive him over to Jackson's house and turn him loose. Tell him to kill everyone inside, and you get the call from an anonymous number telling you there's screaming and yelling and a murder going on there." He reached into his jacket pocket and produced a drop phone and held it in his palm as an unnecessary visual aid. "Then you drive up, find Belcher killing everyone and shoot the son of a bitch. You get your wish, he's out of the way and off Snow's trail, and Jackson's office will be vacant. You step in, finish his term, and when election time comes around, you're a shoo-in because you killed the guy who murdered the sheriff."

Lomax's suspicion was evident in his face. "I thought Belcher was your friend."

"He is, but he's getting sloppy, and we can't have that. I know another old boy out of Tyler who's just as mean and probably more reliable. Belcher's been around too long and knows too much about this whole operation, anyway."

Atchley didn't bother to tell Lomax that he woke up early that morning and saw Belcher slipping out of his bedroom where Priscilla was supposed to be asleep. Atchley had suspected Belcher was knocking off a piece whenever he wasn't around.

It started with looks between Belcher and Priscilla that lasted way too long, and every now and then Atchley smelled smoke when he went to bed. Priscilla smoked, but she didn't exude nicotine from her pores like Belcher. One night a week earlier he smelled it on the sheets and his own pillowcase.

Belcher had been in his bed, and his wife, and Atchley couldn't stand for anyone else to sleep in his room. It was time to get a new dog.

"This new guy don't do drugs, neither, 'less you count beer. I swear, that boy can drink a case and all he does is pee."

Lomax studied his feet, thinking. "Who figured this plan out?"

"Why, it was me."

"No it wasn't. You barely have sense enough to wipe your own ass."

"Hey! There's no call for that. You and me're kin."

"That's the *only* reason you're standing there and breathing my air. This is all your fault. We had a deal with the right suppliers that I vetted and have something on to keep 'em in line. They won't get sideways with us because I have 'em by the short hairs. It's all a delicate balance that you've screwed up by peddling shit out of Pushmataha County, which is a stupid-ass move, if you ask me. Those people up there are crazy as Bessie bugs."

In the late 1800s, the rocky, mountainous landscape was a refuge for outlaws, horse thieves, murderers, and anyone trying to exceed the grasp of the law. Now the Choctaw county in Southeast Oklahoma was known for the timber industry wielded primarily by the enormous Weyerhaeuser Land and Timber Company. Farming, ranching, and a rough way of life rivaling the post–Civil War era produced families who trusted only their own.

The Kiamichi region of the state listed fewer than 12,000 people calling the county their residence, and in that sparse population there were still pockets of untouched land, settlements of old-time people, abandoned and near-defunct farms, and a landscape perfect for meth cookers and dealers.

Atchley scowled and dropped the butt onto the ground. "We make more money off gravel, though."

"Money is one thing, but that shit's poison, and it's you spreading it around. It won't be long before the feds show up, and that's a battle I don't want. Two dumbasses are dead today because of it, not counting them I'm not hearing about. There's no telling how far this stuff travels once you sell it. You need to quit spreading that shit around."

"We get it cheap, and the markup is ten times what we're moving on the other product." Atchley lit another cigarette and inhaled, letting the smoke out through his nose. He felt good. Smoking slow and taking his time in answering, he was in charge for once. "You're seeing it in your envelope every week. I just don't mark the damned bills so you'll know which is our usual product and what we're making from the gravel."

"That don't cut no ice right now. The news is getting wind

of it, and that kind of exposure is bad for us all. I want this stopped now."

Atchley cut his eyes toward the river as if expecting to see landing craft disgorging a division of DEA agents.

Lomax wasn't finished. He wanted to have his say. "I'm afraid that shit's gonna get to someone's high-class kid who dies and a hotshot detective gets on the case. It's dangerous stuff that acts different in everybody who smokes it. They'll start working backward, and before you know it, they'll be sniffing around here. I can cover up Horner and Kehoe…"

"Brock Horner and Dylan Kehoe?"

"Who else would it be? You didn't know about them?"

"No." Atchley felt a chill run up his spine. "Saw 'em last night. They weren't bad kids."

"Don't matter none, now. They're dead, and it's because of you. They were flying high on gravel when they bought it."

"That's why you need to be in Jackson's office. We won't have to worry as much."

"But I'm not the sheriff *yet*." A gust of wind came down the river and spilled over the bank like an ocean breaker, picking up loose, dry sand from the two-track and carrying it into the trees where it hissed against the remaining leaves. Turning their backs to the wind, they ducked down into their coats. "And we'll still have to be careful. Judge Dawson ain't stupid, nor any others on the city council or the commissioner's court…"

"'cept for Councilman Smallwood." Atchley chuckled. "He comes by ever' now and then for a taste. Got to liking that coke, and then when he found crank, whoo weee. Now that guy's a *good* customer."

"All right." Lomax licked his lips, and Atchley could tell he liked the idea of having a councilman in their pocket. "I kinda like your idea that I don't think you thought up. Send your dog over to Jackson's house and let's get this over with."

"You want him hyped up on gravel? That'll be an easy explanation."

Lomax's mouth tightened into a thin line. "What did I just tell you about that stuff? God*damn*, you're a dumbass. Focus for a minute, will ya? Just send him over there and give me a call when he gets to the sheriff's house. It's simple. Don't make it complicated."

Atchley toed the sand, red from embarrassment. "I have to tell you."

"What?"

"You're right. I didn't come up with that idea on my own. Belcher came up with it to get rid of Jackson, before he got sick. We were going to pay the Farm Boys to take Waylon Jackson out and then let you know the play. You'd come in, kill them, and there you'd be, large and in charge."

"Don't do nothing without telling me first. And I don't want to get mixed up any more with those Farm Boys than we already are. Those stupid sonsabitches need to be chained to the porch. Keep them out of our business."

"Fine then. You ready to be sheriff come tomorrow?"

"If things work out."

Chapter Thirty-Eight

Belcher lit another cigarette and adjusted the pillow behind his head, unconcerned about the white cloud rising to the bedroom ceiling. Everyone in the trailer smoked, so having a toonie beside Priscilla shouldn't be a problem, especially since she lit one too.

He exhaled and rested one hand on her bare thigh in the dingy room lit by a single sixty-watt bulb and wondered when she'd last shaved her legs. The only decorations on the walls were a cowboy-themed calendar and a framed print of a marijuana leaf. "I'm not sure, but I'm starting to think Jess might suspect something about us."

She cut her eyes at him before they returned to the stained ceiling. "He don't know a thing."

"You think that, but he's smarter than folks give him credit for."

"So what?"

"Well, it's no skin off my nose, but that'll tear y'all's playhouse down here."

"I was looking for a place to live before I moved in with him."

He took a deep drag. "That brings me to something I've been thinking about."

She moved her leg closer, encouraging him to go on.

"Well, anyway, I'm thinking about going to Dallas, thought you might come with me."

She barked a laugh that became a cough. "What'd I want to do that for?"

"Things are starting to get a little hot around here, and I'm not interested in carrying Jess's water for him anymore. He's getting careless, and that gravel we're selling is gonna get us in trouble."

"*You're* smoking it."

"Sometimes, but I can quit whenever I want." Just the mention of the drug lit a fire inside him that felt like magnetic waves pulling toward the pipe on the scarred nightstand beside her. She glanced at it, and he realized she was just as hooked as he was.

"Neither one of us can quit."

"People do."

"They try, but I only know one person who stopped without going into one of them centers. None of us can afford that. Hell, we can barely afford to feed ourselves."

Belcher wouldn't look at her, knowing that a Spic and Span box full of cash was Atchley's bank. Neither of them worried that she'd find it in there because she seldom ever cleaned anything, and even if she did look under there, a fresh, new open box sat in front.

The cigarette bobbed in his lips as he adjusted Atchley's pillow behind his head. "Let's run off. I know some people there, a couple of Farm Boys who live over in Urbandale."

"That's a Mexican neighborhood now."

"Not all of it. There's a little pocket of white folks still there, and nobody messes with them. We can set up shop there and work the whole east side all the way to Mesquite."

His comment piqued her interest. "I used to live in Mesquite."

"Well, there you go. Me and you and Jimma can move there and get out of this county."

"You get caught there, you won't have Lomax or anybody else to cover for you."

"Don't need 'em. I'm the toughest son of a bitch around here, and you know it."

She grinned and patted his chest. "You're right about that."

"Good. Then we can go?"

"Yeah, but I'm not taking Jimma with us. She's nearly old enough to take care of herself. I left home when I was her age. I've been thinking about taking her to Mama's and letting her live there until she graduates."

The idea both appealed to Belcher and disappointed him. He knew Jess had been slipping into Jimma's room in the middle of the night, and he'd fantasized about the same thing himself. Now Priscilla was ruining half of his plan.

He shook another Camel from the pack on the nightstand and lit it from the butt. Dropping it into the ashtray beside a Makarov handgun, he checked his watch to be sure they still had time before Jess returned. "Let's do it, then."

"Might have to. I can't find anyone to hire me."

Belcher looked at her face that was once full and attractive in a homely sort of way. He met her when she was eating the stuff and still had a fresh look about her. But when she graduated to smoking meth, the drug took its toll, and now her features were harsh and more sharply defined.

She was missing a tooth, and the rest of her teeth were changing color. When he was rubbing her arms earlier, he'd noticed more bumps than usual, and a couple of new lesions, as well as one on the side of her face. Makeup covered them when she was working, but she hadn't used any for the past few months.

He hoped she wouldn't take the needle. Once an addict started injecting meth, their days were numbered. He'd also been watching his customers and had a sneaking suspicion that it wasn't the gravel they were selling that was killing people, but the way they were taking it. Eating, sniffing, and smoking gravel was fine, but in his opinion, injecting the stuff was the trigger to the users' violent behavior.

"They don't hire people like you and me. That's why we have to go and make it on our own." He felt his reasons were getting to her and pressed home. "You know I can make money on my own. It'll be you and me, and without Jimma to worry about, we can be footloose and fancy free."

"You want to be Bonnie and Clyde, huh?"

"Naw, they were stupid. Kept coming back to the same places and then got themselves killed. We're smarter than that. We can live a better life there than here."

She crushed out her cigarette and rolled over toward him. "Okay. Let's do it. When do you want to go?"

"Soon. When the time is right, I'll go back to my place and get a few things." He squatted in a falling-down shack out on a county road not far away that belonged to some guy up in Wisconsin. The guy paid the taxes each year but never came down. People living around that hundred acres assumed Belcher was renting the place and left him alone.

"I'll be ready when you are."

"Fine then. I have a couple of things to do between now and then, and then we'll go. I gotta run to town here in a few minutes, and when I get back, I'll have a surprise for you."

Her face lit up in a girlish grin. "I love surprises. Flowers?"

"It wouldn't be a surprise if I told you."

They heard a car turn into the drive, and thinking it was

Atchley, Belcher bolted from the bed. Priscilla wrapped herself in a ratty old bathrobe and stepped into the bathroom, closing the door behind her. Buttoning his jeans, he heard the shower come on. Slipping into his faded blue shirt, he picked up the pistol and padded barefoot into the hall. The blinds were half open and he peered through the window overlooking the warped porch.

It was only a customer. Sighing in relief, he stuck the pistol into the small of his back and stepped into a pair of rubber mud boots beside the door, ready to make another sale.

Chapter Thirty-Nine

In jeans and a gray lightweight sweatshirt, Chloe watched from the living room window, waiting for Jimma to arrive. Kevin padded into the room and nuzzled her leg. Uncle Harley brought him over that morning, saying the yellow Lab needed to stay there whenever she was alone. Though he was a sweet dog, he had a tendency to protect the kids by growling and showing his teeth whenever he didn't like a stranger who wandered too close.

She was there alone only after a long discussion with her dad, who was reluctant to leave her at the house after all that had happened. Digging in her heels, she insisted that she was old enough to stay there on her own, especially under the protection of the cameras and new security system. He left only when she agreed to set the alarm after he was gone.

The house electronically secure, she unlocked the front door and sighed in frustration. They were in the country, for crying out loud, and should be able to leave their doors open. But the events of the past few days made her mind up for her. Kevin being there was proof of that.

She turned off the security system and unlocked the door when Jimma appeared, walking down the road in nothing but jeans and a T-shirt, as if there was a sidewalk instead of mowed grass and weeds. Chloe watched her come, and though she seemed to be taking her time, there was an air of tension about the girl. Shoulders hunched and arms folded under her breasts, she looked cold and already beaten down by life.

A flash of blue caught Chloe's attention, flickering through the cedars growing through the fence paralleling the road. She realized the two fainting goats were pacing the girl, but they were *blue*.

Odd. She knew those funny little goats fainted at loud sounds, but there was no mention of them changing *color*. Maybe it was something Jimma did, some quirk she had. She thought back. Maybe Jimma had a different side Chloe hadn't noticed. Had Jimma indicated that she had artistic inclinations that would lend itself to quirks such as dyeing fainting goats? Artsy people were strange, so maybe she'd dyed their coats in some way.

Jimma's demeanor changed as she neared Chloe's drive. She broke into a trot as she entered the yard and ducked in, quick as a flash, to step behind a thick cedar growing beside the corner post. Strange. She pushed into the soft, green branches and froze like a frightened quail.

Seconds later, a silver sedan drove by, heading in the direction of Jimma's trailer. It passed slowly, as if the driver was studying the house, and then sped up. Chloe watched the car roll over the bridge, then turn into Atchley's drive.

Once it was past, Jimma darted out from behind the cedar and ran to the porch. She was up the steps in a flash and before she could knock, Chloe opened the door and the youngster slipped inside.

"What was that all about?"

Pasty white, Jimma was breathing hard when the door closed behind her. "Close it, quick."

"What's the matter?"

"That was one of Belcher's skinhead friends. Do you think he saw me?"

Kevin pushed up against her leg, hoping for a rub. Jimma absently dropped her hand to pat the big dog's head as Chloe engaged the security system.

"I don't know. What if he did?"

Jimma suddenly shook like a leaf. "I don't want him to know I'm here. That guy might tell Belcher he saw me on the way over. He's there with Mama right now."

As if someone was peeking through the window, Chloe pulled Jimma deeper into the living room. "What's up? What's the matter?"

Swallowing, Jimma looked around the room. "Is anybody else here?"

"Nope. Just us. Dad and Uncle Harley left a little while ago."

"Can you drive? Is there something we can drive out of here?"

"Well, yeah, but I'd have to ask Dad if we can take the Expedition." Though she only had her beginner's license, her dad allowed Chloe to drive the country roads from time to time to gain experience. She was more than capable of driving anywhere she wanted, but that was only with his permission.

She made a quick decision. "Sure. Where do we need to go?"

Jimma put her mouth close to Chloe's ear. "Your aunt's house. Would anybody know we'd go there?"

Chloe drew back and frowned, not understanding. She whispered. "Who would know where we were?"

"Atchley. I don't want him or Belcher to know…" She threw a look at the front window.

"What?" Chloe followed her look.

"Uh, look, I have something to tell you." Her face twisted as she girl held back a sob. "I did something bad."

"It couldn't be too bad. What was it?"

Instead of answering, Jimma raised a finger and pointed at the front window. "I did that. I had to."

Chloe glanced at the window but saw nothing but the new curtains and beyond that, the front yard and the gravel road. "I don't get it."

"That!" Jimma whispered and pointed again, with emphasis. Kevin heard the tone of her voice and lowered his head.

Again, Chloe examined the window and finally saw a small round suction cup on the outside of the glass. "What's that?"

"A little speaker," Jimma whispered.

"I don't get it."

"A listening device."

Understanding dawned. "You bugged our *house*? How? When?"

"A couple of days ago. Atchley made me do it." Her voice caught and she swallowed. "They've been watching you."

Unable to think of anything thing else to ask, Chloe searched for a logical question. "Why?"

"They think y'all are spying on them."

They kept their voices low. "For what?"

"For what they're doing over there."

"What is it?"

"Selling drugs. Crank mostly. That's how Atchley makes his money. He also sells cocaine for those who need it to come down from the gravel, but it's a river of meth hell over there." Words flowed like water through a broken dam. "He says he runs a backhoe business, but he hasn't cranked it up in months. Him and Belcher have most of the drug business here in this county. You have to have seen all the cars coming in and out."

"I've seen them, and so has Dad, but he hasn't said anything to me."

"That's not all." Her voice broke again, and she took a deep breath before continuing. "Mama and Atchley aren't really married. They've been living together for a couple of years..."

"That means they're married. It's called common law."

"Whatever." Jimma waved a hand as if to shoo away a fly. "He does things to her. He beats her whenever he wants, and he uses her like a whore."

"Why don't y'all leave?"

"And go where? He'll just come and get her like the last time she tried that, and it took her a month to heal up."

Chloe shrugged. "Go to the police."

Jimma's response was a harsh bark. "Hah. Half the sheriff's department is kin to Atchley. All he'd do is beat me, when they told him what I said..." She dissolved into tears. "That's not all."

Chloe's stomach dropped. She instinctively knew what was coming next. "You don't have to tell me."

"I have to say it."

Face impassive, Chloe crossed her arms and waited, prepared to hear whatever Jimma had to tell her.

"Atchley comes into my room sometimes, when Mama's at work or asleep. It's always late and he does whatever he wants, and I can't do anything about it."

"Tell the counselor when we get back to school. They'll know what to do. Dad says when someone tells them what's happening, like this, the law says they have to get the police involved."

"Then CPS will take me away."

"That has to be better than letting Atchley touch you."

"He's bad enough." Jimma shivered and sobbed harder. "But Belcher's been looking at me like he looks at Mama, and he'll come into my room next."

"He's doing your mama too?"

"I told you I was living in hell."

Making up her mind, Chloe plucked the Expedition's keys off the hanger beside the door. "Let's go."

"Where?"

Chloe pointed at the listening device on the window. "They probably heard all this since Belcher is there, or recorded it. We have to get out of here now, and I have just the place to go."

Chloe disarmed the alarm and opened the door. Jimma went first with Kevin on her heels, but Chloe held out a hand when the Lab started to follow. "Kevin, you're not going with us."

She closed and locked the door behind her, and used two fingernails to pry the bug off the window. Dropping it onto the porch, she crushed it with the heel of her boot and rushed down the stairs.

Slipping behind the wheel, she started the engine as Jimma yanked the passenger door open and dropped into the seat. "Hurry."

Chapter Forty

Atchley's burner phone rang, and he took his eyes off the dirt county road to see who was calling. Recognizing the number, he absently pushed at the greasy hair on his forehead and turned the radio down. "Hello."

"It's me."

"I know who it is. I saw the number. What's up?"

"We have big trouble."

"Now what?"

"I'm at the trailer and turned on the bug at that house. Jimma's over there whispering most of the time and talking to Snow's daughter and some guy named Kevin. Jimma's spilling her guts to that kid about the business and everything else that goes on in here. She told her we bugged the house too. We have to do something."

Atchley's stomach dropped. "They still there?"

"Yep. Chattering like magpies."

"Did you hear if they called anybody?"

"Nope. I just tuned in online and they haven't called yet."

Shoving the accelerator to the floor, Atchley sped up on the long straightaway, throwing a huge cloud of dust behind his truck. "Get over there."

"And do what?"

The pickup bottomed out on a low spot and then bounced hard enough for Atchley's head to hit the padded roof. "Get Jimma out of there."

"How? She ain't my kid."

"Dammit! Just do something. I'll be there in a minute."

"They're leaving! Said that girl's driving."

"Hurry and get out there. Don't let 'em get past you."

Chapter Forty-One

Inexperienced with backing up the big SUV, Chloe adjusted the rearview and side mirrors. Shifting into reverse, she took care to avoid a utility pole and the support post of a parking overhang attached to the barn a few yards away.

Absently flicking on her indicator, she used both hands to turn the wheel. A small pickup came rapidly into view from the north. Chloe accelerated with care and pulled through the damaged gate, taking her foot off the gas and wondering if she should try to pull the two pieces together and chain them closed, though it hadn't done much good when the Dodge was stolen.

"That's Atchley's truck!" Jimma pointed. "We have to get out of here!"

The pickup was closing in from their left, looking like a rocket blowing dust exhaust.

Terrified, Chloe hit the gas. Gravel shot from under the SUV's back tires as the sudden acceleration launched the big Expedition in front of the oncoming truck.

Turning sharp, she fishtailed on the loose gravel and fought the wheel to straighten back up. Jimma screamed, and Chloe thought it was because of her driving, but then she saw Belcher's Ford Focus streaking toward them from the other direction.

They were over the culvert bridge, but Belcher's car had them blocked. The steep ditch on both sides provided no way to get around him. Chloe hit the brakes, skidding. A cloud of dust engulfed the SUV.

What would Dad do? Trying to think like her old man, she shoved the transmission into reverse and hit the gas as Atchley's truck slewed sideways behind her to block the road. *Attack with what he had at hand.*

With no other options, she attempted to ram the little pickup, but inexperience worked against her. Unfamiliar with backing up vehicles other than at a slow creep, she turned the wheel more than necessary. The rear end suddenly dropped out from under them, and she was in the ditch with the tires spinning. It was a replay of the night before.

Chloe snatched her phone from her back pocket and hit the home button with her thumb. Swiping once, she found the number at the top and punched it. The phone rang on the other end, and a familiar voice answered. "What's up, sugar babe?"

"Dad!"

The driver's window exploded inward, showering her with glass. She screamed as the same thing happened on the passenger side and a hand reached in to drag Jimma through the opening by her hair.

"Chloe! What's wrong?"

"Atchley!"

A hard, open-handed blow knocked the phone from her hand, and the fist that followed took the fight out of her.

Chapter Forty-Two

Judge Elliot Hiragana was in his mahogany-paneled chambers when we arrived. We'd worked with him for years, and he supported our undercover efforts one hundred percent. No matter the time or day, all Harley and I had to do was give him a call, and he'd sign whatever warrant we needed.

We kept in close touch with him after we left the DPS, and as a stock agent, I still called him with hot warrants, though our visits were further and further apart.

He'd been expecting us and glanced up from his desk when we came through the door.

"Tucker Snow! You're a lot more clean-cut than in the old days." He stood when he saw who was behind me. "Harley, how the hell are you? It's good to see you again."

They shook. "I'm fine, Judge."

"I thought you'd retired."

"I did, but Tuck needed some help on a little situation, and I'm just his man."

"What's up?"

I handed him the warrants for Curtis Bailey and Frank

Cornelison, a.k.a. Spyder. A third warrant was for Jess Atchley. He perched a pair of readers on his nose and scanned the papers. I told him what we'd been working on, and he listened with one ear.

"This all sounds pretty personal, Tuck. A good lawyer could stretch it six ways to Sunday and say it's all a vendetta."

"As an agent for the Cattle Raisers Association, I can investigate rural theft, and that means my own property too."

Harley took out his phone. "I have surveillance photos of cars coming in to make buys."

"Do you have photos of exchange?"

"No." For a moment Harley looked deflated.

Judge Hiragana pursed his lips. "You guys are doing this without any kind of umbrella?"

I knew that question was coming. "We have to. This is one of those inbred counties where the law covers for kinfolk." I told him about the break-in, the incendiary device, and my stolen truck. I followed it up with the Kroger shoot-out, the incident with Tammy and Chloe going to jail, and what we suspected.

The judge listened without comment, his eyes flicking back and forth between me and Harley, who nodded from time to time whenever Hiragana's expression started to show disbelief. When I was finished, he leaned back in his chair. "That's the damndest thing I've ever heard, and all in the space of a few days. Only you two could get into something like this, and right off your front porch."

"Well, there's more. There's a new formula for meth that's about the nastiest stuff I've ever seen. Drives some people crazy, but it's the same old drug for everyone else. It causes people to go insane and they kill people while they're on it, or they kill themselves. The street name is gravel, and I have a sneaking suspicion that it's coming through the house across the road from mine."

"I'll sign this for surveillance, and expect y'all to get me more evidence." Hiragana adjusted his reading glasses. "Do it within the next couple of days, and you can pick these guys up."

I felt Harley behind me, shifting from one foot to the other. From the corner of my eye, I saw him examining the polished bookshelves along the wall to our left. They were filled with law books, which I knew he wasn't interested in, but the shelves were also loaded with personal mementos reaching back to the Second World War.

There were also golf trophies, golf balls encased in clear Lucite, and a signed club I'd noticed resting on the narrow space between the books and the shelf's edge. A history buff and strangely enough, a golfer, Harley was in his element.

Hiragana picked up a pen. "Harley, you can pick those up if you want. There's a club up there signed by Bob Hope."

"I will the next time we're in."

The judge studied him over the top of his reading glasses. "You're kinda operating on the edges with a retirement badge, aren't you?"

"I am. We've always skirted off the edge between the spirit and the letter of the law, but we've never crossed the line."

"We can make it clear this time."

He raised an eyebrow at the judge. "How's that?"

"I can swear you back in for this job."

That was a new one for me. "You can do that?"

He grinned. "I'm a sitting judge. I can do just about anything I want, within the confines of the law. Harley doesn't need to be working without a net. Raise your right hand, Harley."

He did, and Judge Hiragana swore him in, using language so vague I had trouble keeping up with him. "What did that all mean?"

"He's a special investigator for this office. He can now legally work with you."

"We might have to go into Oklahoma. *My* jurisdiction covers that county, but I don't think you can give him that kind of jurisdiction for another state."

Holding up one hand, he picked up a desk phone and dialed. "What county?"

"Well, we don't know. It might be anywhere from north of Durant all the way to the Arkansas border. It's just too early to tell."

"What Oklahoma counties are in your region?"

"Choctaw, McCurtain, and Pushmataha."

He wrote them down on a pad. "What other Texas regions are those up there?"

"Three and five."

A tinny voice answered on the other end, but it was too soft for me to make out. I caught Harley from the corner of my eye, in a golfing stance and swinging a putter. "Good Lord."

The judge smiled and spoke into the receiver. "This is Judge Hiragana in Red River County. I need to speak to Judge Buckmaster." He waved a hand toward a chair beside me. "Sit down, Tuck. You need to learn how to relax like Harley."

I settled onto the seat. "He's about as far from relaxed as he can get."

"He don't look it."

"That's Harley."

He returned to his call. "Larry. How the hell are you? I need to ask a favor. I have a couple of guys in here asking me for warrants that might cross over into your jurisdiction. If it's all right, I'll have my secretary email them to you for your signature."

Hiragana listened for a moment. "It's meth. But here's the

kicker, one of these guys working with my stock agent is a retired DPS undercover agent. I've sworn him in to work on this case, but he might need the same from you so he can work with his brother."

I heard one word. *Brother*, with a question mark at the end.

"That's right. They're the only brothers to ever work undercover together here in the state, and they're back together again. The agent is Tucker Snow, and his brother is Harley." He listened and nodded. "Putting you on speaker."

He punched a button. "Harley, identify yourself."

"Harley Snow."

A deep voice came through the speaker, and Judge Buckmaster swore Harley in over the phone. When my little brother said, "I do," Buckmaster chuckled. "I don't believe I've ever done this before. Y'all come by the office here before you move on these people. I need a signature in person from Harley."

I answered for the both of us. "Will do."

"All right, Larry." Judge Hiragana plucked the glasses from his nose and pitched them onto the desk. "Gotta go. I owe you one."

"You sure do."

They hung up at the same time my phone rang. Chloe's name came up on the screen and I took the call. "What's up, sugar babe?"

Her scream froze my blood. "Dad!"

Harley stopped putting and Judge Hiragana leaned forward. A soft explosion came from the phone, followed by a single word. "Atchley!"

The phone went as silent as the office.

Harley snatched the phone from his back pocket and punched it alive. He swiped the screen a couple of times and stared it. "I see photos of that little gal Jimma walking out onto the road. A car coming out quick…looks like five minutes later. Hang on." He used a forefinger to swipe again. "Shots down the road of Atchley's truck and this sedan pinning your Expedition in. The images are fuzzy, so far away, but it looks like they took Chloe and that girl."

My mind calmed and went into reaction mode. Though I didn't want to, I had to call the sheriff's department in Ganther Bluff. Dispatch answered. "911. What is your emergency?"

"Listen. This is Special Agent Tucker Snow." I gave the male operator my address. "My daughter Chloe has just been kidnapped by Jess Atchley and another unknown person from in front of my house. Atchley is driving a blue pickup I imagine that's registered to him."

Harley read info off his screen, giving me the license place of the sedan. I repeated it to the operator. "That's the other vehicle that was involved. A white sedan. Took her on the road in front of my house. Send a unit now, and I'll be there as soon as I can."

Harley left the putter leaning against the bookshelves. "Judge, we're gonna need an open warrant for Atchley and persons unknown…"

"On it."

We hit the door a second later.

Chapter Forty-Three

The ever-present cigarette hanging from his lips, Belcher dragged Jimma from the Expedition by the hair. She screamed and fought, but was no match for a grown man. The girl clawed at his face with one hand, leaving three long scratches down one cheek that he hardly felt.

He backhanded her and Jimma dropped to the ground, weeping. Belcher yanked the sobbing girl upright and caught sight of Atchley's fist rising and falling. The Snow girl's screaming stopped as if a switch was thrown. Her eyes rolled back in her head until only the whites were visible.

"Don't you move." Belcher jammed a finger at Jimma. "What do you want me to do with her?"

Atchley dragged the limp girl toward his truck. "Bring her over here! Quick, before somebody comes."

Jimma weighed no more than a Labrador retriever. Belcher threw her over his shoulder and rounded the Expedition and saw Atchley dump the other girl into the back of his truck. He threw a look back at the Snow house. "Jess, that guy's still in there."

"Then we have to hurry."

He threw Jimma in after. She landed hard, head bouncing off the metal bed. Still fighting, she somehow managed to get onto all fours. When her face rose of the side of the truck, Belcher hit her in the nose as hard as he could. She went down like a poleaxed steer.

Atchley ran to his driver's door. "I'm going up to the house. You pull yours to the side of the road so cars can get by and bring theirs up around to the back."

"What do we do about that Kevin guy?"

"Probably a kid from school. I'm not worried about him. He's probably got his nose stuck in a phone like all the others."

Belcher sprinted for the SUV as Atchley's truck squeezed by. He stepped on the gas to pull into his drive and behind the cedars. Belcher moved his car off to the side in order to clear the road. That done, he jumped behind the Expedition's wheel and teased it out of the ditch. He drove up to Atchley's trailer and killed the engine.

Lighting a fresh cigarette from the butt between his lips, he raced back down the drive and checked the road. Finding it clear, he jogged back to his sedan and parked up beside Atchley's truck.

By that time Atchley finished tying the girls' hands behind them and sealed their mouths closed with strips of duct tape he kept under his seat. Belcher blew smoke from his nostrils and tried not to show that the sight of Jimma all tied up turned him on.

Belcher shrugged. "You want me to drive back over there and burn the house down with him in it?"

"No." Atchley stopped. "Someone'll see the smoke and call the fire department. We need as much time as possible to clean this up."

"What're we gonna do?"

"Plans have changed. These two little split-tails screwed everything up."

Belcher studied the scene, feeling strangely pleased. "Well, ain't this something?"

Atchley paced beside the truck, breathing hard. "All right. Let's see. We have to do something."

"No shit."

"Hey, I have to think this through."

"Then what?"

"I'm thinking! I think this one called somebody, and it might have gone through. Where's her phone?"

Belcher patted his pockets as if he'd picked it up. "I don't know."

"Well, she probably dropped it in the car."

Dragging deep on his cigarette, Belcher looked around. "So?"

"Go *look*!"

"Why?"

"I need to see who she called."

Irritated that Atchley was ordering him around as if he worked for the man, Belcher took his time opening the SUV's door. Glass rattled inside, and more fell onto the ground. The seat was covered in safety glass, but that was all. He checked the floorboard and looked under the seat.

Nothing. Time was running out, and here he was wasting what they had left looking for that kid's phone.

The two blue goats wandered up to watch as he searched between the seat and console. When he couldn't find it there, he leaned in under the wheel and put his forehead against the hump. Atchley shouted at him. "Hurry up, dammit!"

The phone was caught in the narrow space between the seat frame and the console. He held it up like a trophy. "Found it."

He pitched it to Atchley, who thumbed the home button. "The damned screen's locked. I'll make her unlock it when she wakes up."

Neither of them had considered the safety feature. He watched Atchley stick the phone in his back pocket and disappear into the trailer.

Belcher glanced into the truck bed. A tattered blue tarp covered the girls, held down on the edges with cinder blocks and an old tire. Atchley came out with a worn sports bag.

Lighting another cigarette with the butt of its predecessor, Belcher flicked it into the yard. "What now?"

"We're done here."

"So?"

"We go to Cloudy. They won't be looking for us in Oklahoma."

"We going to the silos?"

"Yep. Then we find another place to set up shop."

Belcher glanced toward the rundown trailer. Priscilla was gone for more cigarettes with his most recent Farm Boys customer. He waved a hand at the patchwork porch and steps. "You taking Priscilla?"

"Naw. I'm done with her."

"Can I have her?"

"You already have, haven't you?"

A jolt of fear went down Belcher's spine for the first time in his life. This was a problem he hadn't anticipated. Atchley was one of those guys who could be laughing at a man one minute and burying him with a backhoe the next. He'd done it more than once. "I don't know what you're talking about."

Atchley studied the girls for a moment without making eye contact with Belcher. He shook his head. "I don't know what I'm thinking right now. Look, she's not here, but we gotta git.

I have to do one thing for Lomax before we leave. I promised him, and I always keep my promises."

"Okay, what's that?"

"We need to get Sheriff Jackson out of the way like you said. We do that, Lomax is a shoo-in for his office, and we can come back and start over when the smoke clears from all this. You need to do that, then put this Snow guy in the ground somewhere so he don't come after us."

"You're taking these two up to Pushmataha County alone while I do your dirty work for you?"

"If that's how you want to put it."

Belcher grinned. "I like the way you think."

"We need to do it fast."

"I like slow, best."

"Whatever. I'll call Lomax and let him know the plan."

"When are you leaving?"

"Right now."

Belcher thought for a moment. Atchley would be gone in a minute. After that, Priscilla was his until he finished with her and burned that rat's nest of a trailer down. He turned to look at the Snow house in the distance and sighed in satisfaction. He'd burn it too before he left.

God, he loved a good fire.

And he was starting to love how gravel made him feel.

Chapter Forty-Four

Harley phoned Tammy to tell her what happened as soon as we were in the truck and on the way to my house. I pushed the gas pedal almost through the floorboard and telephone poles flashed by in a blur.

His voice was level, but I knew what raged beneath. "Baby, take the kids and get out of the house. They've taken Chloe and another girl, and we don't know if they're coming after you or not. Keep your pistol close, and go to your mama's house. Your daddy'll know what to do."

It was the first time there were few lawmen I could trust. The brotherhood failed me in the town where I chose to live, and it kept running over and over in my mind that 99.9 percent of the officers in this country are great, law-abiding men and women. But in this little Northeast Texas burg, I'd stumbled into a scorpion nest of clannish backwater rednecks insulated by their own kinfolk wearing badges.

Harley kept his eyes on the road, as if he were driving, but his left hand fluttered on the seat and his leg like some kind of giant spider looking for somewhere to rest. "We've called a couple of guys, but they're gonna take a while to get there. We don't have that kind of time to wait."

My own phone was in my shirt pocket, but there was no one else to call. It was him and me for the moment. He listened to her response and reached across the cab to take my arm. He held it tight, as if to anchor me both in the seat and emotionally.

It helped.

Harley told Tammy he loved her and thumbed his phone to sleep. Instead of talking, he let go and both hands roamed over his pockets. I knew he was unconsciously checking on the firearms he always carried on his person.

Mostly on our own when we worked undercover, we were usually walking armories and he hadn't changed much through the years. Long ago, we'd hauled a couple of felons into the Garland, Texas, jail. We had to disarm ourselves when we booked them into the strange place, and the desk sergeant watched in stunned disbelief as we pulled handguns from virtually every pocket in our clothes. Once they were emptied, we raised our pant-legs and plucked small-caliber pistols from ankle holsters.

When we were finished, each of us left six guns in the lockbox. And that didn't count the folding and fixed-blade knives we carried. Though our badges were out and legit, every officer in that station kept an eye on us until we left.

This time, there was no kidding between us. This wasn't about just me and Harley and the people we were either working on or going to arrest. It was about our own family in danger, and that changed everything.

"We're headed to your house, I assume."

I nodded. "That's the only place I know to start."

"We're gonna need more guns. I only have three on me."

"We can outfit when we get there."

"And if we have to shoot our way in?"

"There are two under your seat and one in the glove box."

"Ammo?"

"I doubt we'll have time to reload anything if it hits the fan. If nothing happens, then we finish outfitting in the house."

He nodded, but this time his hands rested easy on his thighs, a sure sign of something, but I wasn't sure what.

—

When we rolled close to the house, Harley pointed. "Glass on the road."

The pit of my stomach dropped out. I heard Chloe shriek inside my head and the sound of something breaking. "Safety glass."

Everything looked normal when we pulled into my drive, but of course, we'd been to hundreds of houses and business where everything looked fine from the outside. My Expedition was nowhere in sight. Harley was out of the truck before the tires stopped rolling and came up in a high ready stance.

I swung left and parked with the truck between myself and the house. "Chloe!"

There wasn't an answer from inside, and I didn't expect one, but Kevin answered, his bark muffled from the inside. Harley gave me a hand sign that said he was going around to the back, and I nodded.

The windows were dark as I moved up, pistol at high ready. Something with a suction cup was smashed on the porch, but I couldn't tell what it was. I studied on the unfamiliar device for a moment.

Kevin barked again, knowing I was outside. I ducked past the window, looking out on to the porch and approached the door. There were no scratch marks on the lock and my key slipped in easily. Standing to the side, I opened the door and Kevin loped out, sniffing and excited to see me. The security system's warning beeper hammered at my ears until I waved the dog back in and punched in the code. The alarm wasn't set in the "stay" mode, which meant the house was empty.

And silent.

I went into the kitchen and opened the back door to let Harley in. He jerked a thumb over his shoulder. "Nothing out back."

"House is empty."

"What do we do now?"

"We're going over there." I pointed toward the trailer and stopped. "Wait."

I plucked my cellphone from the back pocket of my jeans and punched it awake and found the app I was looking for. It was something I'd installed a couple of years earlier and forgotten about. Two more swipes to a third page, and there it was.

Find a Friend.

I thumbed it alive, and Chloe's name came up. Hers was the only one on my list. It blinked for a second and then a big circle appeared with the words, Your Friend Is Somewhere Within This Circle.

The blinking target was northeast of us, across the Red River in Oklahoma.

"I know where she is."

"It could be her phone without her."

I pointed toward the trailer. "We check that place first. Then we'll know, but I'm certain it's with her."

"They're not stupid enough to keep her that close."

"We don't know that for sure. Bailey took my truck there five minutes after he stole it. We have to check."

"Good point."

Chapter Forty-Five

Belcher knew better than to stay at the trailer after Atchley left. He planned to come back later and get Priscilla, and then light his fires, but right then he had to go. After a quick search, he saw Atchley took most of the product they had on hand, along with the cash usually stashed in a Spic and Span box under the sink.

He drove to town and after checking the back seat and seeing he only had six cartons of smokes left, Belcher swung into a convenience store for a few more cartons. It pissed him off that Atchley was issuing orders that he expected to be followed without question.

Although he dearly loved his role as a private hit man, this one pissed him off for some reason, probably because everything was dissolving around them and instead of contracting someone else for a hit, Atchley wanted him to take out a sheriff with one foot in the grave.

He came out of the store with four extra cartons and added them to the pile in the back seat. He was starting to feel that familiar tug pulling him toward another session with the pipe. It wasn't bad yet, but bad was coming, and he needed to get his dominoes lined up before that happened.

He felt a little flash of fear that something different was going on inside his body. They'd warned others that gravel seemed to build up in a person's system, unlike the effects of typical street crystal. They'd heard rumors that it eventually reached a critical breaking point that drove users over the edge and into a dark, violent place.

He'd felt a little different the past day or two, but it could be anything, including too much nicotine in such a short amount of time. Once all this started with Snow, he hadn't taken a breath that wasn't pulled through a cigarette filter, and maybe it was catching up to him. He thought about going back inside for some nicotine gum, but he needed to start the ball rolling on his plan.

Instead of going to Sheriff Jackson's house and making the hit, Belcher leaned on the back of his sedan and dialed Spyder's number. What he was doing might have serious repercussions, but there was no way he planned to hang around after they kidnapped two kids and some guy named Kevin might have been looking through a window. The guy was the perfect witness, and there was no telling what he was telling the FBI right that minute. "I have a job for you."

Spyder answered the phone. "What?"

"This is Belcher."

"Christ. This is why we use burners. Names can be traced, you idiot. Spill it quick so I can dump this phone."

"Atchley wants you to do a job for him."

"What kind?"

"The contents of a house." Belcher gave him Sheriff Jackson's address.

"When?"

"Can you do it right now?"

"I'm in McCurtain County, putting together a team for another job."

"Dammit. I need this done quick."

"Flea's close by. He can get some men if the price is right."

Belcher had worked with Flea in the past. "Are they any good?"

"They have operable index fingers."

"That doesn't answer my question."

"Ex-military."

"All right. Now I have to ask you for a favor."

"What?"

"I'm supposed to do it, but I'm on the way out of here, and you remember both of those jobs I handled for you a couple of years ago?"

Spyder was in a turf war with another gang in Dallas, and when he found out Belcher was good at burning things down, he asked for a favor in return for more work in the future...sort of paying it forward. Belcher had a hard-on for that gang and agreed to do it for nothing, with the promise that Spyder would return the favor someday.

It was that day.

Spyder drew a long breath into the phone. "Why isn't your friend setting this up?"

"He's in the wind."

"To where?"

"The silos."

"Ten large?"

"That works." Belcher grinned. "I have another job for you too."

"What's that?"

"You'll like this one. No pay, but you'll get the satisfaction of taking out those two guys who killed our friends."

"The Kroger lot?"

"That's it. His name's Agent Tucker Snow, and I know that guy well enough now that he's on his way to the silos somehow."

"Hot damn! I'll be waiting for his ass. It'll be a pleasure."

Belcher grinned and watched a car hauler pass with a load of covered vehicles. He had Spyder on the hook and was confident that he'd established the groundwork for his new life in Dallas. "I knew it would be."

Chapter Forty-Six

Sirens wailed somewhere past the trees while I called my supervisor, Jimmy Meeks. "Harley and I are on the way to Pushmataha County. Somebody's taken my daughter, and we're going to get her back."

His shocked intake of breath was the only thing that came through for several seconds. I visualized him thinking on the other end. "You know this for sure?"

"I do. I'm standing at the kidnapper's trailer, and my Expedition's parked in front of it with the glass busted out on both front doors."

"Tell me there's no blood inside."

"No, there's not." My knees went weak at the thought of what might have happened, and how it could have been even worse.

"How do you know who the kidnapper is?"

"Two of 'em. One's Jess Atchley. Not sure about the other." I told him about the cameras and he went silent for a moment.

"Him again. I take it no one's in the trailer."

"Nope. We called the sheriff's department, but they weren't gonna come out until I told them I was going in." The sirens were a long way off, but I knew where they were headed.

"They're on the way now?"

"Yep, but I intend to find him myself."

"You're in the clear going to Oklahoma, but Harley can get into trouble up there. We might be able to cover for him down here, but Oklahoma law is different, and if you guys get on Choctaw land, it'll be out of our hands."

"He's sworn in to work with me, and we have an Oklahoma judge's authority for him to act as his agent."

"Already?" His voice was full of surprise. "You guys work in mysterious ways. What do you need from me?"

"I can't trust anyone back home, so we're doing this on our own."

"I can send a couple of agents up there with you."

"Nossir. It's too dangerous, and I couldn't live with it if anyone got hurt."

"This means you're calling me for authorization. You know, I have a bad feeling here that you're getting too far afield with this one."

"It's my daughter and another little girl. What would you do?"

He sighed. "The same thing. Y'all keep me posted."

"You know, up there we might get out of cell phone range."

"How do you know where she is?"

"I'm using an app on my phone that tracks her. It was pretty vague when I first fired it up, but now its narrowed down to Choctaw County, and she's still moving, or at least her phone is, and that's all I have to go on."

"You think she's separated from her phone?"

"There's that possibility. We know who took her, and like I said, we went to her ratty old trailer, but nobody was there, and it looked to me'n Harley like they'd cleared out. Our only lead's to follow that phone."

"Let me contact the sheriff's department."

"They're on the way right now, but I don't have faith in any of 'em." I didn't have time to get into the details of all the corruption we'd uncovered.

"The FBI involved yet?"

"It's a kidnapping, so I'd expect the sheriff's department to contact them pretty soon, if they haven't."

"Call 'em yourself."

"Nope. They'll take over and pull me off. I'm not trusting anyone with my daughter's life."

"The feds won't like you plowing ahead of them."

"Don't care. I think we're reacting faster than they'd expect and Chloe's moving right now, so there's no concrete destination. I bet these guys feel pretty safe up there. They might be kin to some others wearing a badge wherever it is they're going, like here in this town. Look, I don't trust a damned soul right now, and can't risk my daughter's life."

"All right. Y'all need any gear?"

"We have what we need…except for a satellite phone? Like I said, the signal up in the country might be weak, if there's any at all."

He was silent for a moment. "All right. I'll call Agent Hardin up there who works for the FBI."

"I don't want the damned *feebs* in on this." I hit that word a little harder than I should have, but the sirens pulling into my front yard were loud, even several hundred yards away.

"They won't be. Hardin and I've worked together for several years. He has a SAT phone that you can use."

"I don't want to meet him. I don't want to talk to anyone."

"Fine." His voice was sharp, and I knew I was pushing him to the edge of his tolerance for all that cloak-and-dagger stuff. "Here's an address for a mailbox up there." He recited a location on an Oklahoma county road. "There's an old house there with a black mailbox in front. No one lives there, but it's a drop for certain alphabet organizations. The phone will be there in half an hour."

"It'll take us longer than that."

"Ten-four. Use that phone to reach us if you need anything. Where is Chloe's phone now?"

The way he put it struck like a lightning bolt. He didn't ask where Chloe was. He asked about her phone, and that spoke volumes.

I thumbed up the app and saw where the signal was at that moment. "They're through Choctaw County. Now they're in Pushmataha County."

"That's rough country up there."

"I'm afraid these're rough men."

Harley looked toward my house and a swarm of cars coming down the road. "You know we're driving straight into the storm."

"So is Chloe."

Chapter Forty-Seven

Gray clouds covered the sky as Flea and three other Farm Boys pulled to the curb in front of Sheriff Jackson's house in a ten-year-old Chevy Suburban. He pointed through the windshield at the neatly trimmed house sitting on a street that looked as if it were a movie set. "We do this fast, and then we get to burn down them that killed our brothers in Dallas."

His words were like gasoline on a fire. The Farm Boy in the front passenger seat half-raised his hand. Flea had come to think of him as Groucho, because the man's thick, black mustache resembled that of the famous Marx brother. "What do we do here?"

"Clean house."

While Flea stayed behind the wheel, the other three opened their doors and stepped out. In addition to Groucho, two two-time losers named Stamford and Musk emerged with semi-automatic pistols, carrying them in the open as casually as if they were car tools.

As a group, they walked up the sidewalk. Groucho and Stamford stepped onto the porch. Musk went around back as Groucho held a sawed-off twelve-gauge close against his leg like a cane and knocked on the door hard and loud. A voice came from next door, causing Stamford and Groucho to stop.

"Can I help you gentlemen?"

They turned as one to find a plump woman on the porch next to Sheriff Jackson's house. Groucho's shotgun was hidden on his off side, and he flashed her a big smile, answering loud enough to be heard across the way. "We're here to see the guy who lives here."

"Well, his hospice nurse is in there, and they're gonna be busy. Can y'all come back later?"

Groucho shook his head. "We have to talk to him now."

"Is this official business?"

Groucho hammered the door a second time, frustrated that the women was interfering with their job. Stamford took two steps toward the woman and scowled. Irritated at the interference, Groucho used his free hand to wave her away. "Mind your own damn business, bitch!"

Now they'd have to take her out, because you can't leave witnesses behind. He nodded his head toward her. "Go burn her down."

Still acting as if carrying an AR platform weapon like a broom was normal, Stamford started down the steps.

There was still no response from within, and Groucho had reached the end of his patience. He pointed the sawed-off chest-high and braced himself to kick the door in when a shotgun blast blew out the lower of three small, staggered windows, shredding his chest with an entire load of buckshot.

As Groucho collapsed in a heap, the distinct sound of someone racking in another round was followed by a second load that blew through the same hole and caught Stamford in the shoulder and chest. He wilted from a half-dozen double-ought buck pellets that penetrated his heart and lungs, and he landed at the bottom of the steps.

The woman on the next-door porch screamed and disappeared back into the house as Flea opened his door and stepped outside the Suburban to see what was happening. None of this should have been taking place outside in the first place. They should have gone in and cut them down away from eyes and ears. It was nuts to make a hit like this in the daylight, but orders were orders.

Several beats later, a third blast came from around the back of the house, and he froze in place, stunned that their hit had collapsed from the start.

The neighborhood was silent until a slender barefoot man with short gray hair and an untucked khaki shirt opened the door and stepped through with a shotgun in hand. Flea instinctively drew a Glock 43 pistol from the small of his back and leveled the little automatic across the sedan's roof.

The world clicked into slow motion as he fired at the man in the door. It missed by a mile and the round buried itself in a support post. Flea pulled the trigger again and again, until the gray-haired man shouldered the pump twelve-gauge and brought the huge muzzle to bear. Fire belched from the barrel, seeming to reach halfway across the yard, and electric jolts of liquid fire shot through Flea's left shoulder, jaw, cheek, and forehead.

He fell back, his skull cracking against the hard concrete street.

Panicked voices.

Screaming.

Footsteps.

Sirens.

Someone kicked his Glock across the concrete, and Flea

registered a number of voices coming through the darkness that gathered around him. "Wha?"

More voices. A woman wept. "What's this all about, Waylon?"

A gruff voice cut through the gathering fog. "Somebody's bad idea."

"They all have guns."

The bright world from only a few seconds earlier grew dark, as if the sun was in eclipse.

"Looks to me like they all *had* guns." The gruff voice stepped away. "That's why I shot the sonsabitches. Lomax? This is Jackson. I need everyone you have available over here at the house."

Flea's eyes flickered uncontrollably. His head felt as if he'd been drinking whiskey all day, that light-headed feeling that drifted from his brain down to his body. He tried to form words that inexplicably came out as gurgles. He registered the old man was barefoot.

"Four men. Three DRT front and back. I'm looking at the fourth one bleeding out here. How'n hell do I know who they are? Looks like a hit team to me. They came up on my front porch and all of 'em throwing guns on me. Stupid bastards. They didn't have sense enough to keep 'em hid."

Flea wanted to explain that it was a routine job. Just a knock and shoot, their own version of a drive-by, but more surgical. Nothing worked and the words he spoke only came out as soft mutters.

"You're how close? Damn, that's lucky."

"You were supposed to be half dead." Flea's gurgle was weaker, and didn't sound anything like the words flowing through his head. His left side was numb. He wondered if he was having a stroke. Yeah, that's what it was. He was having a stroke. Of all the damned luck. There were sirens coming. Maybe the paramedics would help.

The gruff voice cut through the fog surrounding Flea. "I should put another round into this bastard's chest and finish this off."

A woman's voice. "Waylon, you all right?"

"A helluva lot better than these dumbass gangsters."

"What did they want?"

"Me, for some reason, but they tangled with the wrong he-bull."

A different man's voice drifted through the gathering fog in Flea's brain. "It looks like you were ready for them."

"I was. A little birdie told me something might happen, and he was right."

"A little birdie?"

"Yep, one that brought me a helluva lot more information too."

The fog gathered around Flea. "This was supposed to be easy."

The only thing Sheriff Waylon Jackson, Loretta, and their neighbors heard was a death rattle.

"But then again, finishing this son of a bitch off would have been the waste of a twelve-gauge shell."

Chapter Forty-Eight

Slaps of gunfire not far away faded, and Deputy Lomax closed his eyes, waiting in front of a little frame house just around the corner for dispatch to call over the radio. The phone in his uniform shirt pocket vibrated, and he saw Deputy Baker's name.

"Lomax."

"Bad news. Looks like Atchley and Belcher took the Snow girl for some reason."

"They did what?" Deputy Lomax shouted into his cell phone.

"Atchley called me to tell you what he'd done. He's on the road and asking for help."

"Those stupid bastards!"

The cruiser's radio came to life. "All units, shots fired at 814 Phillip. Multiple reports of armed individuals."

Numb with shock at Lomax's stupid movie, Deputy Lomax looked through the windshield at the Phillip Street sign. He was parked around the corner and halfway down the street.

He picked up the microphone. "This is Lomax. I'm almost there."

Baker also responded on the radio that he was less than five minutes away, then his voice came through Lomax's phone that he still held against his ear. "What do you want me to do? Forget Atchley right now? DPS and one of our guys is on the way out to the Snow house about a kidnapping."

Lomax felt his face go hot. He wanted to unload on someone, but Baker hadn't done anything. It was that damned stupid cousin of his who acted without thought. "There's nothing we can do there. Stay out of it and meet me at Jackson's house. I think there's been a hit on him."

"What?"

"Just get over there." Lomax's phone vibrated with an incoming call. He glanced at the screen to see Sheriff Jackson's name and he went cold. Jackson shouldn't be making calls. He should be dead. "Gotta go." He hung up, drew a deep breath to calm himself and took the call, hoping it was Jackson's wife on the phone. That would make sense.

"Lomax. What's up, Sheriff?"

"I've just been involved in a shooting at my house. I need you to get over here now."

"Just heard it on the radio. Be there in a couple of minutes. Hang on." Resisting the urge to go right that second, he leaned back in the seat to gather himself. He and Sheriff Jackson continued the conversation, but the remainder of what they said flew in one ear and out the other. Distant sirens told him first responders were on the way, and that would include fire and rescue, the local police, and likely any DPS cruisers that were close by.

When he thought enough time had passed, he shifted into gear and pulled around the corner from where he'd been waiting for the call from dispatch about the gunshots coming from Jackson's street.

Lights flashing and to make it look legit, he squealed to a stop beside a still body lying half under a black Suburban's open door. A crowd was gathered around Sheriff Jackson, who cradled a shotgun in the crook of his arm.

Graying hair cut short and looking better than a man with cancer should, Jackson was down to a hundred and thirty pounds, but he was well enough to handle the pump shotgun with ease.

Slamming the gearshift lever into Park, Lomax popped the door open and emerged with his hand on the butt of his pistol. More neighbors drifted toward the scene, and he waved them back. "Y'all stay away! Waylon, what'n hell happened?"

Leaning on the strange Suburban for support, Jackson held up one hand. "You can keep that in the holster, son. All these people standing around like they're at a church social should have let you know the war was over."

Someone chuckled, and Lomax felt his face redden. "You all right?"

Two more units rolled to a stop, sirens screeching. Jackson frowned and waved them down. "Turn all that off."

Both drivers killed the sirens and stepped out, leaving their lights on. One was Deputy Baker. Deputy Frank Gibson hurried up the sidewalk and checked on the body lying by the front steps.

"Gibson," Sheriff Jackson's voice was sharp and in command. "That one's dead. Check on the one in the back, but he took most of a load in his heart so I'd say he's done too. Baker, you stay right where you are."

The deputy frowned, but did as he was told and remained beside his front bumper. "Yessir."

"What's up, Waylon?" Lomax came close. "You need to sit down?"

"Yeah, but not right this minute." More sirens approached.

His eyes bored into Lomax. "Tell me something, Butch, how'd you get here so fast?"

Lomax paused. "I was just down the street."

"No siren?" Keeping the shotgun cradled, Sheriff Jackson tilted his head, watching. "Everybody else is rolling in hot, and you just cruised up here and got out."

Feeling a chill run down his spine, Lomax couldn't believe this man who was half dead a week ago could have any indication of what had happened. He took a deep breath to steady his voice. "What're you asking, Sheriff?"

Still another car arrived and Jackson flicked his fingers at the Ganther Bluff police officer who emerged to push the crowd back. "Officer, would you come here please? And you," he called to Deputy Gibson who came back around from behind the house. Though the local police department was under the command of the city police chief, Sheriff Jackson was the situation commander and had the authority to issue orders. Deputy Gibson was one of his department's more experienced men, and Jackson had faith in the man's character and experience. "Gibson, come here please. Everyone else, step back."

The neighbors shuffled away and still another uniformed Ganther Bluff officer came through the crowd. Proving he was definitely in charge, Jackson pointed to him. "You, Officer. Come here. What's your name?"

"Garcia, sir."

Sheriff Jackson tilted the muzzle of his shotgun toward Lomax's chest, though it was getting heavier by the minute. "Garcia, you and that other officer will think this is gonna sound strange, but I'm ordering you to arrest Chief Deputy Lomax there."

Surprised at the order, they paused, but Jackson spoke over his shoulder. "Gibson, you place Deputy Baker under arrest."

Lomax's hand lowered close to his service weapon but stopped short at the sheriff's command. "Nope." He clicked off the pump's safety with an index finger.

The older of the two officers, Garcia, saw Lomax's reaction and drew his weapon. "Deputy Lomax. Hands away from your weapon and turn around, now!"

Sheriff Jackson swung the shotgun to cover Deputy Baker, but it felt heavier and he knew the shallow reservoir of adrenaline-fueled strength he'd tapped was almost gone. "You too. Hands where I can see them. Don't you move."

"What'n hell's going on here?" Lomax's voice rose almost to a falsetto.

"Boys, disarm them now!"

Finally jolted into action, the officers disarmed Lomax and Baker, removing their service weapons with practiced efficiency. An officer plucked a tiny pistol from Lomax's ankle holster and they patted him down. They did the same with Baker, who had a small revolver in his pocket.

Once they were in cuffs, Sheriff Jackson relaxed, feeling a wave of weakness wash over him. An ambulance shrieked to a stop and the first responders emerged and got to work examining the corpses scattered on the property.

Red-faced with fury, Lomax adjusted his hands. "What's this all about, Waylon?"

"You two are under arrest for drug trafficking, conspiracy to commit murder, accessory after the fact, and conspiracy to distribute narcotics," Jackson paused to gather himself, "And generally being assholes."

Lomax's eyes widened. "You don't have a warrant on us!"

A warrant was exactly what Jackson had worked to avoid. After reading the report from Agent Tucker Snow, he called him and they discussed the validity of what he'd included in those pages. Harley Snow forwarded his own report through email after their phone call, along with dozens of photos taken with their home security cameras.

With that information in hand, Sheriff Jackson went directly to the grand jury and requested an indictment, an unusual move, but one that was absolutely necessary. In such a small town, running a warrant past a judge was the same as posting his intent on social media. Instead, he'd bypassed the grapevine and went through the DA he trusted to submit his request to the grand jury an hour after he and the Snows ended their conversation and the photos had come through.

With sufficient evidence to believe that Lomax probably committed the crimes listed in the documents before them, the jury's foreperson threatened the other eleven members with bodily harm if they leaked the contents of the report and signed the true bill only a couple of hours later.

"Nope. A grand jury indictment."

Deputy Baker had heard enough. "I didn't want to do all this. Butch made me, and he makes a lot of us help him and Atchley!"

"Shut up, you idiot!" Despite being cuffed, Lomax lunged to push through the arresting officers who responded to their training and threw him to the ground hard enough to bounce his chin off the pavement.

"Looky here." Officer Garcia withdrew his hand from their prisoner's pocket. A tiny clear bag dangled from between his fingertips. "Looks like crystal, but it's a different color. It might be that gravel they're talking about these days."

"It's evidence from that car wreck..."

"There's another charge." Jackson's head felt heavy, and he knew he'd have to sit down soon. "Read them their rights, boys. I don't have the energy." A lifetime law enforcement officer, he was disgusted with the job and disappointed in a man he used to trust.

Using one hand, he punched in a number he'd only recently loaded into his phone. Tucker Snow answered and Jackson mustered up enough strength to tell him what had happened.

As Lomax and Baker were Mirandized, Sheriff Jackson's knees shook, and he laid his shotgun across the hood of the cruiser beside him and settled to the ground to rest against the tire. Holding his head as if it were about to fall off, he hung up and hoped the information they'd shared with a trusted judge would result in Jess Atchley's arrest.

He closed his eyes when a paramedic knelt beside him. "You need to lay down, Sheriff?"

"Naw. I just need to sit here for a minute and rest. You know, I coached that son of a bitch in Little League when he was a boy, and always figured Atchley would wind up in the pen."

The paramedic paused with a blood pressure cuff in hand. "Sir?"

"Nothing. Just talking to myself." His voice faded away as darkness descended and the world faded away.

Chapter Forty-Nine

Cell phone service was getting spotty. People talk about how wonderful phones are, and I agree they've changed the world, and people as individuals, but once you get into rural areas, service is mostly unreliable.

Flat farmland was behind us and we moved into the rugged Kiamichi Mountains of Southeast Oklahoma. Many don't realize there are mountains and a mixed pine and hardwood wilderness area only three hours from Dallas. Granted, they're not like the mountains in Colorado, but some of the roughest country in the southern United States rises a little over two thousand feet into the air.

We sometimes had three bars, enough for a fair signal and to make calls as we went, and several times Harley growled that there was no service at all. We needed that SAT phone, and were getting close to the drop Jimmy Meeks told us about.

Sunset was coming fast, and that scared me even more. The winding two-lane road we followed brought us to the crest of one of many low-lying mountains covered with pines and hardwoods. The elevation was one of the only things working in our favor.

My phone rang, and I pulled into a pasture road blocked by a gate. "Hello."

"Tucker Snow. Sheriff Jackson." His voice sounded tired.

I punched the speaker icon. "Right here. My brother, Harley's here too."

"I got what you wanted. Deputies Lomax and Baker are in custody. Lomax clammed up, but Baker's spilling his guts, hoping for a plea deal. His lawyer's head is about to explode, but he says he thinks Atchley's heading to a meth lab up in Pushmataha County. That's where this new gravel's coming from. Says they outfitted a couple of old grain silos not far out of Cloudy. That's where he figures Atchley's taking your daughter."

I knew the area. Harley and I went up there dozens of times with Dad to fish the Little River and we always went through Cloudy on the way.

"You have an address?"

His voice broke up, sounding robotic, but we could still make it out. "Kind of. He told me where it was. You have a pen?"

Harley found a pen in the glove box as I rolled down the window to combat a sudden hot flash burning inside my chest. I don't know if it was fear, or relief, but I needed some of that cold air outside the truck. "Go ahead."

The directions were simple and old school. "Go to Rattan, then follow the Cloudy Road northeast out of there. Go through Cloudy to 1858 and take it north."

Harley wrote the directions on the palm of his hand and switched to some indecipherable shorthand when the route left the county road and Jackson identified the rest of the way using landmarks.

"When you reach the top of a hill right after you pass a falling-down barn with three dead trees beside it, Baker said you'll see the silos a mile away on the right."

We were high enough that the view across a small valley was breathtaking, with a wash of golden light to the west. Ready to go, I shifted back into gear and backed out of the gate's drive. The sun winked out behind the trees, and Harley punched what he could into his map app. "Thanks. We're about to pick up a satellite phone. I might call you again, so be ready to see a different number."

His voice sounded tired, as cold air rich with the scent of pines and humus poured inside the cab. "I don't think I'll be here," Jackson said. "I believe my time's up, but thank you boys for what you've done for me and my town and..."

Neither of us were able to say anything else, for as we dropped off the ridge and into a narrow valley, service dropped and we were once again alone. It reminded me of what it must have been like in the late 1800s when U.S. Marshals rode by themselves into this same Indian Territory on the way to arrest some of the most violent and bloodthirsty criminals in history. Most of those old marshals traveled alone, but I had my best friend and brother with me.

Those bastards who had my daughter were about to catch hell.

Chapter Fifty

Chloe awoke in total darkness, lying on her side. The right side of her face throbbed with every beat of her heart. Whatever she was lying on vibrated and bounced underneath, and a tarp slapped and flapped on top of her. Something covered her mouth and she soon realized she was in the back of a truck and cold wind flowed over her like a river.

She tried to move, but her hands were bound behind her. Terror washed over the teenager as she struggled to remember what had happened.

The road in front of the house.

Atchley.

The window exploding inward.

Jimma screaming.

A soft moan cut through the engine noise, and Chloe realized she wasn't alone. Someone was beside her. Jimma. It had to be her after what'd happened. She tried to speak, couldn't open her mouth. Panic rose, and she felt she was suffocating. She needed to take a long, deep breath. Everyone needed to breathe deep sometimes, but even forcing her jaw as hard as possible wouldn't put enough pressure on what she suspected was duct tape.

Thank God her nose wasn't clogged. She paused, and inhaled.

There. She wasn't dying, and she was getting air.

What was it Dad always said? Yeah, slow down, observe, and think.

She wriggled around and managed to lay her legs over Jimma's, hoping the contact would help relieve some of the girl's fear when she woke up.

The truck hit a bump, bouncing them in the darkness. Dad said think, but her mind was in a whirl. They were kidnapped and in a moving truck.

Okay, end of thinking. All those movies where car trunks can open from the inside and the kidnap victims pull a strap and get away won't work here.

There was no way to get her hands free. They were bound tight and since her mouth was taped shut, she figured they'd wrapped it around her wrists and ankles too. Okay. Good. Figuring things out here.

Where are we going?

No lights flickered underneath the tarp that stunk like ass. That probably meant they weren't in town. Out in the country, but where?

Jimma tensed, and Chloe figured she was awake. She wriggled around and laid her head on the younger girl's shoulder. There, she'd know she wasn't alone. Jimma twisted around for a moment or two, fighting the bindings on her arms and feet, the same way Chloe did earlier.

Chloe tried to speak, and realized it was impossible. To form words, air had to move and that couldn't happen with her lips taped.

Jimma stilled for the next several minutes as the pickup shot down the highway. She finally moved, rubbing her cheek against Chloe's shoulder.

She's trying to work the tape off. At least with the tarp fluttering over us, whoever's in the cab won't see what she's doing.

The material of her shirt was too smooth, and after a couple of futile minutes, Jimma bent and flexed at the waist until she'd scooted half the length down Chloe's body. After shifting position again, Chloe felt Jimma's head moving back and forth against her hip, then stomach.

What the hell is she doing!!!???

Jimma rubbed her cheek back and forth against Chloe's hard hip, then it moved across her stomach. It took several minutes to realize the girl was using the waist button flap on her jeans to try and catch the tape to work it loose from her cheek.

The miles rolled past and Jimma's action slowed and finally there was a gasp. "I'm free."

At least her mouth was, but that wasn't going to help.

The next thing she knew, Jimma wriggled back up with her head against Chloe's cheek and things became strange again. This time the younger girl was trying to kiss her! Wait. No. Jimma was biting at the edge of the tape, using her teeth to pick one corner of the sticky material up and then with a better grip, she twisted her head and the tape pulled loose, and Chloe could fully breathe again.

"Oh, God!" She took a deep, refreshing breath. Then another. "You okay?"

"I don't think so." Jimma's voice was soft and weak. "My left eye is swollen shut, and my hands are numb. You hurt?"

"My head's killing me. I think my face is swelled in two or three places. Where do you think we are?"

"In the back of a truck."

Daddy said think! "I bet it's Atchley's truck."

"My hands are cuffed."

"Maybe, but I think it's tape."

The truck hit another bump and something hard bounced against Chloe's side. The tarp came loose there and a stronger current of cold air washed underneath. She felt with her fingertips in the darkness, finding a rough flat rough surface. Wiggling and feeling around, she explored the object and found an edge. It was a cinder block they'd used to hold the tarp down.

Think, girl!

Still on her side, Chloe had an idea.

Cinder blocks are rough on the edges.

She contorted her body, twisting into a pretzel until she was in position to rub the tape against the concrete. Each motion wore at the tape, but also her skin. Soon blood flowed. The sticky moisture worked against her, but after what seemed like a year, she finally wore through the strips and her bleeding hands were free. "I did it!"

"Get mine." Jimma struggled to rise under the tarp, but Chloe laid one bloody hand on her side. "No. They'll see you. Just roll over and do it slow."

Her fingers burned and tingled as the feeling returned to her hands. Finding the tape around Jimma's wrists, she raked the surface with her nails until she felt an edge. Worrying it free, she peeled it loose.

"Be still. I'll get my feet, then yours."

"Then what do we do?"

"I don't know yet."

Chapter Fifty-One

We cruised down an oil road in the middle of nowhere Oklahoma at about thirty miles an hour. Such a slow speed was killing me because I wanted to floor the accelerator and find my daughter who was somewhere in those mountains, but I was convinced I needed that SAT phone. Jimmy Meek's directions were accurate, but it was completely dark and we were looking for a black rural mailbox on a post.

Scattered farms and houses appeared, some dark, some with lights, then winked out in the rearview mirror. Most of the time it felt as if we were driving through leafy tunnels that closed in overhead.

It was too dark to drive without headlights, and we didn't want to alarm anyone who might see a suspicious dark truck passing in the night. Those folks up there were raised on shotguns, and it was entirely possible someone would load up and come after us.

Harley rolled his window down and stuck his head out like a dog. "Smell that?"

I nodded. "Meth lab."

The familiar chemical odor alternately drifted into the truck and back out again. Meth production involves the use of dangerous chemicals that some people say smell like ammonia, glass cleaner, rotten eggs, cat pee, paint, and that hospital smell we all know.

To me it smells like compounded death.

"It's close by."

Tense already, we jolted upright when a massive buck exploded from the trees on our right and leaped into the middle of the road only yards ahead, typical of its species. It froze in the headlights as I slammed on the brakes and we got a clear look at his swollen neck and the magnificent atypical antlers on its head. It was the biggest, most impressive buck I'd ever seen. Bunching its muscles, he made one single leap and disappeared into the trees on the other side.

I looked past where he entered the woods and saw an overgrown drive that vanished into the darkness. On the other side was the battered mailbox Meeks told us about.

I reached out and flipped open the warped door to find a satellite phone, as promised. Passing it to Harley, I accelerated slowly in case another deer popped out of nowhere. Ten minutes later, a pickup shot out of a hidden drive and slammed on its brakes. Stark and contrasty in my headlights, two men emerged, one holding a pistol and the other a long gun.

I slammed on the brakes and instead of doing what they expected, shoved the transmission into reverse and hit the gas. The last thing I saw before looking back over my shoulder to watch the road was a long gun rising and the flash of the other man's pistol.

That was all it took to spin Harley up. He leaned out and opened up with his Beretta M-9, firing so fast it sounded like an automatic weapon.

Moving backward at such a high rate of speed threw off his aim, but he sent an entire fifteen-round magazine downstream, so at least one of them had to have made contact with something. Another gate turnout was half a mile back and we reached it in a flash. I whipped the wheel, backing in and nearly hit the gate before we stopped.

He slammed a full magazine into the pistol as I shifted again and spun the wheel to the left. He twisted to look over his shoulder, and I glanced into the rearview mirror to see nothing but darkness.

"Folks ain't too friendly up in here."

"Nope, but they're not the ones we're after."

Harley holstered his weapon and reached into a canvas bag at his feet. "Well, that was exciting." He opened a box of 9mm ammo and reloaded the spent magazine, acting like the shootout behind us was nothing, but as I followed our high beams back the way we came, he kept glancing into the side mirror to see if anyone was following.

Chapter Fifty-Two

"We have to get out of here!" Jimma whispered into Chloe's ear.

The truck turned off the broken asphalt and onto gravel. Rocks hammered against the undercarriage, and the smell of dust rose around them through cracks in the bed.

"We can't right now." Even though she suspected the driver had the windows up on the cab, and the tarp wasn't flapping as much at the lower speed, they kept their voices low. "We're still going too fast. If we jump out on this gravel it'll peel off every inch of skin we have."

It felt like they'd passed through some kind of small town or community several minutes earlier, but that was before they were free. Since then, the driver had turned off a smooth highway and onto what felt like an oil or asphalt road. The truck's speed alternated between fast and slow as they wound left and right, following a winding lane that constantly rose and fell. But when the pickup hit gravel, he slowed even more, though it was still too fast to chance an escape.

Jimma wouldn't quit. "We can jump out and roll."

"Not in the dark." Chloe considered their options. "We could hit something at the very least."

"We have to do *something*."

"Look, we're going to get out of here, but it has to be the right time."

"When is that?"

"I don't know."

The truck slowed and the distinctive sound of tires rolling through water told Chloe what was happening. "Low water crossing."

"What?"

"It's what you've been wanting. Out now. He's watching the water and the other side. Slide over the tailgate like a snake before he speeds up."

Her description was accurate. They slipped from under the tarp into the night and flowed over the tailgate in one smooth motion. Familiar with trucks, their feet found the back bumper before stepping off.

Misjudging their speed and the resistance of the ice-cold water, the girls' feet went out from under them. Chloe's breath caught. Jimma struggled to stand, but still on her hands and knees, Chloe grabbed her arm. "Hold your breath and get under." Gasping from the frigid water, she pulled the girl beneath the surface and they both disappeared from view.

A slight current pulled them sideways, and Chloe kept them submerged as long as she dared, afraid it might pull them away from the shallow crossing and into a deep hole downstream. Struggling to her knees, she pushed upright to see the truck's taillights going uphill until the road turned and they flickered through trees until it disappeared from sight.

Jimma came up sputtering "My God, that's cold! What'd you do that for?"

"He might have looked into his mirror."

Freezing, soaked, and terrified, they rose to their feet and looked around. The waxing moon provided enough light to make out the shapes of the trees lining the stream. Beyond them, hills rose in the distance, and Chloe had an idea where they were.

"I think we're in Oklahoma."

"How would you know that?"

"Because the only hills close to Red River County are to the northeast and across the river. This is Southeast Oklahoma. The Kiamichi." She pronounced the name as Kymesh. "We're in the Kiamichi Mountains."

She'd been there before with her family one summer. They'd driven up the Talimena Trail and camped later in Beavers Bend State Park, where they hiked, fished, and canoed a couple of streams.

"What does that mean?"

"We're in the wilderness."

Chapter Fifty-Three

Atchley's headlights illuminated the gate pullout he was looking for, bracketed by dark trees that came together overhead. He'd been there a couple of times, so he knew the drill and followed the two-track drive for half a mile to a decaying farmhouse backed by a barn and two grain silos. He waved when he drove past a bluebird house he knew contained a live feed security camera shooting through the round hole.

He waved again, and, after a short distance, Atchley stopped the truck, waiting for the signal to continue. Though he couldn't see in the shadows, there was an armed man stationed there who would empty a magazine into the truck if he was alerted by whoever monitored the bluebird camera. The guard would receive that information from the house through the VOX earpiece he always wore.

Two flashes from a small light said they recognized Atchley and he could continue to the house and the overgrown yard that was a carbon copy of his own back in Red River County. He parked next to a battered Ford pickup, leaned back, and killed the engine. Though the eighty-mile drive was short by Texas standards, he was exhausted by the day's events. All he wanted to do was get the girls into the house and secured in the bedroom they'd used for that purpose a couple of times before, and then sleep.

Floodlights in front and behind him suddenly bathed the junked-up yard in intense white light, and Atchley used one hand to shade his eyes. He opened the door and put one foot on the ground. "Dammit, Chuck. Kill them lights. You know it's me."

"Just wanted to make sure there was nobody else in the front there with you." A man with out-of-control hair and dirty clothes held an AR-15 right inside the front door.

"You saw it was just me on the camera."

Chuck Davis stepped outside and lowered the AR's muzzle. "Never can be too careful, especially after what I've heard today."

The pit of Atchley's stomach dropped. "What's that?"

"Lomax and Baker are in jail. Your sheriff back there picked them up after he shot four of our Farm Boys. You know what's going on?"

Atchley licked his lips and thought fast. "Uh, yeah. Belcher lost his damned mind and tried to take over our operation. Said he was gonna send some boys over there and after I argued with him, it was a done deal anyway."

"And you ran here."

"Had to." He jerked a thumb over his shoulder. He needed to tell them what was under the tarp and get that out of the way. "I got two girls tied up back there. One's my wife's girl and the other belongs to a stock agent who was after us."

"You kidnapped a lawman's kid? That's the stupidest thing I've ever heard of, and why do you have *Priscilla's* kid tied up?"

"Jimma was ratting us out to that agent's girl, and well, look

Chuck, I had to. You know as well as I do this gal was gonna to tell her daddy everything she heard."

"What a dumbass."

The voice from behind him made Atchley jump. He spun around to see Ryan Miller in mismatched camouflage and carrying a tricked-out AR with a holstered pistol on his hip. "Uh, hey, Ryan. Man, I didn't know what else to do. I had to bring 'em here."

"Oh, I know what you thought you had to do, but you're a dumbass for another reason."

Shifting from foot to foot, Atchley wet his lips again. "Why's that?"

Ryan reached into the back of the truck and yanked at the tarp. "Because there ain't nobody back here."

Stunned, Atchley rushed to the bed that contained nothing but tires, cinder blocks, and the tarp. "Oh, shit."

Chapter Fifty-Four

Wet and freezing in the cold north wind, Chloe and Jimma waded out of the stream and ran through the darkness back the way they came, in case the driver figured out where they got out of the truck. High in the sky, the moon cast a dim glow on the tall loblolly pines and hardwoods around them, creating deep shadows on one side of the gravel-and-packed-clay road.

Jimma panted behind her, lagging behind.

"Stay up!"

"I can't." Jimma almost wailed. "God, it's cold!"

Chloe slowed down, thankful she'd put on the sweatshirt that morning. "Jogging will keep us warm. Let's do that."

"We can't run all night."

Her hands were numb and Chloe wrapped them in her shirt-tail. When that didn't work, she tucked them under her arms to warm them up. "No, but we'll die from hypothermia if we stop."

"What's that?"

"We'll get so cold our bodies will shut down."

Jimma started to weep. "You said we're in the wilderness, and all I have on is a T-shirt. What're we gonna do?"

"Keep going is all I know to do. Keep an eye over your shoulder. If that truck comes back after us, we duck into the woods until he passes. There's no way the driver can know where we got out, so he'll have to drive all the way back to the highway."

"Why there?"

"Because until we turned off on the asphalt, we were going way too fast to jump out. He'll know that."

"How do you know what a kidnapper will do?"

"Because I do what Daddy says to do. Think."

Neither spoke for several minutes, and Chloe started running out of steam. She slowed to a walk, and Jimma moved up beside her. "Are we gonna have to walk all night?"

"Maybe."

"I don't think I can."

"We may have to. Look, you can do anything you want to do. You've been through a lot, and this little walk is just that, a walk."

"A cold walk. I wish I had my backpack with my cigarettes."

Shivering, in her wet clothes, Chloe wrung some of the water out of her hair to keep it from continually seeping down her back, then the tail of her sweatshirt, hoping it would help. "You think a cigarette would help?"

"Nope, but I'd have a lighter, and we could go out in the woods and build a fire to warm up."

The thought of a fire was the most wonderful thing in the world right at that moment and she almost moaned. "I wish you had it too, then."

Another mile passed and Chloe started to relax, sensing that their kidnappers weren't coming back. "You think it was your dad driving that truck?"

"I said he ain't my dad. We just live with him." Jimma shrugged, arms crossed against the frigid air. "Maybe it was Atchley, or it could have been Belcher." She thought for a moment. "There are a lot of tough guys who come to the house. They aren't customers. I think they're a gang. I heard him and Belcher talking in the kitchen and more than once they said something about the Farm Boys. It could have been one of them that got us from Atchley and brought us up here."

"Farm Boys. That doesn't sound tough."

"If you saw them you'd change your mind."

Coyotes yapped in the distance, a familiar sound that was frightening out there alone with no adults around. Chloe remembered in bed and under the warm covers back at the ranch, listening to them chase rabbits or other small animals in the bottoms. Now *they* could be the prey, and she wondered what they should do if the pack appeared. Dad always said never run from a wild animal, so they'd have to stand their ground.

She recalled a conversation around a campfire one night. "If you ever see something like a bear or a mountain lion, just make yourself look bigger at least. Kids are more in danger than adults. That works for coyotes and dogs too. Most animals will back off if you shout and wave your arms."

Her dad always carried a pistol, and she wished she had one right then. They needed some kind of weapon, but she didn't even have a pair of fingernail clippers. Chloe started looking for fallen limbs on the lighter side of the road. She paused to pick up one and discarded it because it was too crooked and rotten. She picked up another that was too long, but a third branch was just the right size after she broke off one end, leaving the point splintered and sharp.

"What's that for?"

Not wanting to scare Jimma with thoughts about the

coyotes, she poked one end into the ground. "Hikers use these to increase their stability. You need to get one too."

Jimma picked up a branch as thick as her thigh.

"No, you don't want to carry that thing."

The girl dropped it and picked up one about the length of a baseball bat. She gave it a swing. "You have a spear and I have a club. You stab those coyotes if they get close and I'll bash their heads in."

Despite being cold, tired, miserable, and scared, Chloe grinned. Jimma was sharp, and Chloe's lame explanation hadn't fooled her one bit. "Okay, I just thought we needed weapons."

A satellite flew past the stars on a long, unblinking path that took it out of sight. Walking again at a brisk pace, Chloe threw a glance over her shoulder to be sure the road was still clear and turned back ahead. A mile farther on, they came to a break in the trees and she stopped.

"This looks like a drive." She knelt on one knee to better see the sandy two-track leading away from the road at a right angle. "Look, are those tire tracks?"

"Maybe. I bet there's a house in there."

Relief washed over Chloe. "It can't be far. Probably a farmhouse. Maybe a hermit. Either way, it'll be warm, and we can call someone."

"What if it's just an abandoned house and that's just somebody who drove in to look it over?"

"It might be, but at least we'll have somewhere to spend the night out of the breeze and with something between us and whatever's out here with teeth."

They stepped into even greater darkness as the trees overhead closed off the moonlight and followed the two-track to wherever it led.

At least they were off the road, and that made Chloe feel safe.

A farmhouse, with a family, would be perfect. Then they could get warm and eat something. She realized she hadn't eaten a thing since breakfast, and with that thought, her stomach growled.

Chapter Fifty-Five

Belcher and Priscilla pulled into the parking lot of a run-down motel off Highway 80, not far out of East Dallas. The Big Town Mall, the first indoor shopping center in the country, once sat only a couple of miles away. Nothing much was left except for a broken-up parking lot and a large expo building used for a variety of events such as gun and garden shows, and RV expositions.

He glanced up at the flickering neon sign that read Creekview Motel. He broke into a phlegmy laugh and pointed at a concrete catchwater drain. "Creekview Motel, my ass. That's a damn drainage ditch."

"It's nicer than the trailer. How long we gonna be here?"

"As long as it takes to hear that Snow and Jackson are dead." He glanced at a dirty sports bag on the back seat, containing several grams of crack and a baggie of cocaine. "We'll sell all that back there and it'll give us the cash to make another buy. Then we'll be back in business."

Using two fingers, she plucked the cigarette from her lips and unconsciously rubbed at a sore that had formed on her face the night before. "Maybe we can use a little of that good stuff you have, the gravel? Just a little, to get through the night?"

He reached into his shirt pocket and handed her a piece of twisted plastic wrap. "There's crystal in there, but don't fire the damned thing up in the car. Wait until we get in a room."

She considered the two levels of rooms in the L-shaped '60s-era motel. A second-floor walkway overlooked the busy parking lot full of people loafing around cars. Drifts of trash piled up on one end of the drained swimming pool and the tables around it were occupied by residents drinking from red plastic cups and bottles hidden in brown paper sacks. Several doors were propped open, and she could see figures in the rooms, lying on beds and watching television, or eating and drinking around small tables in front of the windows.

Priscilla scratched at her scalp. "Nobody here will say anything if I fire up. Hell, they'll probably see the pipe and you'll have all the business you can handle."

He shot her a disgusted look and killed the engine. "Christ, just do what I say!" Slamming the door, he went into the lobby and up to the registration counter.

A fleshy girl behind the desk forced herself out of a rolling chair and stood. "Help you?"

"Need a room for two."

"That'll be fifty-nine dollars. I need your driver's license and a credit card."

"I don't have a credit card." He opened his wallet and produced a hundred-dollar bill. "Will this take care of one night?"

She made it disappear with the ease of a practiced magician and ran a plastic key card through the reader. "Room 215."

When Belcher returned to the car, Priscilla was passed out in her seat, the crack pipe cooling in her hand. Two men with dreadlocks contained in bright bags walked past, grinning. One flashed Belcher a smile. "Party!"

He shook his head. So much for being invisible.

Chapter Fifty-Six

Harley had my phone in his hand because we had to plug it in before the stinkin' thing went dead. Using the Find a Friend app along with the map app drained the battery faster than I anticipated. Chloe had the brightness on her screen dimmed down because her eyes were better than mine, but I needed more light, so mine was turned all the way up, which also added to the drain.

When he thumbed it alive in the dark cab, it lit his face the way we used to use flashlights when we were kids to make ourselves look spooky. "She hasn't moved for the past twenty minutes. I think they've stopped."

"Show me."

He tilted the phone so I could see a round spot in the middle of nothing. "How far away are we?"

"Thirty minutes."

"Punch up the map, and let's figure out where we can gear up."

Resisting the urge to push the accelerator to the floor, I kept our speed constant at forty mph. We couldn't afford to skid off the gravel road and into the ditch, or run into a deer or wild hog.

Hogs are dense and low, hitting one of those would be like ramming into a boulder, and that would be disastrous.

He was intent on the device as we ate up the miles. "Dammit!"

"What?"

"It's not responding."

I went cold. We couldn't afford to lose the signal. "What'd you do?"

"I didn't do anything." He pointed at the mountains and trees around us. "We're out in the middle of nowhere. I haven't had any cell service since that last ridge."

"What are we gonna do?"

"I've heard there's a way around this." He picked up the SAT phone and punched up my contact list. "There it is."

"What?"

"Your buddy Don Wells's phone number." He dialed the number and waited, tilting the phone so I could hear. I slowed to reduce the volume of gravel under our tires. "Hello, is this Don?"

"It is. Who is this?"

"Harley Snow. Tuck's here with me, and we're way back up in the mountains here in Southeast Oklahoma. We've lost cell service and need to use the map app, but it won't work. Isn't there a way we can get it back?"

"Sure. First you have to go back to where you still had coverage."

I slammed the wheel with the heel of my hand. "Dammit."

Harley glanced into the mirror on his side, as if he could see where we'd been. "Is that the only way?"

"The only one I know. I'm not a cell phone expert, you know."

Hearing that, I slowed even more, looking for a wide place to turn around. As we drove back to the ridge where we could get a signal, Don told Harley how to restore our guidance system without data.

We were driving away from Chloe and my next fear was that *her* battery would run down before we got there. She was pretty good about charging it every night, but even if it had been at 100 percent that morning, it was likely getting dangerously low. And, depending on how many apps she had up and running, it could be dead in the next minute or two.

Chapter Fifty-Seven

Chloe and Jimma were barely off the gravel road and on the two-track drive when a pair of headlights flickered through the pines. The vehicle approached at a steady rate, and its sudden appearance frightened the girls.

Grabbing Jimma's arm, Chloe pulled her off into the understory growth. "Get down."

"Is it Atchley?"

"Not coming from that direction. It's someone else, but we need to hide until they get past."

Both girls were shivering, and being still for any length of time wasn't what either of them wanted to endure. There might be a house just up there, and getting inside and warm was all they could think of.

The vehicle slowed at the two-track's intersection with the county road and pulled in, its headlights sweeping through the trees. Watching from the shadows, they kept still as the silhouette of a pickup stopped, reversed, and headed back to where they came.

Jimma started to stand, but Chloe didn't like what she saw. "Wait. That didn't look right."

"It looked someone turning around to me."

"Why would someone be driving along out here in the middle of nowhere, then turn around *exactly* where we are?"

"I don't know, why?"

"Because they're looking for us. I didn't think about Atchley calling someone else to help."

"If it *was* Atchley."

"If it was. But it doesn't matter who was driving, I think he finally noticed we were gone." Chloe was overcome with a violent tremor. Shivering was good, wasn't it? When Dad told her about hypothermia, he said shivering was the body's way of generating heat, but when the shivering stopped, they'd be in trouble, because at that point a person's organs were shutting down.

The sound of the truck receded, and they rose. Gripping her makeshift spear, Chloe stepped out of the bushes, and Jimma followed. "Let's go find that house before they come back."

Chapter Fifty-Eight

A miserable Atchley sat at a cluttered table in the farmhouse. Chuck Davis and Ryan Miller glared at him over a small mountain of empty SOLO cups, dirty plates, beer bottles, cans, and empty fast-food wrappers and grease-stained paper bags. A sixty-inch television mounted on the wall blared a reality show throughout the living room.

"How dumb can you be?" Ryan slapped at a mound of trash, knocking it to the floor. He picked up the TV remote and lowered the volume. "Why didn't you just call DEA and have them meet you here?"

"I wasn't thinking right."

"Wow. News flash, Chuck. He wasn't thinking right."

A dirty, old-fashioned beige phone on a dented TV tray rang, and the jangle startled Atchley. Tense as a wound spring, he checked the windows around them, glad they were covered.

Ryan picked up the receiver. "What?"

He listened for several moments, glaring at Atchley. "He won't go anywhere." He hung up. "That's Spyder. He's on the way to pick up a load and he wants to talk to you."

"About what?"

"Everything you screwed up."

"I don't work for him."

"No, we all work *with* him, but he's lost men because of you and this Snow guy. I think you better be ready for anything."

Atchley looked at the door, and Chuck shook his head. "Uh, uh. Don't even think about it."

That same door opened and a gray-haired man came in. Though he looked like a grandpa, his clothes reeked of chemicals, and there was a strange, empty look in his eyes. Atchley had never seen him before, but he knew the guy was the brilliant meth cook who created gravel and built the lab out in one of the silos.

He oversaw nearly a dozen men who worked in there around the clock. The cooks wore disposable hazmat suits and breathing apparatus, but the deadly chemicals used in the process seeped through anyway. Atchley was no stranger to meth labs, but this was the most high-tech factory he'd ever seen.

Barely giving them a glance, Grandpa went straight to the refrigerator and opened the door. "Can we get some decent food in here?" Oblivious to the fact that he smelled like a chemical factory, he opened a flat box and frowned at the contents. "How old is this pizza?"

"Couple of days." Chuck joined him and reached around to get a beer. "I'll eat it if you don't." He made a face. "Can you guys find a way to change your clothes before you come in here?"

"Can you shut the hell up?" Grandpa bit into the end of a cold slice and plucked his own beer off a shelf. "How about you learn to do what we do and make yourself useful."

"Speaking of useful," Ryan addressed Atchley. "You'd make Spyder happy if you'd straddle that backhoe out there and bury some of his trash from the lab."

The tough Okie two-time loser had been running meth labs for years. When he met Grandpa, they came up with the idea to use the abandoned silos there in the mountains to set up a super lab that rivaled any of those high-class operations down in Mexico.

At the mention of Spyder's name, Atchley glanced again at the blacked-out windows in front of the house. Someone had painted them with a brush and flat black. "Now?" He pointed at the glass that wouldn't emit a speck of light at noon. "It's dark."

"It has lights on it."

Grandpa sat down beside Atchley, crowding him with both his close presence and the odor of chemicals. Atchley wanted nothing more than to lie down in one of the back rooms and sleep for days. But getting away from those guys for even an hour appealed to him. "Well, I guess. Where do you want it buried?"

Ryan pointed. "We've cut a road past the silos. It goes out in the woods a piece and comes to a clearing. Chuck usually does it, but I figured since you were a professional with a backhoe business, you can get the job done quick before Spyder shows up."

"How much is there? How big a hole do you need?"

"A lot. How much you say we've made this week, Chuck?"

"About five pounds a day and the last time we buried and burned was three weeks ago..." he tried to do the math in his head, "a lot, I'd say. Three hundred maybe."

Each pound of meth produced about five or six pounds of the most dangerous waste in the country. They burned as much as they could, but the rest went into the ground. Before they found the silos and turned one of them into a lab, they cooked in old houses and trailers until the laws closed in, or they burned down.

Once they moved on and left the houses, the residual effects of the dangerous chemicals often rendered the structures completely uninhabitable. Law enforcement would only go in wearing full hazmat suits and breathing apparatus, and that was to gather evidence and clean out what they needed for a case.

The property owners suffered the most, having to hire an environmental company trained in hazardous waste removal and cleanup, removing building materials and furniture that absorbed contaminants and continued to release chemicals. It wasn't unusual for new owners to bulldoze the entire structure and build new.

"Grandpa there has the formula drilled down to perfection." Chuck was as proud as a new daddy. "The crystal is coming out titty pink and perfect. We already have an ass-load of gravel that'll make us millions and we ain't stopping there."

Atchley knew how dangerous the materials were. "I suppose I have to haul it out there."

"Yep." Ryan chuckled. "It's piled up outside the barn. I'd use the loader to pick it up if I's you."

"Any particular place you want it?"

"Yeah, go straight to the back of the clearing. That's where we've been putting it."

Anxious to get away from those two, Atchley went outside. He thought about leaving, running again and slipped behind the wheel of his truck. He went cold when he saw the keys were gone. He never took them from the ignition.

Knowing he was being watched, he closed the door and walked through the darkness to the barn where they kept the backhoe. He fired up the big John Deere, flicked on the headlights, and drove around the silos to follow the two-track path leading into the woods.

It wound around half a mile until he came to an opening in the piney woods. The clearing was fairly fresh, maybe six months old, and likely made with a forestry drum mulcher on the front of a tractor. Those giants made short work of full-grown trees.

He picked up the first pile of refuse in the loader bucket and drove to the back of the area that looked as if artillery had been called in on it and followed a set of tire tracks to a large area free of stubble. That's where they'd recently buried a large amount of toxic trash. He dug a fresh hole five feet deep and ten feet wide a couple of yards away. Figuring it was big enough, he steered the backhoe around the perimeter of the clearing, just to kill a little more time.

As the lights swung along a line of trees, he saw three smaller piles of fresh dirt. They weren't nearly as large as the previous dumps, and he frowned at them for several minutes before realizing what they were.

He'd dug holes like that back in Red River County, most for large stock like dead cows and horses. But back before he got on the dope and went into business with Spyder, he did even more delicate work at the Chapel Hill Cemetery, digging graves such as the ones in his headlights.

Only these in the dark Oklahoma mountains would never be marked with headstones.

Chapter Fifty-Nine

It didn't take but a few minutes to follow Don Wells's instructions and get the GPS up and working again. We let him go, and I headed back down the country road, trying not to drive too fast.

"While we were up there getting your phone set up, I was looking at this area on Google Maps since we had a signal." Harley was getting real still again, a sure sign that he'd reached that point where nothing around him was safe. "I found where I think we're going, and there's some kind of structure about a mile away from two silos. Maybe an old barn or house. There's no yard I can see, and no cars. That's where we gear up and go creepy-crawling."

"Is it on the road, or is there a drive up to it?"

"Right on the road. Tuck, we have these warrants, but you know what I'm thinking?"

"About men who have my daughter? Yep."

"We might have to kill some people."

"Nope."

I cut a look across the cab. His face was hard in the dash lights. "What do you mean?"

"We're not gonna kill *some* people. This is family we're talking about. I'm gonna do my best to kill *all* the people I see."

"We can't just kick doors in and start shooting." I was caught in a bad place. Men took my daughter, and I'd do what was necessary, but it was hard to wrap my mind around just shooting our way in. The law dictated what we could do. "We're lawmen. We have to follow protocol and serve these warrants the right way."

"None of those have anything to do with kidnapping. We do what we have to do."

I had the same thoughts in my head when it came to Chloe, but I didn't want either of us to wind up in the pen as an aftermath of what we were doing. It would be a tightrope walk.

The satellite phone rang. Keeping both hands on the wheel, I flicked a finger for Harley to answer. "Hello."

He held it between us so we could hear. "Is this Snow?"

"Don't know any Snow." Harley leaned closer to make sure I was hearing the exchange. "Who's this?"

"Agent Vince Bradshaw. FBI."

Harley wasn't giving an inch. "Anyone could say that."

"Yeah, but this *Anyone* called *this* number on the SAT phone you picked up from a mailbox out in the middle of Nowhere, Oklahoma. I know your daughter's been kidnapped by an individual named Jess Atchley."

"You know a lot."

"More than you can imagine. Which one of you Snow brothers am I talking to?"

"Harley. I'm the good-looking one."

I wanted him to hear my voice too. "Both of us. This is Special Agent Tucker Snow."

"Good. Both of you listen to me. This is federal. The FBI

now has this case, and I'm pulling both of you out. Step aside and let us handle it."

"Do you know where my daughter is, Agent Bradshaw?"

"We have some good leads, and my people are on it."

"But you don't know her exact location, do you?"

"If we did, we'd already have her out."

"Well, sir, with all due respect, we know where she is, and we'll get her ourselves." Any time Harley used that phrase "with all due respect," it meant that he didn't give a damn what the other person thought.

The anger in Agent Bradshaw's voice told me he didn't like to be challenged. "You're both aware that when they crossed state lines this became our case."

Harley rolled his eyes in the dash light. "You don't have to repeat yourself; we understood you the first time."

"Then consider yourselves relieved, Snow."

I instinctively slowed when my headlights lit up a rabbit darting across the road, then pressed the accelerator harder than I intended, irritated at the agent's attitude. "Nope. Where'd you get the info you have?"

"Where'd you get yours?"

"What are we, in the fifth grade?" Harley was getting irritated too. "We're following a signal from Chloe's phone. Are you?"

It was silent on the other end, and I thought we'd either lost him, or Agent Bradshaw'd hung up. He came back after a long moment. "Deputies Lomax and Baker are in the custody of the Texas Rangers. Baker told us he thinks Jess Atchley has her, and is on the way to Oklahoma with her. We have a location and address. You two need to get out of the way *right now*."

I figured the Rangers would already be involved. Corrupt law officials in Texas fall under their jurisdiction, and I almost grinned. I figured the boys wearing *cinco peso* badges felt the same way about Bradshaw and the other feds with him.

Harley looked ready spit nails. "Let me ask you, Agent Bradshaw, are you or any of your people in the Kiamichi Mountains at this moment?"

"We're putting our team together right now."

"That's what I thought...hey, you're breaking up...ay... you ne...can't...you." He ended the call and leaned back. "Lost the signal."

"You know that probably can't happen with a SAT phone."

"Hey, you don't know that. There're trees all around us, so the signal *might* get interrupted."

We rolled past a dark track road on our left, leading into the woods where I'd turned around earlier. For a moment I wondered if there was a house tucked back up in there, but it didn't matter. There were no lights in the trees, and what difference would it make anyway if there was?

Chapter Sixty

Chloe gasped at the sight of a faint light ahead. "Look!"

"Is it a house?"

"Who cares?" Chloe broke into a run. "A light means electricity and that means help."

They forgot the cold as they pounded down the drive. Soon the light morphed into a lit window. It was a house, all right, but not much of one. The trailer sitting on blocks was in worse shape than the one Jimma lived in, but it was shelter.

Familiar with country folks, the girls slowed as they drew near the house. Jimma hung back, fretting. "There might be a dog."

"I doubt it. It'd already be barking if there was one." Just to be sure, they stopped a good distance away, and Chloe got a clear look at the long metal box with exposed cinder blocks and piping in the shadows underneath that was in the process of settling into the ground. A simple set of bare, wooden steps led up to the door.

The soft, yellow light they'd followed came from what she took for a bedroom on the nearest end. All the rest of the windows were dark. A burn barrel not far away smelled of ashes and scorched chemicals. Large, white plastic boxes scattered on the ground reflected the moonlight. Tires, something covered with a tarp, and several piles of Natural Light cans formed a low mountain range near the door. Only the sight of a gleaming new satellite dish gave any indication that the trailer was occupied.

"Must be kinfolk," Jimma muttered.

Chloe took a deep breath. "Should we yell, or knock on the door?"

"What're you asking me for?"

"You've lived in the country longer than I have."

Instead of answering, Jimma shouted. "Hey! Help!"

Chloe jumped at the shrill sound and waited for lights to flick on inside or at least the bare bulb over the door, but the trailer remained dark. "Plan B." She threaded her way through the junk and climbed the rickety steps and knocked on the dented metal door with her fist. "Hello! We need help!"

Still nothing. After two full minutes Chloe tried the doorknob. It turned and the door swung open. Uneasy, she remained where she was. "Hello! Anybody home?"

A rush of deliciously warm air smelling of cigarettes with a slight tinge of sewer gas rolled out, and she shivered at the same time Jimma pushed in ahead of her. No one voiced a challenge at the intrusion, and Chloe followed. They paused inside to take in the dim living and kitchen area. A string of rope lights strung over the couch provided enough illumination to see. One single grate in a propane heater glowed beside a dark television.

Jimma crossed to the heater, felt around on top, and turned a dial. The other four grates flamed and turned orange with heat as the burners ignited. Moaning with the cold, the girls moved in as close as possible until their clothes steamed and began to scorch.

Chloe turned around and soaked up more heat on her rear and back. "Oh, God, that feels good."

"I thought we were going to die out there."

"We would have if we hadn't been lucky. Do you see a telephone in here?"

"No, but I see that refrigerator." Jimma left the fire. "I hope there's something to eat in it."

"Well, somebody lives here, or this heater wouldn't have been on. We're gonna have to do some fast talking when they get home."

"At least we'll be alive to talk." Jimma opened the fridge stared into the lighted interior. "I'm gonna eat everything in here."

Now that she was warm, Chloe's wet hair was cold on her neck and shoulders. "I need a towel." She passed Jimma who'd found a package of weenies and already had one between her teeth like a cigar while she unwrapped something covered in foil.

It was a two-bedroom trailer. The first door on the left was the bathroom. Chloe flicked on the light and saw a towel hanging over the shower rod. She took it down and squeezed as much water from her hair as she could, then flipped it over her head and gave it a twist in the back to soak up the rest.

Stepping into the hall, she glanced into the first bedroom that was open, dark, and empty. The bed looked so inviting that she wanted to strip down and curl up under the covers, but she needed to warm up and get dry first.

She turned the knob on the second bedroom and swept the door open, feeling a little like Goldilocks. A table lamp beside the unmade double bed was the light they'd followed. She took in the nightstand stacked with beer cans, a half-empty whiskey bottle, dirty glasses, pill bottles, and two full ashtrays.

She froze in shock when the covers moved, and a sleepy

woman with dirty tousled hair raised up to squint at the door. "Shit!" Chloe held up a hand and took a step back. "Hey, we're sorry. We were lost and cold and thought nobody was home."

The woman rubbed at her forehead. "Wha—?"

"I'm so sorry." Chloe backed down the short hall. "Jimma? There's somebody in the bedroom."

The fridge slammed and Jimma flicked a switch on the wall. Bright light flooded the kitchen at the same time the front door opened and a man stepped inside with a grocery bag in one arm and case of beer in the other hand. At the sight of the two girls, he dropped it all. One can sprung a leak and a jet of beer shot against the wall.

He snatched a semi-automatic from the small of his back and crouched into a firing stance. "Don't you move! Who are you? Who let you in here?"

Jimma squeaked and held up both hands. "Don't shoot! We were lost and cold."

Chloe mimicked her actions. "Please don't shoot. We were freezing out there."

The woman wearing only a T-shirt appeared. She pushed a strand of hair out of her face. "I just woke up and they were in here."

He swung the pistol over the girls, and then around the room, as if someone else might pop up. "Are y'all alone?"

Eyes wide, Chloe nodded. "Honestly, it's just us. We've been kidnapped and got away and were going down the road when we saw your drive and then a light. We were wet and cold and needed somewhere to hide."

The man lowered the weapon. "Well, there's no car out there."

"See?" Jimma turned to the woman. "It's like she said. Me and Chloe. That's all. Do y'all have a phone we can use to call the sheriff, or maybe her dad? He's a special agent. He'll come and get us and tell you everything you need to know."

The man's eyes went cold and flat. "Special agent?"

Chloe didn't like the look on his face. "Yeah, a special agent for the TSCRA."

"What's that?"

"A stock inspector."

"He's the law?" The woman's voice was nervous.

"That's right." Chloe judged the distance between her and the door. It was close, but the slender man who looked as tough as nails prevented their escape. Things were going sour and there was nowhere to run. "He's on the way now."

"Shit, Carl. Her daddy's the law."

"I thought you said you were kidnapped." Carl was working it out in his mind. "How could he be on the way if y'all were taken? Phones don't hardly work up here."

"Well, we don't have our phones, but Dad's smart, and he thinks. He'll figure out where Atchley was taking us, if it was him driving."

A look of dread fell over the woman's face. "I know that name."

Carl swung his attention to Jimma. "Now that we have that settled, who are you?"

"Jimma."

He shook his head and flicked the barrel of the pistol to move them. "You two go sit down on that couch. Tweena, get your britches on."

"My head's not very clear. I took a sleeping pill right after you left."

"Do what I said while I call Ryan and tell him what we have here."

Chapter Sixty-One

Back when Harley and I worked undercover, I usually had some nerves as we geared up to serve a warrant to go creepy-crawling up on a house, but they calmed once we started moving. This time the nerves weren't for us, but for what we might find when we got into the house or the silos Harley saw on the screen.

In our younger days, we worked so closely as a team that each of us knew what the other would do in any situation. I was afraid we were rusty, or at least I was. Harley still stayed in practice with his tactical business course where he trained SWAT teams, military contractor teams, and civilians who took his week-long programs on combat training. He also offered classes on night-shooting, firearms training, active shooter threats, and even fighting with edged weapons, which kept him polished and loose.

I just had to rely on muscle memory and experience. We'd parked out behind a barn so old it was built with rough, hand-cut logs and chinking. Now in the moonlight, the thick horizontal slabs on the crumbling building looked like exposed rib bones on some enormous rotting beast.

I watched Harley secure his tactical vest and smooth the Velcro that held it closed. He almost grinned when he saw me double-checking the magazine pouches. "Almost like the old days."

"Glad you didn't say good old days."

"Thought about it." In the soft glow of a shielded tac light, he picked up his M4 rifle with the sound suppressor and pulled back the charging handle, making sure a round was in the chamber.

I did the same with my own weapon that matched his in every way. We'd changed into black tactical gear, slipped night-vision goggles over our helmets, and checked the headsets and voice-activated throat mics. We'd already discussed our plan, what there was of it.

"You ready?"

"I'm ready when you are." He pointed. "Straight through there. We'll skirt around a clearing and come up behind the two silos. We clear them, then a barn. This late at night, I doubt there'll be much activity. After that, it's the house where I expect them to have the girls."

Heart scudding in my chest, I lowered the NVGs over my eyes, dropped the lenses into place, and the world turned green. He did the same, and I took the lead. He fell in behind and we moved through the woods as quietly as possible.

Woods are full of trails made by different kinds of game. Rabbits wear thin pathways that seem to wind at whim, or around trees, and into deep brush piles and thickets. Bigger animals like deer and hogs create distinct trails that are easy to follow most of the time. We struck such a path almost immediately and, for the most part, it went where we wanted to go.

The forest isn't silent. Tree frogs, crickets, and night birds filled the air with a symphony of natural music. An owl hooted not far away, its voice deep and somehow lonesome. Coyotes tuned up in the distance, and I hoped they were distracting enough that anyone outside would be listening to them and not hearing us if we stepped on a twig or a pile of dry leaves.

I'd been chilly when we first geared up, but by now the combination of nerves and gear kept me warm as we flowed through the pines like shadows. In one sense, I was glad I still had it, the ability to avoid as much noise as possible. One the flip side, I hated being there.

Walking through piney woods is different than a hardwood forest. There, leaves and sticks invariably crunch underfoot. In a pine forest, the fallen needles are a soft carpet, though we had to be sure not to step on pine cones or dried, fallen branches.

Harley's voice was soft in my ear through the communication system, "We're getting close. I got a glimpse of light up ahead."

That didn't make sense. "We haven't gone that far yet."

"I don't care. Look to your two o'clock. See it over there?"

I'd been listening to my own breathing so hard that I hadn't noticed the sound of an engine in the distance. He was right. A bright green glow told me something was going on a few hundred yards away. "Why would somebody be using heavy equipment this time of night?"

"Can't think of a reason."

We slowed as the sound became louder. No one could hear us over that, and it was so dark under the trees that we were invisible to the naked eye. However, the NVGs allowed us to see a backhoe at work.

I watched for a moment, then scanned the area for others. "One man."

"That's all I see too."

"What do we do about him?"

Harley thought for a moment before answering. "We can't ignore this guy. He's somehow involved with whatever's going on at the silos."

"He could just be some good old boy out here trying to make a living on a second or third job."

"Could be. Cuff and stuff him, then, until we can come back and find out who he is."

It was a good idea, but how to get him off the backhoe would be a problem. I moved closer, but the bright lights on his rig were playing hell with the night-vision equipment. I flicked the lenses up as Harley split off and worked his way around between the trees lining the clearing. From where I crouched, I could see the man's back as he manipulated the controls. He was facing the woods and Harley's position.

"Harley. His back's to me."

"You'll have to be in the open to get close enough to wave him down."

"For a minute. It's dark on this side and those lights are bright. Maybe anybody watching what he's doing won't see me in the dark."

"I'm on him."

That meant Harley had the man in his scope. I hoped he'd stay off the trigger. I paused to let my eyes fully adjust to the bright lights in front of the operator. He was using the long arm and bucket to scoop out a deep hole, piling the dirt up on one side. The loader behind him was full of something that looked like garbage.

He adjusted the legs on the backhoe and the bucket took another bite. The big John Deere bucked and something light fluttered to the ground. It looked like a coffee filter and then I knew what he was burying.

"Harley, he's burying waste from a meth lab."

"A good old boy trying to make some cash, huh?"

"Stay off the trigger. I think I have him."

Slinging my own M4 down and around on my back, I slipped an old school sap from my pocket and crept forward. The engine was so loud I could have walked up there singing "I want my MTV" and he wouldn't have heard me. The tricky part was climbing up to the open cab and cracking him in the head.

Intent on what he was doing, the operator kept his eyes on the bucket and hole he was digging. The stabilizer legs were outside the huge back tires, so they wouldn't be an issue, but to get up there, I'd have to climb up at his side and slightly behind; the eight o'clock position. I reached the smaller front tire and knelt beside the vibrating machine to study on how to monkey my way up there.

Harley spoke in my ear. "He's gonna see you."

Before I could answer, the operator's head jerked up and to the right. Catching motion from the corner of my eye, I knew what had happened and took the opportunity Harley provided when he stepped out into the open. Grabbing a handhold, I put one foot on that side's metal step and pulled myself up. The moment I was up there, I saw Harley standing at the edge of the woods. He waved, and damned if the guy didn't raise a hand back.

I cracked him just behind the ear with the sap, and he folded at the waist. His grip on the joystick levers relaxed, and the bucket dropped with a bang. I grabbed him before he could fall off the seat, and I nearly tumbled off when his full weight leaned against me. Harley was at my side in a flash, and he caught the unconscious man's body as I got a handful of collar.

We lowered him to the ground, and Harley pulled out a set of flex cuffs. He zip-tied the guy's wrists, and we rolled him over on his side so he could breathe. That's when we got a good look at his face, and I almost killed him then.

It was Atchley.

"Oh, my God!" Heart pounding in my throat, I rushed around to the loader, praying Chloe's body wasn't in there. I didn't see her, but she could be buried under all that nasty refuse.

"Harley, dump this load!"

He scrambled up and, unfamiliar with the controls, almost took longer than I could stand to find the right position on the joystick. The big bucket rose as if to take another bite of what might have been Chloe's grave, then it fell, and the rig adjusted itself on the stabilizer legs.

"Hang on." He worked them again and the loader rose, then tipped, the big bucket spilling its contents. Flashlight in hand, I watched the material spill onto the ground.

"Nothing." I had to lean on the backhoe as my knees trembled.

Chapter Sixty-Two

Ryan answered the beige phone half a second before Spyder and four men stepped inside. Alone in the trailer, he threw up a hand in greeting and waved for the newcomers to sit down. "What?"

Spyder snatched a beer from the fridge, cracked it, and dropped onto the couch. He took a sip and watched with interest as Ryan's face broke into a big grin.

"You're shittin' me!" It was one of Ryan's old buddies who lived about twenty miles away with some outstanding news. The girls Atchley lost had turned up on Carl's doorstep, or rather, actually *inside* his trailer.

"You sure it's them?"

The voice on the other end snorted. "Yep. Two little ol' gals by name of Jimma and Chloe. And get this, Jimma finally gave me her last name and it's Bailey."

Ryan's eyes widened. He glanced over at Spyder on the couch and knew they had a golden opportunity at the same time he had great news for his boss. "Keep them there for right now. We don't want them to know where the silos are if anything else happens. I'll send a couple of boys over there in a little while."

He hung up and studied the four strangers who'd come in with Spyder. The burr cut and tattooed guys were badass, and looked to be ex-military to him. "New men?"

"New *good* men," Spyder answered with a proud look.

"You growing the organization? I could use one or two new men around here. A couple of these bastards are getting lazy. They need some remedial training."

"Not these four." The hard-edged men remained standing, as if ready for action at any time and not aware that Spyder and Ryan were talking about them. "This is the beginning of my new elite team. My version of the SS. I call 'em the Fab Four."

At the mention of the Nazi party's black uniformed elite corps, Ryan studied them even harder. This was something brand new.

"What brought the change?"

"I've lost several of what I thought were good men to a bunch of local..." he searched for a word, "gendarmes." He sipped his beer, looking satisfied at his vocabulary.

His term went right over Ryan's head. "Huh?"

"Po-po."

Understanding dawned. "Oh."

"Killed 'em easy as pie, so we had to up our game."

"You have my shipment ready?"

"Sure do, and more than that."

"What?"

"There's a friend of yours here, and I think you're gonna be wanting to talk to him."

"I don't have any friends."

"How about business associate?" Ryan felt good about his own vocabulary.

"I'm waiting. Hurry up and quit fooling around, I need to get this dope loaded and out of here."

He'd played around with his new information as much as he dared. "Jess Atchley rolled in here, and he says the laws are on his tail."

"It ain't the laws after him." Spyder's eyes narrowed. "Where's here?"

Ryan extended his index finger and pointed at the floor. "Sure 'nuff."

Spyder rose and pulled a handgun from the small of his back. "Where is he? I'm gonna kill the son of a bitch right now." He turned to the newcomers who'd tensed at the sight of the pistol like hungry wolves eyeing a crippled deer. "Can any of y'all operate a backhoe?"

All four raised their hands.

"You don't need them to dig." Ryan was busting with news and couldn't wait to tell Spyder. "I've got Atchley digging his own grave out back right now."

"Where is he?"

"In the clearing. And I have more news, though I doubt you'll like it. He showed up here thinking he had his daughter and another girl tied up in the back of his truck. Well, they got loose and slipped out somehow..."

Spyder swelled up in a quick rage, but Ryan held out one hand. "Easy, they got away all right, but they went straight to a house for help, and a friend of mine opened the door. He has them now, and they're yours if you want them. Hell, turn 'em over to Flea if you want, he can sell 'em both to that bunch of Czechs who're moving girls out of Dallas."

"Well, you don't want that." Ryan knew better than to string Spyder along with the news. "You know one of those gals."

"I do? Which one?"

"The one that's your daughter. Jimma."

He watched the expression on Spyder's face tighten and wondered if he'd made a mistake. The man looked downright evil.

"I'm not sure she's mine. That slut she calls her mother laid down for anyone who had drugs in their pocket. Thought she went by Atchley now, anyway. How'd you know about her?"

"I heard you talking to Grandpa about her once, and Jimma ain't no common name. I put two and two together when she told my buddy Atchley at first, then changed her mind."

Spyder weighed the pistol in his hand and chilled Ryan to the bone. "Them Czechs'd buy 'em for sure, but it won't be Flea doing the deal."

"Why not?"

"He's dead, shot by some Barney in Ganther Bluff."

"You ain't gonna sell your own daughter, are you?"

"Said she ain't mine for sure, so I don't care one damned bit what happens to her."

Stunned, Ryan waited. Spyder laid the pistol on the arm of his chair and drained the beer. "All right. Let's see what you boys have." He nodded toward his new recruits. "Go out past the silos and take that road to the clearing. You'll hear the backhoe before you get there. Get a little creepy-crawly practice and bury the son of a bitch in the hole he's digging."

One of the Fab Four nodded and led the way outside. "Let's gear up."

Ryan looked at Spyder. "They don't need gear for this. Atchley's alone, and if he has a gun, it'll be in a holster."

"They like to keep in practice." Spyder picked up the remote and scrolled through a selection of apps on the flat panel TV. "Where's YouTube?"

—

Outside, the men gathered around the back of Spyder's black Suburban. The assumed leader, Enrique, opened the back and pulled out an AR-15. The shortest of the four reached for a ballistic vest, but Enrique shook his head.

"We don't need full gear for this. Grab a couple of mags and let's get on with it."

Shrugging, Shorty picked up an AR-style rifle and stepped back so the others could do the same. Seconds later, they rounded the silos on foot and followed the dirt road.

Chapter Sixty-Three

Harley wanted to pitch Atchley's unconscious carcass in the hole, but I wanted to wake him up and make him tell me where Chloe was. I slapped his face a few times, but my old neighbor only moaned and went back under.

"Dammit! I shouldn't have hit him so hard."

"He'll be awake when we get back and we'll have her then. If he's here, then she is too."

"I hope so, or he could die from a brain bleed. Leave the backhoe running with the lights on, in case somebody comes by. They might think he's still working."

"They'll know something's up when they see the seat's empty."

"It might buy a few minutes. Let's go."

I turned and stepped into the woods. Harley grunted in my earpiece and before I slipped the NVGs back into place, I looked over my shoulder to see him kick Atchley into the hole anyway.

He shrugged when he realized I'd seen him. "I didn't bring any blue paint with me, and anyway, he landed on his side, so he can breathe."

Shaking my head, I tilted the goggles back over my eyes and headed for the silos.

We hadn't taken ten steps when I saw a flicker of movement through the trees. Thinking at first it was a deer, I paused, then held up a hand. Harley's voice came into my ear. "'sup?"

The beauty of throat mikes is that you can barely make a sound and anyone on that channel can hear as clear as a bell. "Hang on."

The dirt road Atchley drove in on was only a few yards away and because there was little understory in the pines, I could see them clearly. "Armed men, on the road."

We took a knee. "I see 'em."

"Count four."

"Me too. They're loaded for bear."

"What do you want to do?"

"They're headed for the clearing." I was glad we'd left the backhoe running. "They're going to have the headlights in their eyes when get there. Let 'em pass and come in behind them."

"We gonna have a visit?"

"That's up to them."

The men passed, and I waited a little longer before moving. When I looked for Harley, he was gone. There was still too much chance of stepping on something in the woods, so I eased out into the lane where it was clear footing and followed the men.

The team wasn't concerned about keeping watch behind them and seemed to be out for a midnight stroll. They all carried rifles, and I knew they weren't armed just for the fun of it. The moon was settling toward the trees, leaving one side of the lane darker than the other. Keeping in the shadows, I followed with my rifle at high ready.

A minute later, as I expected, they were silhouetted with the backhoe in front of them. The big rig's diesel growl filled the air, and they stopped to study the area, probably because they saw the cab was empty.

Three of them turned to one guy who seemed to be in charge. He waved a hand, and two of them vanished into the trees. He spoke to the other guy, the shortest of the quartet, apparently issuing instructions. He released his rifle to hang muzzle-down on its sling, and his minion did the same.

I liked that a lot. It was a relaxed position, and though they could quickly get them into action, it might shave off a second or so. It also told me those two were some kind of decoys, because the other two went in ready for trouble.

It was the same technique we'd used on Atchley only a few minutes earlier.

But now I was in a bad position. The NVGs are great when it's dark, but we were facing the backhoe's front lights. I had to tilt them up, and that put the woods in shadow. Maybe Harley had a better field of view, but I had to be ready.

The only safe thing to do was step back into the trees and avoid the lights. Keeping my head angled as much as possible to preserve what little night vision I had, I followed the Mutt and Jeff pair as they approached the big rig.

Sitting in a dark pocket of shadow, I considered the four. They all looked military and every one resembled the other. I wasn't sure if they were some kind of gang, or some kind of mercenary squad who might be working for a meth operation.

I bet on the last, but no matter, they all looked mean and tough as hell.

That's when I heard laughter and it dawned on me the first two had crept up on the backhoe and found Atchley in his hole. A voice called over the diesel engine. "Well, looky here."

With little sense of professional security, all four of them stepped to the edge of the pit. "What'd he do, get out to take a piss and fall in?"

"I don't know. It's dark in there. Hey, stupid. You awake?"

Two of them stepped to the edge of the pit and peered in. "I think the dumb bastard's dead. Looks like he fell in and broke his neck."

The presumed leader turned his attention from the pit and scanned the area. "One of y'all climb up there and push this dirt in on him. I want one of those beers back there."

"I want all of the beers," another said and like a couple of kids, two men pushed toward the rig, pushing each other in fun. It was like watching a pack of young wolves playing on a quiet night.

I couldn't let them murder Atchley, though I wanted to do it myself. Shouldering my rifle, I called over the diesel engine. "Stock agents! Let me see your hands! Let me see your hands!"

They froze at the sound, not sure where it was coming from.

"Po-lice!" Harley's voice was a sharp slap and distinct so there was no mistake. "We're the po-lice. Hands! Hands!"

The night went quiet, and I didn't hear the growling engine any longer. My world shrank down to a few square yards, focusing on the apparent leader, who finally figured out where I was. I had the crosshairs on his chest and my finger on the trigger. "Don't do it!"

"Drop your weapons now!" Harley's shout was louder, and I knew that tone. He was a heartbeat away from firing. "Do it!"

The short guy started the ball rolling. I don't know if he intended to fire, or if Harley's voice startled him, but raising the muzzle was the absolute wrong thing to do. The moment that barrel came level, Harley's rifle opened up on full auto.

Because of television and movies, most folks think sound

suppressors completely silence a rifle's report, but that's not true. Acting like mufflers, they significantly reduce muzzle blast and flash, but the lighter cracks are still there, and much louder than I was comfortable with.

The leader brought his weapon up and started firing way too early. The first two or three blasts that shattered the night flashed down low. I shot him with a three-round burst. Seeing his body recoil with the impact of the 5.56 rounds, I shifted my aim toward the two would-be heavy machinery operators. One twisted sideways from the impact of Harley's rounds and I swung on the other.

Being last, he had the best chance for return fire. I was apparently far enough in the shadows that he wasn't sure where I stood. He threw hot rounds my direction that snapped past me only a foot away. More than one struck the pines, the ricochets whining away into the darkness.

I squeezed off another burst that blended with Harley's return fire and the guy fell, a little heavier from three extra lead slugs. Trembling from nerves and reaction, I advanced on the still forms, ready to shoot again at the slightest twitch.

Harley appeared from my right. "Good thing they were all on this side." Still in firing position, he swept the muzzle over the lane to make sure there were no more surprises.

I had to step around the pit to kick the nearest rifle away and saw it was on a sling. I dropped a knee onto the man's back, hard. There was no response. Keeping an eye on the others, I checked the next. "Wonder what the hell this was all about?"

He turned his back on the shooting scene to keep an eye out. "Looks like a hit team to me."

"Four men to hit Atchley?"

"He pissed *you* off, didn't he?"

Chapter Sixty-Four

It took us an hour and a half to make our way up to the silos, crawling and listening. I was shocked that truckloads of armed men hadn't roared down the lane to see what all the shooting was about. The night was quiet, though, and I knew better than to think they hadn't heard all the shooting, even though our weapons had sound suppressors.

Once we came within a hundred yards, we crawled slow as cold lizards. That was our specialty back in the olden days, and we were still good at it. Even though we were dressed all in black, I wished I'd thought to bring my ghillie suit for extra camouflage.

We finally reached the old farm and peered through a growth of young saplings and tall grass I couldn't identify on a bet. The two round silos stood tall and silver in a slice of moonlight.

A steady humming sound filled the still air, and it took a few minutes to realize it was coming from the silos. I gave Harley the sign to stay put, and I went on a quick creep around the twin buildings. On the far side I found drainpipes sticking through the sides and realized both had new high-tech Mitsubishi window units installed in the sides.

Beyond them was a tired farmhouse. A barn sat between them, set back a ways and forming a shallow triangle. The grounds between the structures were dark and scattered with piles of garbage.

That's when it hit me. "The silos are where they have the lab." My words were little more than expelled breath into the throat mike.

Harley studied the scene. Waves of music came from the farmhouse. Somebody inside liked AC/DC. "I think you're right."

"That's why they didn't send the army down on us."

He was silent, sweeping the area though his NVGs. "Nope."

What was I missing? "You think there are men stationed out here somewhere." It was a statement, not a question.

"Yep, and they heard the shooting. It might sound like they're having a party in the house, but you can bet this place has guards and surveillance."

With that determination, we settled in to wait some more as the temperature continued to fall. We both felt we had time on our side, even though I was scared to death for Chloe.

I wanted to check my watch to see what time it was. The minutes pass slowly when you're lying in the cold shadows, not knowing what's going to happen next. The only movement from Harley was the occasional slight turn of his head as he studied the terrain around us through his NVGs.

It had grown colder in the last hour, a sure sign that sunrise was close. I finally noticed it was almost imperceptibly lighter in the east. Our waiting game finally paid off when I saw movement ahead. "Eleven o'clock."

Harley's head didn't move, but he saw it too. "One man. Rifle."

The sentry's movement sparked another guy to show himself.

This one was farther out, watching the driveway. Apparently thinking that if his partner was relaxed and could let down his guard, then he could too. Guard Number 2 stood and stretched and remained standing where he was.

"Two."

My little brother answered. "Saw him first."

"No, you didn't."

I checked the house that still blared hard rock. Green light through my goggles showed a well-beaten path through the trash connecting the house with the nearest round building. Peeled battery cases where they stripped out the lithium were everywhere, empty cans of Coleman fuel, from which they extracted sodium hydroxide, and empty boxes of decongestants were everywhere. Stained coffee filters were scattered on the ground like giant, dirty snowflakes, all solid evidence they were cooking meth inside.

Harley's voice was soft in my ear. "These guys are good. I saw that one on the left quite a while ago, but the guy on the drive didn't move at all."

"You already saw him?" I swear I could feel him grinning.

"Wasn't sure until you said something."

"Time to move?"

"We'll have to. It's gonna be light in a little while."

"So how do you want to do this?"

He shouldered his rifle with glacial speed. "I'm gonna shoot that one up there by the drive. You shoot the other one."

"You can't just shoot the man. We need to identify ourselves first."

"Then I can shoot him."

"Only if he poses a threat."

"He's armed, guarding a meth lab, and we've already been shot at. I'd call that a threat."

"We still have to identify ourselves. We're the law..."

"I will, when we get closer. One."

"Stop counting and watch that guy on the left." Staying on my belly, I lined the crosshairs on the figure to our right and took a deep breath. "Special agent! Put down your weapon."

"Two."

The guard I was looking at raised his weapon in my direction, firing even before he could bring it to bear. I squeezed the trigger at the same time Harley's rifle fired.

It didn't matter that the guy fired first. Harley never gets to three.

Chapter Sixty-Five

Early morning sunlight filtered through the thin drapes in the cheap motel room. Belcher woke up beside Priscilla, and it took him a minute to remember where they were. A single beam of light leaked through a hole in one drape and the beam fell on the mirror over a scarred desk.

He rolled over to see her propped on two stained pillowcases. A reality show blared from the television mounted on the wall loud enough to require earplugs. Belcher rubbed his head and buried his face in the pillow. "Turn that damned thing down."

Ignoring him, she rustled around on the other side of the bed and made several adjustments, her weight on the broken-down mattress irritating him. Frustrated that he couldn't go back to sleep, Belcher rose on one elbow and saw her remove a needle from her arm and put the syringe on the night table beside her.

A packet of pink crystals lay beside a half-empty bottle of beer. "Dammit, Priscilla. Where'd you get that?"

"From your bag." Her voice went soft and dreamy. "This stuff's *good*."

"You don't need to be shooting that shit! How long has it been since your last hit from the pipe?"

"I don't remember." She turned toward him, eyes half-lidded. "Smoking it wasn't doing it for me anymore. Neither was snorting. This is the *way*! What a great high!"

He flipped the thin sheet off them both and swung his legs over the edge of the bed. She coughed behind him as he waited for his head to quit spinning.

"I told you to stay off the gravel. Use those rocks over there on the table." Lipping a cigarette out of the pack, he flicked a lighter and inhaled his first cigarette of the day.

Her voice came low and soft. "Ohhhhhh."

"What?"

"It's hot in here."

He exhaled and watched her in the mirror through a cloud of smoke.

"Something's…I'm…" She convulsed and doubled over. Half a second later she folded so far back he thought her spine would snap.

He looked over his shoulder to see her rise up in nothing but a dingy white T-shirt, like some kind of ascending specter in the dim light. The next thing he knew, she threw herself onto his back and buried her teeth in his neck.

Shrieking at the sudden pain, he bent forward, reaching back to grab her hair at the same time, and threw the growling woman over his shoulder. Her feet flew overhead and slammed the round table in front of the closed drapes with enough force to turn it over. Whiskey bottles, beer cans, half-full glasses of liquid, and the remains of a chicken dinner cascaded onto the filthy carpet.

Rolling onto her knees, she attempted to stand and fell

instead when her broken ankles collapsed in opposite directions. Unfazed, she threw her weight at the shocked man and grabbed his shoulders. Her leverage was enough to lunge forward and head-butt him square in the nose.

Belcher's face exploded into pain, and he fell backward onto the bed. With abnormal strength, she used her arms to crawl up his body and on top of him. Fire shot through his damaged nose when she bit it off and he shrieked in both pain and terror when she lunged in like a mad dog to bite again.

Screaming like a banshee, he threw her to the side and rolled off the end, holding his mangled face. Gaining his feet at the same time she grabbed a handful of his boxers, he struggled to reach the sports bag and the pistol lying on top of the dope.

Horrific screams erupted from the raging woman as she slashed at him with her nails, drawing three long lines down his neck, all the time filling the room with animal growls.

It was impossible for Belcher to comprehend what was happening. Fire lanced through his face. Priscilla was between him and the door, and instead of retreating into the bathroom and locking himself inside, he wanted out, away from the nightmarish creature that kept coming at him taking bites out of his living body.

He swung a fist that caught her on the side of the head, knocking her into the overturned table a second time. She landed hard, snarling like a wild animal. Belcher reached the door, fumbling with the cheap safety chain, then the dead bolt that refused to turn in his bloodied hand.

She slammed into him again, and this time white-hot lava shot through his neck as she bit out another chunk of flesh. Setting his feet, he shouldered her back over the table yet again and this time, yanked the door open.

"Help!" Belcher fell out onto the walkway. "Help!"

Something was wrong. Hot liquid flowed over his shoulder, soaking his shirt. A couple in jeans and concert T-shirts came out of the room next to his. The man backed away, pulling the woman with him. "Hey, man, you're bleeding out."

The woman screamed at the sight of his mangled face. More people came from their rooms, and those in the parking lot below pointed and shouted.

A terrified shout cut above the noise of frightened people. "Zombie!"

Belcher's hand felt a deep, ragged gash in the side of his neck. He instinctively understood his artery was severed and stopped in horror at the amount of blood pumping from his body. "Call..."

Priscilla flew through the open door, catching him in the small of the back with all her weight. He crashed face-first into the metal railing with a meaty crunch, and his neck snapped.

More screams filled the air, both from Priscilla as she slashed at his body with the jagged neck of a broken Wild Turkey bottle, along with those witnessing the horrifying scene unfolding before their very eyes.

The hard slap of a gunshot cut off Priscilla's shrieks. Another shot threw her sideways and she collapsed beside Belcher's corpse, jabbing at him with weak thrusts. A uniformed security guard approached and flipped her over.

Her eyes fluttered as she looked up at the shocked man. She took a deep breath and let it out to form one dying sentence. "Gravel...so hot..."

Chapter Sixty-Six

The world filled with gunfire coming from the house when we dropped those two guards. The windows exploded outward from at least two guns. I rolled left, and Harley went right, crawfishing back toward a blue pickup I recognized as Atchley's ride as slugs punched holes in the air and everything solid around us.

A roll of automatic rifle fire came from my right, stitching the ground only feet away. I registered a partially open door on the left-hand silo. More rounds came through an open barn door. Harley's rifle opened up, driving at least two guns back into the silo. He shifted his aim to the barn and held the trigger down, giving me enough cover fire to throw myself behind a pile of trash.

Hidden behind drifts of lumber and branches, I found an opening in the debris and followed Harley's lead. We poured rounds into the dark barn, ending from the threat from there.

My weapon ran dry. "Reloading!"

That single word told him not to run his magazine empty.

I slammed a fresh one into my rifle's receiver. "Loaded."

"Reloading!" He mirrored my actions. "Loaded."

I took advantage of the silence. "Search warrants! Stock agents! Put down your weapons and come out."

My orders irritated someone in the house, and another roll of automatic fire raked over Atchley's hood. Harley crouched beside the front wheel, using it and the motor as cover. "Police! Put down your weapons!"

I could see through a small hole in the mound of trash, and I lined the scope on the shattered window they were shooting through. We couldn't just ventilate the trailer if the girls were somewhere inside. It had to be surgical. I saw movement inside. When the barrel of a rifle pushed through a shot-out window, I fired a three-round burst.

The figure fell back, and their fire ceased, at least for a moment.

Chapter Sixty-Seven

Chuck Davis rose up beside the broken window and glanced outside. "I think there's only two."

"Can you get a shot?" Spyder knelt beside a second blown-out window, and studied their situation.

Ryan Miller took cover behind the overturned table in the kitchen. "Then let's slip out the back door and get the hell out of here."

"Not with all that gravel in the silo." Spyder shook his head. "I'm not leaving all that cash for them."

"It won't do us any good if we're dead."

"We ain't gonna be dead. Call those cowards in the lab and tell them to help us."

"Nobody in Number Two's gonna shoot anything. That whole place will go up and kill us all. Grandpa's smarter than that."

"How many are in the bunkhouse?"

Silo One was a makeshift sleeping quarters with a dozen beds for the men who worked in shifts.

Ryan shrugged. "Depends. There's no telling. They're back and forth all the time."

"Call 'em!"

"Signal won't go through all that metal. We never put a repeater in there because we didn't want them making calls."

"There he is." Chuck Davis shifted position, raised his AR through the window and leaned over the sights. Three quick shots struck him in the chest, and the dead man fell where he stood.

"Dammit!" Ryan ducked. "We've got to get out of there."

Spyder looked at the back door, then at the short hallway leading to the bedrooms. "Not without that crank. I have an idea. You go out with your hands up. I'll take care of the rest."

"What're you gonna do?"

"Kill 'em all while they're concentrating on you." Crouching, Spyder ran into the hallway and opened a narrow door, revealing an empty space where the central air-conditioning unit once stood. He knelt and yanked a piece of plywood out of the way, revealing a hole in the floor.

"Give 'em a taste of their own medicine." He lowered himself into the hole, stuffed his handgun into the small of his back, and waved at the front door. "Give me that rifle and give yourself up."

Chapter Sixty-Eight

I'd had enough. "Come out!"

"You'll kill us." The man's voice was high with fear and tension.

"I'll kill you if you don't." Harley's response was a matter-of-fact shout, full of finality.

There was silence for a moment. "All right. Coming out!"

"Do it!" Harley sidestepped to the rear of the pickup and surprised me by looking at something other than the door.

"Hands up where we can see them!" I kept one eye on the front door and the other on the silos that remained closed. "Hands out and come down the steps backward!"

"Good idea." Harley knelt and went to his stomach.

The door opened and a bald-headed guy stuck his empty hands into the open.

"Turn around and back out!"

He did it, carefully, feeling with his toes for each step.

"Harley, he's not watching his feet. He's looking to your left."

We were still using VOX to communicate with each other. He answered. "There's movement under the house."

I raised my voice again. "You! Keep coming, but if anything happens, I'm gonna shoot you off those steps."

The man stopped, as if he'd stepped on a live wire. "I'm doing what you say!"

Harley's turn. "Who's under the house?"

He glanced to his left again, and I knew we had him. "Harley, watch out."

The crack of a single gunshot startled me. A flash from underneath the trailer told me we were right. An automatic rifle opened up in a deadly cadence.

Harley returned fire, but he never shot just once.

His rifle spat three-round bursts as if he were taking target practice.

There was silence for a second, and then he saw something that concerned him and hosed the underside of the trailer on full auto. The lighter pop of a handgun came seconds later, the round snapping past Harley's ear.

"Dammit!" Harley snatched the Beretta from the holster strapped to his thigh and holding it with both hands, emptied the mag until there was no more return fire or movement in the shadows.

The guy at the door forgot he wasn't on the ground and he missed the last step, falling back as if he'd been shot.

I had the scope on him. "Get up!"

"Don't shoot!"

"I won't!"

"You just shot Spyder!"

Harley's voice was flat. "That was me and it was his fault, so don't you do anything else stupid."

"Get up and keep backing to my voice!" I had the rifle on him, expecting at any minute to hear more gunshots.

Trembling, the man backed up to my trash pile.

"Stop!" I saw Harley was waiting. "Sidestep to your left with your hands still out."

He took a step to the right.

"My way, dumbass!" Harley was out of patience. "Your other left!"

The man followed our directions and jumped when he saw Harley only feet away.

"On your stomach." Harley was on him in a flash, dropping his knee into the middle of the man's back while I swung to cover the quiet silos, then back to the house. He cuffed him. "Anyone else in there?"

"No. It was just the three of us, and you shot Chuck in the window. That was Spyder under there."

Harley met my gaze. Neither of us expected to hear that name.

"Where's my daughter?"

The guy's head snapped toward me. "They aren't here."

He knew about them and my stomach lurched. "Where?"

Lying on his belly, he pointed with his chin. "Back through there a few miles. They're safe with a friend of mine, and his wife...in their trailer."

"They better be. Where's your phone?"

"Back pocket."

I slipped it out. "Password."

"That's it. Password."

Harley shook his head.

I was shocked to see he had full coverage. "Name."

"Carl."

"Carl how much?"

"Just Carl."

I found the name and called. A voice answered. "Ryan. It's about time. What do we do about these girls?"

My knees went weak, and I put the phone to his ear. "Tell him."

"Hey, it's over. You need to do what this guy says. Let 'em go."

I took over. "Carl. This is Special Agent Tucker Snow, and you have my daughter. Let me talk to her."

He made no response. The next sound I heard was Chloe's voice. "Dad?"

A lump formed in my throat and I nearly couldn't talk. "Baby, you all right?"

"Dad. We're fine."

"Where are you?"

"In a trailer, but I don't know where. I think we're somewhere in the mountains, in Oklahoma."

"You're not far away. I'm here too. I'll be there to get y'all in a few minutes. Give the phone back to Carl."

"I can't."

"Why not?"

"Him and his wife just ran out of the house and got in a truck. They're gone."

"You stay right there, then."

"I love you, Dad."

I had to fight the sobs boiling up in my chest. "Me too. Stay right there until me or someone else gets there, and keep that phone handy."

Chapter Sixty-Nine

His knee still in Ryan's back, Harley gave me a big grin. "Let's finish this up."

"Don't kill me!" Ryan started crying.

"Shut up, idiot." Harley stood and yanked him to his feet. "Tell me about those silos."

"The one on the left's a bunkhouse. The other one is the lab."

"How many people?"

"Eight."

"Guns?"

"Not in the lab. There are a couple in the bunkhouse, but those guys won't fight."

"One of 'em shot at us."

"I'm surprised."

I got in Ryan's face. "You better tell me the truth. Anyone else in the trailer?"

"No. I swear."

"Let's go find out." Harley grabbed Ryan's collar and yanked the guy around between him and the trailer. Slinging his rifle, he reached into the pocket of his utility pants and plucked out a flashbang. He pulled the pin. "You stay in front of me all the way to that back window."

His face went white. "What're you gonna do?"

"I don't believe a damned word you say. Let's clear the house. Ready, Tuck?"

"Let's go."

Harley used his forearm and rushed Ryan toward the house, staying close and using him for cover. I moved parallel, alternately sweeping the trailer with my rifle muzzle, then swinging back to the silent silos.

Harley slammed Ryan face-first into the side of the trailer and then, staying close to the outside wall, he pitched the flashbang through the window. Throwing Ryan to the ground, he charged the open door, plucked out another grenade, and tossed it through the next blown-out window and rushed the length of the trailer.

The first flashbang went off, shattering the rest of the windows on the far end. By the time the second explosion detonated, he'd pitched another into the open door. The string of three close-quarter blasts should have incapacitated anyone inside before we charged up the steps.

Rifle at my shoulder, I crept inside to find the interior a shambles. Morning light slanted through the broken windows, but the rooms were empty, except for the still body of a male lying in the living room. Breathing hard, we took up positions to see the silos through the empty window frames.

The two buildings seemed to be anchored by a thick tangle of overgrown bushes and vines. A trail beaten by thousands of footsteps led from the thick brush at one door to the other.

Harley tucked the rifle against his shoulder. "Ready to serve those warrants?"

I started to answer when the doors on the lab opened. A gray-haired man who looked like a church elder stepped out, hands high and empty. "We're coming out!"

Before I could order him down, the door on the barracks silo opened and a string of men emerged, hands high in the air. Harley flowed down the steps, rifle at high ready, shouting orders.

"Down! Down! Down! Hands out! Show me your hands!" The men dropped to their knees and lay facedown, hands wide.

Harley passed them and stopped outside the bunkhouse silo. Knowing I had the men and lab covered, he rolled around the door and disappeared from sight. Seconds later, he came back outside.

"Clear!"

He took up a position to cover our prisoners, I approached the second silo and peeked inside to find the most high-tech meth lab I'd ever seen. More organized than a legitimate development laboratory, the entire floor space was filled with rows of fifty-five-gallon stainless-steel drums and heating mantles capable of producing thousands of pounds or more at a time. I took a moment to admire the craftsmanship of the drums fitted with custom-made stainless-steel condensers standing eight feet tall.

I whistled.

The grandpa-looking man turned his head. "Thank you."

"Your lab?"

"It was."

Harley pointed above the door. "Tuck."

I looked up to see a hand-painted sign that read, "The Finest Gravel Ever Made."

Sara Beth, my baby Peyton, dead people I didn't know, and ruined lives—it all came from this lab, and this man.

I swung the muzzle of my rifle to the back of that son of a bitch's head...

...and Sara Beth whispered, *No baby*...

and I swear she pushed my arm upward, but then it was Harley shoving the muzzle skyward...

...and I screamed and emptied the entire magazine into the morning air.

—

"We have to get gone." The gray-haired cook sounded concerned.

Harley flex-cuffed the man. "Why?"

"Because something bad might happen if those guys in the trailer did what they said they'd do."

I moved on to another prisoner, patting each one down as Harley cuffed them up. "Something bad such as?"

A sound I'd been hearing became clear. The pounding in my ears was gone, replaced by the thumping of a helicopter converging on the farm. It swept overhead then tilted back toward the clearing where they buried their refuse.

The SAT phone rang, and I regained control of myself. Wiping my mouth with one hand, I answered. "Snow."

"Get out of there!"

"What?"

"Get out of there now. This is Agent Vince Bradshaw, FBI! Baker told us there's explosives wired to timers around those silos. We think they'll blow it."

I glanced down at the grandpa-looking guy who overhead the conversation. He gave me a wink. "That's what I was saying. We need to get gone."

Harley stiffened. "How long do we have?"

The gray-haired guy looked at the silo. "It's wired with C-4, but they told me it was on a delay. Now, your guess is as good as mine on anything else. Spyder said it was to take out as many of y'all as he could if they all went down, so maybe we have enough time if we run."

I yanked him up by his collar. "Run, then." One by one Harley and I helped the others to their knees and shoved them forward. "And the rest of y'all stay with him or we'll shoot you down."

"Haul ass to that clearing!" Harley gave the last guy a push.

I was fully expecting them to scatter like quail, but the group thundered down the dirt track, running as awkward as dodo birds with their hands behind their backs. We emerged into the clearing to find the backhoe still running, and I had an idea. "Everybody into that hole!"

Lordy, I hoped it was big enough, and it was. The helicopter tilted away from the area as men leaped feetfirst into the excavation like soldiers jumping into a foxhole, and that's what it became. I was the last in and heard the concussion as one of the silos went up.

The very process of making meth creates explosive gasses, and that, along with all the stored chemicals and the C-4 detonators, created a fireball that rose high into the air. I hit something soft as I landed and registered a loud grunt before the shock wave rolled over us.

Trees bent with the force of the explosion and snapped back up as a storm of dust filled the air. Debris rained down on the clearing. I found my footing in the hole and leaned back against the dirt wall to see Jess Atchley still lying on the ground, covered in dirt, and looking as if he'd been stomped by a herd of wild elephants.

Chapter Seventy

Harley and I were out of the hole and watching our prisoners who were still in there when the SAT phone rang again. "Snow here."

"Daddy?"

My knees went weak. "Baby, where are you?"

"With the FBI. We met them on the road."

A second helicopter swooped in like a bird and landed in the middle of the clearing.

"You all right?"

"I'm fine. Jimma is too. They said they'd bring us to you. Is that all right?"

I looked at the helicopter and the men dropping to the ground. Sirens filled the air as a flood of responders converged on the area. "That's fine. How would you like to go home on a helicopter?"

Chapter Seventy-One

It was late in the evening two months later. Sheriff Jackson had passed, replaced by Chief Deputy Frank Gibson, who held the office until the next election. Frank reached out to Harley, asking him to join the department as *his* chief deputy, based on what he heard about us taking down the Oklahoma drug lab.

Harley laughed and laughed, and thanked him, saying he'd retired once from law enforcement, and didn't intend to get back into it. I didn't blame him one bit and was kinda glad because we'd worked so well together I wanted him available if I ever needed help again.

So that's what we were doing, he and I were creepy-crawling through tall grass up to the house sitting on a hill. The cold sky was awash with color as clouds swept in from the west. Geese and mallard ducks paddled across the lake behind us, setting in for the night.

Covered head to toe in ghillie suits, we'd been moving only inches at a time for the past three hours and didn't have much longer before the light failed. Both of us had rifles in the crooks of our arms and crept so slowly that not even the dog on the porch had noticed anything awry. Two people in chairs on the back porch talked quietly from time to time.

He spoke through the VOX, though we were only feet from each other. "I'm close enough to take the shot."

"Wait. That chicken is looking at us. They might notice it and see us out here."

"People don't pay attention to what chickens are looking at."

I watched. "*Those* two might."

A Dominicker hen stopped scratching at the ground and turned her head away from our position to watch us with one eye.

Harley froze in place. "I hate putting the sneak on a place with animals, but at least that dumb dog's not paying attention to anything."

I moved a couple of inches forward. "I have to get past this clump of grass before we can shoot."

"You should have planned for that all the way up here. Move easy, or they'll see you."

I gently shifted several inches to the right and raised a pair of binoculars to my eyes with glacial speed.

A young woman in a coat adjusted a blanket across her lap. We stopped again. She looked up from a phone in her hands and studied the pasture for a minute before turning to her friend. We were so close her voice came across clear as a bell. "You get the feeling we're being watched?"

A dark-haired girl similarly wrapped up against the late evening chill glanced up from the cell phone in her hand. "I always feel like that."

I was afraid they'd take more notice of the pasture and see us. It was time to end this. "All right. Do it now."

Harley raised the rifle and leaned his cheek against the stock to peer down the scope. "Taking the shot. One..."

The blond girl stood and held her camera up. The Lab rose at her movement and tilted his head in our direction. I realized she was taking a photo, and then she lowered it and spoke in a loud voice. "I saw y'all coming a mile away. Jimma, that's Dad on the left and Harley on the right."

"Two, dammit." Harley fired anyway and the .177 caliber pellet rang in the bullet trap at the base of the porch.

Jimma shook her head. "And y'all shouldn't be shooting air rifles at the house, neither, right, Chloe?"

My daughter, looking older than her age, reached into a container at her feet and pitched a handful of chicken feed into yard. She was acting more like her mama after their experience in Oklahoma and the resulting visits with her therapist, who said she was well on the road to recovery. "You remembered."

"Sure do." Jimma was living with Harley and Tammy as they waded through the adoption process that would take months. "I'll never point a gun at anyone again."

The hen rushed forward and pecked at the ground as Kevin barked once at us before he followed the girls into the house. Tammy appeared at the door to squint in our direction. "Tuck, phone call from a guy named Steve Knagg, says somebody stole his trailer and wants you to call him. Supper's ready too."

Seconds later, Danny and Matt raced out the door and headed in our direction like two little missiles.

I stood and stretched as the boys charged their daddy. "You should wait to shoot on the count of three for once."

Preparing for the attack from his boys, Harley rolled onto his back and stared at the late evening sky. "I never remember what comes after two."

THE END

Powderly, Texas
February 24, 2022

AUTHOR'S NOTE

Though this is a work of fiction, there's a lot of truth in here.

The Texas and Southwestern Cattle Raisers Association (TSCRA) was founded in 1877. The Stock-Raisers' Association of North-West Texas was created back then to fight cattle theft in the region. These special rangers are commissioned as peace officers by the Texas Department of Public Safety. In Oklahoma, they are commissioned by the Oklahoma State Bureau of Investigation, and yes, they can, and often do, cross state lines to investigate and make arrests.

In ten years, 2010–2020, the association's thirty special rangers have recovered more than $48 million worth of livestock and equipment, but they did it differently than Tucker and Harley Snow. It isn't the Old West here in the Lone Star State anymore, and these real officers have moved far from their gunslinging days and into technology.

Today they see their fair share of cattle theft (it's still big business in some regions of Texas and Oklahoma) and complex financial scams that boggle the mind. Because they deal with down-and-dirty rural farm and ranch crime, these men and women investigate "the thefts of cattle, horses, saddles, trailers, equipment, and even poaching. They pursue white-collar criminals who commit agricultural fraud, inspect livestock to determine ownership, educate landowners on how to prevent theft and spoil the plans of thieves, and...keep the peace."

That's where Tucker Snow comes in. A significant amount of methamphetamine is cooked up in the country, and these law enforcement professionals encounter it more than they'd like. Mixed in hell by demons who have no regard for human life, meth is making headlines across the United States, and one, "flakka," is the basis for the new fictional meth called gravel in these books.

Because investigations can be slow, boring, and detailed, crime writers lean more toward action, and that's where thrillers come in. I may have stretched some of the legal boundaries to make the story more interesting, but any exaggerations or mistakes are my own and in no way reflect how these exemplary agents operate within the law. It is my sincere prayer that none of these special rangers ever encounter anything I've described in these pages, but I think "stretching the truth" makes for an entertaining read.

Much of the technology detailed in the Dodge's "black box" is real, though I stretched the vehicle's ability to collect even *more* data to fit the plot of this story (or maybe it exists and we don't yet know the full ramifications of their data-collecting methods). You're essentially driving another computer these days if you have a newer car or truck, and all this personal data, (including GPS, driving habits, music, and purchasing history) is harvested through the vehicle itself, and your cell phone.

It's true. Look it up.

I've already thanked the retired Easterwood brothers in this book's dedication, but I want my readers to know they were invaluable in creating these characters and the plot of this book. We've spent a lot of hours drinking brown water and sharing recollections, along with my mentor and running buddy bestselling author John Gilstrap, and some of those memories made their way into the plot in dramatically altered fashion.

Thanks also to Scott Williamson, TSCRA Executive Director of Law Enforcement, Brand and Inspection Services, for his time and patience as I asked many, many questions. Thanks also to Kaycee Anderson, TSCRA Law Enforcement Department, for her assistance in tracking down specific details of these officers' day-to-day jobs.

As always, it's a sincere pleasure to work with the great staff at Sourcebooks—Dominique Raccah, Anna Michels, Diane DiBiase, Beth Deveny, and Mandy Chahal. You guys make this process fun and smooth.

Thanks again to my wonderful agent and friend, Anne Hawkins, who is always supportive.

And of course, this writing career's foundation is the love of my life, Shana, who is good and right in all things.

CAN'T GET ENOUGH OF REAVIS Z. WORTHAM'S WRITING? GO ON AN ADVENTURE TO RURAL TEXAS WITH

THE ROCK HOLE

Chapter One

We're from up on the river.

I came to live with my grandparents up on the Red River in the summer of 1964. Their hardscrabble farm sat exactly one mile from the domino hall in Center Springs, a one-horse settlement named after the clear-water spring that feeds Sanders Creek, which then drains into the Red.

When I climbed down the metal steps of that hot old bus outside the Greyhound station in the much larger town of Chisum, Grandpa and my grandmother, Miss Becky, were waiting on the blistering sidewalk. I was so proud to see them I could have busted, Grandpa especially. There he stood in his sweat-stained old straw hat and overalls, with a tiny badge pinned to his blue work shirt.

I knew a revolver was in one of those big pockets, because he was the Law in Lamar County, though you couldn't rightly tell if you didn't know.

He hugged me against his big belly. Miss Becky was nearly dancing with excitement when he turned me loose to throw my suitcase into the truck bed among the baling wire, empty feed sacks, and loose hay. He'd parked right at the curb, and the bus's front bumper was almost against the tailgate. When the bus driver stopped a few minutes before, I could tell he was aggravated because the truck was in his way, but he didn't say anything.

"Why, Top, you've growed a foot since we last saw you!" When Miss Becky hugged my neck, she smelled like the bath powder she kept in a round tin on her dresser.

"C'mon, Mama, we have to go." Grandpa opened the door for us. "Get in, hoss, and let's go look at a dead dog." He was always in a hurry to get out of town and back to the country. I crawled onto the dusty seat full of holes, and Miss Becky gathered her long skirts and climbed in behind me.

"Ned," Miss Becky softly scolded him when he pulled away from the curb.

"Aw, Mama, it ain't nothin' but a dead dog, and we're liable to see two or three in the same condition on the side of the highway before we get back to the house. It won't hurt him none."

"Well, y'all can drop me off at the house first, then."

"I intend to."

Ten-year-old boys are always up for an adventure, so twenty minutes later, we let her out at the house, and fifteen minutes after that, I followed him through a field of chest-high corn. Grandpa led us between the rows with a hoe thrown over his shoulder and a 'toe sack dangling from the back pocket of his overalls. I wasn't sure how he knew where we were going until I looked down at his brogans and saw footprints leading through the rows in the sand.

He heard me cock my Daisy air rifle he'd remembered to bring. The BB gun's barrel was hot to the touch from the blazing summer sun. "Glad we have a gun." He always enjoyed kidding me. "You never know if you're gonna run across a booger-bear out here."

I rattled the air rifle to see how many BBs were left. "Is this your corn?"

"Nope. It belongs to Isaac Reader. I usually don't like being alone in another man's field. It feels like trespassing, but since Ike called me, here we are."

Turkey buzzards drifted on the thermals high above the thick cornstalks surrounding us. Locusts sang in the trees at the edge of the field. Grandpa stopped and wrinkled his nose at the edge of a tramped-down area in the corn. "Sheew. That stinks."

I almost gagged. The sight of what lay at our feet nearly made me fall out. Someone had used a heated two-handed screwdriver to torture a poor bird dog lying beside the cold remains of a fire. Dark stains on the blade and the German shorthair's wounds told us what had happened in the clearing. Burn marks made crisscross patterns in the animal's hide. Deep puncture wounds from the once red-hot blade still oozed fluid.

Despite the heat, a chill ran up my spine. I'd seen dead dogs on the side of the highway, but I'd never seen one intentionally mistreated. My stomach rose, but I choked it down. The stink made my asthma act up, causing me to wheeze. I dug my puffer out of my jeans pocket, stuck the atomizer end in my mouth, and gave the bulb a squeeze. My lungs tickled deep down inside, and I began to breathe better.

"Bastard." Grandpa had a habit of talking quietly to himself. He hooked the sharp blade of his hoe under the stiff corpse and lifted it off the ground. Flies rose and buzzed all around us. "This one makes five now."

"Five what, Grandpa?"

"Just you never mind."

I waved flies out of my face as he knelt on one knee and pulled a damp scrap of paper free from the sand. He unfolded the raggedly torn advertisement from *The Chisum News*. I got a peek at the drawing of a boy and girl playing catch.

He stood with a grunt and backed off a step.

I'd never seen anything so horrible in my life, and I wished Grandpa hadn't brought me. Center Springs was always my safe place, where I didn't have to worry about anything except running outside, hunting, and fishing. That's part of why I came to live with them up on the river.

Another truck rattled down the dirt road and pulled into the shade beside ours parked under a huge red oak where folks used to rest their mules. Grandpa slipped the folded clipping into the deep pocket of his overalls, removed his hat, and wiped the sweat from his bald head with a blue bandanna. "That's your Uncle Cody's bird dog someone stole out of his pen last week. But you don't say anything to him about it. I'll tell him."

"Why?"

He stared down at me with those pale blue eyes of his. "Because I said not to."

Behind him, I saw the tops of several cornstalks twitch, but there was no wind. I started to say something about it, but a man got out of the truck and hollered across the field. Had I known someone was creeping through the field with us that morning, I could have told Grandpa, and we might have ended what was coming for us right then and there.

He also might not have had to do what he did.

But at the time, I didn't know I'd been slapped square in the path of a maniac who had it in for our family.

READING GROUP GUIDE

1. What was your first impression of Jess Atchley? How did that change as you read further into the book?

2. What motivates Deputy Lomax to help Atchley? What benefits does he get to balance out the headaches of cleaning up messes and covering for their drug operation with his colleagues?

3. Tuck and Harley are rare as a sibling crime-fighting team. Why do you think they're some of the only brothers who can work cases together?

4. How would you describe Jimma? What propels her toward the Snows?

5. For the first half of the book, Tuck's investigation is completely unofficial. Why does he first take matters into his own hands? Why does he officially return from his leave when he does?

6. "Gravel" appears to turn its users into homicidal maniacs regardless of their own personalities or backgrounds. How does that compare to depictions of addicts in other books you've read? Do you think these fictional representations change the way we think about real people struggling with addiction?

7. When challenged over the consequences of buying and consuming his meth, Atchley argues that he provides a service to willing customers and is not responsible for anything beyond that. What do you think of his stance?

8. What does Tuck think of Harley's anger? How does it affect their rapport?

9. Why do Atchley and Lomax decide to go forward with the plan to assassinate Sheriff Jackson when they do? Atchley mentions that he considered a similar plan even before Jackson fell ill.

10. How are Harley and Tuck able to overcome the much larger group at the Silos? How do the meth cooks' priorities ruin their chances of winning?

A CONVERSATION WITH THE AUTHOR

What was your inspiration for *Hard Country*?

While doing a signing several years ago in Paris, Texas, I met Constable Rick Easterwood, who was already a big fan of my newspaper columns that have, to date, been running for thirty-four years. We built a solid friendship and eventually became hunting buddies.

Sitting beside a campfire one night, he began telling stories of his work as an undercover narcotics officer for the Texas Department of Public Safety. As the evening progressed, we found that we knew many of the same people in law enforcement. Rick opened up even more, relating experiences with his younger brother, Dan, who also worked undercover for the DPS, and how they spent several years fighting illegal drugs as a team. They had to receive special dispensation from then-governor Mark Williams to work together, and that sparked a concept as he and Dan spoke with enthusiasm of their undercover years.

Not long after, I approached the brothers with the idea of writing a series *loosely* based on their experiences but with generous amounts of fiction thrown in to keep a reader's interest. Police work is mostly a slow investigative plod, punctuated by brief jolts of adrenaline. Police procedurals are interesting in their own right, but thrillers require those bursts of rocket fuel.

Both agreed without hesitation and provided even more material I could use in the future. Of course, I manipulated their adventures to fit the story line and action, and spun the book in my own way, but many of their personality traits helped develop Tucker and Harley Snow.

What are your biggest priorities when writing the first book in a new series?

One is to give readers a quality product, followed by a great plot and characters. In my opinion, a sense of place is important also. Readers of a favorite series often remember where a book is set and the geography of an area before they can recall the complete plot. That's why I use all of our senses in describing settings throughout the novel.

I think that's successful, because reviewers often mention a sense of place in my work.

Next is family, *always* an essential ingredient in my books. Family is important in real life, and that's not exclusive to blood relations. We pick up friends who eventually become family members as we go through life, and a combination of the two is essential.

Character traits and desires are fundamental, and that third priority develops as we get to know these fictional people. Readers of my work won't get that in an info dump either. It's scattered throughout the novel in bits and pieces, eventually adding up to a whole. Think about what it's like meeting a new person and learning about them over the course of several months. Soon you know them, as much as they'll let you.

Hopefully by the end of the novel, my fans have grown to love (or, in the case of the antagonists, hate) those who populate these pages.

It's my hope I've done all three with *Hard Country* and that it drew all y'all into Tucker Snow's world.

You tell the story from many different perspectives, including those surrounding Atchley's drug outfit. Why was it important to you to include those points of view?

For the most part, a single POV isn't as exciting as writing from different viewpoints. Unlike mysteries, thrillers are a roller-coaster ride to the end. In a mystery, we know about the crime, but the road to unraveling the details to find the antagonist is what drives the story, with the knowledge there is a payoff at the end.

In a thriller, we know who the bad guys are, but we hang on for the ride to the end in which justice is served. In order to amp up the action, authors provide a look at the world through the eyes of several characters. This allows the reader to get inside the mind of antagonists and see the events unfold through *their* eyes. To point at a person and say they're bad guys is easy. To get inside their mind and *show* they're evil and dangerous is a whole 'nother animal.

Switching these viewpoints also increases the pacing, as readers subconsciously wonder what's going to happen next with the other characters and how that one particular point of view reacts with the others.

Your previous series, the Texas Red River mysteries, are set in the 1960s. What was the biggest challenge about shifting focus to a series set in the present day?

Technology!

Oh, sure, you can look back at the '60s, which is the setting for my Red River series, and say there's technology, but that pretty much ends with telephones attached to a wall, automatic transmissions, Telstar, and direct dialing. Now with the world at our fingertips via cell phones, it's difficult to create situations people can't get out of by calling for help or information. We can simply dial 911 or look up a location on mapping apps.

A good or bad guy on the run, for example, can no longer escape as easily by car. BOLOs by law enforcement agencies, cameras everywhere, license plate scanners, and much more all add a level of difficulty to something that was once simple in books.

Cell phones create hardships for writers. That's why I had to get Tucker and Harley out into the country here in *Hard Country*, where signals are spotty.

When it comes to technology in vehicles, we're talking about an entirely different situation. I heard on the radio one Saturday morning about how *vehicles* are now tracking devices, and companies mine the computers in them for information. To my knowledge, everything in this novel about computers in vehicles is true, and I suspect there's more.

The whole world is a news crew now that we have camera and video capabilities in our phones. There are cameras everywhere, and it's difficult to get away from them in urban areas. But you'll recall there's a lot of technology that advances the plot. Security cameras at Tucker's house lead to details involving the girl's kidnapping. I use it when I can, but I don't have to like it.

That old song by Rockwell "Somebody's Watching Me" is chillingly accurate. Somebody is *always* watching, or listening, to you. Don't believe it? Look up an obscure item on your cell phone, or discuss at length something like paint-by-number art close to an Alexa or Echo Dot and see how many pop up in your social media feeds within the next few minutes, days, or weeks. It'll be there.

I always feel like somebody's watching me...

What's next for Tucker Snow?

Kill Slot is the working title for the next book in this series. While picking up a stray cow from a local ranch, Tucker Snow finds himself investigating a local judge involved with wild cattle that becomes the source of mysterious funds added to a community's treasury and, ultimately, an individual's bank account.

At the same time, a series of suspicious medical issues reported by a local rancher become a concern to Tuck when the man is diagnosed with what appears to be radiation poisoning.

When Tuck discovers the unsuspecting rancher used contaminated drill rods from West Texas oil fields to build corrals and fences, they are suddenly targeted by mysterious individuals who do their best to put Tuck and Harley in shallow graves to bury a dangerous secret leading back to Big Oil.

But then again, I don't outline my books. I tried once and abandoned it after the third page. Who knows what happens in *Kill Slot* as the manuscript advances past the opening chapter? You'll find out the same way I did, and I hope it's a surprise to all of us.

ABOUT THE AUTHOR

© Shana Wortham

Two-time Spur Award–winning author Reavis Z. Wortham also pens the Texas Red River historical mystery series, and the high-octane Sonny Hawke contemporary Western thrillers. The Texas Red River novels are set in rural Northeast Texas in the 1960s. In a Starred Review, *Kirkus Reviews* listed his first novel, *The Rock Hole,* as one of the "Top 12 Mysteries of 2011." *The Rock Hole* was reissued in 2020 by Poisoned Pen Press with new material added, including an introduction by Joe R. Lansdale.

"*Burrows,* Wortham's outstanding sequel to *The Rock Hole,* combines the gonzo sensibility of Joe R. Lansdale and the elegiac mood of *To Kill a Mockingbird* to strike just the right balance between childhood innocence and adult horror."

—*Publishers Weekly,* Starred Review

"The cinematic characters have substance and a pulse. They walk off the page and talk Texas."

—*Dallas Morning News*

His series from Kensington Publishing features Texas Ranger Sonny Hawke and debuted in 2018. *Hawke's War,* the second in the Sonny Hawke series, won the Spur Award from the Western Writers Association of America as the Best Mass Market Paperback of 2019. In 2020, the third book in the series, *Hawke's Target,* won a Spur Award in the same category.

Wortham has been a newspaper columnist and magazine writer since 1988, penning nearly two thousand columns and articles, and has been the humor editor for *Texas Fish & Game Magazine* for twenty-four years. He and his wife, Shana, live in Northeast Texas.

All his works are available at your favorite bookstore or online, in all formats.

Check out his website at reaviszwortham.com.